Second Variety

Philip K. Dick was born in Chicago in 1928 and lived most of his life in California. He attended college for a year at Berkeley. Apart from writing, his main interest was music. He won the Hugo Award for his classic novel of alternative history, *The Man in the High Castle* (1962). He was married five times and had three children. He died in March 1982.

D1796217

Novels

Solar Lottery
Eye in the Sky
Vulcan's Hammer
The Man Who Japed
The Cosmic Puppets
The World Jones Made
Time Out of Joint
Dr Futurity
The Man in the High Castle
The Game Players of Titan
Clans of the Alphane Moon
*Flow My Tears, the
    Policeman Said*
The Penultimate Truth
The Simulacra
Martian Time-Slip
*Dr Bloodmoney, or How We
    Got Along After the Bomb*
The Zap Gun
Now Wait for Last Year
Counter-Clock World
Ubik
Our Friends from Frolix 8
Glactic Pot-Healer
*The Three Stigmata of
    Palmer Eldritch*
A Scanner Darkly
Valis
The Divine Invasion
*The Transmigration of
    Timothy Archer*
Confessions of a Crap Artist
The Ganymede Takeover
    (with Ray Nelson)

Deus Irae
    (With Roger Zelazny)
A Maze of Death
Lies, Inc.
    (*The Unteleported Man*)
*The Man Whose Teeth Were
    All Exactly Alike*
In Milton Lumky Territory
*Puttering About in a
    Small Land*
Humpty Dumpty in Oakland
Radio Free Albemuth
We Can Build You
Mary and the Giant
The Broken Bubble

Short Stories

A Handful of Darkness
I Hope I Shall Arrive Soon
The Variable Man
The Book of Philip K. Dick
The Golden Man
The Preserving Machine
*Collected Stories 1:
    Beyond Lies the Wub*
*Collected Stories 2:
    Second Variety*
*Collected Stories: 3
    The Father-Thing*
*Collected Stories 4:
    The Days of Perky Pat*
*Collected Stories 5:
    We Can Remember it for
    you Wholesale*

Voyager

PHILIP K. DICK

Second Variety

Volume 2
The Collected Stories of Philip K. Dick

Introduction by Norman Spinrad

HarperCollins*Publishers*

Voyager
An Imprint of HarperCollins*Publishers*
77–85 Fulham Palace Road,
Hammersmith, London W6 8JB

The *Voyager* World Wide Web site address is
http://www.harpercollins.co.uk/voyager

This paperback edition 1996
1 3 5 7 9 8 6 4 2

Previously published in paperback by
HarperCollins Science Fiction and Fantasy 1994
and by Grafton 1990

First published in Great Britain by
Victor Gollancz Ltd 1989

The excerpt by Philip K. Dick which appears at the beginning of this
volume is from a collection of inverviews with the author conducted by
Paul Williams and published in *Only Apparently Real*, Arbor House, 1986.
Used with permission.

ISBN 0 586 20765 1

Set in Times

Printed and bound in Great Britain by
Caledonian International Book Manufacturing Ltd, Glasgow

Contents

Introduction

By Norman Spinrad

Philip K. Dick's debut story, *Beyond Lies the Wub*, was first published in 1952. This volume, *SECOND VARIETY*, contains 27 short stories published between 1952 and 1955, when his first novel, *SOLAR LOTTERY*, appeared. What is more, it does not include every story he published during the first four years of his career either.

That in itself is quite remarkable. Few writers could boast such prodigious publication in the first four years of their careers, even in this period, when markets for short sf were relatively abundant and editors had many slots to fill. And while it must be admitted that there are a certain number of fairly trivial gimmick stories in this book, the majority of them already show many of the unique virtues of Dick's more mature work, and even the least of them are written in his unmistakable voice.

Considering that they were written in such a brief period by a new writer in the first flush of his career, that Dick must have been churning them out rapidly to make money and a name, these 27 stories are also quite remarkable for what they are not.

There is not really an action-adventure formula story in here. No space opera. No nuts and bolts. No fully-developed alien civilizations. No intrepid stock heroes, villains, mad scientists, no real good guys versus bad guys at all. From the very outset, Dick wrote as if the commercial conventions of the sf genre did not exist. Even the one-punch gimmick stories are *Dickian* gimmicks. From the beginning, Dick was reinventing science fiction, turning it into a literary instrument for his own concerns, and yes, obsessions.

What we have here is a kind of fascinating time capsule, 27

stories published before Philip K. Dick's first novel, the compressed short fiction apprenticeship of a writer who was to go on to become one of the great novelists of the twentieth century and arguably the greatest metaphysical novelist of all time.

Dick began writing during what at least in a publishing sense was the greatest transformation that science fiction has ever seen. In the early 1950s, the magazines were still the dominant mode of sf publication, meaning that short fiction was still the dominant form. By the time he published *SOLAR LOTTERY* in 1955, the paperback book was on its way to becoming the dominant publishing mode, and the novel therefore the dominant form.

In the 1950s, with the standard advance for an sf novel being about $1500, any writer trying to eke out a precarious living writing sf was still constrained to crank out short stories for the magazines. And what with novel slots still being limited, one was also constrained to make one's mark as a short story writer before a publisher was about to grant a novel contract at all.

Nor, in hindsight, as evidenced by this volume, was this, in literary terms at least, a bad thing, even for a writer like Dick, whose natural metier was the novel. These 27 stories, and the others published before *SOLAR LOTTERY*, were an apprenticeship in the best sense of the term.

Reading these stories one after the other in a single volume, one is indeed struck by a certain sameness, a certain repetitiveness, a certain series of recurrences, a sense of a writer staking out the territory of his future oeuvre. We would see the same thing in the short fiction of other writers of the period, and even much later, in the early short fiction, for example, of John Varley, William Gibson, Lucius Shepard, Kim Stanley Robinson.

But in this book, what we see is a uniquely Dickian sameness.

Most sf writers who stake out a territory in their early short fiction that they will later explore at greater length and depth tend to create a consistent universe like Larry Niven's 'Known Space' or recurring characters like Keith Laumer's Retief or a historical template like Robert A. Heinlein's 'Future History,' and not infrequently all three.

In part this is a commercial strategy. A new writer naive or crazy enough to actually attempt a career as a full-time sf short story writer has to write a lot of fiction rather rapidly to stay afloat. It is much easier to reuse settings, history, and characters than to begin from zero each time out, and, as network TV has long proven, the episodic series is the fastest way to build an audience too.

That, however, is not what Philip K. Dick did. There are no real recurring characters in these stories. There is no attempt to set them all in a consistent universe. Except for some rather tenuous connections between *Second Variety*, *Jon's World*, and *James P. Crow*, there is really no attempt at a consistent future history either.

But there most certainly *are* recurrences of theme, imagery, and metaphysical concerns, and we will see them again and again in Dick's subsequent novels, expanded upon, recomplicated, deepened, made quite vast.

The Earth reduced to a nuclear ash heap. Robot weapons systems evolving towards baleful anti-empathetic pseudo-life. Human freedom ground down in the name of military security, economic prosperity, or even order for its own sake. Interpenetrating realities. Ironic time-loops and paradoxes. Ordinary people holding ordinary jobs as the heroes and heroines trying to muddle through.

These stories were written during the fever pitch of the Cold War, the height of the anti-Communist hysteria engendered by Senator Joseph McCarthy and the House Un-American Activities Committee, the nadir of the nuclear war paranoia, when school children were taught to hide under their desks when the air raid sirens went off. And on an obvious level they reflect this quite overtly. They show that Dick was a writer of deep political concern from the very outset.

But they show something much more. At a time when there was no little danger in voicing such views, Dick spoke out loud and clear *against* the prevailing hysterias of the times – against militarism, security obsession, xenophobia, and chauvinism.

Further, what these stories juxtapose against these large scale political evils are not equally large scale political virtues but the intimate small scale human and spiritual virtues of modest heroism, caritas, and most of all the empathy that, in the end, is finally what distinguishes the human from the machine, the spiritual from the mechanical, authentic being from even the most cunningly crafted pseudo-life.

And if we already see here what was to be the great theme and the spiritual core of Philip K. Dick's whole career, so too do we see in these stories the genesis of the characteristic literary technique which so cogently brings it down to an intimate and specific human level – Dick's use of multiple viewpoint characters.

True, his use of multiple viewpoint techniques is not always perfect in these early stories. Sometimes he cavalierly shifts viewpoint within a scene for mere narrative convenience. Sometimes he introduces a new viewpoint character in media res just to give us a scene he cannot easily render from viewpoints he has already established. Sometimes a viewpoint character appears for only a few paragraphs and then disappears.

Dick is learning multiple viewpoint technique in these stories. Indeed, it may be more accurate to say that he is *inventing* it, for few if any writers had really used multiple viewpoint this way before Dick, and all of us who were to adopt it later owe a great debt to him, whether we consciously realize it or not.

For what the Dickian multiple viewpoint technique allows the writer to do is to tell the story from within the consciousness, the spirit, the heart, of several characters, not merely one. It allows intimacy, it grants the reader empathy, with the *multiplexity* of the human spirit within the confines of a single tale. And in the hands of a master like Philip K. Dick, it becomes a series of windows into the metaphysical multiplexity of reality itself, the perfect merger of theme and form.

These 27 stories are not perfect. It would be a disservice to the truth and to Philip K. Dick's literary reputation to contend that they represent the full flowering of the mature talent to come. But they too are a series of windows, windows into the past, into the beginnings of a great spirit's long and mighty journey, and windows too into the future, into the fully developed vision of the mature master the talented young apprentice who wrote them was one day destined to become.

Norman Spinrad
October, 1986

Paranoia, in some respects, I think, is a modern-day development of an ancient, archaic sense that animals still have – quarry-type animals – that they're being watched . . . I say paranoia is an atavistic sense. It's a lingering sense, that we had long ago, when we were – our ancestors were – very vulnerable to predators, and this sense tells them they're being watched. And they're being watched probably by something that's going to get them . . .

And often my characters have this feeling.

But what really I've done is, I have atavized their society. That although it's set in the future, in many ways they're living – there is a retrogressive quality in their lives, you know? They're living like our ancestors did. I mean, the hardware is in the future, the scenery's in the future, but the situations are really from the past.

– Philip K. Dick in an interview, 1974

The Cookie Lady

'Where you going, Bubber?' Ernie Mill shouted from across the street, fixing papers for his route.

'No place,' Bubber Surle said.

'You going to see your lady friend?' Ernie laughed and laughed. 'What do you go visit that old lady for? Let us in on it!'

Bubber went on. He turned the corner and went down Elm Street. Already, he could see the house, at the end of the street, set back a little on the lot. The front of the house was overgrown with weeds, old dry weeds that rustled and chattered in the wind. The house itself was a little gray box, shabby and unpainted, the porch steps sagging. There was an old weather-beaten rocking chair on the porch with a torn piece of cloth hanging over it.

Bubber went up the walk. As he started up the rickety steps he took a deep breath. He could smell it, the wonderful warm smell, and his mouth began to water. His heart thudding with anticipation, Bubber turned the handle of the bell. The bell grated rustily on the other side of the door. There was silence for a time, then the sounds of someone stirring.

Mrs Drew opened the door. She was old, very old, a little dried-up old lady, like the weeds that grew along the front of the house. She smiled down at Bubber, holding the door wide for him to come in.

'You're just in time,' she said. 'Come on inside, Bernard. You're just in time – they're just now ready.'

Bubber went to the kitchen door and looked in. He could see them, resting on a big blue plate on top of the stove. Cookies, a plate of warm, fresh cookies right out of the oven. Cookies with nuts and raisins in them.

'How do they look?' Mrs Drew said. She rustled past him, into the kitchen. 'And maybe some cold milk, too. You like cold milk with them.' She got the milk pitcher from the window box on the back porch. Then she poured a glass of milk for him and set some of the cookies on a small plate. 'Let's go into the living room,' she said.

Bubber nodded. Mrs Drew carried the milk and the cookies in and set them on the arm of the couch. Then she sat down in her own chair, watching Bubber plop himself down by the plate and begin to help himself.

Bubber ate greedily, as usual, intent on the cookies, silent except for chewing sounds. Mrs Drew waited patiently, until the boy had finished, and his already ample sides bulged that much more. When Bubber was done with the plate he glanced toward the kitchen again, at the rest of the cookies on the stove.

'Wouldn't you like to wait until later for the rest?' Mrs Drew said.

'All right,' Bubber agreed.

'How were they?'

'Fine.'

'That's good.' She leaned back in her chair. 'Well, what did you do in school today? How did it go?'

'All right.'

The little old lady watched the boy look restlessly around the room. 'Bernard,' she said presently, 'won't you stay and talk to me for a while?' He had some books on his lap, some school books. 'Why don't you read to me from your books? You know, I don't see too well any more and it's a comfort to me to be read to.'

'Can I have the rest of the cookies after?'

'Of course.'

Bubber moved over towards her, to the end of the couch. He opened his books, World Geography, Principles of Arithmetic, Hoyte's Speller. 'Which do you want?'

She hesitated. 'The geography.'

Bubber opened the big blue book at random. PERU. 'Peru is bounded on the north by Ecuador and Columbia, on the south by Chile, and on the east by Brazil and Bolivia. Peru is divided into three main sections. These are, first – '

The little old lady watched him read, his fat cheeks wobbling as he read, holding his finger next to the line. She was silent, watching him, studying the boy intently as he read, drinking in each frown of concentration, every motion of his arms and hands. She relaxed, letting herself sink back in her chair. He was very close to her, only a little way off. There was only the table and lamp between them. How nice it was to have him come; he had been coming for over a month, now, ever since the day she had been sitting on her porch and seen him go by and thought to call to him, pointing to the cookies by her rocker.

Why had she done it? She did not know. She had been alone so long that she found herself saying strange things and doing strange things. She saw so few people, only when she went down to the store or the mailman came with her pension check. Or the garbage men.

The boy's voice droned on. She was comfortable, peaceful and relaxed. The little old lady closed her eyes and folded her hands in her lap. And as she sat, dozing and listening, something began to happen. The little old lady was beginning to change, her gray wrinkles and lines dimming away. As she sat in the chair she was growing younger, the thin fragile body filling out with youth again. The gray hair thickened and darkened, color coming to the wispy strands. Her arms filled, too, the mottled flesh turning a rich hue as it had been once, many years before.

Mrs Drew breathed deeply, not opening her eyes. She could feel *something* happening, but she did not know just what. *Something* was going on; she could feel it, and it was good. But what it was she did not exactly know. It had happened before, almost every time the boy came and sat by her. Especially of late, since she had moved her chair nearer to the couch. She took a deep breath. How good it felt, the warm fullness, a breath of warmth inside her cold body for the first time in years!

In her chair the little old lady had become a dark-haired matron of perhaps thirty, a woman with full cheeks and plump arms and legs. Her lips were red again, her neck even a little too fleshy, as it had been once in the long forgotten past.

Suddenly the reading stopped. Bubber put down his book and stood up. 'I have to go,' he said. 'Can I take the rest of the cookies with me?'

She blinked, rousing herself. The boy was in the kitchen, filling his pockets with cookies. She nodded, dazed, still under the spell. The boy took the last cookies. He went across the living room to the door. Mrs Drew stood up. All at once the warmth left her. She felt tired, tired and very dry. She caught her breath, breathing quickly. She looked down at her hands. Wrinkled, thin.

'Oh!' she murmured. Tears blurred her eyes. It was gone, gone again as soon as he moved away. She tottered to the mirror above the mantel and looked at herself. Old faded eyes stared back, eyes deep-set in a withered face. Gone, all gone, as soon as the boy had left her side.

'I'll see you later,' Bubber said.

'Please,' she whispered. 'Please come back again. Will you come back?'

'Sure,' Bubber said listlessly. He pushed the door open. 'Good-bye.' He went down the steps. In a moment she heard his shoes against the sidewalk. He was gone.

'Bubber, you come in here!' May Surle stood angrily on the porch. 'You get in here and sit down at the table.'

'All right.' Bubber came slowly up on to the porch, pushing inside the house.

'What's the matter with you?' She caught his arm. 'Where you been? Are you sick?'

'I'm tired.' Bubber rubbed his forehead.

His father came through the living room with the newspapers, in his undershirt. 'What's the matter?' he said.

'Look at him,' May Surle said. 'All worn out. What you been doing, Bubber?'

'He's been visiting that old lady,' Ralf Surle said. 'Can't you tell? He's always washed out after he's been visiting her. What do you go there for, Bub? What goes on?'

'She gives him cookies,' May said. 'You know how he is about things to eat. He'd do anything for a plate of cookies.'

'Bub,' his father said, 'listen to me. I don't want you hanging around that crazy old lady anymore. Do you hear me? I don't care how many cookies she gives you. You come home too tired! No more of that. You hear me?'

Bubber looked down at the floor, leaning against the door. His heart beat heavily, labored. 'I told her I'd come back,' he muttered.

'You can go once more,' May said, going into the dining room, 'but only once more. Tell her you won't be able to come back again, though. You make sure you tell her nice. Now go upstairs and get washed up.'

'After dinner better have him lie down,' Ralf said, looking up the stairs, watching Bubber climb slowly, his hand on the banister. He shook his head. 'I don't like it,' he murmured. 'I don't want him going there any more. There's something strange about that old lady.'

'Well, it'll be the last tine,' May said.

Wednesday was warm and sunny. Bubber strode along, his hands in his pockets. He stopped in front of McVane's drugstore for a minute, looking speculatively at the comic books. At the soda fountain a woman was drinking a big chocolate soda. The sight of it made Bubber's mouth water. That settled it. He turned and continued on his way, even increasing his pace a little.

A few minutes later he came up on the the gray sagging porch and rang the bell. Below him the weeds blew and rustled with the wind. It was almost four o'clock; he could not stay too long. But then, it was the last time anyhow.

The door opened. Mrs Drew's wrinkled face broke into smiles. 'Come in, Bernard. It's good to see you standing there. It makes me feel so young again to have you come visit.'

He went inside, looking around.

'I'll start the cookies. I didn't know if you were coming.' She padded into the kitchen. 'I'll get them started right away. You sit down on the couch.'

Bubber went over and sat down. He noticed that the table

and lamp were gone; the chair was right up next to the couch.
He was looking at the chair in perplexity when Mrs Drew came
rustling back into the room.

'They're in the oven. I had the batter all ready. Now.' She
sat down in the chair with a sigh. 'Well, how did it go today?
How was school?'

'Fine.'

She nodded. How plump he was, the little boy, sitting just a
little distance from her, his cheeks red and full! She could touch
him, he was so close. Her aged heart thumped. Ah, to be
young again. Youth was so much. It was everything. What did
the world mean to the old? _When all the world is old, lad. . ._

'Do you want to read to me, Bernard?' she asked presently.

'I didn't bring any books.'

'Oh.' She nodded. 'Well, I have some books,' she said
quickly. 'I'll get them.'

She got up, crossing to the bookcase. As she opened the
doors, Bubber said, 'Mrs Drew, my father says I can't come
here anymore. He says this is the last time. I thought I'd tell
you.'

She stopped, standing rigid. Everything seemed to leap
around her, the room twisting furiously. She took a harsh,
frightened breath. 'Bernard, you're – you're not coming back?'

'No, my father says not to.'

There was silence. The old lady took a book at random and
came slowly back to her chair. After a while she passed the
book to him, her hands trembling. The boy took it without
expression, looking at its cover.

'Please, read, Bernard. Please.'

'All right.' He opened the book. 'Where'll I start?'

'Anywhere. Anywhere, Bernard.'

He began to read. It was something by Trollope; she only
half heard the words. She put her hand to her forehead, the
dry skin, brittle and thin, like old paper. She trembled with
anguish. The last time?

Bubber read on, slowly, monotonously. Against the window
a fly buzzed. Outside the sun began to set, the air turning cool.
A few clouds came up, and the wind in the trees rushed
furiously.

The old lady sat, close by the boy, closer than ever, hearing him read, the sound of his voice, sensing him close by. Was this really the last time? Terror rose up in her heart and she pushed it back. The last time! She gazed at him, the boy sitting so close to her. After a time she reached out her thin, dry hand. She took a deep breath. He would never be back. There would be no more times, no more. This was the last time he would sit there.

She touched his arm.

Bubber looked up. 'What is it?' he murmured.

'You don't mind if I touch your arm, do you?'

'No, I guess not.' He went on reading. The old lady could feel the youngness of him, flowing between her fingers, through her arm. A pulsating vibrating youngness, so close to her. It had never been that close, where she could actually touch it. The feel of life made her dizzy, unsteady.

And presently it began to happen, as before. She closed her eyes, letting it move over her, filling her up, carried into her by the sound of the voice and the feel of the arm. The change, the flow, was coming over her, the warm, rising feeling. She was blooming again, filling with life, swelling into richness, as she had been, once, long ago.

She looked down at her arms. Rounded, they were, and the nails clear. Her hair. Black again, heavy and black against her neck. She touched her cheek. The wrinkles had gone, the skin pliant and soft.

Joy filled her, a growing bursting joy. She stared around her, at the room. She smiled, feeling her firm teeth and gums, red lips, strong white teeth. Suddenly she got to her feet, her body secure and confident. She turned a little, lithe, quick circle.

Bubber stopped reading. 'Are the cookies ready?' he said.

'I'll see.' Her voice was alive, deep with a quality that had dried out many years before. Now it was there again, *her* voice, throaty and sensual. She walked quickly to the kitchen and opened the oven. She took out the cookies and put them on top of the stove.

'All ready,' she called gaily. 'Come and get them.'

Bubber came past her, his gaze fastened on the sight of the cookies. He did not even notice the woman by the door.

Philip K. Dick

Mrs Drew hurried from the kitchen. She went into the bedroom, closing the door after her. Then she turned, gazing into the full-length mirror on the door. Young – she was young again, filled out with the sap of vigorous youth. She took a deep breath, her steady bosom swelling. Her eyes flashed, and she smiled. She spun, her skirts flying. Young and lovely.

And this time it had not gone away.

She opened the door. Bubber had filled his mouth and his pockets. He was standing in the center of the living room, his face fat and dull, a dead white.

'What's the matter?' Mrs Drew said.

'I'm going.'

'All right, Bernard. And thanks for coming to read to me.' She laid her hand on his shoulder. 'Perhaps I'll see you again some time.'

'My father – '

'I know.' She laughed gaily, opening the door for him. 'Good-bye, Bernard. Good-bye.'

She watched him go slowly down the steps, one at a time. Then she closed the door and skipped back into the bedroom. She unfastened her dress and stepped out of it, the worn gray fabric suddenly distasteful to her. For a brief second she gazed at her full, rounded body, her hands on her hips.

She laughed with excitement, turning a little, her eyes bright. What a wonderful body, bursting with life. A swelling breast – she touched herself. The flesh was firm. There was so much, so many things to do! She gazed about her, breathing quickly. So many things! She started the water running in the bathtub and then went to tie her hair up.

The wind blew around him as he trudged home. It was late, the sun had set and the sky overhead was dark and cloudy. The wind that blew and nudged against him was cold, and it penetrated through his clothing, chilling him. The boy felt tired, his head ached, and he stopped every few minutes, rubbing his forehead and resting, his heart laboring. He left Elm Street and went up Pine Street. The wind screeched around him, pushing him from side to side. He shook his head, trying to clear it. How weary he was, how tired his arms and legs were. He felt the wind hammering at him, pushing and plucking at him.

He took a breath and went on, his head down. At the corner he stopped, holding on to a lamp-post. The sky was quite dark, the street lights were beginning to come on. At last he went on, walking as best he could.

'Where is that boy?' May Surle said, going out on the porch for the tenth time. Ralf flicked on the light and they stood together. 'What an awful wind.'

The wind whistled and lashed at the porch. The two of them looked up and down the dark street, but they could see nothing but a few newspapers and trash being blown along.

'Let's go inside,' Ralf said. 'He sure is going to get a licking when he gets home.'

They sat down at the dinner table. Presently May put down her fork. 'Listen! Do you hear something?'

Ralf listened.

Outside, against the front door, there was a faint sound, a tapping sound. He stood up. The wind howled outside, blowing the shades in the room upstairs. 'I'll go see what it is,' he said.

He went to the door and opened it. Something gray, something gray and dry was blowing up against the porch, carried by the wind. He stared at it, but he could not make it out. A bundle of weeds, weeds and rags blown by the wind, perhaps.

The bundle bounced against his legs. He watched it drift past him, against the wall of the house. Then he closed the door again slowly.

'What was it?' May called.

'Just the wind,' Ralf Surle said.

Beyond the Door

That night at the dinner table he brought it out and set it down beside her plate. Doris stared at it, her hand to her mouth. 'My God, what is it?' She looked up at him, bright-eyed.

'Well, open it.'

Doris tore the ribbon and paper from the square package with her sharp nails, her bosom rising and falling. Larry stood watching her as she lifted the lid. He lit a cigarette and leaned against the wall.

'A cuckoo clock!' Doris cried. 'A real old cuckoo clock like my mother had.' She turned the clock over and over. 'Just like my mother had, when Pete was still alive.' Her eyes sparkled with tears.

'It's made in Germany,' Larry said. After a moment he added, 'Carl got it for me wholesale. He knows some guy in the clock business. Otherwise I wouldn't have – ' he stopped.

Doris made a funny little sound.

'I mean, otherwise, I wouldn't have been able to afford it.' He scowled. 'What's the matter with you? You've got your clock, haven't you? Isn't that what you want?'

Doris sat holding onto the clock, her fingers pressed against the brown wood.

'Well,' Larry said, 'what's the matter?'

He watched in amazement as she leaped up and ran from the room, still clutching the clock. He shook his head. 'Never satisfied. They're all that way. Never get enough.'

He sat down at the table and finished his meal.

The cuckoo clock was not very large. It was hand-made, however, and there were countless frets on it, little indentations and ornaments scored in the soft wood. Doris sat on the bed drying her eyes and winding the clock. She set the hands by her wristwatch. Presently she carefully moved the hands to two minutes of ten. She carried the clock over to the dresser and propped it up.

Then she sat waiting, her hands twisted together in her lap – waiting for the cuckoo to come out, for the hour to strike.

As she sat she thought about Larry and what he had said. And what she had said, too, for that matter – not that she could be blamed for any of it. After all, she couldn't keep listening to him forever without defending herself; you had to blow your own trumpet in the world.

She touched her handkerchief to her eyes suddenly. Why did he have to say that, about getting it wholesale? Why did he have to spoil it all? If he felt that way he needn't have got it in the first place. She clenched her fists. He was so mean, so damn mean.

But she was glad of the little clock sitting there ticking to itself, with its funny grilled edges and the door. Inside the door was the cuckoo, waiting to come out. Was he listening, his head cocked on one side, listening to hear the clock strike so that he would know to come out?

Did he sleep between hours? Well, she would soon see him: she could ask him. And she would show the clock to Bob. He would love it; Bob loved old things, even old stamps and buttons. Of course, it was a little *awkward*, but Larry had been staying at the office so much, and that helped. If only Larry didn't call up sometimes to –

There was a whirr. The clock shuddered and all at once the door opened. The cuckoo came out, sliding swiftly. He paused and looked around solemnly, scrutinizing her, the room, the furniture.

It was the first time he had seen her, she realized, smiling to herself in pleasure. She stood up, coming toward him shyly. 'Go on,' she said, 'I'm waiting.'

The cuckoo opened his bill. He whirred and chirped, quickly, rhythmically. Then, after a moment of contemplation, he retired. And the door snapped shut.

She was delighted. She clapped her hands and spun in a little circle. He was marvelous, perfect! And the way he had looked around, studying her, sizing her up. He liked her; she was certain of it. And she, of course, loved him at once, completely. He was just what she had hoped would come out of the little door.

Doris went to the clock. She bent over the little door, her lips close to the wood. 'Do you hear me?' she whispered. 'I think you're the most wonderful cuckoo in the world.' She paused, embarrassed. 'I hope you'll like it here.'

Then she went downstairs again, slowly, her head high.

Larry and the cuckoo clock really never got along well from the start. Doris said it was because he didn't wind it right, and it didn't like being only half-wound all the time. Larry turned the job of winding over to her; the cuckoo came out every quarter hour and ran the spring down without remorse, and someone had to be ever after it, winding it up again.

Doris did her best, but she forgot a good deal of the time. Then Larry would throw his newspaper down with an elaborate weary motion and stand up. He would go into the dining-room where the clock was mounted on the wall over the fireplace. He would take the clock down and making sure that he had his thumb over the little door, he would wind it up.

'Why do you put your thumb over the door?' Doris asked once.

'You're supposed to.'

She raised an eyebrow. 'Are you sure? I wonder if it isn't that you don't want him to come out while you're standing so close.'

'Why not?'

'Maybe you're afraid of him.'

Larry laughed. He put the clock back on the wall and gingerly removed his thumb. When Doris wasn't looking he examined his thumb.

There was still a trace of the nick cut out of the soft part of it. Who – or what – had pecked at him?

One Saturday morning, when Larry was down at the office working over some important special accounts, Bob Chambers came to the front porch and rang the bell.

Doris was taking a quick shower. She dried herself and

slipped into her robe. When she opened the door Bob stepped inside, grinning.

'Hi,' he said, looking around.

'It's all right. Larry's at the office.'

'Fine.' Bob gazed at her slim legs below the hem of the robe. 'How nice you look today.'

She laughed. 'Be careful! Maybe I shouldn't let you in after all.'

They looked at one another, half amused, half frightened. Presently Bob said, 'If you want, I'll – '

'No, for God's sake.' She caught hold of his sleeve. 'Just get out of the doorway so I can close it. Mrs Peters across the street, you know.'

She closed the door. 'And I want to show you something,' she said. 'You haven't seen it.'

He was interested. 'An antique? Or what?'

She took his arm, leading him toward the dining-room. 'You'll love it, Bobby.' She stopped wide-eyed. 'I hope you will. You must; you must love it. It means so much to me – *he* means so much.'

'He?' Bob frowned. 'Who is he?'

Doris laughed. 'You're jealous! Come on.' A moment later they stood before the clock, looking up at it. 'He'll come out in a few minutes. Wait until you see him. I know you two will get along fine.'

'What does Larry think of him?'

'They don't like each other. Sometimes when Larry's here he won't come out. Larry gets mad if he doesn't come out on time. He says – '

'Says what?'

Doris looked down. 'He always says he's been robbed, even if he did get it wholesale.' She brightened. 'But I know he won't come out because he doesn't like Larry. When I'm here alone he comes right out for me, every fifteen minutes, even though he really only has to come out on the hour.'

She gazed up at the clock. 'He comes out for me because he wants to. We talk; I tell him things. Of course, I'd like to have him upstairs in my room, but it wouldn't be right.'

There was a sound of footsteps on the front porch. They looked at each other, horrified.

Larry pushed the front door open, grunting. He set his briefcase down and took off his hat. Then he saw Bob for the first time.

'Chambers. I'll be damned.' His eyes narrowed. 'What are you doing here?' He came into the dining-room. Doris drew her robe about her helplessly, backing away.

'I – ' Bob began. 'That is, we – ' He broke off, glancing at Doris. Suddenly the clock began to whirr. The cuckoo came rushing out, bursting into sound. Larry moved toward him.

'Shut that din off,' he said. He raised his fist toward the clock. The cuckoo snapped into silence and retreated. The door closed. 'That's better.' Larry studied Doris and Bob, standing mutely together.

'I came over to look at the clock,' Bob said. 'Doris told me that it's a rare antique and that – '

'Nuts. I bought it myself.' Larry walked up to him. 'Get out of here.' He turned to Doris. 'You too. And take that damn clock with you.'

He paused, rubbing his chin. 'No. Leave the clock here. It's mine; I bought it and paid for it.'

In the weeks that followed after Doris left, Larry and the cuckoo clock got along even worse than before. For one thing, the cuckoo stayed inside most of the time, sometimes even at twelve o'clock when he should have been busiest. And if he did come out at all he usually spoke only once or twice, never the correct number of times. And there was a sullen, uncooperative note in his voice, a jarring sound that made Larry uneasy and a little angry.

But he kept the clock wound, because the house was very still and quiet and it got on his nerves not to hear someone running around, talking and dropping things. And even the whirring of a clock sounded good to him.

But he didn't like the cuckoo at all. And sometimes he spoke to him.

'Listen,' he said late one night to the closed little door. 'I know you can hear me. I ought to give you back to the Germans – back to the Black Forest.' He paced back and forth.

'I wonder what they're doing now, the two of them. That young punk with his books and his antiques. A man shouldn't be interested in antiques; that's for women.'

He set his jaw. 'Isn't that right?'

The clock said nothing. Larry walked up in front of it. 'Isn't that right?' he demanded. 'Don't you have anything to say?'

He looked at the face of the clock. It was almost eleven, just a few seconds before the hour. 'All right. I'll wait until eleven. Then I want to hear what you have to say. You've been pretty quiet the last few weeks since she left.'

He grinned wryly. 'Maybe you don't like it here since she's gone.' He scowled. 'Well, I paid for you, and you're coming out whether you like it or not. You hear me?'

Eleven o'clock came. Far off, at the end of town, the great tower clock boomed sleepily to itself. But the little door remained shut. Nothing moved. The minute hand passed on and the cuckoo did not stir. He was someplace inside the clock, beyond the door, silent and remote.

'All right, if that's the way you feel,' Larry murmured, his lips twisting. 'But it isn't fair. It's your job to come out. We all have to do things we don't like.'

He went unhappily into the kitchen and opened the great gleaming refrigerator. As he poured himself a drink he thought about the clock.

There was no doubt about it – the cuckoo should come out, Doris or no Doris. He had always liked her, from the very start. They had got along well, the two of them. Probably he liked Bob too – probably he had seen enough of Bob to get to know him. They would be quite happy together, Bob and Doris and the cuckoo.

Larry finished his drink. He opened the drawer at the sink and took out the hammer. He carried it carefully into the dining-room. The clock was ticking gently to itself on the wall.

'Look,' he said, waving the hammer. 'You know what I have here? You know what I'm going to do with it? I'm going to start on you – first.' He smiled. 'Birds of a feather, that's what you are – the three of you.'

The room was silent.

'Are you coming out? Or do I have to come in and get you?'

The clock whirred a little.

'I hear you in there. You've got a lot of talking to do, enough for the last three weeks. As I figure it, you owe me – '

The door opened. The cuckoo came out fast, straight at him. Larry was looking down, his brow wrinkled in thought. He glanced up, and the cuckoo caught him squarely in the eye.

Down he went, hammer and chair and everything, hitting the floor with a tremendous crash. For a moment the cuckoo paused, its small body poised rigidly. Then it went back inside its house. The door snapped tight-shut after it.

The man lay on the floor, stretched out grotesquely, his head bent over to one side. Nothing moved or stirred. The room was completely silent, except, of course, for the ticking of the clock.

'I see,' Doris said, her face tight. Bob put his arm around her, steadying her.

'Doctor,' Bob said, 'can I ask you something?'

'Of course,' the doctor said.

'Is it very easy to break your neck, falling from so low a chair? It wasn't very far to fall. I wonder if it might not have been an accident. Is there any chance it might have been – '

'Suicide?' the doctor rubbed his jaw. 'I never heard of anyone committing suicide that way. It was an accident; I'm positive.'

'I don't mean suicide,' Bob murmured under his breath, looking up at the clock on the wall. 'I meant *something else*.'

But no one heard him.

Second Variety

The Russian soldier made his way nervously up the rugged side of the hill, holding his gun ready. He glanced around him, locking his dry lips, his face set. From time to time he reached up a gloved hand and wiped perspiration from his neck, pushing down his coat collar.

Eric turned to Corporal Leone. 'Want him? Or can I have him?' He adjusted the view sight so the Russian's features squarely filled the glass, the lines cutting across his hard, somber features.

Leone considered. The Russian was close, moving rapidly, almost running. 'Don't fire. Wait.' Leone tensed. 'I don't think we're needed.'

The Russian increased his pace, kicking ash and piles of debris out of his way. He reached the top of the hill and stopped, panting, staring around him. The sky was overcast, with drifting clouds of gray particles. Bare trunks of trees jutted up occasionally; the ground was level and bare, rubble-strewn, with the ruins of buildings standing here and there like yellowing skulls.

The Russian was uneasy. He knew something was wrong. He started down the hill. Now he was only a few paces away from the bunker. Eric was getting fidgety. He played with his pistol, glancing at Leone.

'Don't worry,' Leone said. 'He won't get here. They'll take care of him.'

'Are you sure? He's got damn far.'

'They hang around close to the bunker. He's getting into the bad part. Get set!'

The Russian began to hurry, sliding down the hill, his boots sinking into the heaps of gray ash, trying to keep his gun up. He stopped for a moment, lifting his field glasses to his face.

'He's looking right at us,' Eric said.

The Russian came on. They could see his eyes, like two blue stones. His mouth was open a little. He needed a shave; his chin was stubbled. On one bony cheek was a square of tape, showing blue at the edge. A fungoid spot. His coat was muddy and torn. One glove was missing. As he ran, his belt counter bounced up and down against him.

Leone touched Eric's arm. 'Here one comes.'

Across the ground something small and metallic came, flashing in the dull sunlight of midday. A metal sphere. It raced up the hill after the Russian, its treads flying. It was small, one of the baby ones. Its claws were out, two razor projections spinning in a blur of white steel. The Russian heard it. He turned instantly, firing. The sphere dissolved into particles. But already a second had emerged and was following the first. The Russian fired again.

A third sphere leaped up the Russian's leg, clicking and whirring. It jumped to the shoulder. The spinning blades disappeared into the Russian's throat.

Eric relaxed. 'Well, that's that. God, those damn things give me the creeps. Sometimes I think we were better off before them.'

'If we hadn't invented them, they would have.' Leone lit a cigarette shakily. 'I wonder why a Russian would come all this way alone. I didn't see anyone covering him.'

Lieutenant Scott came slipping up the tunnel, into the bunker. 'What happened? Something entered the screen.'

'An Ivan.'

'Just one?'

Eric brought the viewscreen around. Scott peered into it. Now there were numerous metal spheres crawling over the prostrate body, dull metal globes clicking and whirring, sawing up the Russian into small parts to be carried away.

'What a lot of claws,' Scott murmured.

'They came like flies. Not much game for them anymore.'

Scott pushed the sight away, disgusted. 'Like flies. I wonder why he was out there. They know we have claws all around.'

A larger robot had joined the smaller spheres. A long blunt tube with projecting eyepieces, it was directing operations. There was not much left of the soldier. What remained was brought down the hillside by the host of claws.

'Sir,' Leone said. 'If it's all right, I'd like to go out there and take a look at him.'

'Why?'

'Maybe he came with something.'

Scott considered. He shrugged. 'All right. But be careful.'

'I have my tab.' Leone patted the metal band at his wrist. 'I'll be out of bounds.'

He picked up his rifle and stepped carefully up to the mouth of the bunker, making his way between blocks of concrete and steel prongs, twisted and bent. The air was cold at the top. He crossed over the ground toward the remains of the soldier, striding across the soft ash. A wind blew around him, swirling gray particles up in his face. He squinted and pushed on.

The claws retreated as he came close, some of them stiffening into immobility. He touched his tab. The Ivan would have given something for that! Short hard radiation emitted from the tab neutralized the claws, put them out of commission. Even the big robot with its two waving eyestalks retreated respectfully as he approached.

He bent down over the remains of the soldier. The gloved hand was closed tightly. There was something in it. Leone pried the fingers apart. A sealed container, aluminum. Still shiny.

He put it in his pocket and made his way back to the bunker. Behind him the claws came back to life, moving into operation again. The procession resumed, metal spheres moving through the gray ash with their loads. He could hear their treads scrabbling against the ground. He shuddered.

Scott watched intently as he brought the shiny tube out of his pocket. 'He had that?'

'In his hand.' Leone unscrewed the top. 'Maybe you should look at it, sir.'

Scott took it. He emptied the contents out in the palm of his hand. A small piece of silk paper, carefully folded. He sat down by the light and unfolded it.

'What's it say?' Eric said. Several officers came up the tunnel. Major Hendricks appeared.

'Major,' Scott said. 'Look at this.'

Hendricks read the slip. 'This just come?'

'A single runner. Just now.'

'Where is he?' Hendricks asked sharply.

'The claws got him.'

Major Hendricks grunted. 'Here.' He passed it to his companions. 'I think this is what we've been waiting for. They certainly took their time about it.'

'So they want to talk terms,' Scott said. 'Are we going along with them?'

'That's not for us to decide.' Hendricks sat down. 'Where's the communications officer? I want the Moon Base.'

Leone pondered as the communications officer raised the outside antenna cautiously, scanning the sky above the bunker for any sign of a watching Russian ship.

'Sir,' Scott said to Hendricks. 'It's sure strange they suddenly came around. We've been using the claws for almost a year. Now all of a sudden they start to fold.'

'Maybe claws have been getting down in their bunkers.'

'One of the big ones, the kind with stalks, got into an Ivan bunker last week,' Eric said. 'It got a whole platoon of them before they got their lid shut.'

'How do you know?'

'A buddy told me. The thing came back with – with remains.'

'Moon Base, sir,' the communications officer said.

On the screen the face of the lunar monitor appeared. His crisp uniform contrasted to the uniforms in the bunker. And he was cleanshaven. 'Moon Base.'

'This is forward command L-Whistle. On Terra. Let me have General Thompson.'

The monitor faded. Presently General Thompson's heavy features came into focus. 'What is it, Major?'

'Our claws got a single Russian runner with a message. We don't know whether to act on it – there have been tricks like this in the past.'

'What's the message?'

'The Russians want us to send a single officer on policy level over to their lines. For a conference. They don't state the nature of the conference. They say that matters of – ' He consulted the slip: ' – matters of grave urgency make it advisable that discussion be opened between a representative of the UN forces and themselves.'

He held the message up to the screen for the General to scan. Thompson's eyes moved.

'What should we do?' Hendricks said.

'Send out a man.'

'You don't think it's a trap?'

'It might be. But the location they give for their forward command is correct. It's worth a try, at any rate.'

'I'll send an officer out. And report the results to you as soon as he returns.'

'All right, Major.' Thompson broke the connection. The screen died. Up above, the antenna came slowly down.

Hendricks rolled up the paper, deep in thought.

'I'll go,' Leone said.

'They want somebody at policy level.' Hendricks rubbed his jaw. 'Policy level. I haven't been outside in months. Maybe I could use a little air.'

'Don't you think it's risky?'

Hendricks lifted the view sight and gazed into it. The remains of the Russian were gone. Only a single claw was in sight. It was folding itself back, disappearing into the ash, like a crab. Like some hideous metal crab . . . 'That's the only thing that bothers me.' Hendricks rubbed his wrist. 'I know I'm safe as long as I have this on me. But there's something about them. I hate the damn things. I wish we'd never invented them. There's something wrong with them. Relentless little –'

'If we hadn't invented them, the Ivans would have.'

Hendricks pushed the sight back. 'Anyhow, it seems to be winning the war. I guess that's good.'

'Sounds like you're getting the same jitters as the Ivans.'

Hendricks examined his wristwatch. 'I guess I had better get started, if I want to be there before dark.'

He took a deep breath and then stepped out onto the gray rubbled ground. After a minute he lit a cigarette and stood gazing around him. The landscape was dead. Nothing stirred. He could see for miles, endless ash and slag, ruins of buildings. A few trees without leaves or branches, only the trunks. Above him the eternal rolling clouds of gray, drifting between Terra and the sun.

Major Hendricks went on. Off to the right something scuttled, something round and metallic. A claw, going lickety-split after something. Probably after a small animal, a rat. They got rats, too. As a sort of sideline.

He came to the top of the little hill and lifted his field glasses. The Russian lines were a few miles ahead of him. They had a forward command post there. The runner had come from it.

A squat robot with undulating arms passed by him, its arms weaving inquiringly. The robot went on its way, disappearing under some debris. Hendricks watched it go. He had never seen that type before. There were getting to be more and more types he had never seen, new varieties and sizes coming up from the underground factories.

Hendricks put out his cigarette and hurried on. It was interesting, the use of artificial forms of warfare. How had they got started? Necessity. The Soviet Union had gained great initial success, usual with the side that got the war going. Most of North America had been blasted off the map. Retaliation was quick in coming, of course. The sky was full of circling diskbombers long before the war began; they had been up there for years. The disks began sailing down all over Russia within hours after Washington got it.

But that hadn't helped Washington.

The American bloc governments moved to the Moon Base the first year. There was not much else to do. Europe was gone, a slag heap with dark weeds growing from the ashes and bones. Most of North America was useless; nothing could be planted, no one could live. A few million people kept going up in Canada and down in South America. But during the second year Soviet parachutists began to drop, a few at first, then more and more. They wore the first really effective anti-radiation equipment; what was left of American production moved to the Moon along with the governments.

All but the troops. The remaining troops stayed behind as

best they could, a few thousand here, a platoon there. No one knew exactly where they were; they stayed where they could, moving around at night, hiding in ruins, in sewers, cellars, with the rats and snakes. It looked as if the Soviet Union had the war almost won. Except for a handful of projectiles fired off from the Moon daily, there was almost no weapon in use against them. They came and went as they pleased. The war, for all practical purposes, was over. Nothing effective opposed them.

And then the first claws appeared. And overnight the complexion of the war changed.

The claws were awkward, at first. Slow. The Ivans knocked them off almost as fast as they crawled out of their underground tunnels. But then they got better, faster and more cunning. Factories, all on Terra, turned them out. Factories a long way underground, behind the Soviet lines, factories that had once made atomic projectiles, now almost forgotten.

The claws got faster, and they got bigger. New types appeared, some with feelers, some that flew. There were a few jumping kinds. The best technicians on the Moon were working on designs, making them more and more intricate, more flexible. They became uncanny; the Ivans were having a lot of trouble with them. Some of the little claws were learning to hide themselves, burrowing down into the ash, lying in wait.

And they started getting into the Russian bunkers, slipping down when the lids were raised for air and a look around. One claw inside a bunker, a churning sphere of blades and metal – that was enough. And when one got in others followed. With a weapon like that the war couldn't go on much longer.

Maybe it was already over.

Maybe he was going to hear the news. Maybe the Politburo had decided to throw in the sponge. Too bad it had taken so long. Six years. A long time for war like that, the way they had waged it. The automatic retaliation disks, spinning down all over Russia, hundreds of thousands of them. Bacteria crystals. The Soviet guided missiles, whistling through the air. The chain bombs. And now this, the robots, the claws –

The claws weren't like other weapons. They were *alive*, from any practical standpoint, whether the Governments wanted to admit it or not. They were not machines. They were living things, spinning, creeping, shaking themselves up suddenly from the gray ash and darting toward a man, climbing up him, rushing for his throat. And that was what they had been designed to do. Their job.

They did their job well. Especially lately, with the new designs coming up. Now they repaired themselves. They were on their own. Radiation tabs protected the UN troops, but if a man lost his tab he was fair game for the claws, no matter what his uniform. Down below the surface automatic machinery stamped them out. Human beings stayed a long way off. It was too risky; nobody wanted to be around them. They were left to themselves. And they seemed to be doing all right. The new designs were faster, more complex. More efficient.

Apparently they had won the war.

Major Hendricks lit a second cigarette. The landscape depressed him. Nothing but ash and ruins. He seemed to be alone, the only living thing in the whole world. To the right the ruins of a town rose up, a few walls and heaps of debris. He tossed the dead match away, increasing his pace. Suddenly he stopped, jerking up his gun, his body tense. For a minute it looked like –

From behind the shell of a ruined building a figure came, walking slowly toward him, walking hesitantly.

Hendricks blinked. 'Stop!'

The boy stopped. Hendricks lowered his gun. The boy stood silently, looking at him. He was small, not very old. Perhaps eight. But it was hard to tell. Most of the kids who remained were stunted. He wore a faded blue sweater, ragged with dirt, and short pants. His hair was long and matted. Brown hair. It hung over his face and around his ears. He held something in his arms.

'What's that you have?' Hendricks said sharply.

The boy held it out. It was a toy, a bear. A teddy bear. The boy's eyes were large, but without expression.

Hendricks relaxed. 'I don't want it. Keep it.'

The boy hugged the bear again.

'Where do you live?' Hendricks said.

'In there.'

'The ruins?'

'Yes.'

'Underground?'

'Yes.'

'How many are there?'

'How – how many?'

'How many of you? How big's your settlement?'

The boy did not answer.

Hendricks frowned. 'You're not all by yourself, are you?'

The boy nodded.

'How do you stay alive?'

'There's food.'

'What kind of food?'

'Different.'

Hendricks studied him. 'How old are you?'

'Thirteen.'

It wasn't possible. Or was it? The boy was thin, stunted. And probably sterile. Radiation exposure, years straight. No wonder he was so small. His arms and legs were like pipe cleaners, knobby and thin. Hendricks touched the boy's arm. His skin was dry and rough; radiation skin. He bent down, looking into the boy's face. There was no expression. Big eyes, big and dark.

'Are you blind?' Hendricks said.

'No. I can see some.'

'How do you get away from the claws?'

'The claws?'

'The round things. That run and burrow.'

'I don't understand.'

Maybe there weren't any claws around. A lot of areas were free. They collected mostly around bunkers, where there were people. The claws had been designed to sense warmth, warmth of living things.

'You're lucky.' Hendricks straightened up. 'Well? Which way are you going? Back – back there?'

'Can I come with you?'

'With *me*?' Hendricks folded his arms. 'I'm going a long way.

Miles. I have to hurry.' He looked at his watch. 'I have to get there by nightfall.'

'I want to come.'

Hendricks fumbled in his pack. 'It isn't worth it. Here.' He tossed down the food cans he had with him. 'You take these and go back. Okay?'

The boy said nothing.

'I'll be coming back this way. In a day or so. If you're around here when I come back you can come along with me. All right?'

'I want to come with you now.'

'It's a long walk.'

'I can walk.'

Hendricks shifted uneasily. It made too good a target, two people walking along. And the boy would slow him down. But he might not come back this way. And if the boy were really all alone –

'Okay. Come along.'

The boy fell in beside him. Hendricks strode along. The boy walked silently, clutching his teddy bear.

'What's your name?' Hendricks said, after a time.

'David Edward Derring.'

'David? What – what happened to your mother and father?'

'They died.'

'How?'

'In the blast.'

'How long ago?'

'Six years.'

Hendricks slowed down. 'You've been alone six years?'

'No. There were other people for a while. They went away.'

'And you've been alone since?'

'Yes.'

Hendricks glanced down. The boy was strange, saying very little. Withdrawn. But that was the way they were, the children who had survived. Quiet. Stoic. A strange kind of fatalism gripped them. Nothing came as a surprise. They accepted anything that came along. There was no longer any *normal*, any natural course of things, moral or physical, for them to expect. Custom, habit, all the determining forces of learning were gone; only brute experience remained.

'Am I walking too fast?' Hendricks said.

'No.'

'How did you happen to see me?'

'I was waiting.'

'Waiting?' Hendricks was puzzled. 'What were you waiting for?'

'To catch things.'

'What kind of things?'

'Things to eat.'

'Oh.' Hendricks set his lips grimly. A thirteen-year-old boy, living on rats and gophers and half-rotten canned food. Down in a hole under the ruins of a town. With radiation pools and claws, and Russian dive-mines up above, coasting around in the sky.

'Where are we going?' David asked.

'To the Russian lines.'

'Russian?'

'The enemy. The people who started the war. They dropped the first radiation bombs. They began all this.'

The boy nodded. His face showed no expression.

'I'm an American,' Hendricks said.

There was no comment. On they went, the two of them, Hendricks walking a little ahead, David trailing behind him, hugging his dirty teddy bear against his chest.

About four in the afternoon they stopped to eat. Hendricks built a fire in a hollow between some slabs of concrete. He cleared the weeds away and heaped up bits of wood. The Russians' lines were not very far ahead. Around him was what had once been a long valley, acres of fruit trees and grapes. Nothing remained now but a few bleak stumps and the mountains that stretched across the horizon at the far end. And the clouds of rolling ash that blew and drifted with the wind, settling over the weeds and remains of buildings, walls here and there, once in a while what had been a road.

Hendricks made coffee and heated up some boiled mutton and bread. 'Here.' He handed bread and mutton to David. David squatted by the edge of the fire, his knees knobby and white. He examined the food and then passed it back, shaking his head.

'No.'

'No? Don't you want any?'

'No.'

Hendricks shrugged. Maybe the boy was a mutant, used to special food. It didn't matter. When he was hungry he would find something to eat. The boy was strange. But there were many strange changes coming over the world. Life was not the same anymore. It would never be the same again. The human race was going to have to realize that.

'Suit yourself,' Hendricks said. He ate the bread and mutton by himself, washing it down with coffee. He ate slowly, finding the food hard to digest. When he was done he got to his feet and stamped the fire out.

David rose slowly, watching him with his young-old eyes.

'We're going,' Hendricks said.

'All right.'

Hendricks walked along, his gun in his arms. They were close; he was tense, ready for anything. The Russians should be expecting a runner, an answer to their own runner, but they were tricky. There was always the possibility of a slip-up. He scanned the landscape around him. Nothing but slag and ash, a few hills, charred trees. Concrete walls. But some place ahead was the first bunker of the Russian lines, the forward command. Underground, buried deep, with only a periscope showing, a few gun muzzles. Maybe an antenna.

'Will we be there soon?' David asked.

'Yes. Getting tired?'

'No.'

'Why, then?'

David did not answer. He plodded carefully along behind, picking his way over the ash. His legs and shoes were gray with dust. His pinched face was streaked, lines of gray ash in riverlets down the pale white of his skin. There was no color to his face. Typical of the new children, growing up in cellars and sewers and underground shelters.

Hendricks slowed down. He lifted his field glasses and studied the ground ahead of him. Were they there, some place, waiting for him? Watching him, the way his men had watched the Russian runner? A chill went up his back. Maybe they were getting their guns ready, preparing to fire, the way his men had prepared, made ready to kill.

Hendricks stopped, wiping perspiration from his face. 'Damn.' It made him uneasy. But he should be expected. The situation was different.

He strode over the ash, holding his gun tightly with both hands. Behind him came David. Hendricks peered around, tight-lipped. Any second it might happen. A burst of white light, a blast, carefully aimed from inside a deep concrete bunker.

He raised his arm and waved it around in a circle.

Nothing moved. To the right a long ridge ran, topped with dead tree trunks. A few wild vines had grown up around the trees, remains of arbors. And the eternal dark weeds. Hendricks studied the ridge. Was anything up there? Perfect place for a lookout. He approached the ridge warily, David coming silently behind. If it were his command he'd have a sentry up there, watching for troops trying to infiltrate into the command area. Of course, if it were his command there would be claws around the area for full protection.

He stopped, feet apart, hands on his hips.

'Are we there?' David said.

'Almost.'

'Why have we stopped?'

'I don't want to take any chances.' Hendricks advanced slowly. Now the ridge lay directly beside him, along his right. Overlooking him. His uneasy feeling increased. If an Ivan were up there he wouldn't have a chance. He waved his arm again. They should be expecting someone in the UN uniform, in response to the note capsule. Unless the whole thing was a trap.

'Keep up with me.' He turned toward David. 'Don't drop behind.'

'With you?'

'Up beside me. We're close. We can't take any chances. Come on.'

'I'll be all right.' David remained behind him, in the rear, a few paces away, still clutching his teddy bear.

'Have it your way.' Hendricks raised his glasses again,

suddenly tense. For a moment – had something moved? He scanned the ridge carefully. Everything was silent. Dead. No life up there, only tree trunks and ash. Maybe a few rats. The big black rats that had survived the claws. Mutants – built their own shelters out of saliva and ash. Some kind of plaster. Adaptation. He started forward again.

A tall figure came out on the ridge above him, cloak flapping. Gray-green. A Russian. Behind him a second soldier appeared, another Russian. Both lifted their guns, aiming.

Hendricks froze. He opened his mouth. The soldiers were kneeling, sighting down the side of the slope. A third figure had joined them on the ridge top, a smaller figure in gray-green. A woman. She stood behind the other two.

Hendricks found his voice. 'Stop!' He waved up at them frantically. 'I'm – '

The two Russians fired. Behind Hendricks there was a faint *pop*. Waves of heat lapped against him, throwing him to the ground. Ash tore at his face, grinding into his eyes and nose. Choking, he pulled himself to his knees. It was all a trap. He was finished. He had come to be killed, like a steer. The soldiers and the woman were coming down the side of the ridge toward him, sliding down through the soft ash. Hendricks was numb. His head throbbed. Awkwardly, he got his rifle up and took aim. It weighed a thousand tons; he could hardly hold it. His nose and cheeks stung. The air was full of the blast smell, a bitter acrid stench.

'Don't fire,' the first Russian said, in heavily accented English.

The three of them came up to him. Surrounding him. 'Put down your rifle, Yank,' the other said.

Hendricks was dazed. Everything had happened so fast. He had been caught. And they had blasted the boy. He turned his head. David was gone. What remained of him was strewn across the ground.

The three Russians studied him curiously. Hendricks sat, wiping blood from his nose, picking out bits of ash. He shook his head, trying to clear it. 'Why did you do it?' he murmured thickly. 'The boy.'

'Why?' One of the soldiers helped him roughly to his feet. He turned Hendricks around. 'Look.'

Hendricks closed his eyes.

'Look!' The two Russians pulled him forward. 'See. Hurry up. There isn't much time to spare, Yank!'

Hendricks looked. And gasped.

'See now? Now do you understand?'

From the remains of David a metal wheel rolled. Relays, glinting metal. Parts, wiring. One of the Russians kicked at the heap of remains. Parts popped out, rolling away, wheels and springs and rods. A plastic section fell in, half charred. Hendricks bent shakily down. The front of the head had come off. He could make out the intricate brain, wires and relays, tiny tubes and switches, thousands of minute studs –

'A robot,' the soldier holding his arm said. 'We watched it tagging you.'

'Tagging me?'

'That's their way. They tag along with you. Into the bunker. That's how they get in.'

Hendricks blinked, dazed. 'But – '

'Come on.' They led him toward the ridge. 'We can't stay here. It isn't safe. There must be hundreds of them all around here.'

The three of them pulled him up the side of the ridge, sliding and slipping on the ash. The woman reached the top and stood waiting for them.

'The forward command,' Hendricks muttered. 'I came to negotiate with the Soviet – '

'There is no more forward command. *They* got in. We'll explain.' They reached the top of the ridge. 'We're all that's left. The three of us. The rest were down in the bunker.'

'This way. Down this way.' The woman unscrewed a lid, a gray manhole cover set in the ground. 'Get in.'

Hendricks lowered himself. The two soldiers and the woman came behind him, following him down the ladder. The woman closed the lid after them, bolting it tightly into place.

'Good thing we saw you,' one of the two soldiers grunted. 'It had tagged you about as far as it was going to.'

'Give me one of your cigarettes,' the woman said. 'I haven't had an American cigarette for weeks.'

Hendricks pushed the pack to her. She took a cigarette and passed the pack to the two soldiers. In the corner of the small room the lamp gleamed fitfully. The room was low-ceilinged, cramped. The four of them sat around a small wood table. A few dirty dishes were stacked to one side. Behind a ragged curtain a second room was partly visible. Hendricks saw the corner of a coat, some blankets, clothes hung on a hook.

'We were here,' the soldier beside him said. He took off his helmet, pushing his blond hair back. 'I'm Corporal Rudi Maxer. Polish. Impressed in the Soviet Army two years ago.' He held out his hand.

Hendricks hesitated and then shook. 'Major Joseph Hendricks.'

'Klaus Epstein.' The other soldier shook with him, a small dark man with thinning hair. Epstein plucked nervously at his ear. 'Austrian. Impressed God knows when. I don't remember. The three of us were here, Rudi and I, with Tasso.' He indicated the woman. 'That's how we escaped. All the rest were down in the bunker.'

'And – and *they* got in?'

Epstein lit a cigarette. 'First just one of them. The kind that tagged you. Then it let others in.'

Hendricks became alert. 'The *kind*? Are there more than one kind?'

'The little boy. David. David holding his teddy bear. That's Variety Three. The most effective.'

'What are the other types?'

Epstein reached into his coat. 'Here.' He tossed a packet of photographs onto the table, tied with a string. 'Look for yourself.'

Hendricks untied the string.

'You see,' Rudi Maxer said, 'that was why we wanted to talk terms. The Russians, I mean. We found out about a week ago. Found out that your claws were beginning to make up new designs on their own. New types of their own. Better types. Down in your underground factories behind our lines. You let them stamp themselves, repair themselves. Made them more and more intricate. It's your fault this happened.'

Hendricks examined the photos. They had been snapped hurriedly; they were blurred and indistinct. The first few showed – David. David walking along a road, by himself. David and another David. Three Davids. All exactly alike. Each with a ragged teddy bear.

All pathetic.

'Look at the others,' Tasso said.

The next pictures, taken at a great distance, showed a towering wounded soldier sitting by the side of a path, his arm in a sling, the stump of one leg extended, a crude crutch on his lap. Then two wounded soldiers, both the same, standing side by side.

'That's Variety One. The Wounded Soldier.' Klaus reached out and took the pictures. 'You see, the claws were designed to get to human beings. To find them. Each kind was better than the last. They got farther, closer, past most of our defenses, into our lines. But as long as they were merely *machines*, metal spheres with claws and horns, feelers, they could be picked off like any other object. They could be detected as lethal robots as soon as they were seen. Once we caught sight of them – '

'Variety One subverted our whole north wing,' Rudi said. 'It was a long time before anyone caught on. Then it was too late. They came in, wounded soldiers, knocking and begging to be let in. So we let them in. And as soon as they were in they took over. We were watching out for machines . . .'

'At that time it was thought there was only one type,' Klaus Epstein said. 'No one suspected there were other types. The pictures were flashed to us. When the runner was sent to you, we knew of just one type. Variety One. The Wounded Soldier. We thought that was all.'

'Your line fell to – '

'To Variety Three. David and his bear. That worked even better.' Klaus smiled bitterly. 'Soldiers are suckers for children. We brought them in and tried to feed them. We found out the hard way what they were after. At least, those who were in the bunker.'

'The three of us were lucky,' Rudi said. 'Klaus and I were – '

were visiting Tasso when it happened. This is her place.' He waved a big hand around. 'This little cellar. We finished and climbed the ladder to start back. From the ridge we saw that they were all around the bunker. Fighting was going on. David and his bear. Hundreds of them. Klaus took the pictures.'

Klaus tied up the photographs again.

'And it's going on all along your line?' Hendricks said.

'Yes.'

'How about *our* lines?' Without thinking, he touched the tab on his arm. 'Can they – '

'They're not bothered by your radiation tabs. It makes no difference to them. Russian, American, Pole, German. It's all the same. They're doing what they were designed to do. Carrying out the original idea. They track down life, wherever they find it.'

'They go by warmth,' Klaus said. 'That was the way you constructed them from the very start. Of course, those you designed were kept back by the radiation tabs you wear. Now they've got around that. These new varieties are lead-lined.'

'What's the other variety?' Hendricks asked. 'The David type, the Wounded Soldier – what's the other?'

'We don't know.' Klaus pointed up at the wall. On the wall were two metal plates, ragged at the edges. Hendricks got up and studied them. They were bent and dented.

'The one on the left came off a Wounded Soldier,' Rudi said. 'We got one of them. It was going along toward our old bunker. We got it from the ridge, the same way we got the David tagging you.'

The plate was stamped: *I-V*. Hendricks touched the other plate. 'And this came from the David type?'

'Yes.' The plate was stamped: *III-V*.

Klaus took a look at them, leaning over Hendricks's broad shoulder. 'You can see what we're up against. There's another type. Maybe it was abandoned. Maybe it didn't work. But there must be a Second Variety. There's One and Three.'

'You were lucky,' Rudi said. 'The David tagged you all the way here and never touched you. Probably thought you'd get it into a bunker, somewhere.'

'One gets in and it's all over,' Klaus said. 'They move fast.

One lets all the rest inside. They're inflexible. Machines with one purpose. They were built for only one thing.' He rubbed sweat from his lip. 'We saw.'

They were silent.

'Let me have another cigarette, Yank,' Tasso said. 'They are good. I almost forgot how they were.'

It was night. The sky was black. No stars were visible through the rolling clouds of ash. Klaus lifted the lid cautiously so that Hendricks could look out.

Rudi pointed into the darkness. 'Over that way are the bunkers. Where we used to be. Not over half a mile from us. It was just chance that Klaus and I were not there when it happened. Weakness. Saved by our lusts.'

'All the rest must be dead,' Klaus said in a low voice. 'It came quickly. This morning the Politburo reached their decision. They notified us – forward command. Our runner was sent out at once. We saw him start toward the direction of your lines. We covered him until he was out of sight.'

'Alex Radrivsky. We both knew him. He disappeared about six o'clock. The sun had just come up. About noon Klaus and I had an hour relief. We crept off, away from the bunkers. No one was watching. We came here. This used to be a town here, a few houses, a street. This cellar was part of a big farmhouse. We knew Tasso would be here, hiding down in her little place. We had come here before. Others from the bunkers came here. Today happened to be our turn.'

'So we were saved,' Klaus said. 'Chance. It might have been others. We – we finished, and then we came up to the surface and started back along the ridge. That was when we saw them, the Davids. We understood right away. We had seen the photos of the First Variety, the Wounded Soldier. Our Commissar distributed them to us with an explanation. If we had gone another step they would have seen us. As it was we had to blast two Davids before we got back. There were hundreds of them, all around. Like ants. We took pictures and slipped back here, bolting the lid tight.'

'They're not so much when you catch them alone. We moved faster than they did. But they're inexorable. Not like living things. They came right at us. And we blasted them.'

Major Hendricks rested against the edge of the lid, adjusting his eyes to the darkness. 'Is it safe to have the lid up at all?'

'If we're careful. How else can you operate your transmitter?'

Hendricks lifted the small belt transmitter slowly. He pressed it against his ear. The metal was cold and damp. He blew against the mike, raising up the short antenna. A faint hum sounded in his ear. 'That's true, I suppose.'

But he still hesitated.

'We'll pull you under if anything happens,' Klaus said.

'Thanks.' Hendricks waited a moment, resting the transmitter against his shoulder. 'Interesting, isn't it?'

'What?'

'This, the new types. The new varieties of claws. We're completely at their mercy, aren't we? By now they've probably gotten into the UN lines, too. It makes me wonder if we're not seeing the beginning of a new species. *The* new species. Evolution. The race to come after man.'

Rudi grunted. 'There is no race after man.'

'No? Why not? Maybe we're seeing it now, the end of human beings, the beginning of a new society.'

'They're not a race. They're mechanical killers. You made them to destroy. That's all they can do. They're machines with a job.'

'So it seems now. But how about later on? After the war is over. Maybe, when there aren't any humans to destroy, their real potentialities will begin to show.'

'You talk as if they were alive!'

'Aren't they?'

There was silence. 'They're machines,' Rudi said. 'They look like people, but they're machines.'

'Use your transmitter, Major,' Klaus said. 'We can't stay up here forever.'

Holding the transmitter tightly, Hendricks called the code of the command bunker. He waited, listening. No response. Only silence. He checked the leads carefully. Everything was in place.

'Scott!' he said into the mike. 'Can you hear me?'

Silence. He raised the gain up full and tried again. Only static.

'I don't get anything. They may hear me but they may not want to answer.'

'Tell them it's an emergency.'

'They'll think I'm being forced to call. Under your direction.' He tried again, outlining briefly what he had learned. But still the phone was silent, except for the faint static.

'Radiation pools kill most transmission,' Klaus said, after a while. 'Maybe that's it.'

Hendricks shut the transmitter up. 'No use. No answer. Radiation pools? Maybe. Or they hear me, but won't answer. Frankly, that's what I would do, if a runner tried to call from the Soviet lines. They have no reason to believe such a story. They may hear everything I say – '

'Or maybe it's too late.'

Hendricks nodded.

'We better get the lid down,' Rudi said nervously. 'We don't want to take unnecessary chances.'

They climbed slowly back down the tunnel. Klaus bolted the lid carefully into place. They descended into the kitchen. The air was heavy and close around them.

'Could they work that fast?' Hendricks said. 'I left the bunker this noon. Ten hours ago. How could they move so quickly?'

'It doesn't take them long. Not after the first one gets in. It goes wild. You know what the little claws can do. Even *one* of these is beyond belief. Razors, each finger. Maniacal.'

'All right.' Hendricks moved away impatiently. He stood with his back to them.

'What's the matter?' Rudi said.

'The Moon Base. God, if they've gotten there – '

'The Moon Base?'

Hendricks turned around. 'They couldn't have got to the Moon Base. How would they get there? It isn't possible. I can't believe it.'

'What is this Moon Base? We've heard rumors, but nothing definite. What is the actual situation? You seem concerned.'

'We're supplied from the Moon. The governments are there, under the lunar surface. All our people and industries. That's what keeps us going. If they should find some way of getting off Terra, onto the Moon – '

Philip K. Dick

'It only takes one of them. Once the first one gets in it admits the others. Hundreds of them, all alike. You should have seen them. Identical. Like ants.'

'Perfect socialism,' Tasso said. 'The ideal of the communist state. All citizens interchangeable.'

Klaus grunted angrily. 'That's enough. Well? What next?'

Hendricks paced back and forth, around the small room. The air was full of smells of food and perspiration. The others watched him. Presently Tasso pushed through the curtain, into the other room. 'I'm going to take a nap.'

The curtain closed behind her. Rudi and Klaus sat down at the table, still watching Hendricks. 'It's up to you,' Klaus said. 'We don't know your situation.'

Hendricks nodded.

'It's a problem.' Rudi drank some coffee, filling his cup from a rusty pot. 'We're safe here for a while, but we can't stay here forever. Not enough food or supplies.'

'But if we go outside – '

'If we go outside they'll get us. Or probably they'll get us. We couldn't go very far. How far is your command bunker, Major?'

'Three or four miles.'

'We might make it. The four of us. Four of us could watch all sides. They couldn't slip up behind us and start tagging us. We have three rifles, three blast rifles. Tasso can have my pistol.' Rudi tapped his belt. 'In the Soviet Army we didn't have shoes always, but we had guns. With all four of us armed one of us might get to your command bunker. Preferably you, Major.'

'What if they're already there?' Klaus said.

Rudi shrugged. 'Well, then we come back here.'

Hendricks stopped pacing. 'What do you think the chances are they're already in the American lines?'

'Hard to say. Fairly good. They're organized. They know exactly what they're doing. Once they start they go like a horde of locusts. They have to keep moving, and fast. It's secrecy and speed they depend on. Surprise. They push their way in before anyone has any idea.'

'I see,' Hendricks murmured.

From the other room Tasso stirred. 'Major?'

Hendricks pushed the curtain back. 'What?'

Tasso looked up at him lazily from the cot. 'Have you any more American cigarettes left?'

Hendricks went into the room and sat down across from her, on a wood stool. He felt in his pockets. 'No. All gone.'

'Too bad.'

'What nationality are you?' Hendricks asked after a while.

'Russian.'

'How did you get here?'

'Here?'

'This used to be France. This was part of Normandy. Did you come with the Soviet Army?'

'Why?'

'Just curious.' He studied her. She had taken off her coat, tossing it over the end of the cot. She was young, about twenty. Slim. Her long hair stretched out over the pillow. She was staring at him silently, her eyes dark and large.

'What's on your mind?' Tasso said.

'Nothing. How old are you?'

'Eighteen.' She continued to watch him, unblinking, her arms behind her head. She had on Russian army pants and shirt. Gray-green. Thick leather belt with counter and cartridges. Medicine kit.

'You're in the Soviet Army?'

'No.'

'Where did you get the uniform?'

She shrugged. 'It was given to me,' she told him.

'How – how old were you when you came here?'

'Sixteen.'

'That young?'

Her eyes narrowed. 'What do you mean?'

Hendricks rubbed his jaw. 'Your life would have been a lot different if there had been no war. Sixteen. You came here at sixteen. To live this way.'

'I had to survive.'

'I'm not moralizing.'

'Your life would have been different, too,' Tasso murmured. She reached down and unfastened one of her boots. She kicked the boot off, onto the floor. 'Major, do you want to go in the other room? I'm sleepy.'

'It's going to be a problem, the four of us here. It's going to be hard to live in these quarters. Are there just the two rooms?'

'Yes.'

'How big was the cellar originally? Was it larger than this? Are there other rooms filled up with debris? We might be able to open one of them.'

'Perhaps. I really don't know.' Tasso loosened her belt. She made herself comfortable on the cot, unbuttoning her shirt. 'You're sure you have no more cigarettes?'

'I only had the one pack.'

'Too bad. Maybe if we get back to your bunker we can find some.' The other boot fell. Tasso reached up for the light cord. 'Good night.'

'You're going to sleep?'

'That's right.'

The room plunged into darkness. Hendricks got up and made his way past the curtain, into the kitchen. And stopped, rigid.

Rudi stood against the wall, his face white and gleaming. His mouth opened and closed but no sounds came. Klaus stood in front of him, the muzzle of his pistol in Rudi's stomach. Neither of them moved. Klaus, his hand tight around the gun, his features set. Rudi, pale and silent, spreadeagled against the wall.

'What – ' Hendricks muttered, but Klaus cut him off.

'Be quiet, Major. Come over here. Your gun. Get out your gun.'

Hendricks drew his pistol. 'What is it?'

'Cover him.' Klaus motioned him forward. 'Beside me. Hurry!'

Rudi moved a little, lowering his arms. He turned to Hendricks, licking his lips. The whites of his eyes shone wildly. Sweat dripped from his forehead, down his cheeks. He fixed his gaze on Hendricks. 'Major, he's gone insane. Stop him.' Rudi's voice was thin and hoarse, almost inaudible.

'What's going on?' Hendricks demanded.

Without lowering his pistol Klaus answered. 'Major, remember our discussion? The Three Varieties? We knew about One

and Three. But we didn't know about Two. At least, we didn't
know before.' Klaus's fingers tightened around the gun butt.
'We didn't know before, but we know now.'

He pressed the trigger. A burst of white heat rolled out of
the gun, licking around Rudi.

'Major, this is the Second Variety.'

Tasso swept the curtain aside. 'Klaus! What did you do?'

Klaus turned from the charred form, gradually sinking down
the wall onto the floor. 'The Second Variety, Tasso. Now we
know. We have all three types identified. The danger is less.
I – '

Tasso stared past him at the remains of Rudi, at the blackened, smoldering fragments and bits of cloth. 'You killed him.'

'Him? *It*, you mean. I was watching. I had a feeling, but I
wasn't sure. At least, I wasn't sure before. But this evening I
was certain.' Klaus rubbed his pistol butt nervously. 'We're
lucky. Don't you understand? Another hour and it might – '

'You were *certain*?' Tasso pushed past him and bent down,
over the steaming remains on the floor. Her face became hard.
'Major, see for yourself. Bones. Flesh.'

Hendricks bent down beside her. The remains were human
remains. Seared flesh, charred bone fragments, part of a skull.
Ligaments, viscera, blood. Blood forming a pool against the
wall.

'No wheels,' Tasso said calmly. She straightened up. 'No
wheels, no parts, no relays. Not a claw. Not the Second
Variety.' She folded her arms. 'You're going to have to be able
to explain this.'

Klaus sat down at the table, all the color drained suddenly
from his face. He put his head in his hands and rocked back
and forth.

'Snap out of it.' Tasso's fingers closed over his shoulder.
'Why did you do it? Why did you kill him?'

'He was frightened,' Hendricks said. 'All this, the whole
thing, building up around us.'

'Maybe.'

'What, then? What do you think?'

'I think he may have had a reason for killing Rudi. A good
reason.'

'What reason?'

'Maybe Rudi learned something.'

Hendricks studied her bleak face. 'About what?' he asked.

'About him. About Klaus.'

Klaus looked up quickly. 'You can see what she's trying to say. She thinks I'm the Second Variety. Don't you see, Major? Now she wants you to believe I killed him on purpose. That I'm –'

'Why did you kill him, then?' Tasso said.

'I told you.' Klaus shook his head wearily. 'I thought he was a claw. I thought I knew.'

'Why?'

'I had been watching him. I was suspicious.'

'Why?'

'I thought I had seen something. Heard something. I thought I –' He stopped.

'Go on.'

'We were sitting at the table. Playing cards. You two were in the other room. It was silent. I thought I heard him – *whirr*.'

There was silence.

'Do you believe that?' Tasso said to Hendricks.

'Yes. I believe what he says.'

'I don't. I think he killed Rudi for a good purpose.' Tasso touched the rifle, resting in the corner of the room. 'Major –'

'No.' Hendricks shook his head. 'Let's stop it right now. One is enough. We're afraid, the way he was. If we kill him we'll be doing what he did to Rudi.'

Klaus looked gratefully up at him. 'Thanks. I was afraid. You understand, don't you? Now she's afraid, the way I was. She wants to kill me.'

'No more killing.' Hendricks moved toward the end of the ladder. 'I'm going above and try the transmitter once more. If I can't get them we're moving back toward my lines tomorrow morning.'

Klaus rose quickly. 'I'll come up with you and give you a hand.'

The night air was cold. The earth was cooling off. Klaus took a deep breath, filling his lungs. He and Hendricks stepped onto the ground, out of the tunnel. Klaus planted his feet wide apart, the rifle up, watching and listening. Hendricks crouched by the tunnel mouth, tuning the small transmitter.

'Any luck?' Klaus asked presently.

'Not yet.'

'Keep trying. Tell them what happened.'

Hendricks kept trying. Without success. Finally he lowered the antenna. 'It's useless. They can't hear me. Or they hear me and won't answer. Or – '

'Or they don't exist.'

'I'll try once more.' Hendricks raised the antenna. 'Scott, can you hear me? Come in!'

He listened. There was only static. Then, still very faintly –

'This is Scott.'

His fingers tightened. 'Scott! Is it you?'

'This is Scott.'

Klaus squatted down. 'Is it your command?'

'Scott, listen. Do you understand? About them, the claws. Did you get my message? Did you hear me?'

'Yes.' Faintly. Almost inaudible. He could hardly make out the word.

'You got my message? Is everything all right at the bunker? None of them got in?'

'Everything is all right.'

'Have they tried to get in?'

The voice was weaker.

'No.'

Hendricks turned to Klaus. 'They're all right.'

'Have they been attacked?'

'No.' Hendricks pressed the phone tighter to his ear. 'Scott, I can hardly hear you. Have you notified the Moon Base? Do they know? Are they alerted?'

No answer.

'Scott! Can you hear me?'

Silence.

Hendricks relaxed, sagging. 'Faded out. Must be radiation pools.'

Hendricks and Klaus looked at each other. Neither of them

said anything. After a time Klaus said, 'Did it sound like any of your men? Could you identify the voice?'

'It was too faint.'

'You couldn't be certain?'

'No.'

'Then it could have been – '

'I don't know. Now I'm not sure. Let's go back down and get the lid closed.'

They climbed back down the ladder slowly, into the warm cellar. Klaus bolted the lid behind them. Tasso waited for them, her face expressionless.

'Any luck?' she asked.

Neither of them answered. 'Well?' Klaus said at last. 'What do you think, Major? Was it your officer, or was it one of *them*?'

'I don't know.'

'Then we're just where we were before.'

Hendricks stared down at the floor, his jaw set. 'We'll have to go. To be sure.'

'Anyhow, we have food here for only a few weeks. We'd have to go up after that, in any case.'

'Apparently so.'

'What's wrong?' Tasso demanded. 'Did you get across to your bunker? What's the matter?'

'It may have been one of my men,' Hendricks said slowly. 'Or it may have been one of *them*. But we'll never know standing here.' He examined his watch. 'Let's turn in and get some sleep. We want to be up early tomorrow.'

'Early?'

'Our best chance to get through the claws should be early in the morning,' Hendricks said.

The morning was crisp and clear. Major Hendricks studied the countryside through his field glasses.

'See anything?' Klaus said.

'No.'

'Can you make out our bunkers?'

'Which way?'

'Here.' Klaus took the glasses and adjusted them. 'I know where to look.' He looked a long time, silently.

Tasso came to the top of the tunnel and stepped up onto the ground. 'Anything?'

'No.' Klaus passed the glasses back to Hendricks. 'They're out of sight. Come on. Let's not stay here.'

The three of them made their way down the side of the ridge, sliding in the soft ash. Across a flat rock a lizard scuttled. They stopped instantly, rigid.

'What was it?' Klaus muttered.

'A lizard.'

The lizard ran on, hurrying through the ash. It was exactly the same color as the ash.

'Perfect adaptation,' Klaus said. 'Proves we were right. Lysenko, I mean.'

They reached the bottom of the ridge and stopped, standing close together, looking around them.

'Let's go.' Hendricks started off. 'It's a good long trip, on foot.'

Klaus fell in beside him, Tasso walked behind, her pistol held alertly. 'Major, I've been meaning to ask you something,' Klaus said. 'How did you run across the David? The one that was tagging you.'

'I met it along the way. In some ruins.'

'What did it say?'

'Not much. It said it was alone. By itself.'

'You couldn't tell it was a machine? It talked like a living person? You never suspected?'

'It didn't say much. I noticed nothing unusual.'

'It's strange, machines so much like people that you can be fooled. Almost alive. I wonder where it'll end.'

'They're doing what you Yanks designed them to do,' Tasso said. 'You designed them to hunt out life and destroy. Human life. Wherever they find it.'

Hendricks was watching Klaus intently. 'Why did you ask me? What's on your mind?'

'Nothing,' Klaus answered.

'Klaus thinks you're the Second Variety,' Tasso said calmly, from behind them. 'Now he's got his eye on you.'

Klaus flushed. 'Why not? We sent a runner to the Yank lines and *he* comes back. Maybe he thought he'd find some good game here.'

Hendricks laughed harshly. 'I came from the UN bunkers. There were human beings all around me.'

'Maybe you saw an opportunity to get into the Soviet lines. Maybe you saw your chance. Maybe you –'

'The Soviet lines had already been taken over. Your lines had been invaded before I left my command bunker. Don't forget that.'

Tasso came up beside him. 'That proves nothing at all, Major.'

'Why not?'

'There appears to be little communication between the varieties. Each is made in a different factory. They don't seem to work together. You might have started for the Soviet lines without knowing anything about the work of the other varieties. Or even what the other varieties were like.'

'How do you know so much about the claws?' Hendricks said.

'I've seen them. I've observed them take over the Soviet bunkers.'

'You know quite a lot,' Klaus said. 'Actually, you saw very little. Strange that you should have been such an acute observer.'

Tasso laughed. 'Do you suspect me, now?'

'Forget it,' Hendricks said. They walked on in silence.

'Are we going the whole way on foot?' Tasso said, after a while. 'I'm not used to walking.' She gazed around at the plain of ash, stretching out on all sides of them, as far as they could see. 'How dreary.'

'It's like this all the way,' Klaus said.

'In a way I wish you had been in your bunker when the attack came.'

'Somebody else would have been with you, if not me,' Klaus muttered.

Tasso laughed, putting her hands in her pockets. 'I suppose so.'

They walked on, keeping their eyes on the vast plain of silent ash around them.

The sun was setting. Hendricks made his way forward slowly, waving Tasso and Klaus back. Klaus squatted down, resting his gun butt against the ground.

Tasso found a concrete slab and sat down with a sigh. 'It's good to rest.'

'Be quiet,' Klaus said sharply.

Hendricks pushed up to the top of the rise ahead of them. The same rise the Russian runner had come up, the day before. Hendricks dropped down, stretching himself out, peering through his glasses at what lay beyond.

Nothing was visible. Only ash and occasional trees. But there, not more than fifty yards ahead, was the entrance of the forward command bunker. The bunker from which he had come. Hendricks watched silently. No motion. No sign of life. Nothing stirred.

Klaus slithered up beside him. 'Where is it?'

'Down there.' Hendricks passed him the glasses. Clouds of ash rolled across the evening sky. The world was darkening. They had a couple of hours of light left, at the most. Probably not that much.

'I don't see anything,' Klaus said.

'That tree there. The stump. By the pile of bricks. The entrance is to the right of the bricks.'

'I'll have to take your word for it.'

'You and Tasso cover me from here. You'll be able to sight all the way to the bunker entrance.'

'You're going down alone?'

'With my wrist tab I'll be safe. The ground around the bunker is a living field of claws. They collect down in the ash. Like crabs. Without tabs you wouldn't have a chance.'

'Maybe you're right.'

'I'll walk slowly all the way. As soon as I know for certain – '

'If they're down inside the bunker you won't be able to get back up here. They go fast. You don't realize.'

'What do you suggest?'

Klaus considered. 'I don't know. Get them to come to the surface. So you can see.'

Hendricks brought out his transmitter from his belt, raising the antenna. 'Let's get started.'

Klaus signaled to Tasso. She crawled expertly up the side of the rise to where they were sitting.

'He's going down alone,' Klaus said. 'We'll cover him from here. As soon as you see him start back, fire past him at once. They come quick.'

'You're not very optimistic,' Tasso said.

'No, I'm not.'

Hendricks opened the breech of his gun, checking it carefully. 'Maybe things are all right.'

'You didn't see them. Hundreds of them. All the same. Pouring out like ants.'

'I should be able to find out without going down all the way.' Hendricks locked his gun, gripping it in one hand, the transmitter in the other. 'Well, wish me luck.'

Klaus put out his hand. 'Don't go down until you're sure. Talk to them from here. Make them show themselves.'

Hendricks stood up. He stepped down the side of the rise.

A moment later he was walking slowly toward the pile of bricks and debris beside the dead tree stump. Toward the entrance of the forward command bunker.

Nothing stirred. He raised the transmitter, clicking it on. 'Scott? Can you hear me?'

Silence.

'Scott! This is Hendricks. Can you hear me? I'm standing outside the bunker. You should be able to see me in the view sight.'

He listened, the transmitter gripped tightly. No sound. Only static. He walked forward. A claw burrowed out of the ash and raced toward him. It halted a few feet away and then slunk off. A second claw appeared, one of the big ones with feelers. It moved toward him, studied him intently, and then fell in behind him, dogging respectfully after him, a few paces away. A moment later a second big claw joined it. Silently, the claws trailed him as he walked slowly toward the bunker.

Hendricks stopped, and behind him, the claws came to a halt. He was close now. Almost to the bunker steps.

'Scott! Can you hear me? I'm standing right above you. Outside. On the surface. Are you picking me up?'

He waited, holding his gun against his side, the transmitter tightly to his ear. Time passed. He strained to hear, but there was only silence. Silence, and faint static.

Then, distantly, metallically –

'This is Scott.'

The voice was neutral. Cold. He could not identify it. But the earphone was minute.

'Scott! Listen. I'm standing right above you. I'm on the surface, looking down into the bunker entrance.'

'Yes.'

'Can you see me?'

'Yes.'

'Through the view sight? You have the sight trained on me?'

'Yes.'

Hendricks pondered. A circle of claws waited quietly around him, gray-metal bodies on all sides of him. 'Is everything all right in the bunker? Nothing unusual has happened?'

'Everything is all right.'

'Will you come up to the surface? I want to see you for a moment.' Hendricks took a deep breath. 'Come up here with me. I want to talk to you.'

'Come down.'

'I'm giving you an order.'

Silence.

'Are you coming?' Hendricks listened. There was no response. 'I order you to come to the surface.'

'Come down.'

Hendricks set his jaw. 'Let me talk to Leone.'

There was a long pause. He listened to the static. Then a voice came, hard, thin, metallic. The same as the other. 'This is Leone.'

'Hendricks. I'm on the surface. At the bunker entrance. I want one of you to come up here.'

'Come down.'

'Why come down? I'm giving you an order!'

Silence. Hendricks lowered the transmitter. He looked carefully around him. The entrance was just ahead. Almost at his feet. He lowered the antenna and fastened the transmitter to his belt. Carefully, he gripped his gun with both hands. He moved forward, a step at a time. If they could see him they knew he was starting toward the entrance. He closed his eyes a moment.

Then he put his foot on the first step that led downward.

Two Davids came up at him, their faces identical and expressionless. He blasted them into particles. More came rushing silently up, a whole pack of them. All exactly the same.

Hendricks turned and raced back, away from the bunker, back toward the rise.

At the top of the rise Tasso and Klaus were firing down. The small claws were already streaking up toward them, shining metal spheres going fast, racing frantically through the ash. But he had no time to think about that. He knelt down, aiming at the bunker entrance, gun against his cheek. The Davids were coming out in groups, clutching their teddy bears, their thin knobby legs pumping as they ran up the steps to the surface. Hendricks fired into the main body of them. They burst apart, wheels and springs flying in all directions. He fired again, through the mist of particles.

A giant lumbering figure rose up in the bunker entrance, tall and swaying. Hendricks paused, amazed. A man, a soldier. With one leg, supporting himself with a crutch.

'Major!' Tasso's voice came. More firing. The huge figure moved forward, Davids swarming around it. Hendricks broke out of his freeze. The First Variety. The Wounded Soldier. He aimed and fired. The soldier burst into bits, parts and relays flying. Now many Davids were out on the flat ground, away from the bunker. He fired again and again, moving slowly back, half-crouching and aiming.

From the rise, Klaus fired down. The side of the rise was alive with claws making their way up. Hendricks retreated toward the rise, running and crouching. Tasso had left Klaus and was circling slowly to the right, moving away from the rise.

A David slipped up toward him, its small white face expressionless, brown hair hanging down in its eyes. It bent over suddenly, opening its arms. Its teddy bear hurtled down and leaped across the ground, bounding toward him. Hendricks fired. The bear and the David both dissolved. He grinned, blinking. It was like a dream.

'Up here!' Tasso's voice. Hendricks made his way toward her. She was over by some columns of concrete, walls of a ruined building. She was firing past him, with the hand pistol Klaus had given her.

'Thanks.' He joined her, gasping for breath. She pulled him back, behind the concrete, fumbling at her belt.

'Close your eyes!' She unfastened a globe from her waist, Rapidly, she unscrewed the cap, locking it into place. 'Close your eyes and get down.'

She threw the bomb. It sailed in an arc, an expert, rolling and bouncing to the entrance of the bunker. Two Wounded Soldiers stood uncertainly by the brick pile. More Davids poured from behind them, out onto the plain. One of the Wounded Soldiers moved toward the bomb, stooping awkwardly down to pick it up.

The bomb went off. The concussion whirled Hendricks around, throwing him on his face. A hot wind rolled over him. Dimly he saw Tasso standing behind the columns, firing slowly and methodically at the Davids coming out of the raging clouds of white fire.

Back along the rise Klaus struggled with a ring of claws circling around him. He retreated, blasting at them and moving back, trying to break through the ring.

Hendricks struggled to his feet. His head ached. He could hardly see. Everything was licking at him, raging and whirling. His right arm would not move.

Tasso pulled back toward him. 'Come on. Let's go.'

'Klaus – he's still up there.'

'Come on!' Tasso dragged Hendricks back, away from the columns. Hendricks shook his head, trying to clear it. Tasso led him rapidly away, her eyes intense and bright, watching for claws that had escaped the blast.

One David came out of the rolling clouds of flame. Tasso blasted it. No more appeared.

'But Klaus. What about him?' Hendricks stopped, standing unsteadily. 'He – '

'Come on!'

They retreated, moving farther and farther away from the bunker. A few small claws followed them for a little while and then gave up, turning back and going off.

At last Tasso stopped. 'We can stop here and get our breaths.'

Hendricks sat down on some heaps of debris. He wiped his neck, gasping. 'We left Klaus back there.'

Tasso said nothing. She opened her gun, sliding a fresh round of blast cartridges into place.

Hendricks stared at her, dazed. 'You left him back there on purpose.'

Tasso snapped the gun together. She studied the heaps of rubble around them, her face expressionless. As if she were watching for something.

'What is it?' Hendricks demanded. 'What are you looking for? Is something coming?' He shook his head, trying to understand. What was she doing? What was she waiting for? He could see nothing. Ash lay all around them, ash and ruins. Occasional stark tree trunks, without leaves or branches. 'What – '

Tasso cut him off. 'Be still.' Her eyes narrowed. Suddenly her gun came up. Hendricks turned, following her gaze.

Back the way they had come a figure appeared. The figure walked unsteadily toward them. Its clothes were torn. It limped as it made its way along, going very slowly and carefully. Stopping now and then, resting and getting its strength. Once it almost fell. It stood for a moment, trying to steady itself. Then it came on.

Klaus.

Hendricks stood up. 'Klaus!' He started toward him. 'How the hell did you – '

Tasso fired. Hendricks swung back. She fired again, the blast passing him, a searing line of heat. The beam caught Klaus in the chest. He exploded, gears and wheels flying. For a moment he continued to walk. Then he swayed back and forth. He crashed to the ground, his arms flung out. A few more wheels rolled away.

Silence.

Tasso turned to Hendricks. 'Now you understand why he killed Rudi.'

Hendricks sat down again slowly. He shook his head. He was numb. He could not think.

'Do you see?' Tasso said. 'Do you understand?'

Hendricks said nothing. Everything was slipping away from him, faster and faster. Darkness, rolling and plucking at him.

He closed his eyes.

Hendricks opened his eyes slowly. His body ached all over. He tried to sit up but needles of pain shot through his arm and shoulder. He gasped.

'Don't try to get up,' Tasso said. She bent down, putting her cold hand against his forehead.

It was night. A few stars glinted above, shining through the drifting clouds of ash. Hendricks lay back, his teeth locked. Tasso watched him impassively. She had built a fire with some wood and weeds. The fire licked feebly, hissing at a metal cup suspended over it. Everything was silent. Unmoving darkness, beyond the fire.

'So he was the Second Variety,' Hendricks murmured.

'I had always thought so.'

'Why didn't you destroy him sooner?' He wanted to know.

'You held me back.' Tasso crossed to the fire to look into the metal cup. 'Coffee. It'll be ready to drink in a while.'

She came back and sat down beside him. Presently she opened her pistol and began to disassemble the firing mechanism, studying it intently.

'This is a beautiful gun,' Tasso said, half aloud. 'The construction is superb.'

'What about them? The claws.'

'The concussion from the bomb put most of them out of action. They're delicate. Highly organized, I suppose.'

'The Davids, too?'

'Yes.'

'How did you happen to have a bomb like that?'

Tasso shrugged. 'We designed it. You shouldn't underestimate our technology, Major. Without such a bomb you and I would no longer exist.'

'Very useful.'

Tasso stretched out her legs, warming her feet in the heat of the fire. 'It surprised me that you did not seem to understand, after he killed Rudi. Why did you think he – '

'I told you. I thought he was afraid.'

'Really? You know, Major, for a little while I suspected you. Because you wouldn't let me kill him. I thought you might be protecting him.' she laughed.

'Are we safe here?' Hendricks asked presently.

'For a while. Until they get reinforcements from some other area.' Tasso began to clean the interior of the gun with a bit of rag. She finished and pushed the mechanism back into place. She closed the gun, running her finger along the barrel.

'We were lucky,' Hendricks murmured.

'Yes. Very lucky.'

'Thanks for pulling me away.'

Tasso did not answer. She glanced up at him, her eyes bright in the firelight. Hendricks examined his arm. He could not move his fingers. His whole side seemed numb. Down inside him was a dull steady ache.

'How do you feel?' Tasso asked.

'My arm is damaged.'

'Anything else?'

'Internal injuries.'

'You didn't get down when the bomb went off?'

Hendricks said nothing. He watched Tasso pour the coffee from the cup into a flat metal pan. She brought it over to him.

'Thanks.' He struggled up enough to drink. It was hard to swallow. His insides turned over and he pushed the pan away. 'That's all I can drink now.'

Tasso drank the rest. Time passed. The clouds of ash moved across the dark sky above them. Hendricks rested, his mind blank. After a while he became aware that Tasso was standing over him, gazing down at him.

'What is it?' he murmured.

'Do you feel any better?'

'Some.'

'You know, Major, if I hadn't dragged you away they would have got you. You would be dead. Like Rudi.'

'I know.'

'Do you want to know why I brought you out? I could have left you. I could have left you there.'

'Why did you bring me out?'

'Because we have to get away from here.' Tasso stirred the fire with a stick, peering calmly down into it. 'No human being can live here. When their reinforcements come we won't have a chance. I've pondered about it while you were unconscious. We have perhaps three hours before they come.'

'And you expect me to get us away?'

'That's right. I expect you to get us out of here.'

'Why me?'

'Because I don't know any way.' Her eyes shone at him in the half light, bright and steady. 'If you can't get us out of here they'll kill us within three hours. I see nothing else ahead. Well, Major? What are you going to do? I've been waiting all night. While you were unconscious I sat here, waiting and listening. It's almost dawn. The night is almost over.'

Hendricks considered. 'It's curious,' he said at last.

'Curious?'

'That you should think I can get us out of here. I wonder what you think I can do.'

'Can you get us to the Moon Base?'

'The Moon Base? How?'

'There must be some way.'

Hendricks shook his head. 'No. There's no way that I know of.'

Tasso said nothing. For a moment her steady gaze wavered. She ducked her head, turning abruptly away. She scrambled to her feet. 'More coffee?'

'No.'

'Suit yourself.' Tasso drank silently. He could not see her face. He lay back against the ground, deep in thought, trying to concentrate. It was hard to think. His head still hurt. And the numbing daze still hung over him.

'There might be one way,' he said suddenly.

'Oh?'

'How soon is dawn?'

'Two hours. The sun will be coming up shortly.'

'There's supposed to be a ship near here. I've never seen it. But I know it exists.'

'What kind of a ship?' Her voice was sharp.

'A rocket cruiser.'

'Will it take us off? To the Moon Base?'

'It's supposed to. In case of emergency.' He rubbed his forehead.

'What's wrong?'

'My head. It's hard to think. I can hardly – hardly concentrate. The bomb.'

'Is the ship near here?' Tasso slid over beside him, settling down on her haunches. 'How far is it? Where is it?'

'I'm trying to think.'

Her fingers dug into his arm. 'Nearby?' Her voice was like iron. 'Where would it be? Would they store it underground? Hidden underground?'

'Yes. In a storage locker.'

'How do we find it? Is it marked? Is there a code marker to identify it?'

Hendricks concentrated. 'No. No marking. No code symbol.'

'What then?'

'A sign.'

'What sort of sign?'

Hendricks did not answer. In the flickering light his eyes were glazed, two sightless orbs. Tasso's fingers dug into his arm.

'What sort of sign? What is it?'

'I – I can't think. Let me rest.'

'All right.' She let go and stood up. Hendricks lay back against the ground, his eyes closed. Tasso walked away from him, her hands in her pockets. She kicked a rock out of her way and stood staring up at the sky. The night blackness was already beginning to fade into gray. Morning was coming.

Tasso gripped her pistol and walked around the fire in a circle, back and forth. On the ground Major Hendricks lay, his eyes closed, unmoving. The grayness rose in the sky, higher and higher. The landscape became visible, fields of ash stretching out in all directions. Ash and ruins of buildings, a wall here and there, heaps of concrete, the naked trunk of a tree.

The air was cold and sharp. Somewhere a long way off a bird made a few bleak sounds.

Hendricks stirred. He opened his eyes. 'Is it dawn? Already?'

'Yes.'

Hendricks sat up a little. 'You wanted to know something. You were asking me.'

'Do you remember now?'

'Yes.'

'What is it?' She tensed. 'What?' she repeated sharply.

'A well. A ruined well. It's in a storage locker under a well.'

'A well.' Tasso relaxed. 'Then we'll find a well.' She looked at her watch. 'We have about an hour, Major. Do you think we can find it in an hour?'

'Give me a hand,' Hendricks said.

Tasso put her pistol away and helped him to his feet. 'This is going to be difficult.'

'Yes it is.' Hendricks set his lips tightly. 'I don't think we're going to go very far.'

They began to walk. The early sun cast a little warmth down on them. The land was flat and barren, stretching out gray and lifeless as far as they could see. A few birds sailed silently, far above them, circling slowly.

'See anything?' Hendricks said. 'Any claws?'

'No. Not yet.'

They passed through some ruins, upright concrete and bricks. A cement foundation. Rats scuttled away. Tasso jumped back warily.

'This used to be a town,' Hendricks said. 'A village. Provincial village. This was all grape country, once. Where we are now.'

They came onto a ruined street, weeds and cracks crisscrossing it. Over to the right a stone chimney stuck up.

'Be careful,' he warned her.

A pit yawned, an open basement. Ragged ends of pipes jutted up, twisted and bent. They passed part of a house, a bathtub turned on its side. A broken chair. A few spoons and bits of china dishes. In the center of the street the ground had sunk away. The depression was filled with weeds and debris and bones.

'Over here,' Hendricks murmured.

'This way?'

'To the right.'

They passed the remains of a heavy-duty tank. Hendricks's belt counter clicked ominously. The tank had been radiation-blasted. A few feet from the tank a mummified body lay sprawled out, mouth open. Beyond the road was a flat field. Stones and weeds, and bits of broken glass.

'There,' Hendricks said.

A stone well jutted up, sagging and broken. A few boards lay across it. Most of the well had sunk into rubble. Hendricks walked unsteadily toward it, Tasso beside him.

'Are you certain about this?' Tasso said. 'This doesn't look like anything.'

'I'm sure.' Hendricks sat down at the edge of the well, his teeth locked. His breath came quickly. He wiped perspiration from his face. 'This was arranged so the senior command officer could get away. If anything happened. If the bunker fell.'

'That was you?'

'Yes.'

'Where is the ship? Is it here?'

'We're standing on it.' Hendricks ran his hands over the surface of the well stones. 'The eye-lock responds to me, not to anybody else. It's my ship. Or it was supposed to be.'

There was a sharp click. Presently they heard a low grating sound from below them.

'Step back,' Hendricks said. He and Tasso moved away from the well.

A section of the ground slid back. A metal frame pushed slowly up through the ash, shoving bricks and weeds out of the way. The action ceased as the ship nosed into view.

'There it is,' Hendricks said.

The ship was small. It rested quietly, suspended in its mesh frame like a blunt needle. A rain of ash sifted down into the dark cavity from which the ship had been raised. Hendricks made his way over to it. He mounted the mesh and unscrewed the hatch, pulling it back. Inside the ship the control banks and the pressure seat were visible.

Tasso came and stood beside him, gazing into the ship. 'I'm not accustomed to rocket piloting,' she said after a while.

Hendricks glanced at her. 'I'll do the piloting.'

'Will you? There's only one seat, Major. I can see it's built to carry only a single person.'

Hendricks's breathing changed. He studied the interior of the ship intently. Tasso was right. There was only one seat. The ship was built to carry only one person. 'I see,' he said slowly. 'And the one person is you.'

She nodded.

'Of course.'

'Why?'

'*You* can't go. You might not live through the trip. You're injured. You probably wouldn't get there.'

'An interesting point. But you see, I know where the Moon Base is. And you don't. You might fly around for months and not find it. It's well hidden. Without knowing what to look for – '

'I'll have to take my chances. Maybe I won't find it. Not by myself. But I think you'll give me all the information I need. Your life depends on it.'

'How?'

'If I find the Moon Base in time, perhaps I can get them to send a ship back to pick you up. *If* I find the Base in time. If not, then you haven't a chance. I imagine there are supplies on the ship. They will last me long enough – '

Hendricks moved quickly. But his injured arm betrayed him. Tasso ducked, sliding lithely aside. Her hand came up, lightning fast. Hendricks saw the gun butt coming. He tried to ward off the blow, but she was too fast. The metal butt struck against the side of his head, just above his ear. Numbing pain rushed through him. Pain and rolling clouds of blackness. He sank down, sliding to the ground.

Dimly, he was aware that Tasso was standing over him, kicking him with her toe.

'Major! Wake up!'

He opened his eyes, groaning.

'Listen to me.' She bent down, the gun pointed at his face. 'I have to hurry. There isn't much time left. The ship is ready to go, but you must give me the information I need before I leave.'

Hendricks shook his head, trying to clear it.

'Hurry up! Where is the Moon Base? How do I find it? What do I look for?'

Hendricks said nothing.

'Answer me!'

'Sorry.'

'Major, the ship is loaded with provisions. I can coast for weeks. I'll find the Base eventually. And in a half-hour you'll be dead. Your only chance of survival – ' She broke off.

Along the slope, by some crumbling ruins, something moved. Something in the ash. Tasso turned quickly, aiming. She fired. A puff of flame leaped. Something scuttled away, rolling across the ash. She fired again. The claw burst apart, wheels flying.

'See?' Tasso said. 'A scout. It won't be long.'

'You'll bring them back here to get me?'

'Yes. As soon as possible.'

Hendricks looked up at her. He studied her intently. 'You're telling the truth?' A strange expression had come over his face, an avid hunger. 'You will come back for me? You'll get me to the Moon Base?'

'I'll get you to the Moon Base. But tell me where it is! There's only a little time left.'

'All right.' Hendricks picked up a piece of rock, pulling himself to a sitting position. 'Watch.'

Hendricks began to scratch in the ash. Tasso stood by him, watching the motion of the rock. Hendricks was sketching a crude lunar map.

'This is the Appenine Range. Here is the Crater of Archimedes. The Moon Base is beyond the end of the Appenine, about two hundred miles. I don't know exactly where. No one on Terra knows. But when you're over the Appenine, signal with one red flare and a green flare, followed by two red flares in quick succession. The Base monitor will record your signal. The Base is under the surface, of course. They'll guide you down with magnetic controls.'

'And the controls? Can I operate them?'

'The controls are virtually automatic. All you have to do is give the right signal at the right time.'

'I will.'

'The seat absorbs most of the takeoff shock. Air and temperature are automatically controlled. The ship will leave Terra and pass out into free space. It'll line itself up with the Moon, falling into an orbit around it, about a hundred miles above the surface. The orbit will carry you over the Base. When you're in the region of the Appenine, release the signal rockets.'

Tasso slid into the ship and lowered herself into the pressure seat. The arm locks folded automatically around her. She fingered the controls. 'Too bad you're not going, Major. All this put here for you, and you can't make the trip.'

'Leave me the pistol.'

Tasso pulled the pistol from her belt. She held it in her hand, weighing it thoughtfully. 'Don't go too far from this location. It'll be hard to find you, as it is.'

'No, I'll stay here by the well.'

Tasso gripped the takeoff switch, running her fingers over the smooth metal. 'A beautiful ship, Major. Well built. I admire your workmanship. You people have always done good work. You build fine things. Your work, your creations, are your greatest achievement.'

'Give me the pistol,' Hendricks said impatiently, holding out his hand. He struggled to his feet.

'Good-bye, Major!' Tasso tossed the pistol past Hendricks. The pistol clattered against the ground, bouncing and rolling away. Hendricks hurried after it. He bent down, snatching it up.

The hatch of the ship clanged shut. The bolts fell into place. Hendricks made his way back. The inner door was being sealed. He raised the pistol unsteadily.

There was a shattering roar. The ship burst up from its metal cage, fusing the mesh behind it. Hendricks cringed, pulling back. The ship shot up into the rolling clouds of ash, disappearing into the sky.

Hendricks stood watching a long time, until even the streamer had dissipated. Nothing stirred. The morning air was chill and silent. He began to walk aimlessly back the way they had come. Better to keep moving around. It would be a long time before help came – if it came at all.

He searched his pockets until he found a package of cigarettes. He lit one grimly. They had all wanted cigarettes from him. But cigarettes were scarce.

A lizard slithered by him, through the ash. He halted, rigid. The lizard disappeared. Above, the sun rose higher in the sky. Some flies landed on a flat rock to one side of him. Hendricks kicked at them with his foot.

It was getting hot. Sweat trickled down his face, into his collar. His mouth was dry.

Presently he stopped walking and sat down on some debris. He unfastened his medicine kit and swallowed a few narcotic capsules. He looked around him. Where was he?

Something lay ahead. Stretched out on the ground. Silent and unmoving.

Hendricks drew his gun quickly. It looked like a man. Then he remembered. It was the remains of Klaus. The Second Variety. Where Tasso had blasted him. He could see wheels and relays and metal parts, strewn around on the ash. Glittering and sparkling in the sunlight.

Hendricks got to his feet and walked over. He nudged the inert form with his foot, turning it over a little. He could see the metal hull, the aluminum ribs and struts. More wiring fell out. Like viscera. Heaps of wiring, switches and relays. Endless motors and rods.

He bent down. The brain cage had been smashed by the fall. The artificial brain was visible. He gazed at it. A maze of circuits. Miniature tubes. Wires as fine as hair. He touched the brain cage. It swung aside. The type plate was visible. Hendricks studied the plate.

And blanched.

IV-V.

For a long time he stared at the plate. Fourth Variety. Not the Second. They had been wrong. There were more types. Not just three. Many more, perhaps. At least four. And Klaus wasn't the Second Variety.

But if Klaus wasn't the Second Variety –

Suddenly he tensed. Something was coming, walking through the ash beyond the hill. What was it? He strained to see. Figures. Figures coming slowly along, making their way through the ash.

Coming toward him.

Hendricks crouched quickly, raising his gun. Sweat dripped down into his eyes. He fought down rising panic, as the figures neared.

The first was a David. The David saw him and increased its pace. The other hurried behind it. A second David. A third. Three Davids, all alike, coming toward him silently, without expression, their thin legs rising and falling. Clutching their teddy bears.

He aimed and fired. The first two Davids dissolved into particles. The third came on. And the figure behind it. Climbing silently toward him across the gray ash. A Wounded Soldier, towering over the David. And –

And behind the Wounded Soldier came two Tassos, walking side by side. Heavy belt, Russian army pants, shirt, long hair. The familiar figure, as he had seen her only a little while before. Sitting in the pressure seat of the ship. Two slim, silent figures, both identical.

They were very near. The David bent down suddenly, dropping its teddy bear. The bear raced across the ground. Automatically Hendricks's fingers tightened around the trigger. The bear was gone, dissolved into mist. The two Tasso Types moved on, expressionless, walking side by side, through the gray ash.

When they were almost to him, Henricks raised the pistol waist high and fired.

The two Tassos dissolved. But already a new group was starting up the rise, five or six Tassos, all identical, a line of them coming rapidly toward him.

And he had given her the ship and the signal code. Because of him she was on her way to the Moon, to the Moon Base. He had made it possible.

He had been right about the bomb, after all. It had been designed with knowledge of other types, the David Type and the Wounded Soldier Type. And the Klaus Type. Not designed by human beings. It had been designed by one of the underground factories, apart from all human contact.

The line of Tassos came up to him. Hendricks braced himself, watching them calmly. The familiar face, the belt, the heavy shirt, the bomb carefully in place.

The bomb –

As the Tassos reached for him, a last ironic thought drifted through Hendricks's mind. He felt a little better, thinking about it. The bomb. Made by the Second Variety to destroy the other varieties. Made for that end alone.

They were already beginning to design weapons to use against each other.

Jon's World

Kastner walked around the ship without speaking. He climbed the ramp and entered, disappearing cautiously inside. For a time his outline could be seen, stirring around. He appeared again, his broad face dimly alight.

'Well?' Caleb Ryan said. 'What do you think?'

Kastner came down the ramp. 'Is it ready to go? Nothing left to work out?'

'It's almost ready. Workmen are finishing up the remaining sections. Relay connections and feed lines. But no major problems exist. None we can predict, at least.'

The two men stood together, looking up at the squat metal box with its ports and screens and observation grills. The ship was not lovely. There were no trim lines, no chrome and rexeroid struts to ease the hull into a gradually tapering tear-drop. The ship was square and knobby, with turrets and projections rising up everywhere.

'What will they think when we emerge from that?' Kastner murmured.

'We had no time to beautify it. Of course, if you want to wait another two months – '

'Couldn't you take off a few of the knobs? What are they for? What do they do?'

'Valves. You can examine the plans. They drain off the power load when it peaks too far up. Time travel is going to be dangerous. A vast load is collected as the ship moves back. It has to be leaked off gradually – or we'll be an immense bomb charged with millions of volts.'

'I'll take your word on it.' Kastner picked up his briefcase. He moved toward one of the exits. League Guards stepped out of his way. 'I'll tell the Directors it's almost ready. By the way, I have something to reveal.'

'What is it?'

'We've decided who's going along with you.'

'Who?'

'I'm going. I've always wanted to know what things were like before the war. You see the history spools, but it isn't the same. I want to *be* there. Walk around. You know, they say there was no ash before the war. The surface was fertile. You could walk for miles without seeing ruins. This I would like to see.'

'I didn't know you were interested in the past.'

'Oh, yes. My family preserved some illustrated books showing how it was. No wonder USIC wants to get hold of Schonerman's papers. If reconstruction could begin – '

'That's what we all want.'

'And maybe we'll get it. I'll see you later.'

Ryan watched the plump little businessman depart, his briefcase clutched tightly. The row of League Guards stepped aside for him to pass, filling in behind him as he disappeared through the doorway.

Ryan returned his attention to the ship. So Kastner was to be his companion. USIC – United Synthetic Industries Combine – had held out for equal representation on the trip. One man from the League, one from USIC. USIC had been the source of supply, both commercial and financial, for Project Clock. Without its help the Project would never have got out of the paper stage. Ryan sat down at the bench and sent the blueprints racing through the scanner. They had worked a long time. There was not much left to be done. Only a few finishing touches here and there.

The vidscreen clicked. Ryan halted the scanner and swung to catch the call.

'Ryan.'

The League monitor appeared on the screen. The call was coming through League cables. 'Emergency call.'

Ryan froze. 'Put it through.'

The monitor faded. After a moment an old face appeared, florid and lined. 'Ryan – '

'What's happened?'

'You had better come home. As soon as you can.'

'What is it?'

'Jon.'

Ryan forced himself to be calm. 'Another attack?' His voice was thick.

'Yes.'

'Like the others?'

'Exactly like the others.'

Ryan's hand jerked to the cut-off switch. 'All right. I'll be home at once. Don't let anyone in. Try to keep him quiet. Don't let him out of his room. Double the guard, if necessary.'

Ryan broke the circuit. A moment later he was on his way to the roof, toward his inter-city ship parked above him, at the roof field of the building.

His inter-city ship rushed above the unending gray ash, automatic grapples guiding it toward City Four. Ryan stared blankly out the port, only half-seeing the sight below.

He was between cities. The surface was wasted, endless heaps of slag and ash as far as the eye could see. Cities rose up like occasional toadstools, separated by miles of gray. Toadstools here and there, towers and buildings, men and women working. Gradually the surface was being reclaimed. Supplies and equipment were being brought down from the Lunar Base.

During the war human beings had left Terra and gone to the Moon. Terra was devastated. Nothing but a globe of ruin and ash. Men had come back gradually, when the war was over.

Actually there had been two wars. The first was man against man. The second was man against the claws – complex robots that had been created as a war weapon. The claws had turned on their makers, designing their own new types and equipment.

Ryan's ship began to descend. He was over City Four. Presently the ship came to rest on the roof of his massive private residence at the center of the city. Ryan leaped quickly out and crossed the roof to the lift.

A moment later he entered his quarters and made his way toward Jon's room.

He found the old man watching Jon through the glass side of

the room, his face grave. Jon's room was partly in darkness.
Jon was sitting on the edge of his bed, his hands clasped tightly
together. His eyes were shut. His mouth was open a little, and
from time to time his tongue came out, stiff and rigid.

'How long has he been like that?' Ryan said to the old man
beside him.

'About an hour.'

'The other attacks followed the same pattern?'

'This is more severe. Each has been more severe.'

'No one has seen him but you?'

'Just the two of us. I called you when I was certain. It's
almost over. He's coming out of it.'

On the other side of the glass Jon stood up and walked away
from his bed, his arms folded. His blond hair hung down
raggedly in his face. His eyes were still shut. His face was pale
and set. His lips twitched.

'He was completely unconscious at first. I had left him alone
for awhile. I was in another part of the building. When I came
back I found him lying on the floor. He had been reading. The
spools were scattered all around him. His face was blue. His
breathing was irregular. There were repeated muscular spasms,
as before.'

'What did you do?'

'I entered the room and carried him to the bed. He was rigid
at first, but after a few minutes he began to relax. His body
became limp. I tested his pulse. It was very slow. Breathing
was coming more easily. And then it began.'

'It?'

'The talk.'

'Oh.' Ryan nodded.

'I wish you could have been here. He talked more than ever
before. On and on. Streams of it. Without pause. As if he
couldn't stop.'

'Was – was it the same talk as before?'

'Exactly the same as it's always been. And his face was lit
up. Glowing. As before.'

Ryan considered. 'Is it all right for me to go into the room?'

'Yes. It's almost over.'

Ryan moved to the door. His fingers pressed against the code lock and the door slid back into the wall.

Jon did not notice him as he came quietly into the room. He paced back and forth, eyes shut, his arms wrapped around his body. He swayed a little, rocking from side to side. Ryan came to the center of the room and stopped.

'Jon!'

The boy blinked. His eyes opened. He shook his head rapidly. 'Ryan? What – what did you want?'

'Better sit down.'

Jon nodded. 'Yes. Thank you.' He sat down on the bed uncertainly. His eyes were wide and blue. He pushed his hair back out of his face, smiling a little at Ryan.

'How do you feel?'

'I feel all right.'

Ryan sat down across from him, drawing a chair over. He crossed his legs, leaning back. For a long time he studied the boy. Neither of them spoke. 'Grant says you had a little attack,' Ryan said finally.

Jon nodded.

'You're over it now?'

'Oh, yes. How is the time ship coming?'

'Fine.'

'You promised I could see it, when it's ready.'

'You can. When it's completely done.'

'When will that be?'

'Soon. A few more days.'

'I want to see it very much. I've been thinking about it. Imagine going into time. You could go back to Greece. You could go back and see Pericles and Xenophon and – and Epictetus. You could go back to Egypt and talk to Ikhnaton.' He grinned. 'I can't wait to see it.'

Ryan shifted. 'Jon, do you really think you're well enough to go outside? Maybe – '

'Well enough? What do you mean?'

'Your attacks. You really think you should go out? Are you strong enough?'

Jon's face clouded. 'They're not attacks. Not really. I wish you wouldn't call them attacks.'

'Not attacks? What are they?'

Jon hesitated. 'I – I shouldn't tell you, Ryan. You wouldn't understand.'

Ryan stood up. 'All right, Jon. If you feel you can't talk to me I'll go back to the lab.' He crossed the room to the door. 'It's a shame you can't see the ship. I think you'd like it.'

Jon followed him plaintively. 'Can't I see it?'

'Maybe if I knew more about your – your attacks I'd know whether you're well enough to go out.'

Jon's face flickered. Ryan watched him intently. He could see thoughts crossing Jon's mind, written on his features. He struggled inwardly.

'Don't you want to tell me?'

Jon took a deep breath. 'They're *visions*.'

'What?'

'They're visions.' Jon's face was alive with radiance. 'I've known it a long time. Grant says they're not, but they are. If you could see them you'd know, too. They're not like anything else. More real than, well, than this.' He thumped the wall. 'More real than that.'

Ryan lit a cigarette slowly. 'Go on.'

It all came with a rush. 'More real than *anything* else! Like looking through a window. A window into another world. A real world. Much more real than this. It makes all this just a shadow world. Only dim shadows. Shapes. Images.'

'Shadows of an ultimate reality?'

'Yes! Exactly. The world behind all this.' Jon paced back and forth, animated by excitement. 'This, all these things. What we see here. Buildings. The sky. The cities. The endless ash. None is quite real. It's so dim and vague! I don't really feel it, not like the other. And it's becoming less real, all the time. The other is growing, Ryan. Growing more and more vivid! Grant told me it's only my imagination. But it's not. It's real. More real than any of these things here, these things in this room.'

'Then why can't we all see it?'

'I don't know. I wish you could. You ought to see it, Ryan. It's beautiful. You'd like it, after you got used to it. It takes time to adjust.'

Ryan considered. 'Tell me,' he said at last. 'I want to know exactly what you see. Do you always see the same thing?'

'Yes. Always the same. But more intensely.'

'What is it? What do you see that's so real?'

Jon did not answer for awhile. He seemed to have withdrawn. Ryan waited, watching his son. What was going on in his mind? What was he thinking? The boy's eyes were shut again. His hands were pressed together, the fingers white. He was off again, off in his private world.

'Go on,' Ryan said aloud.

So it was *visions* the boy saw. Visions of ultimate reality. Like the Middle Ages. His own son. There was a grim irony in it. Just when it seemed they had finally licked that proclivity in man, his eternal inability to face reality. His eternal dreaming. Would science never be able to realize its ideal? Would man always go on preferring illusion to reality?

His own son. Retrogression. A thousand years lost. Ghosts and gods and devils and the secret inner world. The world of ultimate reality. All the fables and fictions and metaphysics that man had used for centuries to compensate for his fear, his terror of the world. All the dreams he had made up to hide the truth, the harsh world of reality. Myths, religions, fairy tales. A better land, beyond and above. Paradise. All coming back, reappearing again, and in his own son.

'Go on,' Ryan said impatiently. 'What do you see?'

'I see fields,' Jon said. 'Yellow fields as bright as the sun. Fields and parks. Endless parks. Green, mixed in with the yellow. Paths, for people to walk.'

'What else?'

'Men and women. In robes. Walking along the paths, among the trees. The air fresh and sweet. The sky bright blue. Birds. Animals. Animals moving through the parks. Butterflies. Oceans. Lapping oceans of clear water.'

'No cities?'

'Not like our cities. Not the same. People living in the parks. Little wood houses here and there. Among the trees.'

'Roads?'

'Only paths. No ships or anything. Only walking.'

'What else do you see?'

'That's all.' Jon opened his eyes. His cheeks were flushed. His eyes sparkled and danced. 'That's all, Ryan. Parks and yellow fields. Men and women in robes. And so many animals. The wonderful animals.'

'How do they live?'

'What?'

'How do the people live? What keeps them alive?'

'They grow things. In the fields.'

'Is that all? Don't they build? Don't they have factories?'

'I don't think so.'

'An agrarian society. Primitive.' Ryan frowned. 'No business or commerce.'

'They work in the fields. And discuss things.'

'Can you *hear* them?'

'Very faintly. Sometimes I can hear them a little, if I listen very hard. I can't make out any words, though.'

'What are they discussing?'

'Things.'

'What kind of things?'

Jon gestured vaguely. 'Great things. The world. The universe.'

There was silence. Ryan grunted. He did not say anything. Finally he put out his cigarette. 'Jon – '

'Yes?'

'You think what you see is *real*?'

Jon smiled. 'I know it's real.'

Ryan's gaze was sharp. 'What do you mean, real? In what way is this world of yours real?'

'It exists.'

'Where does it exist?'

'I don't know.'

'Here? Does it exist here?'

'No. It's not here.'

'Some place else? A long way off? Some other part of the universe beyond our range of experience?'

'Not another part of the universe. It has nothing to do with space. It's here.' Jon waved around him. 'Close by. It's very close. I see it all around me.'

'Do you see it now?'

'No. It comes and goes.'

'It ceases to exist? It only exists sometimes?'

'No, it's always there. But I can't always make contact with it.'

'How do you know it's always there?'

'I just know.'

'Why can't *I* see it? Why are you the only one who can see it?'

'I don't know.' Jon rubbed his forehead wearily. 'I don't know why I'm the only one who can see it. I wish you could see it. I wish everybody could see it.'

'How can you demonstrate it isn't an hallucination? You have no objective validation of it. You have only your own inner sense, your state of consciousness. How could it be presented for empirical analysis?'

'Maybe it can't. I don't know. I don't care. I don't *want* to present it for empirical analysis.'

There was silence. Jon's face was set and grim, his jaw tight. Ryan sighed. Impasse.

'All right, Jon.' He moved slowly toward the door. 'I'll see you later.'

Jon said nothing.

At the door Ryan halted, looking back. 'Then your visions are getting stronger, aren't they? Progressively more vivid.'

Jon nodded curtly.

Ryan considered awhile. Finally he raised his hand. The door slid away and he passed outside the room, into the hall.

Grant came up to him. 'I was watching through the window. He's quite withdrawn, isn't he?'

'It's difficult to talk to him. He seems to believe these attacks are some kind of vision.'

'I know. He's told me.'

'Why didn't you let me know?'

'I didn't want to alarm you more. I know you've been worried about him.'

'The attacks are getting worse. He says they're more vivid. More convincing.'

Grant nodded.

Ryan moved along the corridor, deep in thought, Grant a

little behind. 'It's difficult to be certain of the best course of action. The attacks absorb him more and more. He's beginning to take them seriously. They're usurping the place of the outside world. And in addition – '

'And in addition you're leaving soon.'

'I wish we knew more about time travel. A great number of things may happen to us.' Ryan rubbed his jaw. 'We might not come back. Time is a potent force. No real exploration has been done. We have no idea what we may run into.'

He came to the lift and stopped.

'I'll have to make my decision right away. It has to be made before we leave.'

'Your decision?'

Ryan entered the lift. 'You'll know about it later. Watch Jon constantly from now on. Don't be away from him for even a moment. Do you understand?'

Grant nodded. 'I understand. You want to be sure he doesn't leave his room.'

'You'll hear from me either tonight or tomorrow.' Ryan ascended to the roof and entered his inter-city ship.

As soon as he was in the sky he clicked on the vidscreen and dialed the League Offices. The face of the League Monitor appeared. 'Offices.'

'Give me the medical center.'

The monitor faded. Presently Walter Timmer, the medical director, appeared on the screen. His eyes flickered as he recognized Ryan. 'What can I do for you, Caleb?'

'I want you to get out a medical car and a few good men and come over here to City Four.'

'Why?'

'It's a matter I discussed with you several months ago. You recall, I think.'

Timmer's expression changed. 'Your son?'

'I've decided. I can't wait any longer. He's getting worse, and we'll be leaving soon on the time trip. I want it performed before I leave.'

'All right.' Timmer made a note. 'We'll make immediate arrangements here. And we'll send a ship over to pick him up at once.'

Ryan hesitated. 'You'll do a good job?'

'Of course. We'll have James Pryor perform the actual operation.' Timmer reached up to cut the vidscreen circuit. 'Don't worry, Caleb. He'll do a good job. Pryor is the best lobotomist the center has.'

Ryan laid out the map, stretching the corners flat against the table. 'This is a time map, drawn up in the form of a space projection. So we can see where we're going.'

Kastner peered over his shoulder. 'Will we be confined to the one Project – getting Schonerman's papers? Or can we move around?'

'Only the one Project is contemplated. But to be certain of success we should make several stops on this side of Schonerman's continuum. Our time map may be inaccurate, or the drive itself may act with some bias.'

The work was finished. All the final sections were put in place.

In a corner of the room Jon sat watching, his face expressionless. Ryan glanced toward him. 'How does it look to you?'

'Fine.'

The time ship was like some stubby insect, overgrown with warts and knobs. A square box with windows and endless turrets. Not really a ship at all.

'I guess you wish you could come,' Kastner said to Jon. 'Right?'

Jon nodded faintly.

'How are you feeling?' Ryan asked him.

'Fine.'

Ryan studied his son. The boy's color had come back. He had regained most of his original vitality. The visions, of course, no longer existed.

'Maybe you can come next time,' Kastner said.

Ryan returned to the map. 'Schonerman did most of his work between 2030 and 2037. The results were not put to any use until several years later. The decision to use his work in the war was reached only after long consideration. The Government seemed to have been aware of the dangers.'

'But not sufficiently so.'

'No.' Ryan hesitated. 'And we may be getting ourselves into the same situation.'

'How do you mean?'

'Schonerman's discovery of the artificial brain was lost when the last claw was destroyed. None of us have been able to duplicate his work. If we bring his papers we may put society back in jeopardy. We may bring back the claws.'

Kastner shook his head. 'No. Schonerman's work was not implicitly related to the claws. The development of an artificial brain does not imply lethal usage. Any scientific discovery can be used for destruction. Even the wheel was used in the Assyrian war chariots.'

'I suppose so.' Ryan glanced up at Kastner. 'Are you certain USIC doesn't intend to use Schonerman's work along military lines?'

'USIC is an industrial combine. Not a government.'

'It would ensure its advantage for a long time.'

'USIC is strong enough as it is.'

'Let it go.' Ryan rolled up the map. 'We can start any minute. I'm anxious to get going. We've worked a long time on this.'

'I agree.'

Ryan crossed the room to his son. 'We're leaving, Jon. We should be back fairly soon. Wish us luck.'

Jon nodded. 'I wish you luck.'

'You're feeling all right?'

'Yes.'

'Jon – you feel better now, don't you? Better than before?'

'Yes.'

'Aren't you glad they're gone? All the troubles you were having?'

'Yes.'

Ryan put his hand awkwardly on the boy's shoulder. 'We'll see you later.'

Ryan and Kastner made their way up the ramp to the hatch of the time ship. From the corner, Jon watched them silently. A few League Guards lounged at the entrances to the work lab, watching with idle interest.

Ryan paused at the hatch. He called one of the guards over. 'Tell Timmer I want him.'

The guard went off, pushing through the exit.

'What is it?' Kastner said.

'I have some final instructions to give him.'

Kastner shot him a sharp glance. 'Final? What's the matter? You think something's going to happen to us?'

'No. Just a precaution.'

Timmer came striding in. 'You're leaving, Ryan?'

'Everything's ready. There's no reason to hold back any longer.'

Timmer came up the ramp. 'What did you want me for?'

'This may be unnecessary. But there's always the possibility something might go wrong. In case the ship doesn't reappear according to schedule I've filed with the League members – '

'You want me to name a protector for Jon.'

'That's right.'

'There's nothing to worry about.'

'I know. But I'd feel better. Someone should watch out for him.'

They both glanced at the silent, expressionless boy sitting in the corner of the room. Jon stared straight ahead. His face was blank. His eyes were dull, listless. There was nothing there.

'Good luck,' Timmer said. He and Ryan shook hands. 'I hope everything works out.'

Kastner climbed inside the ship, setting down his briefcase. Ryan followed him, lowering the hatch into place and bolting it into position. He sealed the inner lock. A bank of automatic lighting came on. Controlled atmosphere began to hiss into the cabin of the ship.

'Air, light, heat,' Kastner said. He peered out the port at the League Guards outside. 'It's hard to believe. In a few minutes all this will disappear. This building. These guards. Everything.'

Ryan seated himself at the control board of the ship, spreading out the time map. He fastened the map into position, crossing the surface with the cable leads from the board before him. 'It's my plan to make several observation stops along the way, so we can view some of the past events relevant to our work.'

'The war?'

'Mainly. I'm interested in seeing the claws in actual operation. At one time they were in complete control of Terra, according to the War Office records.'

'Let's not get too close, Ryan.'

Ryan laughed. 'We won't land. We'll make our observations from the air. The only actual contact we'll make will be with Schonerman.'

Ryan closed the power circuit. Energy flowed through the ship around them, flooding into the meters and indicators on the control board. Needles jumped, registering the load.

'The main thing we have to watch is our energy peak,' Ryan explained. 'If we build up to much of a load of time ergs the ship won't be able to come out of the time stream. We'll keep moving back into the past, building up a greater and greater charge.'

'An enormous bomb.'

'That's right.' Ryan adjusted the switches before him. The meter readings changed. 'Here we go. Better hang on.'

He released the controls. The ship shuddered as it polarized into position, easing into the time flow. The vanes and knobs changed their settings, adjusting themselves to the stress. Relays closed, braking the ship against the current sweeping around them.

'Like the ocean,' Ryan murmured. 'The most potent energy in the universe. The great dynamic behind all motion. The Prime Mover.'

'Maybe this is what they used to mean by God.'

Ryan nodded. The ship was vibrating around them. They were in the grip of a giant hand, an immense fist closing silently. They were in motion. Through the port the men and walls had begun to waver, fading out of existence as the ship slipped out of phase with the present, drifting farther and farther into the flow of the time stream.

'It won't be long,' Ryan murmured.

All at once the scene beyond the port winked out. There was nothing there. Nothing beyond them.

'We've not phased with any space-time objects,' Ryan explained. 'We're out of focus with the universe itself. At this moment we exist in non-time. There's no continuum in which we're operating.'

'I hope we can get back again.' Kastner sat down nervously, his eyes on the blank port. 'I feel like the first man who went down in a submarine.'

'That was during the American Revolution. The submarine was propelled by a crank which the pilot turned. The other end of the crank was a propeller.'

'How could he go very far?'

'He didn't. He cranked his ship under a British frigate and then bored a hole in the frigate's hull.'

Kastner glanced up at the hull of the time ship, vibrating and rattling from stress. 'What would happen if this ship should break open?'

'We'd be atomized. Dissolved into the stream around us.' Ryan lit a cigarette. 'We'd become a part of the time flow. We'd move back and forth endlessly, from one end of the universe to the other.'

'End?'

'The time ends. Time flows both ways. Right now we're moving back. But energy must move both ways to keep a balance. Otherwise time ergs in vast amounts would collect at one particular continuum and the result would be catastrophic.'

'Do you suppose there's some purpose behind all of this? I wonder how the time flow ever got started.'

'Your question is meaningless. Questions of purpose have no objective validity. They can't be subjected to any form of empirical investigation.'

Kastner lapsed into silence. He picked at his sleeve nervously, watching the port.

Across the time map the cable arms moved, tracing a line from the present back into the past. Ryan studied the motion of the arms. 'We're reaching the latter part of the war. The final stages. I'm going to rephase the ship and bring it out of the time flow.'

'Then we'll be back in the universe again?'

'Among objects. In a specific continuum.'

Ryan gripped the power switch. He took a deep breath. The first great test of the ship had passed. They had entered the time stream without accident. Could they leave it as easily? He opened the switch.

The ship leaped. Kastner staggered, catching hold of the wall support. Outside the port a gray sky twisted and wavered. Adjustments fell into place, leveling the ship in the air. Down below them Terra circled and tilted as the ship gained equilibrium.

Kastner hurried to the port to peer out. They were a few hundred feet above the surface, rushing parallel to the ground. Gray ash stretched out in all directions, broken by the occasional mounds of rubbish. Ruins of towns, buildings, walls. Wrecks of military equipment. Clouds of ash blew across the sky, darkening the sun.

'Is the war still on?' Kastner asked.

'The claws still possess Terra. We should be able to see them.'

Ryan raised the time ship, increasing the scope of their view. Kastner scanned the ground. 'What if they fire at us?'

'We can always escape into time.'

'They might capture the ship and use it to come to the present.'

'I doubt it. At this stage in the war the claws were busy fighting among themselves.'

To their right ran a winding road, disappearing into the ash and reappearing again later on. Bomb craters gaped here and there, breaking the road up. Something was coming slowly along it.

'There,' Kastner said. 'On the road. A column of some sort.'

Ryan maneuvered the ship. They hung above the road, the two of them peering out. The column was dark brown, a marching file making its way steadily along. Men, a column of men, marching silently through the landscape of ash.

Suddenly Kastner gasped. 'They're identical! All of them are the same!'

They were seeing a column of claws. Like lead toys, the robots marched along, tramping through the gray ash. Ryan caught his breath. He had expected such a sight, of course. There were only four types of claws. These he saw now had all been turned out in the same underground plant, from the same dies and stampers. Fifty or sixty robots, shaped like young men, marched calmly along. They moved very slowly. Each had only one leg.

'They must have been fighting among themselves,' Kastner murmured.

'No. This type was made this way. The Wounded Soldier Type. Originally they were designed to trick human sentries to gain entrance into regular bunkers.'

It was weird, watching the silent column of men, identical men, each the same as the next, plodding along the road. Each soldier supported himself with a crutch. Even the crutches were identical. Kastner opened and closed his mouth in revulsion.

'Not very pleasant, is it?' Ryan said. 'We're lucky the human race got away to Luna.'

'Didn't any of these follow?'

'A few, but by that time we had identified the four types and were ready for them.' Ryan took hold of the power switch. 'Let's go on.'

'Wait.' Kastner raised his hand. 'Something's going to happen.'

To the right of the road a group of figures were slipping rapidly down the side of a rise, through the ash. Ryan let go of the power switch, watching. The figures were identical. Women. The women, in uniforms and boots, advanced quietly toward the column on the road.

'Another variety,' Kastner said.

Suddenly the column of soldiers halted. They scattered, hobbling awkwardly in all directions. Some of them fell, stumbling and dropping their crutches. The women rushed out on the road. They were slender and young, with dark hair and eyes. One of the Wounded Soldiers began to fire. A woman fumbled at her belt. She made a throwing motion.

'What – ' Kastner muttered. There was a sudden flash. A cloud of white light rose from the center of the road, billowing in all directions.

'Some kind of concussion bomb,' Ryan said.

'Maybe we better get out of here.'

Ryan threw the switch. The scene below them began to waver. Abruptly it faded. It winked out.

'Thank God that's over,' Kastner said. 'So that's what the war was like.'

'The second part. The major part. Claw against claw. It's a good thing they started fighting with each other. Good for us, I mean.'

'Where to now?'

'We'll make one more observation stop. During the early part of the war. Before claws came into use.'

'And then Schonerman?'

Ryan set his jaw. 'That's right. One more stop and then Schonerman.'

Ryan adjusted the controls. The meters moved slightly. Across the map the cable arm traced their path. 'It won't be long,' Ryan murmured. He gripped the switch, setting the relays in place. 'This time we have to be more careful. There'll be more war activity.'

'Maybe we shouldn't even – '

'I want to see. This was man against man. The Soviet region against the United Nations. I'm curious to see what it was like.'

'What if we're spotted?'

'We can get away quickly.'

Kastner said nothing. Ryan manipulated the controls. Time passed. At the edge of the board Ryan's cigarette burned to an ash. At last he straightened up.

'Here we go. Get set.' He opened the switch.

Below them green and brown plains stretched out, pocked with bomb craters. Part of a city swept past. It was burning. Towering columns of smoke rose up, drifting into the sky. Along the roads black dots moved, vehicles and people streaming away.

'A bombing,' Kastner said. 'Recent.'

The city fell behind. They were over open country. Military trucks rushed along. Most of the land was still intact. They could see a few farmers working the fields. The farmers dropped down as the time ship moved over them.

Ryan studied the sky. 'Watch out.'

'Air craft?'

'I'm not sure where we are. I don't know the location of the sides in this part of the war. We may be over UN territory, or Soviet territory.' Ryan held on tight to the switch.

From the blue sky two dots appeared. The dots grew. Ryan watched them intently. Beside him Kastner gave a nervous grunt. 'Ryan, we better – '

The dots separated. Ryan's hand closed over the power switch. He yanked it closed. As the scene dissolved the dots swept past. Then there was nothing but grayness outside.

In their ears the roar of the two planes still echoed.

'That was close,' Kastner said.

'Very. They didn't waste any time.'

'I hope you don't want to stop any more.'

'No. No more observation stops. The Project itself comes next. We're close to Schonerman's time area. I can begin to slow down the velocity of the ship. This is going to be critical.'

'Critical?'

'There are going to be problems getting to Schonerman. We must hit his continuum exactly, both in space as well as time. He may be guarded. In any case they won't give us much time to explain who we are.' Ryan tapped the time map. 'And there's always the chance the information given here is incorrect.'

'How long before we rephase with a continuum? Schonerman's continuum?'

Ryan looked at his wristwatch. 'About five or ten minutes. Get ready to leave the ship. Part of this is going to be on foot.'

It was night. There was no sound, only unending silence. Kastner strained to hear, his ear against the hull of the ship. 'Nothing.'

'No. I don't hear anything either.' Carefully, Ryan unbolted the hatch, sliding the locks back. He pushed the hatch open, his gun gripped tight. He peered out into the darkness.

The air was fresh and cold. Full of smells of growing things. Trees and flowers. He took a deep breath. He could see nothing. It was pitch black. Far off, a long way off, a cricket chirruped.

'Hear that?' Ryan said.

'What is it?'

'A beetle.' Ryan stepped gingerly down. The ground was soft underfoot. He was beginning to adjust to the darkness. Above him a few stars glinted. He could make out trees, a field of trees. And beyond the trees a high fence.

Kastner stepped down beside him. 'What now?'

'Keep your voice down.' Ryan indicated the fence. 'We're going that way. Some kind of building.'

They crossed the field to the fence. At the fence Ryan aimed his gun, setting the charge at minimum. The fence charred and sank, the wire glowed red.

Ryan and Kastner stepped over the fence. The side of the building rose, concrete and iron. Ryan nodded to Kastner. 'We'll have to move quickly. And low.'

He crouched, taking a breath. Then he ran, bent over, Kastner beside him. They crossed the ground to the building. A window loomed up in front of them. Then a door. Ryan threw his weight against the door.

The door opened. Ryan fell inside, staggering. He caught a quick glimpse of startled faces, men leaping to their feet.

Ryan fired, sweeping the interior of the room with his gun. Flame rushed out, crackling around him. Kastner fired past his shoulder. Shapes moved in the flame, dim outlines falling and rolling.

The flames died. Ryan advanced, stepping over charred heaps on the floor. A barracks. Bunks, remains of a table. An overturned lamp and radio.

By the rays of the lamp Ryan studied a battle map pinned on the wall. He traced the map with his fingers, deep in thought.

'Are we far?' Kastner asked, standing by the door with his gun ready.

'No. Only a few miles.'

'How do we get there?'

'We'll move the time ship. It's safer. We're lucky. It might have been on the other side of the world.'

'Will there be many guards?'

'I'll tell you the facts when we get there.' Ryan moved to the door. 'Come on. Someone may have seen us.'

Kastner grabbed up a handful of newspapers from the

remains of the table. 'I'll bring these. Maybe they'll tell us something.'

'Good idea.'

Ryan set the ship down in a hollow between two hills. He spread the newspapers out, studying them intently. 'We're earlier than I thought. By a few months. Assuming these are new.' He fingered the newsprint. 'Not turned yellow. Probably only a day or so old.'

'What is the date?'

'Autumn, 2030. September 21.'

Kastner peered out the port. 'The sun is going to be coming up soon. The sky is beginning to turn gray.'

'We'll have to work fast.'

'I'm a little uncertain. What am I supposed to do?'

'Schonerman is in a small village beyond this hill. We're in the United States. In Kansas. This area is surrounded by troops, a circle of pillboxes and dugouts. We're inside the periphery. Schonerman is virtually unknown at this continuum. His research has never been published. At this time he's working as part of a large Government research project.'

'Then he's not especially protected.'

'Only later on, when his work has been turned over to the Government will he be protected day and night. Kept in an underground laboratory and never let up to the surface. The Government's most valuable research worker. But right now – '

'How will we know him?'

Ryan handed Kastner a sheaf of photographs. 'This is Schonerman. All the pictures that survived up to our own time.'

Kastner studied the pictures. Schonerman was a small man with horn-rimmed glasses. He smiled feebly at the camera, a thin nervous man with a prominent forehead. His hands were slender, the fingers long and tapered. In one photograph he sat at his desk, a pipe beside him, his thin chest covered by a sleeveless wool sweater. In another he sat with his legs crossed, a tabby cat in his lap, a mug of beer in front of him. An old German enamel mug with hunting scenes and Gothic letters.

'So that's the man who invented the claws. Or did the research work.'

'That's the man who worked out the principles for the first workable artificial brain.'

'Did he know they were going to use his work to make the claws?'

'Not at first. According to reports, Schonerman first learned about it only when the initial batch of claws was released. The United Nations were losing the war. The Soviets gained an original advantage, due to their opening surprise attacks. The claws were hailed as a triumph of Western development. For a time they seemed to have turned the tide of the war.'

'And then – '

'And then the claws began to manufacture their own varieties and attack Soviets and Westerners alike. The only humans that survived were those at the UN base on Luna. A few dozen million.'

'It was a good thing the claws finally turned on each other.'

'Schonerman saw the whole development of his work to the last stages. They say he became greatly embittered.'

Kastner passed the pictures back. 'And you say he's not especially well guarded?'

'Not at this continuum. No more than any other research worker. He's young. In this continuum he's only twenty-five. Remember that.'

'Where'll we find him?'

'The Government Project is located in what was once a school house. Most of the work is done on the surface. No big underground development has begun yet. The research workers have barracks about a quarter mile from their labs.' Ryan glanced at his watch. 'Our best chance is to nab him as he begins work at his bench in the lab.'

'Not in the barracks?'

'The papers are all in the lab. The Government doesn't allow any written work to be taken out. Each worker is searched as he leaves.' Ryan touched his coat gingerly. 'We have to be careful. Schonerman must not be harmed. We only want his papers.'

'We won't use our blasters?'

'No. We don't dare take the chance of injuring him.'

'His papers will definitely be at his bench?'

'He's not allowed to remove them for any reason. We know exactly where we'll find what we want. There's only one place the papers can be.'

'Their security precautions play right into our hands.'

'Exactly,' Ryan murmured.

Ryan and Kastner slipped down the hillside, running between the trees. The ground was hard and cold underfoot. They emerged at the edge of the town. A few people were already up, moving slowly along the street. The town had not been bombed. There was no damage, as yet. The windows of the stores had been boarded up and huge arrows pointed to the underground shelters.

'What do they have on?' Kastner said. 'Some of them have something on their faces.'

'Bacteria masks. Come on.' Ryan gripped his blast pistol as he and Kastner made their way through the town. None of the people paid any attention to them.

'Just two more uniformed people,' Kastner said.

'Our main hope is surprise. We're inside the wall of defense. The sky is patrolled against Soviet craft. No Soviet agents could be landed here. And in any case, this is a minor research lab, in the center of the United States. There would be no reason for Soviet agents to come here.'

'But there will be guards.'

'Everything is guarded. All science. All kinds of research work.'

The school house loomed up ahead of them. A few men were milling around the doorway. Ryan's heart constricted. Was Schonerman one of them?

The men were going inside, one by one. A guard in helmet and uniform was checking their badges. A few of the men wore bacteria masks, only their eyes visible. Would he recognize Schonerman? What if he wore a mask? Fear gripped Ryan suddenly. In a mask Schonerman would look like anyone else.

Ryan slipped his blast pistol away, motioning Kastner to do the same. His fingers closed over the lining of his coat pocket.

Sleep-gas crystals. No one this early would have been immunized against sleep-gas. It had not been developed until a year or so later. The gas would put everyone for several hundred feet around into varying periods of sleep. It was a tricky and unpredictable weapon – but perfect for this situation.

'I'm ready,' Kastner murmured.

'Wait. We have to wait for *him*.'

They waited. The sun rose, warming the cold sky. More research workers appeared, filing up the path and inside the building. They puffed white clouds of frozen moisture and slapped their hands together. Ryan began to become nervous. One of the guards was watching him and Kastner. If they became suspicious –

A small man in a heavy overcoat and horn-rimmed glasses came up the path, hurrying toward the building.

Ryan tensed. Schonerman! Schonerman flashed his badge to the guard. He stamped his feet and went inside the building, stripping off his mittens. It was over in a second. A brisk young man, hurrying to get to his work. To his papers.

'Come on,' Ryan said.

He and Kastner moved forward. Ryan pulled the gas crystals loose from the lining of his pocket. The crystals were cold and hard in his hand. Like diamonds. The guard was watching them coming, his gun alert. His face was set. Studying them. He had never seen them before. Ryan, watching the guard's face, could read his thoughts without trouble.

Ryan and Kastner halted at the doorway. 'We're from the FBI,' Ryan said calmly.

'Identify yourselves.' The guard did not move.

'Here are our credentials,' Ryan said. He drew his hand out from his coat pocket. And crushed the gas crystals in his fist.

The guard sagged. His face relaxed. Limply, his body slid to the ground. The gas spread. Kastner stepped through the door, peering around, his eyes bright.

The building was small. Lab benches and equipment stretched out on all sides of them. The workers lay where they had been standing, inert heaps on the floor, their arms and legs out, their mouths open.

'Quick.' Ryan passed Kastner, hurrying across the lab. At

the far end of the room Schonerman lay slumped over his bench, his head resting against the metal surface. His glasses had fallen off. His eyes were open, staring. He had taken his papers out of the drawer. The padlock and key were still on the bench. The papers were under his head and between his hands.

Kastner ran to Schonerman and snatched the papers up, stuffing them into his briefcase.

'Get them all!'

'I have them all.' Kastner pulled open the drawer. He grabbed the remaining papers in the drawer. 'Every one of them.'

'Let's go. The gas will dissipate rapidly.'

They ran back outside. A few sprawled bodies lay across the entrance, workers who had come into the area.

'Hurry.'

They ran through the town, along the single main street. People gaped at them in astonishment. Kastner gasped for breath, holding on tight to his briefcase as he ran. 'I'm – winded.'

'Don't stop.'

They reached the edge of the town and started up the hillside. Ryan ran between the trees, his body bent forward, not looking back. Some of the workers would be reviving. And other guards would be coming into the area. It would not be long before the alarm would be out.

Behind them a siren whirred into life.

'Here they come.' Ryan paused at the top of the hill, waiting for Kastner. Behind them men were swelling rapidly into the street, coming up out of the underground bunkers. More sirens wailed, a dismal echoing sound.

'Down!' Ryan ran down the hillside toward the time ship, sliding and slipping on the dry earth. Kastner hurried after him, sobbing for breath. They could hear orders being shouted. Soldiers swarming up the hillside after them.

Ryan reached the ship. He grabbed Kastner and pulled him inside. 'Get the hatch shut. Get it closed!'

Ryan ran to the control board. Kastner dropped his briefcase and tugged at the rim of the hatch. At the top of the hill a line of soldiers appeared. They made their way down the hillside, aiming and firing as they ran.

'Get down,' Ryan barked. Shells crashed against the hull of the ship. 'Down!'

Kastner fired back with his blast pistol. A wave of flame rolled up the hillside at the soldiers. The hatch came shut with a bang. Kastner spun the bolts and slid the inner lock into place. 'Ready. All ready.'

Ryan threw the power switch. Outside, the remaining soldiers fought through the flame to the side of the ship. Ryan could see their faces through the port, seared and scorched by the blast.

One man raised his gun awkwardly. Most of them were down, rolling and struggling to rise. As the scene dimmed and faded he saw one of them crawling to his knees. The man's clothing was on fire. Smoke billowed from him, from his arms and shoulders. His face was contorted with pain. He reached out, toward the ship, reaching up at Ryan, his hands shaking, his body bent.

Suddenly Ryan froze.

He was still staring fixedly when the scene winked out and there was nothing. Nothing at all. The meters changed reading. Across the time map the arms moved calmly, tracing their lines.

In the last moment Ryan had looked directly into the man's face. The pain-contorted face. The features had been twisted, screwed up out of shape. And the horn-rimmed glasses were gone. But there was no doubt – it was Schonerman.

Ryan sat down. He ran a shaking hand through his hair.

'You're certain?' Kastner said.

'Yes. He must have come out of the sleep very quickly. It reacts differently on each person. And he was at the far end of the room. He must have come out of it and followed after us.'

'Was he badly injured?'

'I don't know.'

Kastner opened his briefcase. 'Anyhow, we have the papers.'

Ryan nodded, only half hearing. Schonerman injured, blasted, his clothing on fire. That had not been part of the plan.

But more important – *had it been part of history?*

For the first time the ramification of what they had done was beginning to emerge in his mind. Their own concern had been to obtain Schonerman's papers, so that USIC could make use of the artificial brain. Properly used, Schonerman's discovery could have great value in aiding the restoration of demolished Terra. Armies of worker-robots replanting and rebuilding. A mechanical army to make Terra fertile again. Robots could do in a generation what humans would toil at for years. Terra could be reborn.

But in returning to the past had they introduced new factors? Had a new past been created? Had some kind of balance been upset?

Ryan stood up and paced back and forth.

'What is it?' Kastner said. 'We got the papers.'

'I know.'

'USIC will be pleased. The League can expect aid from now on. Whatever it wants. This will set up USIC forever. After all, USIC will manufacture the robots. Worker-robots. The end of human labor. Machines instead of men to work the ground.'

Ryan nodded. 'Fine.'

'Then what's wrong?'

'I'm worried about our continuum.'

'What are you worried about?'

Ryan crossed to the control board and studied the time map. The ship was moving back toward the present, the arms tracing a path back. 'I'm worried about new factors we may have introduced into past continuums. There's no record of Schonerman being injured. There's no record of this event. It may have set a different causal chain into motion.'

'Like what?'

'I don't know. But I intend to find out. We're going to make a stop right away and discover what new factors we've set into motion.'

Ryan moved the ship into a continuum immediately following the Schonerman incident. It was early October, a little over a week later. He landed the ship in a farmer's field outside of Des Moines, Iowa, at sunset. A cold autumn night with the ground hard and brittle underfoot.

Ryan and Kastner walked into town, Kastner holding tightly

onto his briefcase. Des Moines had been bombed by Russian guided missiles. Most of the industrial sections were gone. Only military men and construction workers still remained in the city. The civilian population had been evacuated.

Animals roamed around the deserted streets, looking for food. Glass and debris lay everywhere. The city was cold and desolate. The streets were gutted and wrecked from the fires following the bombing. The autumn air was heavy with the decaying smells of vast heaps of rubble and bodies mixed together in mounds at intersections and open lots.

From a boarded-up newsstand Ryan stole a copy of a news magazine, *Week Review*. The magazine was damp and covered with mold. Kastner put it into his briefcase and they returned to the time ship. Occasional soldiers passed them, moving weapons and equipment out of the city. No one challenged them.

They reached the time ship and entered, locking the hatch behind them. The fields around them were deserted. The farm building had been burned down, and the crops were withered and dead. In the driveway the remains of a ruined automobile lay on its side, a charred wreck. A group of ugly pigs nosed around the remains of the farmhouse, searching for something to eat.

Ryan sat down, opened the magazine. He studied it for a long time, turning the damp pages slowly.

'What do you see?' Kastner asked.

'All about the war. It's still in the opening stages. Soviet guided missiles dropping down. American disk bombs showering all over Russia.'

'Any mention of Schonerman?'

'Nothing I can find. Too much else going on.' Ryan went on studying the magazine. Finally, on one of the back pages, he found what he was looking for. A small item, only a paragraph long.

SOVIET AGENTS SURPRISED

A group of Soviet agents, attempting to demolish a Government research station at Harristown, Kansas, were fired on by guards and quickly routed. The agents escaped, after attempting to slip past the guards into the work offices of the station. Passing themselves off as FBI men, the Soviet agents tried to gain entry as the early morning shift was beginning work. Alert guards intercepted them and gave chase. No damage was done to the research labs or equipment. Two guards and one worker were killed in the encounter. The names of the guards

Ryan clutched the magazine.

'What is it?' Kastner hurried over.

Ryan read the rest of the article. He laid down the magazine, pushing it slowly towards Kastner.

'What is it?' Kastner searched the page.

'Schonerman died. Killed by the blast. We killed him. We've changed the past.'

Ryan stood up and walked to the port. He lit a cigarette, some of his composure returning. 'We set up new factors and started a new line of events. There's no telling where it will end.'

'What do you mean?'

'Someone else may discover the artificial brain. Maybe the shift will rectify itself. The time flow will resume its regular course.'

'Why should it?'

'I don't know. As it stands, we killed him and stole his papers. There's no way the Government can get hold of his work. They won't even know it ever existed. Unless someone else does the same work, covers the same material – '

'How will we know?'

'We'll have to take more looks. It's the only way to find out.'

Ryan selected the year 2051.

In 2051 the first claws had begun to appear. The Soviets had almost won the war. The UN was beginning to bring out the claws in the last desperate attempt to turn the tide of the war.

Ryan landed the time ship at the top of a ridge. Below them a level plain stretched out, criss-crossed with ruins and barbed wire and the remains of weapons.

Kastner unscrewed the hatch and stepped gingerly out onto the ground.

'Be careful,' Ryan said. 'Remember the claws.'

Kastner drew his blast gun. 'I'll remember.'

'At this stage they were small. About a foot long. Metal. They hid down in the ash. The humanoid types hadn't come into existence, yet.'

The sun was high in the sky. It was about noon. The air was warm and thick. Clouds of ash rolled across the ground, blown by the wind.

Suddenly Kastner tensed. 'Look. What's that? Coming along the road.'

A truck bumped slowly toward them, a heavy brown truck, loaded with soldiers. The truck made its way along the road to the base of the ridge. Ryan drew his blast gun. He and Kastner stood ready.

The truck stopped. Some of the soldiers leaped down and started up the side of the ridge, striding through the ash.

'Get set,' Ryan murmured.

The soldiers reached them, halted a few feet away. Ryan and Kastner stood silently, their blast guns up.

One of the soldiers laughed. 'Put them away. Don't you know the war's over?'

'*Over?*'

The soldiers relaxed. Their leader, a big man with a red face, wiped sweat from his dirty forehead and pushed his way up to Ryan. His uniform was ragged and dirty. He wore boots, split and caked with ash. 'That war's been over for a week. Come on! There's a lot to do. We'll take you on back.'

'Back?'

'We're rounding up all the outposts. You were cut off? No communications?'

'No,' Ryan said.

'Be months before everyone knows the war's over. Come along. No time to stand here jawing.'

Ryan shifted. 'Tell me. You say the war is really over? But – '

'Good thing, too. We couldn't have lasted much longer.' The officer tapped his belt. 'You don't by any chance have a cigarette, do you?'

Ryan brought out his pack slowly. He took the cigarettes

from it and handed them to the officer, crumpling the pack carefully and restoring it to his pocket.

'Thanks.' The officer passed the cigarettes around to his men. They lit up. 'Yes, it's a good thing. We were almost finished.'

Kastner's mouth opened. 'The claws. What about the claws?'

The officer scowled. 'What?'

'Why did the war end so – so suddenly?'

'Counter-revolution in the Soviet Union. We had been dropping agents and material for months. Never thought anything would come of it, though. They were a lot weaker than anyone realized.'

'Then the war's really ended?'

'Of course.' The officer grabbed Ryan by the arm. 'Let's go. We have work to do. We're trying to clear this god damn ash away and get things planted.'

'Planted? Crops?'

'Of course. What would *you* plant?'

Ryan pulled away. 'Let me get this straight. The war is over. No more fighting. And you know nothing about any claws? Any kind of weapon called claws?'

The officer's face wrinkled. 'What do you mean?'

'Mechanical killers. Robots. As a weapon.'

The circle of soldiers drew back a little. 'What the hell is he talking about?'

'You better explain,' the officer said, his face suddenly hard. 'What's this about claws?'

'No weapon was ever developed along those lines?' Kastner asked.

There was silence. Finally one of the soldiers grunted. 'I think I know what he means. He means Dowling's mine.'

Ryan turned. 'What?'

'An English physicist. He's been experimenting with artificial mines, self-governing. Robot mines. But the mines couldn't repair themselves. So the Government abandoned the project and increased its propaganda work instead.'

'That's why the war's over,' the officer said. He started off. 'Let's go.'

The soldiers trailed after him, down the side of the ridge.

'Coming?' The officer halted, looking back at Ryan and Kastner.

'We'll be along later,' Ryan said. 'We have to get our equipment together.'

'All right. The camp is down the road about half a mile. There's a settlement there. People coming back from the Moon.'

'From the Moon?'

'We had started moving units to Luna, but now there isn't any need. Maybe it's a good thing. Who the hell wants to leave Terra?'

'Thanks for the cigarettes,' one the soldiers called back. The soldiers piled in the back of the truck. The officer slid behind the wheel. The truck started up and continued on its way, rumbling along the road.

Ryan and Kastner watched it go.

'Then Schonerman's death was never balanced,' Ryan murmured. 'A whole new past – '

'I wonder how far the change carries. I wonder if it carries up to our own time.'

'There's only one way to find out.'

Kastner nodded. 'I want to know right away. The sooner the better. Let's get started.'

Ryan nodded, deep in thought. 'The sooner the better.'

They entered the time ship. Kastner sat down with his briefcase. Ryan adjusted the controls. Outside the port the scene winked out of existence. They were in the time flow again, moving toward the present.

Ryan's face was grim. 'I can't believe it. The whole structure of the past changed. An entire new chain set in motion. Expanding through every continuum. Altering more and more of our stream.'

'Then it won't be our present, when we get back. There's no telling how different it will be. All stemming from Schonerman's death. A whole new history set in motion from one incident.'

'Not from Schonerman's death,' Ryan corrected.

'What do you mean?'

'Not from his death but from the loss of his papers. Because

Schonerman died the Government didn't obtain a successful methodology by which they could build an artificial brain. Therefore the claws never came into existence.'

'It's the same thing.'

'Is it?'

Kastner looked up quickly. 'Explain.'

'Schonerman's death is of no importance. The loss of his papers to the Government is the determining factor.' Ryan pointed at Kastner's briefcase. 'Where are the papers? In there. We have them.'

Kastner nodded. 'That's true.'

'We can restore the situation by moving back into the past and delivering the papers to some agency of the Government. Schonerman is unimportant. It's his papers that matter.'

Ryan's hand moved toward the power switch.

'Wait!' Kastner said. 'Don't we want to see the present? We should see what changes carry down to our own time.'

Ryan hesitated. 'True.'

'Then we can decide what we want to do. Whether we want to restore the papers.'

'All right. We'll continue to the present and then make up our minds.'

The fingers crossing the time map had returned almost to their original position. Ryan studied them for a long time, his hand on the power switch. Kastner held on tightly to the briefcase, his arms wrapped around it, the heavy leather bundle resting in his lap.

'We're almost there,' Ryan said.

'To our own time?'

'In another few moments.' Ryan stood up, gripping the switch. 'I wonder what we'll see.'

'Probably very little we'll recognize.'

Ryan took a deep breath, feeling the cold metal under his fingers. How different would their world be? Would they recognize anything? Had they swept everything familiar out of existence?

A vast chain had been started in motion. A tidal wave moving through time, altering each continuum, echoing down through all the ages to come. The second part of the war had never happened. Before the claws could be invented the war had ended. The concept of the artificial brain had never been transformed into workable practice. The most potent engine of war had never come into existence. Human energies had turned from war to rebuilding of the planet.

Around Ryan the meters and dials vibrated. In a few seconds they would be back. What would Terra be like? Would anything be the same?

The Fifty Cities. Probably they would not exist. Jon, his son, sitting quietly in his room reading. USIC. The Government. The League and its labs and offices, its buildings and roof fields and guards. The whole complicated social structure. Would it all be gone without a trace? Probably.

And what would he find instead?

'We'll know in a minute,' Ryan murmured.

'It won't be long.' Kastner got to his feet and moved to the port. 'I want to see it. It should be a very unfamiliar world.'

Ryan threw the power switch. The ship jerked, pulling out of the time flow. Outside the port something drifted and turned, as the ship righted itself. Automatic gravity controls slipped into place. The ship was rushing above the surface of the ground.

Kastner gasped.

'What do you see?' Ryan demanded, adjusting the velocity of the ship. 'What's out there?'

Kastner said nothing.

'What do you see?'

After a long time Kastner turned away from the port. 'Very interesting. Look for yourself.'

'What's out there?'

Kastner sat down slowly, picking up his briefcase. 'This opens up a whole new line of thought.'

Ryan made his way to the port and gazed out. Below the ship lay Terra. But not the Terra they had left.

Fields, endless yellow fields. And parks. Parks and yellow fields. Squares of green among the yellow, as far as the eye could see. Nothing else.

'No cities,' Ryan said thickly.

'No. Don't you remember? The people are all out in the fields. Or walking in the parks. Discussing the nature of the universe.'

'This is what Jon saw.'

'Your son was extremely accurate.'

Ryan moved back to the controls, his face blank. His mind was numb. He sat down and adjusted the landing grapples. The ship sank lower and lower until it was coasting over the flat fields. Men and women glanced up at the ship, startled. Men and women in robes.

They passed over a park. A herd of animals rushed frantically away. Some kind of deer.

This was the world his son had seen. This was his vision. Fields and parks and men and women in long flowing robes. Walking along the paths. Discussing the problems of the universe.

And the other world, his world, no longer existed. The League was gone. His whole life's work destroyed. In this world it did not exist. Jon. His son. Snuffed out. He would never see him again. His work, his son, everything he had known had winked out of existence.

'We have to go back,' Ryan said suddenly.

Kastner blinked. 'Beg pardon?'

'We have to take the papers back to the continuum where they belong. We can't recreate the situation exactly, but we can place the papers in the Government's hands. That will restore all the relevant factors.'

'Are you serious?'

Kastner stepped back, whipping out his blaster. Ryan lunged. His shoulder caught Kastner, bowling the little businessman over. The blaster skidded across the floor of the ship, clattering against the wall. The papers fluttered in all directions.

'You damn fool!' Ryan grabbed at the papers, dropping down to his knees.

Kastner chased after the blaster. He scooped it up, his round face set with owlish determination. Ryan saw him out of the corner of his eye. For a moment the temptation to laugh almost overcame him. Kastner's face was flushed, his cheeks burning red. He fumbled with the blaster, trying to aim it.

'Kastner, for God's sake – '

The little businessman's fingers tightened around the trigger. Abrupt fear chilled Ryan. He scrambled to his feet. The blaster roared, flame crackling across the time ship. Ryan leaped out of the way, singed by the trail of fire.

Schonerman's papers flared up, glowing where they lay scattered over the floor. For a brief second they burned. Then the glow died out, flickering into charred ash. The thin acrid smell of the blast drifted to Ryan, tickling his nose and making his eyes water.

'Sorry,' Kastner murmured. He laid the blaster down on the control board. 'Don't think you better get us down? We're quite close to the surface.'

Ryan moved mechanically to the control board. After a moment he took his seat and began to adjust the controls, decreasing the velocity of the ship. He said nothing.

'I'm beginning to understand about Jon,' Kastner murmured. 'He must have had some kind of parallel time sense. Awareness of other possible futures. As work progressed on the time ship his visions increased, didn't they? Every day his visions became more real. Every day the time ship became more actual.'

Ryan nodded.

'This opens up whole new lines of speculation. The mystical visions of medieval saints. Perhaps they were of other futures, other time flows. Visions of hell would be worse time flows. Visions of heaven would be better time flows. Ours must stand some place in the middle. And the vision of the eternal unchanging world. Perhaps that's an awareness of non-time. Not another world but this world, seen outside of time. We'll have to think more about that, too.'

The ship landed, coming to rest at the edge of one of the parks. Kastner crossed to the port and gazed out at the trees beyond the ship.

'In the books my family saved there were some pictures of trees,' he said thoughtfully. 'These trees here, by us. They're pepper trees. Those over there are what they call evergreen trees. They stay that way all year around. That's why the name.'

Kastner picked up his briefcase, gripping it tightly. He moved toward the hatch.

'Let's go find some of the people. So we can begin discussing things. Metaphysical things.' He grinned at Ryan. 'I always did like metaphysical things.'

The Cosmic Poachers

'What kind of ship is it?' Captain Shure demanded, staring fixedly at the viewscreen, his hands gripping the fine adjustment.

Navigator Nelson peered over his shoulder. 'Wait a minute.' He swung the control camera over and snapped a photograph from the screen. The photograph disappeared down the message tube to the chart room. 'Keep calm. We'll get a determination from Barnes.'

'What are they doing here? What are they after? They must know the Sirius system is closed.'

'Notice the balloon sides.' Nelson traced the screen with his finger. 'It's a freighter. Look at the bulge. It's a cargo carrier.'

'And while you're looking, notice *that*.' Shure whirled the enlarger. The image of the ship bloated, expanding until it filled the screen. 'See that row of projections?'

'So?'

'Heavy guns. Countersunk. For deep-space firing. It's a freighter, but it's also armed.'

'Pirates, maybe.'

'Maybe.' Shure toyed with the communications mike. 'I'm tempted to put a call back to Terra.'

'Why?'

'This may be a scout.'

Nelson's eyes flickered. 'You think they're in the process of sounding us out? But if there are more, why don't our screens pick them up?'

'The rest may be out of range.'

'More than two light years? I have the screens up to maximum. And they're the best screens available.'

The determination popped up the tube from the chart room,

skidding out on the table. Shure broke it open and scanned it rapidly. He passed it to Nelson. 'Here.'

The ship was Adharan design. First-class, from a recent freighter group. Barnes had noted in his own hand: 'But not supposed to be armed. Must have added the cannon. Not standard equipment on Adharan freighters.'

'Then it's not bait,' Shure murmured. 'We can rule that out. What's the story on Adhara? Why would an Adharan ship be in the Sirius system? Terra has closed this whole region off for years. They must know they can't trade here.'

'No one knows much about Adharans. They participated in the All-galaxy Trade Conference, but that's all.'

'What race are they?'

'Arachnid type. Typical of this area. Based on the Great Murzim Stem. They're a variant of the Murzim original. They keep mostly to themselves. Complex social structure, very rigid patterns. Organic-state grouping.'

'You mean they're insects.'

'I suppose. In the same sense we're lemurs.'

Shure turned his attention back to the viewscreen. He reduced magnification, watching intently. The screen followed the Adharan ship automatically, maintaining a direct alignment with it.

The Adharan ship was heavy and black, awkward in comparison to the sleek Terran cruiser. It bulged like a well-fed worm, its somber sides swollen almost to a full sphere. An occasional guide light blinked on and off as the ship approached the outermost planet of the Sirius system. It moved slowly, cautiously, feeling its way along. It entered the orbit of the tenth planet and began maneuvering for descent. Brake jets burst on, flashing red. The bloated worm drifted down, lowering itself toward the surface of the planet.

'They're landing,' Nelson murmured.

'That's fine. They'll be stationary. Good target for us.'

On the surface of the tenth planet the Adharan freighter lay resting, its jets dying into silence. A cloud of exhaust particles rose from it. The freighter had landed between two mountain ranges, on a barren waste of gray sand. The surface of the tenth planet was utterly barren. No life, atmosphere or water existed.

The planet was mostly rock, cold gray rock, with vast shadows and pits, a corroded sickly surface, hostile and bleak.

Abruptly the Adharan ship came to life. Hatches popped open. Tiny black dots rushed from the ship. The dots increased in number, a flood of specks pouring out of the freighter, scurrying across the sand. Some of them reached the mountains and disappeared among the craters and peaks. Others gained the far side, where they were lost in the long shadows.

'I'll be damned,' Shure muttered. 'It doesn't make sense. What are they after? We've gone over these planets with a fine tooth comb. There's nothing anyone would want, down there.'

'They may have different wants, or different methods.'

Shure stiffened. 'Look. Their cars are coming back to the ship.'

The black dots had reappeared, emerging from the shadows and craters. They hurried back toward the mother worm, racing across the sand. The hatches opened. One by one the cars popped into the ship and disappeared. A few belated cars made their way to the ship and entered. The hatches clamped shut.

'What in hell could they have found?' Shure said.

Communications Officer Barnes entered the control room, craning his neck. 'Still down there? Let me have a look. I've never seen an Adharan ship.'

On the surface of the planet the Adharan ship stirred. Suddenly it shuddered, quivering from stem to stern. It rose from the surface, gaining altitude rapidly. It headed for the ninth planet. For a time it circled the ninth planet, observing the pitted, eroded surface below. Empty basins of dried-up oceans stretched on like immense pie pans.

The Adharan ship selected one of the basins and settled down to a landing, blowing clouds of exhaust up into the sky.

'The same damn thing again,' Shure murmured.

Hatches opened. Black specks leaped out onto the surface and rushed off in all directions.

Shure's jaw jutted out angrily. 'We have to find out what they're after. Look at them go! They know exactly what they're doing.' He grabbed up the communication mike. Then he dropped it. 'We can handle this alone. We won't need Terra.'

'It's armed, don't forget.'

'We'll catch it as it lands. They're stopping at each planet in order. We'll go all the way in to the fourth planet.' Shure moved rapidly, bringing the command chart into position. 'When they land on the fourth planet we'll be there waiting for them.'

'They may put up a fight.'

'Maybe. But we have to find out what they're loading – and whatever it is, it belongs to us.'

The fourth planet of the Sirius system had an atmosphere, and some water. Shure landed his cruiser in the ruins of an ancient city, long deserted.

The Adharan freighter had not appeared. Shure scanned the sky and then raised the main hatch. He and Barnes and Nelson stepped outside cautiously, armed with heavy-duty Slem rifles. Behind them the hatch slammed back in place and the cruiser took off, soaring up into the sky.

They watched it go, standing together with their rifles ready. The air was cold and thin. They could feel it blowing around their pressure suits.

Barnes turned up the temperature of his suit. 'Too cold for me.'

'Makes you realize we're still Terrans, even though we're light years from home,' Nelson said.

'Here's the outline,' Shure said. 'We can't blast them. That's out. We're after their cargo. If we blast them we'll blast the cargo along with them.'

'What'll we use?'

'We'll shoot a vapor cloud around them.'

'A vapor cloud? But – '

'Captain,' Nelson said, 'we can't use a vapor cloud. We won't be able to get near them until the vapor has become inert.'

'There's a wind. The vapor will dissipate very quickly. Anyhow, it's all we can do. We'll have to take the chance. As soon as the Adharan is sighted, we must be ready to open fire.'

'What if the cloud misses?'

'Then we're in for a fight.' Shure studied the sky intently. 'I think it's coming. Let's go.'

They hurried to a hill of piled up rocks, remains of columns and towers heaped in great mounds, mixed with debris and rubble.

'This will do.' Shure crouched down, his Slem rifle held tightly. 'Here they come.'

The Adharan ship had appeared above them. It was preparing to land. Down it settled, its jets roaring, exhaust particles rising. With a crash it struck the ground, bouncing a little and finally coming to rest.

Shure gripped his phone. 'Okay.'

Above them in the sky the cruiser appeared, sweeping down over the Adharan. From the cruiser a blue-white cloud shot, drilled out by pressure jets directly at the black Adharan ship. The cloud reached the parked freighter. It billowed around it, fusing into it.

The surface of the Adharan hull glowed briefly. It began to fall in, eaten away. Corroded. The Terran cruiser swept past, completing its run. It disappeared into the sky.

From the Adharan ship figures were emerging, jumping out onto the ground. The figures sprang in all directions, long-legged, leaping wildly around. Most of the figures hopped excitedly up onto their ship, dragging hoses and equipment, working frantically, disappearing into the vapor cloud.

'They're spraying.'

More Adharans appeared, leaping frantically up and down, onto their ship, onto the ground, some this way, others in no particular direction at all.

'Like when you step on an ant hill,' Barnes muttered.

The hull of the Adharan ship was covered with clinging Adharans, spraying desperately, trying to halt the corrosive action of the vapor. Above them the Terran cruiser reappeared, entered a second run. It grew, swelling from a dot into a tear-shaped needle, flashing in the sunlight from Sirius. The freighter's bank of guns jutted up desperately, trying to align themselves with the swiftly moving cruiser.

'Bomb close by,' Shure ordered into his phone. 'But no direct hits. I want to save the cargo.'

The cruiser's bomb racks opened. Two bombs fell, singing down in an expert arc. They straddled the inert freighter, bursting on both sides. Towering clouds of rock and debris rose up, billowing over the freighter. The black form shuddered, Adharans sliding off the hull onto the ground. The bank of guns fired a few futile blasts and the cruiser swept past and disappeared.

'They haven't got a chance,' Nelson murmured. 'They can't leave the ground until they've got their hull sprayed.'

Most of the Adharans were beginning to flee from their ship, scattering onto the ground.

'It's almost over,' Shure said. He got to his feet and stepped out from the ruins. 'Let's go.'

A white flare burst up from the Adharans, showering sparks in the sky. The Adharans milled aimlessly around, confused by the attack. The cloud of vapor had virtually dissipated. The flare was the conventional signal of capitulation. The cruiser was circling again, above the freighter, waiting for orders from Shure.

'Look at them,' Barnes said. 'Insects, big as people.'

'Come on!' Shure said impatiently. 'Let's go. I'm anxious to see what's inside.'

The Adharan commander met them outside its ship. It moved toward them, apparently dazed from the attack.

Nelson and Shure and Barnes gazed at it in revulsion. 'Lord,' Barnes muttered. 'So that's what they're like.'

The Adharan stood almost five feet tall, enclosed in a black chitin shell. It stood on four slender legs, two more weaving uncertainly half-way up its body. It wore a loose belt, holding its gun and equipment. Its eyes were complex, multi-lensed. Its mouth was a narrow slit at the base of its elongated skull. It had no ears.

Behind the Adharan commander a group of crew members stood uncertainly, some of them with weapon tubes partly raised. The Adharan commander made a series of sharp clicks with its mouth, waving its antennae. The other Adharans lowered their tubes.

'How is communication with this race possible?' Barnes asked Nelson.

Shure moved forward. 'It doesn't matter. We have nothing

to say to them. They know they are illegally here. It's the cargo we're interested in.'

He pushed past the Adharan commander. The group of Adharans made way for him. He entered the ship, Nelson and Barnes following after him.

The interior of the Adharan ship reeked and dripped with slime. The passages were narrow and dark, like long tunnels. The floor was slippery underfoot. A few crew members scuttled around in the darkness, their claws and antennae waving nervously. Shure flashed his light down one of the corridors.

'This way. It looks like the main passage.'

The Adharan commander followed close behind them. Shure ignored him. Outside, the cruiser had landed nearby. Nelson could see Terran soldiers standing around on the surface.

Ahead of them a metal door closed off the corridor. Shure indicated the door, making an opening motion.

'Open it.'

The Adharan commander retreated, making no move to open the door. A few more Adharans scuttled up, all of them with weapon tubes.

'They may fight yet,' Nelson said calmly.

Shure raised his Slem rifle at the door. 'I'll have to blast it.'

The Adharans clicked excitedly. None of them approached the door.

'All right,' Shure said grimly. He fired. The door dissolved, smoking into ruins. It sank down, leaving an opening wide enough to pass through. The Adharans rushed around wildly, clicking to each other. More of them left the hull and poured into the ship, flocking around the three Terrans.

'Come on,' Shure said, stepping through the gaping hole. Nelson and Barnes followed him, Slem rifles ready.

The passage led down. The air was heavy and thick, and as they walked down the passage, Adharans pressed behind them.

'Get back.' Shure spun, his rifle up. The Adharans halted. 'Stay back. Come on. Let's go.'

The Terrans turned a corner. They were in the hold. Shure advanced cautiously, moving with care. Several Adharan guards stood with drawn weapon tubes.

'Get out of the way.' Shure waved his Slem rifle. Reluctantly, the guards moved aside. 'Come on!'

The guards separated. Shure advanced.

And stopped, amazed.

Before them was the cargo of the ship. The hold was half-filled with carefully stacked orbs of milky fire, giant jewels like immense pearls. Thousands of them. As far back as they could see. Disappearing back into the recesses of the ship, endless stacks of them. All glowing with a soft radiance, an inner illumination that lit up the vast hold of the ship.

'Incredible!' Shure muttered.

'No wonder they were willing to slip in here without permission.' Barnes took a deep breath, his eyes wide. 'I think I'd do the same. Look at them!'

'Big, aren't they?' Nelson said.

They glanced at each other.

'I've never seen anything like it,' Shure said, dazed. The Adharan guards were watching them warily, their weapon tubes ready. Shure advanced toward the first row of jewels, stacked neatly with mathematical precision. 'It doesn't seem possible. Jewels piled up like – like a warehouse full of doorknobs.'

'They may have belonged to the Adharans at one time,' Nelson said thoughtfully. 'Maybe they were stolen by the city-builders of the Sirius system. Now they're getting them back.'

'Interesting,' Barnes said. 'Might explain why the Adharans found them so easily. Perhaps charts or maps existed.'

Shure grunted. 'In any case they're *ours*, now. Everything in the Sirius system belongs to Terra. It's all been signed, sealed and agreed on.'

'But if these were originally stolen from the Adharans – '

'They shouldn't have agreed to the closed-system treaties. They have their own system. This belongs to Terra.' Shure reached up toward one of the jewels. 'I wonder how it feels.'

'Careful, Captain. It may be radioactive.'

Shure touched one of the jewels.

The Adharans grabbed him, throwing him back. Shure struggled. An Adharan caught hold of his Slem rifle and twisted it out of his hands.

Barnes fired. A group of Adharans puffed out of existence.

Nelson was down on one knee, firing at the passage entrance. The passage was choked with Adharans. Some were firing back. Thin heat beams cut over Nelson's head.

'They can't get us,' Barnes gasped. 'They're afraid to fire. Because of the jewels.'

The Adharans were retreating into the passage, away from the hold. Those with weapons were being ordered back by the commander.

Shure snatched Nelson's rifle and blasted a knot of Adharans into particles. The Adharans were closing the passage. They rolled heavy emergency plates into position and welded them rapidly into place.

'Burn a hole,' Shure barked. He turned his gun on the wall of the ship. 'They're trying to seal us in here.'

Barnes turned his gun on the wall. The two Slem beams ate into the side of the ship. Abruptly the wall gave way, a circular hole falling out.

Outside the ship Terran soldiers were fighting with the Adharans. The Adharans were retreating, making their way back as best they could, firing and hopping. Some of them hopped up onto their ship. Others turned and fled, throwing their guns down. They milled about in helpless confusion, running and leaping in all directions, clicking wildly.

The parked cruiser glowed into life, its heavy guns lowering into position.

'Don't fire,' Shure ordered through his phone. 'Leave their ship alone. It isn't necessary.'

'They're finished,' Nelson gasped, jumping onto the ground. Shure and Barnes leaped after him, out of the Adharan ship onto the surface. 'They don't have a chance. They don't know how to fight.'

Shure waved a group of Terran soldiers over to him. 'Over here! Hurry up, damn it.'

Milky jewels were spilling out of the ship onto the ground, rolling and bouncing through the hole. Part of the containing struts had been blasted away. Stacks of jewels cascaded down and rolled around their feet, getting in their way.

Barnes scooped one up. It burned his gloved hand faintly,

tingling his fingers. He held it to the light. The globe was opaque. Vague shapes swam in the milky fire, drifting back and forth. The globe pulsed and glowed, as if it were alive.

Nelson grinned at him. 'Really something, isn't it?'

'Lovely.' Barnes picked up another. On the hull of the ship an Adharan fired down at him futilely. 'Look at them all. There must be thousands of them.'

'We'll get one of our merchant ships here and have them loaded up,' Shure said. 'I won't feel safe until they're on their way back to Terra.'

Most of the fighting had ceased. The remaining Adharans were being rounded up by the Terran soldiers.

'What about them?' Nelson said.

Shure didn't answer. He was examining one of the jewels, turning it over and over. 'Look at it,' he murmured. 'Brings out different colors each way you hold it. Did you ever see anything like it?'

The big Terran freighter bumped to a landing. Its loading hatches dropped down. Jitney cars rumbled out, a fleet of stubby trucks. The jitney cars crossed to the Adharan ship. Ramps dropped into place, as robot scoops prepared to go to work.

'Shovel them up,' Silvanus Fry rambled, crossing over to Captain Shure. The Manager of Terran Enterprises wiped his forehead with a red handkerchief. 'Astonishing haul, Captain. Quite a find.' He put out his moist palm and they shook.

'I can't understand how we could have missed them,' Shure said. 'The Adharans walked in and picked them up. We watched them going from one planet to the next, like some sort of honey bee. I don't know why our own teams didn't find them.'

Fry shrugged. 'What does it matter?' He examined one of the jewels, tossing it up in the air and catching it. 'I imagine every woman on Terra will have one of these around her neck – or will want one of these around her neck. In six months they won't know how they ever lived without them. That's the way people are, Captain.' He put the globe into his briefcase, snapping it shut. 'I think I'll take one home to my own wife.'

The Adharan commander was brought over by a Terran soldier. He was silent, clicking nothing. The surviving Adharans had been stripped of their weapons and allowed to resume work on their ship. They had got the hull patched and most of the corrosion repaired.

'We're letting you go,' Shure said to the Adharan commander. 'We could try you as pirates and shoot you, but there wouldn't be much point in it. Better tell your government to stay out of the Sirius system from now on.'

'He can't understand you,' Barnes said mildly.

'I know. This is a formality. He gets the general idea, though.'

The Adharan commander stood silently, waiting.

'That's all.' Shure waved impatiently toward the Adharan ship. 'Go on. Take off. Clear out of here. And don't come back.'

The soldier released the Adharan. The Adharan made his way slowly back to his ship. He disappeared through the hatch. The Adharans working on the hull of the ship gathered up their equipment and followed their commander inside.

The hatches closed. The Adharan ship shuddered, as its jets roared into life. Awkwardly it lifted from the surface, rising up into the sky. It turned, heading toward outer space.

Shure watched it until it was gone.

'That's that.' He and Fry walked rapidly toward the cruiser. 'You think these jewels will attract some attention on Terra?'

'Of course. Is there any doubt?'

'No.' Shure was deep in thought. 'They got to only five of the ten planets. There should be more on the remaining inner planets. After this load gets back to Terra we can begin work on the inner planets. If the Adharans found them we should be able to.'

Fry's eyes glittered behind his glasses. 'Fine. I didn't realize there would be more.'

'There are.' Shure frowned, rubbing his jaw. 'At least, there ought to be.'

'What's wrong?'

'I can't understand why we never found them.'

Fry clapped him on the back. 'Don't worry!'

Shure nodded, still deep in thought. 'But I can't understand why we never found them ourselves. Do you think it means anything?'

The Adharan commander sat at his control screen, adjusting his communication circuits.

The Check Base on the second planet of the Adharan system came into focus. The commander raised the sound cone to his neck.

'Bad luck.'

'What occurred?'

'Terrans attacked us and seized the balance of our cargo.'

'How much was still aboard?'

'Half. We had been to only five of the planets.'

'That's unfortunate. They took the load to Terra?'

'I presume.'

Silence for a time. 'How warm is Terra?'

'Fairly warm, I understand.'

'Maybe it will work out all right. We didn't contemplate any hatching on Terra, but if – '

'I don't like the idea of Terrans having a good part of our next generation. I'm sorry we hadn't gotten farther in the distribution.'

'Don't worry. We'll petition the Mother to lay a whole new group to make up for it.'

'But what would the Terrans want with our eggs? Nothing but trouble will come, when hatching begins. I can't understand them. Terran minds are beyond comprehension. I shudder to think what it will be like when the eggs hatch. – And on a humid planet, hatching should begin fairly soon . . .'

Progeny

Ed Doyle hurried. He caught a surface car, waved fifty credits in the robot driver's face, mopped his florid face with a red pocket-handkerchief, unfastened his collar, perspired and licked his lips and swallowed piteously all the way to the hospital.

The surface car slid up to a smooth halt before the great white-domed hospital building. Ed leaped out and bounded up the steps three at a time, pushing through the visitors and convalescent patients standing on the broad terrace. He threw his weight against the door and emerged in the lobby, astonishing the attendants and persons of importance moving about their tasks.

'Where?' Ed demanded, gazing around, his feet wide apart, his fists clenched, his chest rising and falling. His breath came hoarsely, like an animal's. Silence fell over the lobby. Everyone turned toward him, pausing in their work. 'Where?' Ed demanded again. 'Where is she? *They?*'

It was fortunate Janet had been delivered of a child on this of all days. Proxima Centauri was a long way from Terra and the service was bad. Anticipating the birth of his child, Ed had left Proxima some weeks before. He had just arrived in the city. While stowing his suitcase in the luggage tread at the station the message had been handed to him by a robot courier: *Los Angeles Central Hospital. At once.*

Ed hurried, and fast. As he hurried he couldn't help feeling pleased he had hit the day exactly right, almost to the hour. It was a good feeling. He had felt it before, during years of business dealings in the 'colonies,' the frontier, the fringe of Terran civilization where the streets were still lit by electric lights and doors opened by hand.

That was going to be hard to get used to. Ed turned toward the door behind him, feeling suddenly foolish. He had shoved it open, ignoring the eye. The door was just now closing, sliding slowly back in place. He calmed down a little, putting his handkerchief away in his coat pocket. The hospital attendants were resuming their work, picking up their activities where they had left off. One attendant, a strapping late-model robot, coasted over to Ed and halted.

The robot balanced his noteboard expertly, his photocell eyes appraising Ed's flushed features. 'May I inquire whom you are looking for, sir? Whom do you wish to find?'

'My wife.'

'Her name, sir?'

'Janet. Janet Doyle. She's just had a child.'

The robot consulted his board. 'This way, sir.' He coasted off down the passage.

Ed followed nervously. 'Is she okay? Did I get here in time?' His anxiety was returning.

'She is quite well, sir.' The robot raised his metal arm and a side door slid back. 'In here, sir.'

Janet, in a chic blue-mesh suit, was sitting before a mahogany desk, a cigarette between her fingers, her slim legs crossed, talking rapidly. On the other side of the desk a well-dressed doctor sat listening.

'Janet!' Ed said, entering the room.

'Hi, Ed.' She glanced up at him. 'You just now get in?'

'Sure. It's – it's all over? You – I mean, it's *happened*?'

Janet laughed, her even white teeth sparkling. 'Of course. Come in and sit. This is Doctor Bish.'

'Hello, Doc.' Ed sat down nervously across from them. 'Then it's all over?'

'The event has happened,' Doctor Bish said. His voice was thin and metallic. Ed realized with a sudden shock that the doctor was a robot. A top-level robot, made in humanoid form, not like the ordinary metal-limbed workers. It had fooled him – he had been away so long. Doctor Bish appeared plump and well fed, with kindly features and eyeglasses. His large fleshy hands rested on the desk, a ring on one finger. Pinstripe suit and necktie. Diamond tie clasp. Nails carefully manicured. Hair black and evenly parted.

But his voice had given him away. They never seemed to be able to get a really human sound into the voice. The compressed air and whirling disc system seemed to fall short. Otherwise, it was very convincing.

'I understand you've been situated near Promixa, Mr Doyle,' Doctor Bish said pleasantly.

Ed nodded. 'Yeah.'

'Quite a long way, isn't it? I've never been out there. I have always wanted to go. Is it true they're almost ready to push on to Sirius?'

'Look, Doc – '

'Ed, don't be impatient.' Janet stubbed out her cigarette, glancing reprovingly up at him. She hadn't changed in six months. Small blond face, red mouth, cold eyes like little blue rocks. And now, her perfect figure back again. 'They're bringing him here. It takes a few minutes. They have to wash him off and put drops in his eyes and take a wave shot of his brain.'

'*He*? Then it's a boy?'

'Of course. Don't you remember? You were with me when I had the shots. We agreed at the time. You haven't changed your mind, have you?'

'Too late to change your mind now, Mr Doyle,' Doctor Bish's toneless voice came, high-pitched and calm. 'Your wife has decided to call him Peter.'

'Peter.' Ed nodded, a little dazed. 'That's right. We did decide, didn't we? Peter.' He let the word roll around in his mind. 'Yeah. That's fine. I like it.'

The wall suddenly faded, turning from opaque to transparent. Ed spun quickly. They were looking into a brightly lit room, filled with hospital equipment and white-clad attendant robots. One of the robots was moving toward them, pushing a cart. On the cart was a container, a big metal pot.

Ed's breathing increased. He felt a wave of dizziness. He went up to the transparent wall and stood gazing at the metal pot on the cart.

Doctor Bish rose. 'Don't you want to see, too, Mrs Doyle?'

'Of course.' Janet crossed to the wall and stood beside Ed. She watched critically, her arms folded.

Doctor Bish made a signal. The attendant reached into the pot and lifted out a wire tray, gripping the handles with his magnetic clamps. On the tray, dripping through the wire, was Peter Doyle, still wet from his bath, his eyes wide with astonishment. He was pink all over, except for a fringe of hair on the top of his head, and his great blue eyes. He was little and wrinkled and toothless, like an ancient withered sage.

'Golly,' Ed said.

Doctor Bish made a second signal. The wall slid back. The attendant robot advanced into the room, holding his dripping tray out. Doctor Bish removed Peter from the tray and held him up for inspection. He turned him around and around, studying him from every angle.

'He looks fine,' he said at last.

'What was the result of the wave photo?' Janet asked.

'Result was good. Excellent tendencies indicated. Very promising. High development of the – ' The doctor broke off. 'What is it, Mr Doyle?'

Ed was holding out his hands. 'Let me have him, Doc. I want to hold him.' He grinned from ear to ear. 'Let's see how heavy he is. He sure looks big.'

Doctor Bish's mouth fell open in horror. He and Janet gasped.

'Ed!' Janet exclaimed sharply. 'What's the matter with you?'

'Good heavens, Mr Doyle,' the doctor murmured.

Ed blinked. 'What?'

'If I had thought you had any such thing in mind – ' Doctor Bish quickly returned Peter to the attendant. The attendant rushed Peter from the room, back to the metal pot. The cart and robot and pot hurriedly vanished, and the wall banged back in place.

Janet grabbed Ed's arm angrily. 'Good Lord, Ed! Have you lost your mind? Come on. Let's get out of here before you do something else.'

'But – '

'Come on.' Janet smiled nervously at Doctor Bish. 'We'll run

along now, Doctor. Thanks so much for everything. Don't pay
any attention to him. He's been out there so long, you know.'

'I understand,' Doctor Bish said smoothly. He had regained
his poise. 'I trust we'll hear from you later, Mrs Doyle.'

Janet pulled Ed out into the hall. 'Ed, what's the matter with
you? I've never been so embarrassed in all my life.' Two spots
of red glowed in Janet's cheeks. 'I could have kicked you.'

'But what – '

'You know we aren't allowed to touch him. What do you
want to do, ruin his whole life?'

'But – '

'Come on.' They hurried outside the hospital, on to the
terrace. Warm sunlight streamed down on them. 'There's no
telling what harm you've done. He may already be hopelessly
warped. If he grows up all warped and – and neurotic and
emotional, it'll be your fault.'

Suddenly Ed remembered. He sagged, his features drooping
with misery. 'That's right. I forgot. Only robots can come near
the children. I'm sorry, Jan. I got carried away. I hope I didn't
do anything they can't fix.'

'How *could* you forget?'

'It's so different out at Prox.' Ed waved to a surface car,
crestfallen and abashed. The driver drew up in front of them.
'Jan, I'm sorry as hell. I really am. I was all excited. Let's go
have a cup of coffee some place and talk. I want to know what
the doctor said.'

Ed had a cup of coffee and Janet sipped at a brandy frappé.
The Nymphite Room was pitch black except for a vague light
oozing up from the table between them. The table diffused a
pale illumination that spread over everything, a ghostly radiation seemingly without source. A robot waitress moved back
and forth soundlessly with a tray of drinks. Recorded music
played softly in the back of the room.

'Go on,' Ed said.

'Go on?' Janet slipped her jacket off and laid it over the back
of her chair. In the pale light her breasts glowed faintly.
'There's not much to tell. Everything went all right. It didn't
take long. I chatted with Doctor Bish most of the time.'

'I'm glad I got here.'

'How was your trip?'

'Fine.'

'Is the service getting any better? Does it still take as long as it did?'

'About the same.'

'I can't see why you want to go all the way out there. It's so – so cut off from things. What do you find out there? Are plumbing fixtures really that much in demand?'

'They need them. Frontier area. Everyone wants the refinements.' Ed gestured vaguely. 'What did he tell you about Peter? What's he going to be like? Can he tell? I guess it's too soon.'

'He was going to tell me when you started acting the way you did. I'll call him on the vidphone when we get home. His wave pattern should be good. He comes from the best eugenic stock.'

Ed grunted. 'On your side, at least.'

'How long are you going to be here?'

'I don't know. Not long. I'll have to go back. I'd sure like to see him again, before I go.' He glanced up hopefully at his wife. 'Do you think I can?'

'I suppose.'

'How long will he have to stay there?'

'At the hospital? Not long. A few days.'

Ed hesitated. 'I didn't mean at the hospital, exactly. I mean with *them*. How long before we can have him? How long before we can bring him home?'

There was silence. Janet finished her brandy. She leaned back, lighting a cigarette. Smoke drifted across to Ed, blending with the pale light. 'Ed, I don't think you understand. You've been out there so long. A lot has happened since you were a child. New methods, new techniques. They've found so many things they didn't know. They're making progress, for the first time. They know what to do. They're developing a real methodology for dealing with children. For the growth period. Attitude development. Training.' She smiled brightly at Ed. 'I've been reading all about it.'

'How long before we get him?'

'In a few days he'll be released from the hospital. He'll go to a child guidance center. He'll be tested and studied. They'll determine his various capacities and his latent abilities. The direction his development seems to be taking.'

'And then?'

'Then he's put in the proper educational division. So he'll get the right training. Ed, you know, I think he's really going to be something! I could tell by the way Doctor Bish looked. He was studying the wave pattern charts when I came in. He had a look on his face. How can I describe it?' She searched for the word. 'Well, almost – almost a greedy look. Real excitement. They take so much interest in what they're doing. He – '

'Don't say he. Say *it*.'

'Ed, really! What's got into you?'

'Nothing.' Ed glared sullenly down. 'Go on.'

'They make sure he's trained in the right direction. All the time he's there ability tests are given. Then, when he's about nine, he'll be transferred to – '

'Nine! You mean nine *years*?'

'Of course.'

'But when do we get him?'

'Ed, I thought you knew about this. Do I have to go over the whole thing?'

'My God, Jan! We can't wait nine years!' Ed jerked himself upright. 'I never heard of such a thing. Nine years? Why, he'll be half grown up then.'

'That's the point.' Janet leaned towards him, resting her bare elbow against the table. 'As long as he's growing he has to be with them. Not with us. Afterwards, when he's finished growing, when he's no longer so plastic, then we can be with him all we want.'

'Afterwards? When he's eighteen?' Ed leaped up, pushing his chair back. 'I'm going down there and get him.'

'Sit down, Ed.' Janet gazed up calmly, one supple arm thrown lightly over the back of her chair. 'Sit down and act like an adult for a change.'

'Doesn't it matter to you? Don't you care?'

'Of course I care.' Janet shrugged. 'But it's necessary. Otherwise he won't develop correctly. It's for *his* good. Not ours. He doesn't exist for us. Do you want him to have conflicts?'

Ed moved away from the table. 'I'll see you later.'

'Where are you going?'

'Just around. I can't stand this kind of place. It bothers me. I'll see you later.' Ed pushed across the room to the door. The door opened and he found himself on the shiny noonday street. Hot sunlight beat down on him. He blinked, adjusting himself to the blinding light. People streamed around him. People and noise. He moved with them.

He was dazed. He had known, of course. It was there in the back of his mind. The new developments in child care. But it had been abstract, general. Nothing to do with him. With *his* child.

He calmed himself, as he walked along. He was getting all upset about nothing. Janet was right, of course. It was for Peter's good. Peter didn't exist for them, like a dog or cat. A pet to have around the house. He was a human being, with his own life. The training was for him, not for them. It was to develop him, his abilities, his powers. He was to be molded, realized, brought out.

Naturally, robots could do the best job. Robots could train him scientifically, according to a rational technique. Not according to emotional whim. Robots didn't get angry. Robots didn't nag and whine. They didn't spank a child or yell at him. They didn't give conflicting orders. They didn't quarrel among themselves or use the child for their own ends. And there could be no *Oedipus Complex*, with only robots around.

No complexes at all. It had been discovered long ago that neurosis could be traced to childhood training. To the way parents brought up the child. The inhibitions he was taught, the manners, the lessons, the punishments, the rewards. Neuroses, complexes, warped development, all stemmed from the subjective relationship existing between the child and the parent. If perhaps the parent could be eliminated as a factor . . .

Parents could never become objective about their children. It was always a biased, emotional projection the parent held toward the child. Inevitably, the parent's view was distorted. No parent could be a fit instructor for his child.

Robots could study the child, analyze his needs, his wants, test his abilities and interests. Robots would not try to force the child to fit a certain mold. The child would be trained along his own lines; wherever scientific study indicated his interest and need lay.

Ed came to the corner. Traffic whirred past him. He stepped absently forward.

A clang and crash. Bars dropped in front of him, stopping him. A robot safety control.

'Sir, be more careful!' the strident voice came, close by him.

'Sorry.' Ed stepped back. The control bars lifted. He waited for the lights to change. It was for Peter's own good. Robots could train him right. Later on, when he was out of growth stage, when he was not so pliant, responsive – 'It's better for him,' Ed murmured. He said it again, half aloud. Some people glanced at him and he colored. Of course it was better for him. No doubt about it.

Eighteen. He couldn't be with his son until he was eighteen. Practically grown up.

The lights changed. Deep in thought, Ed crossed the street with the other pedestrians, keeping carefully inside the safety lane. It was best for Peter. But eighteen years was a long time.

'A hell of a long time,' Ed murmured, frowning. 'Too damn long a time.'

Doctor 2g-Y Bish carefully studied the man standing in front of him. His relays and memory banks clicked, narrowing down the image identification, flashing a variety of comparison possibilities past the scanner.

'I recall you, sir,' Doctor Bish said at last. 'You're the man from Proxima. From the colonies. Doyle, Edward Doyle. Let's see. It was some time ago. It must have been – '

'Nine years ago,' Ed Doyle said grimly. 'Exactly nine years ago, practically to the day.'

Doctor Bish folded his hands. 'Sit down, Mr Doyle. What can I do for you? How is Mrs Doyle? Very engaging wife, as I recall. We had a delightful conversation during her delivery. How – '

'Doctor Bish, do you know where my son is?'

Doctor Bish considered, tapping his fingers on the desk top, the polished mahogany surface. He closed his eyes slightly, gazing off into the distance. 'Yes. Yes, I know where your son is, Mr Doyle.'

Ed Doyle relaxed. 'Fine.' He nodded, letting his breath out in relief.

'I know exactly where your son is. I placed him in the Los Angeles Biological Research Station about a year ago. He's undergoing specialized training there. Your son, Mr Doyle, has shown exceptional ability. He is, shall I say, one of the few, the very few we have found with real possibilities.'

'Can I see him?'

'See him? How do you mean?'

Doyle controlled himself with an effort. 'I think the term is clear.'

Doctor Bish rubbed his chin. His photocell brain whirred, operating at maximum velocity. Switches routed power surges, building up loads and leaping gaps rapidly, as he contemplated the man before him. 'You wish to *view* him? That's one meaning of the term. Or do you wish to talk to him? Sometimes the term is used to cover a more direct contact. It's a loose word.'

'I want to talk to him.'

'I see.' Bish slowly drew some forms from the dispenser on his desk. 'There are a few routine papers that have to be filled out first, of course. Just how long did you want to speak to him?'

Ed Doyle gazed steadily into Doctor Bish's bland face. 'I want to talk to him several hours. *Alone.*'

'Alone?'

'No robots around.'

Doctor Bish said nothing. He stroked the papers he held, creasing the edges with his nail. 'Mr Doyle,' he said carefully, 'I wonder if you're in a proper emotional state to visit your son. You have recently come in from the colonies?'

'I left Proxima three weeks ago.'

'Then you have just arrived here in Los Angeles?'

'That's right.'

'And you've come to see your son? Or have you other business?'

'I came for my son.'

'Mr Doyle, Peter is at a very critical stage. He has just recently been transferred to the Biology Station for his higher training. Up to now his training has been general. What we call the non-differentiated stage. Recently he has entered a new period. Within the last six months Peter has begun advanced work along his specific line, that of organic chemistry. He will – '

'What does Peter think about it?'

Bish frowned. 'I don't understand, sir.'

'How does *he* feel? Is it what he wants?'

'Mr Doyle, your son has the possibility of becoming one of the world's finest bio-chemists. In all the time we have worked with human beings, in their training and development, we have never come across a more alert and integrated faculty for the assimilation of data, construction of theory, formulation of material, than that which your son possesses. All tests indicate he will rapidly rise to the top of his chosen field. He is still only a child, Mr Doyle, but it is the children who must be trained.'

Doyle stood up. 'Tell me where I can find him. I'll talk to him for two hours and then the rest is up to him.'

'The rest?'

Doyle clamped his jaw shut. He shoved his hands in his pockets. His face was flushed and set grim with determination. In the nine years he had grown much heavier, more stocky and florid. His thinning hair had turned iron-gray. His clothes were dumpy and unpressed. He looked stubborn.

Doctor Bish sighed. 'All right, Mr Doyle. Here are your papers. The law allows you to observe your boy whenever you make proper application. Since he is out of his non-differentiated stage, you may also speak to him for a period of ninety minutes.'

'Alone?'

'You can take him away from the Station grounds for that

length of time.' Doctor Bish pushed the papers over to Doyle. 'Fill these out, and I'll have Peter brought here.'

He looked up steadily at the man standing before him.

'I hope you'll remember that any emotional experience at this crucial stage may do much to inhibit his development. He has chosen his field, Mr Doyle. He must be permitted to grow along his selected lines, unhindered by situational blocks. Peter has been in contact with our technical staff throughout his entire training period. He is not accustomed to contact with other human beings. So please be careful.'

Doyle said nothing. He grabbed up the papers and plucked out his fountain pen.

He hardly recognized his son when the two robot attendants brought him out of the massive concrete Station building and deposited him a few yards from Ed's parked surface car.

Ed pushed the door open. 'Pete!' His heart was thumping heavily, painfully. He watched his son come toward the car, frowning in the bright sunlight. It was late afternoon, about four. A faint breeze blew across the parking lot, rustling a few papers and bits of debris.

Peter stood slim and straight. His eyes were large, deep brown, like Ed's. His hair was light, almost blond. More like Janet's. He had Ed's jaw, though, the firm line, clean and well chiseled. Ed grinned at him. Nine years it had been. Nine years since the robot attendant had lifted the rack up from the conveyor pot to show him the little wrinkled baby, red as a boiled lobster.

Peter had grown. He was not a baby any longer. He was a young boy, straight and proud, with firm features and wide, clear eyes.

'Pete,' Ed said. 'How the hell are you?'

The boy stopped by the door of the car. He gazed at Ed calmly. His eyes flickered, taking in the car, the robot driver, the heavy set man in the rumpled tweed suit grinning nervously at him.

'Get in. Get inside.' Ed moved over. 'Come on. We have places to go.'

The boy was looking at him again. Suddenly Ed was conscious of his baggy suit, his unshined shoes, his gray stubbled chin. He flushed, yanking out his red pocket-handkerchief and mopping his forehead uneasily. 'I just got off the ship, Pete. From Proxima. I haven't had time to change. I'm a little dusty. Long trip.'

Peter nodded. '4.3 light years, isn't it?'

'Takes three weeks. Get in. Don't you want to get in?'

Peter slid in beside him. Ed slammed the door.

'Let's go.' The car started up. 'Drive – ' Ed peered out the window. 'Drive up there. By the hill. Out of town.' He turned to Pete. 'I hate big cities. I can't get used to them.'

'There are no large cities in the colonies, are there?' Pete murmured. 'You're unused to urban living.'

Ed settled back. His heart had begun to slow down to its normal beat. 'No, as a matter of fact it's the other way around, Pete.'

'How do you mean?'

'I went to Prox *because* I couldn't stand cities.'

Peter said nothing. The surface car was climbing, going up a steel highway into the hills. The Station, huge and impressive, spread out like a heap of cement bricks directly below them. A few cars moved along the road, but not many. Most transportation was by air, now. Surface cars had begun to disappear.

The road leveled off. They moved along the ridge of the hills. Trees and bushes rose on both sides of them. 'It's nice up here,' Ed said.

'Yes.'

'How – how have you been? I haven't seen you for a long time. Just once. Just after you were born.'

'I know. Your visit is listed in the records.'

'You been getting along all right?'

'Yes. Quite well.'

'They treating you all right?'

'Of course.'

After a while Ed leaned forward. 'Stop here,' he said to the robot driver.

The car slowed down, pulling over to the side of the road. 'Sir, there is nothing – '

'This is fine. Let us out. We'll walk from here.'

The car stopped. The door slid reluctantly open. Ed stepped

quickly out of the car, on to the pavement. Peter got out slowly after him, puzzled. 'Where are we?'

'No place.' Ed slammed the door. 'Go on back to town,' he said to the driver. 'We won't need you.'

The car drove off. Ed walked to the side of the road. Peter came after him. The hill dropped away, falling down to the beginnings of the city below. A vast panorama stretched out, the great metropolis in the late afternoon sun. Ed took a deep breath, throwing his arms out. He took off his coat and tossed it over his shoulder.

'Come on.' He started down the hillside. 'Here we go.'

'Where?'

'For a walk. Let's get off this damn road.'

They climbed down the side of the hill, walking carefully, holding on to the grass and roots jutting out from the soil. Finally they came to a level place by a big sycamore tree. Ed threw himself down on the ground, grunting and wiping sweat from his neck.

'Here. Let's sit here.'

Peter sat down carefully, a little way off. Ed's blue shirt was stained with sweat. He unfastened his tie and loosened his collar. Presently he searched through his coat pockets. He brought out his pipe and tobacco.

Peter watched him fill the pipe and light it with a big sulphur match. 'What's that?' he murmured.

'This? My pipe.' Ed grinned, sucking at the pipe. 'Haven't you ever seen a pipe?'

'No.'

'This is a good pipe. I got this when I first went out to Proxima. That was a long time ago, Pete. It was twenty-five years ago. I was just nineteen, then. Only about twice as old as you.'

He put his tobacco away and leaned back, his heavy face serious, preoccupied.

'Just nineteen. I went out there as a plumber. Repair and sales, when I could make a sale. Terran Plumbing. One of those big ads you used to see. Unlimited opportunities. Virgin lands. Make a million. Gold in the streets.' Ed laughed.

'How did you make out?'

'Not bad. Not bad at all. I own my own line, now, you know. I service the whole Proxima system. We do repairing, maintenance, building, construction. I've got six hundred people working for me. It took a long time. It didn't come easy.'

'No.'

'Hungry?'

Peter turned. 'What?'

'Are you hungry?' Ed pulled a brown paper parcel from his coat and unwrapped it. 'I still have a couple of sandwiches from the trip. When I come in from Prox I bring some food along with me. I don't like to buy in the diner. They skin you.' He held out the parcel. 'Want one?'

'No thank you.'

Ed took a sandwich and began to eat. He ate nervously, glancing at his son. Peter sat silently, a short distance off, staring ahead without expression. His smooth handsome face was blank.

'Everything all right?' Ed said.

'Yes.'

'You're not cold, are you?'

'No.'

'You don't want to catch cold.'

A squirrel crossed in front of them, hurrying toward the sycamore tree. Ed threw it a piece of his sandwich. The squirrel ran off a way, then came back slowly. It scolded at them, standing up on its hind feet, its great gray tail flowing out behind it.

Ed laughed. 'Look at him. Ever see a squirrel before?'

'I don't think so.'

'It's good to come back to Terra once in a while. See some of the old things. They're going, though.'

'Going?'

'Away. Destroyed. Terra is always changing.' Ed waved around at the hillside. 'This will be gone, some day. They'll cut down the trees. Then they'll level it. Some day they'll carve the whole range up and carry it off. Use it for fill, some place along the coast.'

'That's beyond our scope,' Peter said.

'What?'

'I don't receive that type of material. I think Doctor Bish told you. I'm working with bio-chemistry.'

'I know,' Ed murmured. 'Say, how the hell did you ever get mixed up with that stuff? Bio-chemistry?'

'The tests showed that my abilities lie along those lines.'

'You enjoy what you're doing?'

'What a strange thing to ask. Of course I enjoy what I'm doing. It's the work I'm fitted for.'

'It seems funny as hell to me, starting a nine-year-old kid off on something like that.'

'Why?'

'My God, Pete. When I was nine I was bumming around town. In school sometimes, outside mostly, wandering here and there. Playing. Reading. Sneaking into the rocket launching yards all the time.' He considered. 'Doing all sorts of things. When I was sixteen I hopped over to Mars. I stayed there a while. Worked as a hasher. I went on to Ganymede. Ganymede was all sewed up tight. Nothing doing there. From Ganymede I went out to Prox. Got a work-away all the way out. Big freighter.'

'You stayed at Proxima?'

'I sure did. I found what I wanted. Nice place, out there. Now we're starting on to Sirius, you know.' Ed's chest swelled. 'I've got an outlet in the Sirius system. Little retail and service place.'

'Sirius is 8.8 light years from Sol.'

'It's a long way. Seven weeks from here. Rough grind. Meteor swarms. Keeps things hot all the way out.'

'I can imagine.'

'You know what I thought I might do?' Ed turned toward his son, his face alive with hope and enthusiasm. 'I've been thinking it over. I thought maybe I'd go out there. To Sirius. It's a fine little place we have. I drew up the plans myself. Special design to fit with the characteristics of the system.'

Peter nodded.

'Pete – '

'Yes?'

'Do you think maybe you'd be interested? Like to hop out to Sirius and take a look? It's a good place. Four clean planets.

Never touched. Lots of room. Miles and miles of room. Cliffs and mountains. Oceans. Nobody around. Just a few colonists, families, some construction. Wide, level plains.'

'How do you mean, interested?'

'In going all the way out.' Ed's face was pale. His mouth twitched nervously. 'I thought maybe you'd like to come along and see how things are. It's a lot like Prox was, twenty-five years ago. It's good and clean out there. No cities.'

Peter smiled.

'Why are you smiling?'

'No reason.' Peter stood up abruptly. 'If we have to walk back to the Station we'd better start. Don't you think? It's getting late.'

'Sure.' Ed struggled to his feet. 'Sure, but – '

'When are you going to be back in the Sol system again?'

'Back?' Ed followed after his son. Peter climbed up the hill toward the road. 'Slow down, will you?'

Peter slowed down. Ed caught up with him.

'I don't know when I'll be back. I don't come here very often. No ties. Not since Jan and I separated. As a matter of fact I came here this time to – '

'This way.' Peter started down the road.

Ed hurried along beside him, fastening his tie and putting his coat on, gasping for breath. 'Peter, what do you say? You want to hop out to Sirius with me? Take a look? It's a nice place out there. We could work together. The two of us. If you want.'

'But I already have my work.'

'That stuff? That damn chemistry stuff?'

Peter smiled again.

Ed scowled, his face dark red. 'Why are you smiling?' he demanded. His son did not answer. 'What's the matter? What's so damn funny?'

'Nothing,' Peter said. 'Don't become excited. We have a long walk down.' He increased his pace slightly, his supple body swinging in long, even strides. 'It's getting late. We have to hurry.'

Doctor Bish examined his wristwatch, pushing back his pin-striped coat sleeve. 'I'm glad you're back.'

'He sent the surface car away,' Peter murmured. 'We had to walk down the hill on foot.'

It was dark outside. The Station lights were coming on automatically, along the rows of buildings and laboratories.

Doctor Bish rose from his desk. 'Sign this, Peter. Bottom of this form.'

Peter signed. 'What is it?'

'Certifies you saw him in accord with the provisions of the law. We didn't try to obstruct you in any way.'

Peter handed the paper back. Bish filed it away with the others. Peter moved toward the door of the doctor's office. 'I'll go. Down to the cafeteria for dinner.'

'You haven't eaten?'

'No.'

Doctor Bish folded his arms, studying the boy. 'Well?' he said. 'What do you think of him? This is the first time you've seen your father. It must have been strange for you. You've been around us so much, in all your training and work.'

'It was – unusual.'

'Did you gain any impressions? Was there anything you particularly noticed?'

'He was very emotional. There was a distinct bias through everything he said and did. A distortion present, virtually uniform.'

'Anything else?'

Peter hesitated, lingering at the door. He broke into a smile. 'One other thing.'

'What was it?'

'I noticed – ' Peter laughed. 'I noticed a distinct odor about him. A constant pungent smell, all the time I was with him.'

'I'm afraid that's true of all of them,' Doctor Bish said. 'Certain skin glands. Waste products thrown off from the blood. You'll get used to it, after you've been around them more.'

'Do I have to be around them?'

'They're your own race. How else can you work with them? Your whole training is designed with that in mind. When we've taught you all we can, then you will – '

'It reminded me of something. The pungent odor. I kept

thinking about it, all the time I was with him. Trying to place it.'

'Can you identify it now?'

Peter reflected. He thought hard, concentrating deeply. His small face wrinkled up. Doctor Bish waited patiently by his desk, arms folded. The automatic heating system clicked on for the night, warming the room with a soft glow that drifted gently around them.

'I know!' Peter exclaimed suddenly.

'What was it?'

'The animals in the biology lab. It was the same smell. The same smell as the experimental animals.'

They glanced at each other, the robot doctor and the promising young boy. Both of them smiled, a secret, private smile. A smile of complete understanding.

'I believe I know what you mean,' Doctor Bish said. 'In fact, I know *exactly* what you mean.'

Some Kinds of Life

'Joan, for heaven's sake!'

Joan Clarke caught the irritation in her husband's voice, even through the wall-speaker. She left her chair by the vidscreen and hurried into the bedroom. Bob was rooting furiously around in the closet, pulling down coats and suits and tossing them on the bed. His face was flushed with exasperation.

'What are you looking for?'

'My uniform. Where is it? Isn't it here?'

'Of course. Let me look.'

Bob got sullenly out of the way. Joan pushed past him and clicked on the automatic sorter. Suits bobbed by in quick succession, parading for her inspection.

It was early morning, about nine o'clock. The sky was bright blue. Not a single cloud was visible. A warm spring day, late in April. The ground outside the house was damp and black from the rains of the day before. Green shoots were already beginning to poke their way up through the steaming earth. The sidewalk was dark with moisture. Wide lawns glittered in the sparkling sunlight.

'Here it is.' Joan turned off the sorter. The uniform dropped into her arms and she carried it over to her husband. 'Now next time don't get so upset.'

'Thanks.' Bob grinned, embarrassed. He patted the coat. 'But look, it's all creased. I thought you were going to have the darn thing cleaned.'

'It'll be all right.' Joan started up the bed-maker. The bed-maker smoothed out the sheets and blankets, folding them in place. The spread settled carefully around the pillows. 'After you've had it on awhile it'll look just lovely. Bob, you're the fussiest man I know.'

'Sorry, honey,' Bob murmured.

'What's wrong?' Joan came up to him and put her hand on his broad shoulder. 'Are you worried about something?'

'No.'

'Tell me.'

Bob began to unfasten his uniform. 'It's nothing important. I didn't want to bother you. Erickson called me at work yesterday to tell me my group is up again. Seems they're calling two groups at once now. I thought I wouldn't get jerked out for another six months.'

'Oh, Bob! Why didn't you *tell* me?'

'Erickson and I talked a long time. "For God's sake!" I told him. "I was just up." "I know that, Bob," he said, "I'm sorry as hell about it but there's nothing I can do. We're all in the same boat. Anyhow, it won't last long. Might as well get it over with. It's the Martian situation. They're all hot and bothered about it." That's what he said. He was nice about it. Erickson's a pretty good guy for a Sector Organizer.'

'When – when do you have to go?'

Bob looked at his watch. 'I have to get down to the field by noon. Gives me three hours.'

'When will you be back?'

'Oh, I should be back in a couple of days – if everything goes all right. You know how these things are. It varies. Remember last October when I was gone a whole week? But that's unusual. They rotate the groups so fast now you're practically back before you start.'

Tommy came strolling in from the kitchen. 'What's up, Dad?' He noticed the uniform. 'Say, your group up again?'

'That's right.'

Tommy grinned from ear to ear, a delighted teenage grin. 'You going to get in on the Martian business? I was following it over the vidscreen. Those Martians look like a bunch of dry weeds tied together in a bundle. You guys sure ought to be able to blow *them* apart.'

Bob laughed, whacking his son on the back. 'You tell 'em, Tommy.'

'I sure wish I was coming.'

Bob's expression changed. His eyes became hard like gray flint. 'No, you don't, kid. Don't say that.'

There was an uncomfortable silence.

'I didn't mean anything,' Tommy muttered.

Bob laughed easily. 'Forget it. Now all of you clear out so I can change.'

Joan and Tommy left the room. The door slid shut. Bob dressed swiftly, tossing his robe and pajamas on the bed and pulling his dark green uniform around him. He laced his boots up and then opened the door.

Joan had got his suitcase from the hall closet. 'You'll want this, won't you?' she asked.

'Thanks.' Bob picked up the suitcase. 'Let's go out to the car.' Tommy was already absorbed at the vidscreen, beginning his schoolwork for the day. A biology lesson moved slowly across the screen.

Bob and Joan walked down the front steps and along the path to their surface car, parked at the edge of the road. The door opened as they approached. Bob threw his suitcase inside and sat down behind the wheel.

'Why do we have to fight the Martians?' Joan asked suddenly. 'Tell me, Bob. Tell me why.'

Bob lit a cigarette. He let the gray smoke drift around the cabin of the car. 'Why? You know as well as I do.' He reached out a big hand and thumped the handsome control board of the car. 'Because of this.'

'What do you mean?'

'The control mechanism needs rexeroid. And the only rexeroid deposits in the whole system are on Mars. If we lose Mars we lose this.' He ran his hand over the gleaming control board. 'And if we lose this how are we going to get around? Answer me that.'

'Can't we go back to manual steering?'

'We could ten years ago. But ten years ago we were driving less than a hundred miles per hour. No human being could steer at the speeds these days. We couldn't go back to manual steering without slowing down our pace.'

'Can't we do that?'

Bob laughed. 'Sweetheart, it's ninety miles from here to town. You really think I could keep my job if I had to drive the whole way at thirty-five miles an hour? I'd be on the road all my life.'

Joan was silent.

'You see, we must have the darn stuff – the rexeroid. It makes our control equipment possible. We depend on it. We need it. We must keep mining operations going on Mars. We can't afford to let the Martians get the rexeroid deposits away from us. See?'

'I see. And last year it was kryon ore from Venus. We had to have that. So you went and fought on Venus.'

'Darling, the walls of our houses wouldn't maintain an even temperature without kyron. Kryon is the only non-living substance in the system that adjusts itself to temperature changes. Why, we'd – we'd all have to go back to floor furnaces again. Like my grandfather had.'

'And the year before it was lonolite from Pluto.'

'Lonolite is the only substance known that can be used in constructing the memory banks of the calculators. It's the only metal with true retentive ability. Without lonolite we'd lose all our big computing machines. And you know how far we'd get without them.'

'All right.'

'Sweetheart, you know I don't *want* to go. But I have to. We all have to.' Bob waved toward the house. 'Do you want to give that up? You want to go back to the old ways?'

'No.' Joan moved away from the car. 'All right, Bob. I'll see you in a day or two then?'

'I hope so. This trouble should be over soon. Most of the New York groups are being called. The Berlin and Oslo groups are already there. It shouldn't take long.'

'Good luck.'

'Thanks.' Bob closed the door. The motor started up automatically. 'Say goodbye to Tommy for me.'

The car drove off, gaining speed, the automatic control board guiding it expertly into the main stream of traffic flowing down the highway. Joan watched until the car blended with the endless tide of flashing metal hulls, racing across the country-side in a bright ribbon toward the distant city. Then she went slowly back inside the house.

Bob never came back from Mars, so in a manner of speaking, Tommy became the man of the house. Joan got a release from school for him and after a while he began work as a lab technician at the Government Research Project a few miles down the road.

Bryan Erickson, the Sector Organizer, stopped one evening to see how they were getting along. 'Nice little place you have here,' Erickson said, wandering around.

Tommy swelled with pride. 'Sure is, isn't it? Sit down and make yourself comfortable.'

'Thanks.' Erickson peered into the kitchen. The kitchen was in the process of putting out a meal for the evening dinner. 'Quite a kitchen.'

Tommy came up beside him. 'See that unit there on top of the stove?'

'What's it do?'

'It's a selector on the kitchen. It sets up a new combination every day. We don't have to figure out what to eat.'

'Amazing.' Erickson glanced at Tommy. 'You seem to be doing all right.'

Joan looked up from the vidscreen. 'As well as could be expected.' Her voice was toneless, flat.

Erickson grunted. He walked back into the living-room. 'Well, I guess I'll be running along.'

'What did you come for?' Joan asked.

'Nothing in particular, Mrs Clarke.' Erickson hesitated by the door, a big man, red-faced, in his late thirties. 'Oh, there was one thing.'

'What is it?' Her voice was emotionless.

'Tom, have you made out your Sector Unit card?'

'My Sector Unit card!'

'According to law you're supposed to be registered as part of this sector – *my* sector.' He reached in his pocket. 'I have a few blank cards with me.'

'Gee!' Tommy said, a little frightened. 'So soon? I thought it wasn't until I got to be eighteen.'

'They've changed the ruling. We took quite a beating on Mars. Some of the sectors can't fill their quotas. Have to dig deeper from now on.' Erickson grinned good-naturedly. 'This is a good sector, you know. We have a lot of fun drilling and trying out the new equipment. I finally got Washington to consign us a whole squadron of the new double-jet small fighters. Each man in my sector gets the use of a fighter.'

Tommy's eyes lit up. 'Really?'

'In fact the user gets to bring the fighter home over the weekend. You can park it on your lawn.'

'No kidding?' Tommy sat down at the desk. He filled the Unit card out happily.

'Yes, we have a pretty good time,' Erickson murmured.

'Between wars,' Joan said quietly.

'What's that, Mrs Clarke?'

'Nothing.'

Erickson accepted the filled-out card. He put it away in his wallet. 'By the way,' he said.

Tommy and Joan turned toward him.

'I guess you've been seeing the gleco-war on the vidscreen. I guess you know all about that.'

'The gleco-war?'

'We get all our gleco from Callisto. It's made from the hides of some kind of animal. Well, there's been a little trouble with the natives. They claim – '

'What is a gleco?' Joan said tightly.

'That's the stuff that makes your front door open for you only. It's sensitive to your pressure pattern. Gleco is made from these animals.'

There was silence, the kind you can cut with a knife.

'I guess I'll be going.' Erickson moved toward the door. 'We'll see you the next training session, Tom. Right?' He opened the door.

'Right,' Tommy murmured.

'Goodnight.' Erickson left, closing the door after him.

* * *

'But I *have* to go!' Tommy exclaimed.

'Why?'

'The whole sector is going. It's required.'

Joan stared out the window. 'It isn't right.'

'But if I don't go we'll lose Callisto. And if we lose Callisto . . .'

'I know. Then we'll have to go back to carrying door keys. Like our grandfathers did.'

'That's right.' Tommy stuck out his chest, turning from side to side. 'How do I look?'

Joan said nothing.

'How do I look? Do I look all right?'

Tommy looked fine in his deep green uniform. He was slim and straight, much better looking than Bob. Bob had been gaining weight. His hair had been thinning. Tommy's hair was thick and black. His cheeks were flushed with excitement, his blue eyes flashing. He pulled his helmet in place, snapping the strap.

'Okay?' he demanded.

Joan nodded. 'Fine.'

'Kiss me goodbye. I'm off to Callisto. I'll be back in a couple of days.'

'Goodbye.'

'You don't sound very happy.'

'I'm not,' Joan said. 'I'm not very happy.'

Tommy came back from Callisto all right but during the trektone-war on Europa something went wrong with his double-jet small fighter and the Sector Unit came back without him.

'Trektone,' Bryan Erickson explained, 'is used in vidscreen tubes. It's very important, Joan.'

'I see.'

'You know what the vidscreen means. Our whole education and information come over it. The kids learn from it. They get their schooling. And in the evening we use the pleasure-channels for entertainment. You don't want us to have to go back to – '

'No, no – of course not. I'm sorry.' Joan waved a signal and the coffee table slid into the living-room, bearing a pot of steaming coffee. 'Cream? Sugar?'

'Just sugar, thanks.' Erickson took his cup and sat silently on the couch, sipping and stirring. The house was quiet. It was late evening, about eleven o'clock. The shades were down. The vidscreen played softly in the corner. Outside the house the world was dark and unmoving except for a faint wind stirring among the cedar trees at the end of the grounds.

'Any news from the various fronts?' Joan asked after a while, leaning back and smoothing down her skirt.

'The fronts?' Erickson considered. 'Well, some new developments in the iderium-war.'

'Where is that?'

'Neptune. We get our iderium from Neptune.'

'What is iderium used for?' Joan's voice was thin and remote as if she were a long way off. Her face had a pinched look, a kind of strained whiteness. As if a mask had settled into place and remained, a mask through which she looked from a great distance.

'All the newspaper machines require iderium,' Erickson explained. 'Iderium lining makes it possible for them to detect events as they occur and flash them over the vidscreen. Without iderium we'd have to go back to reporting news and writing it up by hand. That would introduce the personal bias. Slanted news. The iderium news machines are impartial.'

Joan nodded. 'Any other news?'

'Not much more. They say some trouble might be going to break out on Mercury.'

'What do we get from Mercury?'

'That's where our ambroline comes from. We use ambroline in all kinds of selector units. In your kitchen – the selector you have in there. The meal selector that sets up the food combinations. That's an ambroline unit.'

Joan gazed vacantly into her coffee cup. 'The natives on Mercury – they're attacking us?'

'There's been some riots, agitation, that sort of thing. Some Sector Units have been called out already. The Paris unit and the Moscow unit. Big units, I believe.'

After a time, Joan said, 'You know, Bryan, I can tell you came here with something on your mind.'

'Oh, no. Why do you say that?'

'I can tell. What is it?'

Erickson flushed, his good-natured face red. 'You're pretty acute, Joan. As a matter of fact I did come for something.'

'What is it?'

Erickson reached into his coat and brought out a folded mimeographed paper. He passed it to Joan. 'It isn't my idea, understand. I'm just a cog in a big machine.' He chewed his lip nervously. 'It's because of the heavy losses in the trektone-war. They need to close ranks. They're up against it, so I hear.'

'What does all this mean?' Joan passed the paper back. 'I can't make out all this legal wording.'

'Well, it means women are going to be admitted into Sector Units in the – in the absence of male members of the family.'

'Oh. I see.'

Erickson got up quickly, relieved that his duty had been done. 'I guess I'll have to run along now. I wanted to bring this over and show it to you. They're handing them out all along the line.' He stuck the paper away in his coat again. He looked very tired.

'It doesn't leave very many people, does it?'

'How do you mean?'

'Men first. Then children. Now women. It seems to take in everybody, just about.'

'Kind of does, I guess. Well, there must be a reason. We have to hold these fronts. The stuff must be kept coming in. We've got to have it.'

'I suppose so.' Joan rose slowly. 'I'll see you later on, Bryan.'

'Yes, I should be around later in the week. I'll see you then.'

Bryan Erickson came back just as the nymphite-war was breaking out on Saturn. He grinned apologetically at Mrs Clarke as she let him in.

'Sorry to bother you so early in the morning,' Erickson said. 'I'm in a big rush, running around all over the sector.'

'What is it?' Joan closed the door after him. He was in his

Organizer's uniform, pale green with silver bands across his shoulders. Joan was still in her dressing robe.

'Nice and warm in here,' Erickson said, warming his hands against the wall. Outside, the day was bright and cold. It was November. Snow lay over everything, a cold blanket of white. A few stark trees jutted up, their branches barren and frozen. Far off along the highway the bright ribbon of surface cars had diminished to a trickle. There were few people going to the city, anymore. Most surface cars were in storage.

'I guess you know about the trouble on Saturn,' Erickson murmured. 'You've heard.'

'I saw some shots, I think. Over the vidscreen.'

'Quite a ruckus. Those Saturn natives are sure big. My golly, they must be fifty feet high.'

Joan nodded absently, rubbing her eyes. 'It's a shame we need anything from Saturn. Have you had breakfast, Bryan?'

'Oh, yes, thanks – I've eaten.' Erickson turned his back to the wall. 'Sure is good to get in out of the cold. You certainly keep your house nice and neat. I wish my wife kept our place this neat.'

Joan crossed to the windows and let up the shades. 'What do we use from Saturn?'

'It would have to be nymphite, of all things. Anything else we could give up. But not nymphite.'

'What is nymphite used for?'

'All aptitude testing equipment. Without nymphite we wouldn't be able to tell who was fit for what occupation, including President of the World Council.'

'I see.'

'With nymphite testers we can determine what each person is good for and what kind of work he should be doing. Nymphite is the basic tool of modern society. With it we classify and grade ourselves. If anything should happen to the supply . . .'

'And it all comes from Saturn?'

'I'm afraid so. Now the natives are rioting, trying to take over the nymphite mines. It's going to be a tough struggle. They're big. The government is having to call up everyone it can get.'

Suddenly Joan gasped. 'Everyone?' Her hand flew to her mouth. 'Even women?'

'I'm afraid so. Sorry, Joan. You know it isn't my idea. Nobody wanted to do it. But if we're going to save all these things we have – '

'But whom will that leave?'

Erickson did not answer. He was sitting down at the desk, making out a card. He passed it to her. Joan took it automatically. 'Your unit card.'

'But who will be left?' Joan asked again. 'Can't you tell me? Will anyone be left?'

The rocketship from Orion landed with a great crashing roar. Exhaust valves poured out clouds of waste material, as the jet compressors cooled into silence.

There was no sound for a time. Then the hatch was unscrewed carefully and swung inward. Cautiously N'tgari-3 stepped out, waving an atmosphere-testing cone ahead of him.

'Results?' his companion queried, his thoughts crossing to N'tgari-3.

'Too thin to breathe. For us. But enough for some kinds of life.' N'tgari-3 gazed around him, across the hills and plains, off in the distance. 'Certainly is quiet.'

'Not a sound. Or any sign of life.' His companions emerged. 'What's that over there?'

'Where?' N'tgari-3 asked.

'Over that way.' Luci'n-6 pointed with his polar antenna. 'See?'

'Looks like some kind of building units. Some sort of mass structure.'

The two Orionians raised their launch to hatch-level and slid it out onto the ground. With N'tgari-3 at the wheel they set off across the plain toward the raised spot visible on the horizon. Plants grew on all sides, some tall and sturdy, some fragile and small with multi-colored blossoms.

'Plenty of immobile forms,' Luci'n-6 observed.

They passed through a field of gray-orange plants, thousands of stalks growing uniformly, endless plants all exactly alike.

'They look as if they were artificially sowed,' N'tgari-3 murmured.

'Slow the launch down. We're coming to some sort of structure.'

N'tgari-3 slowed down the launch almost to a stop. The two Orionians leaned out the port, gazing in interest.

A lovely structure rose up, surrounded by plants of all kinds, tall plants, carpets of low plants, beds of plants with astonishing blossoms. The structure itself was neat and attractive, obviously the artifact of an advanced culture.

N'tgari-3 leaped out of the launch. 'Maybe we're about to encounter the legendary Beings from Terra.' He hurried across the carpet of plants, a long uniform ground-covering, up to the front porch of the structure.

Luci'n-6 followed him. They examined the door. 'How does it open?' Luci'n-6 asked.

They burned a neat hole in the lock and the door slid back. Lights came on automatically. The house was warm, heated by the walls.

'How – how developed! How very advanced.'

They wandered from room to room, gazing around them at the vidscreen, at the elaborate kitchen, at the furniture in the bedroom, at the drapes, the chairs, the bed.

'But where are the Terrans?' N'tgari-3 said at last.

'They'll be right back.'

N'tgari-3 paced back and forth. 'This gives me an odd feeling. I can't put my antenna on it. A sort of uncomfortable feeling.' He hesitated. 'It isn't possible they're *not* coming back, is it?'

'Why not?'

Luci'n-6 began to fiddle with the vidscreen. 'Hardly likely. We'll wait for them. They'll be back.'

N'tgari-3 peered out the window nervously. 'I don't see them. But they *must* be around. They couldn't just walk off and leave all this behind. Where would they go? Why?'

'They'll be back,' Luci'n-6 got some static on the vidscreen. 'This isn't very impressive.'

'I have a feeling they won't.'

'If the Terrans don't return,' Luci'n-6 said thoughtfully, fooling with the vidscreen controls, 'it will be one of the greatest puzzles known to archaeology.'

'I'll keep watching for them,' N'tgari-3 said impassively.

Martians Come in Clouds

Ted Barnes came in all grim-faced and trembling. He threw his coat and newspaper over the chair. 'Another cloud,' he muttered. 'A whole cloud of them! One was up on Johnson's roof. They were getting it down with a long pole of some kind.'

Lena came and took his coat to the closet. 'I'm certainly glad you hurried right on home.'

'I get the shakes when I see one of them.' Ted threw himself down on the couch, groping in his pockets for cigarettes. 'Honest to God it really gets me.'

He lit up, blowing smoke around him in a gray mist. His hands were beginning to quiet down. He wiped sweat from his upper lip and loosened his necktie. 'What's for dinner?'

'Ham.' Lena bent over to kiss him.

'How come? Some sort of occasion?'

'No.' Lena moved back toward the kitchen door. 'It's that canned Dutch ham your mother gave us. I thought it was about time we opened it.'

Ted watched her disappear into the kitchen, slim and attractive in her bright print apron. He sighed, relaxing and leaning back. The quiet living-room, Lena in the kitchen, the television set playing to itself in the corner, made him feel a little better.

He unlaced his shoes and kicked them off. The whole incident had taken only a few minutes but it had seemed much longer. An eternity – standing rooted to the sidewalk, staring up at Johnson's roof. The crowd of shouting men. The long pole. And . . .

. . . and *it*, draped over the peak of the roof, the shapeless gray bundle evading the end of that pole. Creeping this way and that, trying to keep from being dislodged.

Ted shuddered. His stomach turned over. He had stood fixed

to the spot, gazing up, unable to look away. Finally some fellow running past had stepped on his foot, breaking the spell and freeing him. He had hurried on, getting away as fast as he could, relieved and shaken. Lord . . .!

The back door slammed. Jimmy wandered into the living-room, his hands in his pockets. 'Hi, Dad.' He stopped by the bathroom door, looking across at his father. 'What's the matter? You're all funny looking.'

'Jimmy, come over here.' Ted stubbed out his cigarette. 'I want to talk to you.'

'I have to go wash for dinner.'

'Come here and sit down. Dinner can wait.'

Jimmy came over and slid up onto the couch. 'What's the matter? What is it?'

Ted studied his son. Round little face, tousled hair hanging down in his eyes. Smudge of dirt on one cheek. Jimmy was eleven. Was this a good time to tell him? Ted set his jaw grimly. Now was as good a time as any – while it was strong in his mind.

'Jimmy, there was a Martian up on Johnson's roof. I saw it on the way home from the bus depot.'

Jimmy's eyes grew round. 'A buggie?'

'They were getting it with a pole. A cloud of them's around. They come in clouds every few years.' His hands were beginning to shake again. He lit another cigarette. 'Every two or three years. Not as often as they used to. They drift down from Mars in clouds, hundreds of them. All over the world – like leaves.' He shuddered. 'Like a lot of dry leaves blowing down.'

'Gosh!' Jimmy said. He got off the couch onto his feet. 'Is it still there?'

'No, they were getting it down. Listen,' Ted leaned toward the boy. 'Listen to me – I'm telling you this so you'll stay away from them. If you see one of them you turn around and run as fast as you can. You hear? Don't go near it – stay away. Don't . . .'

He hesitated. 'Don't pay any attention to it. You just turn around and run. Get somebody, stop the first man you see and tell him, then come on home. Do you understand?'

Jimmy nodded.

'You know what they look like. They showed you pictures at school. You must have – '

Lena came to the kitchen door. 'Dinner's ready. Jimmy, aren't you washed?'

'I stopped him,' Ted said, getting up from the couch. 'I wanted to have a talk with him.'

'You mind what your father tells you,' Lena said. 'About the buggies – remember what he says or he'll give you the biggest whipping you ever heard of.'

Jimmy ran to the bathroom. 'I'll get washed.' He disappeared, slamming the door behind him.

Ted caught Lena's gaze. 'I hope they get them taken care of soon. I hate even to be outside.'

'They should. I heard on television they're more organized than last time.' Lena counted mentally. 'This is the fifth time they've come. The fifth cloud. It seems to be tapering off. Not as often, any more. The first was in nineteen hundred and fifty-eight. The next in fifty-nine. I wonder where it'll end.'

Jimmy hurried out of the bathroom. 'Let's eat!'

'Okay,' Ted said. 'Let's eat.'

It was a bright afternoon with the sun shining down everywhere. Jimmy Barnes rushed out of the school yard, through the gate and onto the sidewalk. His heart was hammering excitedly. He crossed over to Maple Street and then onto Cedar, running the whole way.

A couple of people were still poking around on Johnson's lawn – a policeman and a few curious men. There was a big ruined place in the center of the lawn, a sort of tear where the grass had been ripped back. The flowers all around the house had been trampled flat. But there was no sign whatsoever of the buggie.

While he was watching Mike Edwards came over and punched him on the arm. 'What say, Barnes.'

'Hi. Did you see it?'

'The buggie? No.'

'My Dad saw it, coming home from work.'

'Bull!'

'No, he really did. He said they were getting it down with a pole.'

Ralf Drake rode up on his bike. 'Where is it? Is it gone?'

'They already tore it up,' Mike said. 'Barnes says his old man saw it, coming home last night.'

'He said they were poking it down with a pole. It was trying to hang onto the roof.'

'They're all dried-up and withered,' Mike said, 'like something that's been hanging out in the garage.'

'How do you know?' Ralf said.

'I saw one once.'

'Yeah. I'll bet.'

They walked along the sidewalk, Ralf wheeling his bike, discussing the matter loudly. They turned down Vermont Street and crossed the big vacant lot.

'The TV announcer said most of them are already rounded up,' Ralf said. 'There weren't very many this time.'

Jimmy kicked a rock. 'I'd sure like to see one before they get them all.'

'I'd sure like to *get* one,' Mike said.

Ralf sneered. 'If you ever saw one you'd run so fast you wouldn't stop until the sun set.'

'Oh, yeah?'

'You'd run like a fool.'

'The heck I would. I'd knock the ol' buggie down with a rock.'

'And carry him home in a tin can?'

Mike chased Ralf around, out into the street and up to the corner. The argument continued endlessly all the way across town and over to the other side of the railroad tracks. They walked past the ink works and the Western Lumber Company loading platforms. The sun sank low in the sky. It was getting to be evening. A cold wind came up, blowing through the palm trees at the end of the Hartly Construction Company lot.

'See you,' Ralf said. He hopped on his bike, riding off. Mike and Jimmy walked back toward town together. At Cedar Street they separated.

'If you see a buggie give me a call,' Mike said.

'Sure thing.' Jimmy walked on up Cedar Street, his hands in

his pockets. The sun had set. The evening air was chill. Darkness was descending.

He walked slowly, his eyes on the ground. The streetlights came on. A few cars moved along the street. Behind curtained windows he saw bright flashes of yellow, warm kitchens and living-rooms. A television set brayed out, rumbling into the gloom. He passed along the brick wall of the Pomeroy Estate. The wall turned into an iron fence. Above the fence great silent evergreens rose dark and unmoving in the evening twilight.

For a moment Jimmy stopped, kneeling down to tie his shoe. A cold wind blew around him, making the evergreens sway slightly. Far off a train sounded, a dismal wail echoing through the gloom. He thought about dinner, Dad with his shoes off, reading the newspapers. His mother in the kitchen – the TV set murmuring to itself in the corner – the warm, bright living-room.

Jimmy stood up. Above him in the evergreens something moved. He glanced up, suddenly rigid. Among the dark branches something rested, swaying with the wind. He gaped, rooted to the spot.

A buggie. Waiting and watching, crouched silently up in the tree.

It was *old*. He knew that at once. There was a dryness about it, an odor of age and dust. An ancient gray shape, silent and unmoving, wrapped around the trunk and branches of the evergreen. A mass of cobwebs, dusty strands and webs of gray wrapped and trailing across the tree. A nebulous wispy presence that made the hackles of his neck rise.

The shape began to move but so slowly he might not have noticed. It was sliding around the trunk, feeling its way carefully, a little at a time. As if it were sightless. Feeling its way inch by inch, an unseeing gray ball of cobwebs and dust.

Jimmy moved back from the fence. It was completely dark. The sky was black above him. A few stars glittered distantly, bits of remote fire. Far down the street a bus rumbled, turning a corner.

A buggie – clinging to the tree above him. Jimmy struggled, pulling himself away. His heart was thumping painfully, choking him. He could hardly breathe. His vision blurred, fading and receding. The buggie was only a little way from him, only a few yards above his head.

Help – he had to get help. Men with poles to push the buggie down – people – right away. He closed his eyes and pushed away from the fence. He seemed to be in a vast tide, a rushing ocean dragging at him, surging over his body, holding him where he was. He could not break away. He was caught. He strained, pushing against it. One step . . . another step . . . a third –

And then he heard it.

Or rather *felt* it. There was no sound. It was like drumming, a kind of murmuring like the sea, inside his head. The drumming lapped against his mind, beating gently around him. He halted. The murmuring was soft, rhythmic. But insistent – urgent. It began to separate, gaining form – form and substance. It flowed, breaking up into distinct sensations, images, scenes.

Scenes – of another world, *its* world. The buggie was talking to him, telling him about its world, spinning out scene after scene with anxious haste.

'Get away,' Jimmy muttered thickly.

But the scenes still came, urgently, insistently, lapping at his mind.

Plains – a vast desert without limit or end. Dark red, cracked and scored with ravines. A far line of blunted hills, dust-covered, corroded. A great basin off to the right, an endless empty piepan with white-crusted salt riming it, a bitter ash where water had once lapped.

'Get away!' Jimmy muttered again, moving a step back.

The scenes grew. Dead sky, particles of sand, whipped along, carried endlessly. Sheets of sand, vast billowing clouds of sand and dust, blowing endlessly across the cracked surface of the planet. A few scrawny plants growing by rocks. In the shadows of the mountains great spiders with old webs, dust-covered, spun centuries ago. Dead spiders, lodged in cracks.

A scene expanded. Some sort of artificial pipe, jutting up from the red-baked ground. A vent – underground quarters. The view changed. He was seeing below, down into the core of the planet – layer after layer of crumpled rock. A withered wrinkled planet without fire or life or moisture of any kind. Its skin cracking, its pulp drying out and blowing up in clouds of dust. Far down in the core a tank of some sort – a chamber sunk in the heart of the planet.

He was inside the tank. Buggies were everywhere, sliding and moving around. Machines, construction of different kinds, buildings, plants in rows, generators, homes, rooms of complex equipment.

Sections of the tank were closed off – bolted shut. Rusty, metal doors – machinery sinking into decay – valves closed, pipes rusting away – dials cracked and broken. Lines clogged – teeth missing from gears – more and more sections closed. Fewer buggies – fewer and fewer . . .

The scene changed. Earth, seen from a long way off – a distant green sphere, turning slowly, cloud-covered. Broad oceans, blue water miles deep – moist atmosphere. The buggies drifting through empty reaches of space, drifting slowly toward Earth, year after year. Drifting endlessly in the dark wastes with agonizing slowness.

Now Earth expanded. The scene was almost familiar. An ocean surface, miles of foaming water, a few gulls above, a distant shore line. The ocean, Earth's ocean. Clouds wandering above in the sky.

On the surface of the water flat spheres drifted, huge metal discs. Floating units, artificially built, several hundred feet around. Buggies rested silently on the discs, absorbing water and minerals from the ocean under them.

The buggie was trying to tell him something, something about itself. Discs on the water – the buggies wanted to use the water, to live on the water, on the surface of the ocean. Big surface discs, covered with buggies – it wanted him to know that, to see the discs, the water discs.

The buggies would live on the water, not on the land. Only the water – they wanted his permission. They wanted to use the water. That was what it was trying to tell him – that they wanted to use the surface of the water between the continents. Now the buggie was asking, imploring. It wanted to know. It wanted him to say, to answer, to give his permission. It was waiting to hear, waiting and hoping – imploring . . .

The scenes faded, winking out of his mind. Jimmy stumbled back, falling against the curb. He leaped up again, wiping damp grass from his hands. He was standing in the gutter. He could still see the buggie resting among the branches of the evergreen. It was almost invisible. He could scarcely make it out.

The drumming had receded, left his mind. The buggie had withdrawn.

Jimmy turned and fled. He ran across the street and down the other side, sobbing for breath. He came to a corner and turned up Douglas Street. At the bus-stop stood a heavy-set man with a lunchbucket under his arm.

Jimmy ran up to the man. 'A buggie. In the tree.' He gasped for breath. 'In the big tree.'

The man grunted. 'Run along, kid.'

'A buggie!' Jimmy's voice rose in panic, shrill and insistent. 'A buggie up in the tree!'

Two men loomed up out of the darkness. 'What? A buggie?' 'Where?'

More people appeared. 'Where is it?'

Jimmy pointed, gesturing. 'Pomeroy Estate. The tree. By the fence.' He waved, gasping.

A cop appeared. 'What's going on?'

'The kid's found a buggie. Somebody get a pole.'

'Show me where it is,' the cop said, grabbing hold of Jimmy's arm. 'Come on.'

Jimmy led them back down the street, to the brick wall. He hung back, away from the fence. 'Up there.'

'Which tree?'

'That one – I think.'

A flashlight flicked on, picking its way among the evergreens. In the Pomeroy house lights came on. The front door opened.

'What's going on there?' Mr Pomeroy's voice echoed angrily.

'Got a buggie. Keep back.'

Mr Pomeroy's door slammed quickly shut.

'*There* it is!' Jimmy pointed up. '*That* tree.' His heart almost stopped beating. 'There. Up *there*!'

'Where?'

'I see it.' The cop moved back, his pistol out.

'You can't shoot it. Bullets go right through.'

'Somebody get a pole.'

'Too high for a pole.'

'Get a torch.'

'Somebody bring a torch!'

Two men ran off. Cars were stopping. A police car slid to a halt, its siren whirring into silence. Doors opened, men came running over. A searchlight flashed on, dazzling them. It found the buggie and locked into place.

The buggie rested unmoving, hugging the branch of the evergreen. In the blinding light it looked like some giant cocoon clinging uncertainly to its place. The buggie began to move hesitantly, creeping around the trunk. Its wisps reached out, feeling for support.

'A torch, damn it! Get a torch here!'

A man came with a blazing board ripped from a fence. They poured gasoline over newspapers heaped in a ring around the base of the tree. The bottom branches began to burn, feebly at first, then more brightly.

'Get more gas!'

A man in a white uniform came lugging a tank of gasoline. He threw the tankful of gas onto the tree. Flames blazed up, rising rapidly. The branches charred and crackled, burning furiously.

Far above them the buggie began to stir. It climbed uncertainly to a higher branch, pulling itself up. The flames licked closer. The buggie increased its pace. It undulated, dragging itself onto the next branch above. Higher and higher it climbed.

'Look at it go.'

'It won't get away. It's almost at the top.'

More gasoline was brought. The flames leaped higher. A crowd had collected around the fence. The police kept them back.

'There it goes.' The light moved to keep the buggie visible.

'It's at the top.'

The buggie had reached the top of the tree. It rested, holding onto the branch, swaying back and forth. Flames leaped from branch to branch, closer and closer to it. The buggie felt hesitantly around, blindly, seeking support. It reached, feeling with its wisps. A spurt of fire touched it.

The buggie crackled, smoke rising from it.

'It's burning!' An excited murmur swept through the crowd. 'It's finished.'

The buggie was on fire. It moved clumsily, trying to get away. Suddenly it dropped, falling to the branch below. For a second it hung on the branch, crackling and smoking. Then the branch gave way with a rending crackle.

The buggie fell to the ground, among the newspapers and gasoline.

The crowd roared. They seethed toward the tree, flowing and milling forward.

'*Step* on it!'

'*Get* it!'

'*Step* on the damn thing!'

Boots stamped again and again, feet rising and falling, grinding the buggie into the ground. A man fell, pulling himself away, his glasses hanging from one ear. Knots of struggling people fought with each other, pressing inward, trying to reach the tree. A flaming branch fell. Some of the crowd retreated.

'I *got* it!'

'Get *back*!'

More branches fell, crashing down. The crowd broke up, streaming back, laughing and pushing.

Jimmy felt the cop's hand on his arm, big fingers digging in. 'That's the end, boy. It's all over.'

'They get it?'

'They sure did. What's your name?'

'My name?' Jimmy started to tell the cop his name but just then some scuffling broke out between two men and the cop hurried over.

Jimmy stood for a moment, watching. The night was cold. A frigid wind blew around him, chilling him through his clothing. He thought suddenly of dinner and his father stretched out on the couch, reading the newspaper. His mother in the kitchen fixing dinner. The warmth, the friendly yellow homey warmth.

He turned and made his way through the people to the edge of the street. Behind him the charred stalk of the tree rose black and smoking into the night. A few glowing remains were being stamped out around its base. The buggie was gone, it was over, there was nothing more to see.

Jimmy hurried home as if the buggie were chasing him.

'What do you say to that?' Ted Barnes demanded, sitting with his legs crossed, his chair back from the table. The cafeteria was full of noise and the smell of food. People pushed their trays along on the racks in front of them, gathering dishes from the dispensers.

'Your kid really did that?' Bob Walters said, across from him, with open curiosity.

'You sure you're not stringing us along?' Frank Hendricks said, lowering his newspaper for a moment.

'It's the truth. The one they got over at the Pomeroy Estate – I'm talking about that one. It was a real son-of-a-gun.'

'That's right,' Jack Green admitted. 'The paper says some kid spotted it first and brought the police.'

'That was my kid,' Ted said, his chest swelling. 'What do you guys think about that?'

'Was he scared?' Bob Walters wanted to know.

'Hell no!' Ted Barnes replied strongly.

'I'll bet he was.' Frank Hendricks was from Missouri.

'He sure wasn't. He got the cops and brought them to the place – last night. We were sitting around the dinner table, wondering where the hell he was. I was getting a little worried.' Ted Barnes was still the proud parent.

Jack Green got to his feet, looking at his watch. 'Time to get back to the office.'

Frank and Bob got up also. 'See you later, Ted.'

Green thumped Ted on the back. 'Some kid you got, Barnes – chip off the old block.'

Ted grinned. 'He wasn't a bit afraid.' He watched them go out of the cafeteria onto the busy noonday street. After a moment he gulped down the rest of his coffee and wiped his chin, standing slowly up. 'Not a damn bit afraid – not one damn bit.'

He paid for his lunch and pushed his way outside onto the street, his chest still swelled up. He grinned at people passing by as he walked back to the office, all aglow with reflected glory.

'Not a bit afraid,' he murmured, full of pride, a deep glowing pride. 'Not one damn bit!'

The Commuter

The little fellow was tired. He pushed his way slowly through the throng of people, across the lobby of the station, to the ticket window. He waited his turn impatiently, fatigue showing in his drooping shoulders, his sagging brown coat.

'Next,' Ed Jacobson, the ticket seller, rasped.

The little fellow tossed a five dollar bill on the counter. 'Give me a new commute book. Used up the old one.' He peered past Jacobson at the wall clock. 'Lord, is it really that late?'

Jacobson accepted the five dollars. 'OK, mister. One commute book. Where to?'

'Macon Heights,' the little fellow stated.

'Macon Heights.' Jacobson consulted his board. 'Macon Heights. There isn't any such place.'

The little man's face hardened in suspicion. 'You trying to be funny?'

'Mister, there isn't any Macon Heights. I can't sell you a ticket unless there is such a place.'

'What do you mean? I live there!'

'I don't care. I've been selling tickets for six years and there is no such place.'

The little man's eyes popped with astonishment. 'But I have a home there. I go there every night. I – '

'Here.' Jacobson pushed him the chart board. 'You find it.'

The little man pulled the board over to one side. He studied it frantically, his finger trembling as he went down the list of towns.

'Find it?' Jacobson demanded, resting his arms on the counter. 'It's not there, is it?'

The little man shook his head, dazed. 'I don't understand. It doesn't make sense. Something must be wrong. There certainly must be – '

Suddenly he vanished. The board fell to the cement floor. The little fellow was gone – winked out of existence.

'Holy Caesar's Ghost,' Jacobson gasped. His mouth opened and closed. There was only the board lying on the cement floor.

The little man had ceased to exist.

'What then?' Bob Paine asked.

'I went around and picked up the board.'

'He was really gone?'

'He was gone, all right.' Jacobson mopped his forehead. 'I wish you had been around. Like a light he went out. Completely. No sound. No motion.'

Paine lit a cigarette, leaning back in his chair. 'Had you ever seen him before?'

'No.'

'What time of day was it?'

'Just about now. About five.' Jacobson moved toward the ticket window. 'Here comes a bunch of people.'

'Macon Heights.' Paine turned the pages of the State city guide. 'No listing in any of the books. If he reappears I want to talk to him. Get him inside the office.'

'Sure. I don't want to have nothing to do with him. It isn't natural.' Jacobson turned to the window. 'Yes, lady.'

'Two round trip tickets to Lewisburg.'

Paine stubbed his cigarette out and lit another. 'I keep feeling I've heard the name before.' He got up and wandered over to the wall map. 'But it isn't listed.'

'There is no listing because there is no such place,' Jacobson said. 'You think I could stand here daily, selling one ticket after another, and not know?' He turned back to his window. 'Yes, sir.'

'I'd like a commute book to Macon Heights,' the little fellow said, glancing nervously at the clock on the wall. 'And hurry it up.'

Jacobson closed his eyes. He hung on tight. When he opened his eyes again the little fellow was still there. Small wrinkled face. Thinning hair. Glasses. Tired, slumped coat.

Jacobson turned and moved across the office to Paine. 'He's back.' Jacobson swallowed, his face pale. 'It's him again.'

Paine's eyes flickered. 'Bring him right in.'

Jacobson nodded and returned to the window. 'Mister,' he said, 'could you please come inside?' He indicated the door. 'The Vice-President would like to see you for a moment.'

The little man's face darkened. 'What's up? The train's about to take off.' Grumbling under his breath, he pushed the door open and entered the office. 'This sort of thing has never happened before. It's certainly getting hard to purchase a commute book. If I miss the train I'm going to hold your company – '

'Sit down,' Paine said, indicating the chair across from the desk. 'You're the gentleman who wants a commute book to Macon Heights?'

'Is there something strange about that? What's the matter with all of you? Why can't you sell me a commute book like you always do?'

'Like – like we *always* do?'

The little man held himself in check with great effort. 'Last December my wife and I moved out to Macon Heights. I've been riding your train ten times a week, twice a day, for six months. Every month I buy a new commute book.'

Paine leaned toward him. 'Exactly which one of our trains do you take, Mr – '

'Critchet. Ernest Critchet. The B train. Don't you know your own schedules?'

'The B train?' Paine consulted a B train chart, running his pencil along it. No Macon Heights was listed. 'How long is the trip? How long does it take?'

'Exactly forty-nine minutes.' Critchet looked up at the wall clock. 'If I ever get on it.'

Paine calculated mentally. Forty-nine minutes. About thirty miles from the city. He got up and crossed to the big wall map.

'What's wrong?' Critchet asked with marked suspicion.

Paine drew a thirty-mile circle on the map. The circle crossed a number of towns, but none of them was Macon Heights. And on the B line there was nothing at all.

'What sort of place is Macon Heights?' Paine asked. 'How many people, would you say?'

'I don't know. Five thousand, maybe. I spend most of my time in the city. I'm a bookkeeper over at Bradshaw Insurance.'

'Is Macon Heights a fairly new place?'

'It's modern enough. We have a little two-bedroom house, a couple years old.' Critchet stirred restlessly. 'How about a commute book?'

'I'm afraid,' Paine said slowly, 'I can't sell you a commute book.'

'What? Why not?'

'We don't have any service to Macon Heights.'

Critchet leaped up. 'What do you mean?'

'There's no such place. Look at the map yourself.'

Critchet gaped, his face working. Then he turned angrily to the wall map, glaring at it intently.

'This is a curious situation, Mr Critchet,' Paine murmured. 'It isn't on the map, and the State city directory doesn't list it. We have no schedule that includes it. There are no commute books made up for it. We don't – '

He broke off. Critchet had vanished. One moment he was there, studying the wall map. The next moment he was gone. Vanished. Puffed out.

'Jacobson!' Paine barked. 'He's gone!'

Jacobson's eyes grew large. Sweat stood out on his forehead. 'So he is,' he murmured.

Paine was deep in thought, gazing at the empty spot Ernest Critchet had occupied. 'Something's going on,' he muttered. 'Something damn strange.' Abruptly he grabbed his overcoat and headed for the door.

'Don't leave me alone!' Jacobson begged.

'If you need me I'll be at Laura's apartment. The number's some place in my desk.'

'This is no time for games with girls.'

Paine pushed open the door to the lobby. 'I doubt,' he said grimly, 'if this is a game.'

Paine climbed the stairs to Laura Nichols's apartment two at a time. He leaned on the buzzer until the door opened.

'Bob!' Laura blinked in surprise. 'To what do I owe this – '

Paine pushed past her, inside the apartment. 'Hope I'm not interrupting anything.'

'No, but – '

'Big doings. I'm going to need some help. Can I count on you?'

'On me?' Laura closed the door after him. Her attractively furnished apartment lay in half shadow. At the end of the deep green couch a single table lamp burned. The heavy drapes were pulled. The phonograph was on low in the corner.

'Maybe I'm going crazy.' Paine threw himself down on the luxuriant green couch. 'That's what I want to find out.'

'How can I help?' Laura came languidly over, her arms folded, a cigarette between her lips. She shook her long hair back out of her eyes. 'Just what did you have in mind?'

Paine grinned at the girl appreciatively. 'You'll be surprised. I want you to go downtown tomorrow morning bright and early and – '

'Tomorrow morning! I have a job, remember? And the office starts a whole new string of reports this week.'

'The hell with that. Take the morning off. Go downtown to the main library. If you can't get the information there, go over to the county courthouse and start looking through the back tax records. Keep looking until you find it.'

'It? Find what?'

Paine lit a cigarette thoughtfully. 'Mention of a place called Macon Heights. I know I've heard the name before. Years ago. Got the picture? Go through the old atlases. Old newspapers in the reading room. Old magazines. Reports. City proposals. Propositions before the State legislature.'

Laura sat down slowly on the arm of the couch. 'Are you kidding?'

'No.'

'How far back?'

'Maybe ten years – if necessary.'

'Good Lord! I might have to – '

'Stay there until you find it.' Paine got up abruptly. 'I'll see you later.'

'You're leaving. You're not taking me out to dinner?'

'Sorry.' Paine moved toward the door. 'I'll be busy. Real busy.'

'Doing what?'

'Visiting Macon Heights.'

Outside the train endless fields stretched off, broken by an occasional farm building. Bleak telephone poles jutted up toward the evening sky.

Paine glanced at his wristwatch. Not far, now. The train passed through a small town. A couple of gas stations, roadside stands, television store. It stopped at the station, brakes grinding. Lewisburg. A few commuters got off, men in overcoats with evening papers. The doors slammed and the train started up.

Paine settled back against his seat, deep in thought. Critchet had vanished while looking at the wall map. He had vanished the first time when Jacobson showed him the chart board . . . When he had been shown there was no such place as Macon Heights. Was there some sort of clue there? The whole thing was unreal, dreamlike.

Paine peered out. He was almost there – if there were such a place. Outside the train the brown fields stretched off endlessly. Hills and level fields. Telephone poles. Cars racing along the State highway, tiny black specks hurrying through the twilight.

But no sign of Macon Heights.

The train roared on its way. Paine consulted his watch. Fifty-one minutes had passed. And he had seen nothing. Nothing but fields.

He walked up the car and sat down beside the conductor, a white-haired old gentleman. 'Ever hear of a place called Macon Heights?' Paine asked.

'No, sir.'

Paine showed his identification. 'You're sure you never heard of any place by that name?'

'Positive, Mr Paine.'

'How long have you been on this run?'

'Eleven years, Mr Paine.'

Paine rode on until the next stop, Jacksonville. He got off and transferred to a B train heading back to the city. The sun had set. The sky was almost black. Dimly, he could make out the scenery out there beyond the window.

He tensed, holding his breath. One minute to go. Forty seconds. Was there anything? Level fields. Bleak telephone poles. A barren, wasted landscape between towns.

Between? The train rushed on, hurtling through the gloom. Paine gazed out fixedly. Was there something out there? Something beside the fields?

Above the fields a long mass of translucent smoke lay stretched out. A homogeneous mass, extended for almost a mile. What was it? Smoke from the engine? But the engine was diesel. From a truck along the highway? A brush fire? None of the fields looked burned.

Suddenly the train began to slow. Paine was instantly alert. The train was stopping, coming to a halt. The brakes screeched, the cars lurched from side to side. Then silence.

Across the aisle a tall man in a light coat got to his feet, put his hat on, and moved rapidly toward the door. He leaped down from the train, onto the ground. Paine watched him, fascinated. The man walked rapidly away from the train across the dark fields. He moved with purpose, heading toward the bank of gray haze.

The man rose. He was walking a foot off the ground. He turned to the right. He rose again, now – three feet off the ground. For a moment he walked parallel to the ground, still heading away from the train. Then he vanished into the bank of haze. He was gone.

Paine hurried up the aisle. But already the train had begun gathering speed. The ground moved past outside. Paine located the conductor, leaning against the wall of the car, a pudding-faced youth.

'Listen,' Paine grated. 'What was that stop!'

'Beg pardon, sir?'

'That stop! Where the hell were we?'

'We always stop there.' Slowly, the conductor reached into his coat and brought out a handful of schedules. He sorted through them and passed one to Paine. 'The B always stops at Macon Heights. Didn't you know that?'

'No!'

'It's on the schedule.' The youth raised his pulp magazine again. 'Always stops there. Always has. Always will.'

Paine tore the schedule open. It was true. Macon Heights was listed between Jacksonville and Lewisburg. Exactly thirty miles from the city.

The cloud of gray haze. The vast cloud, gaining form rapidly. As if something were coming into existence. As a matter of fact, something *was* coming into existence.

Macon Heights!

He caught Laura at her apartment the next morning. She was sitting at the coffee table in a pale pink sweater and dark slacks. Before her was a pile of notes, a pencil and eraser, and a malted milk.

'How did you make out?' Paine demanded.

'Fine. I got your information.'

'What's the story?'

'There was quite a bit of material.' She patted the sheaf of notes. 'I summed up the major parts for you.'

'Let's have the summation.'

'Seven years ago this August the county board of supervisors voted on three new suburban housing tracts to be set up outside the city. Macon Heights was one of them. There was a big debate. Most of the city merchants opposed the new tracts. Said they would draw too much retail business away from the city.'

'Go on.'

'There was a long fight. Finally two of the three tracts were approved. Waterville and Cedar Groves. But not Macon Heights.'

'I see,' Paine murmured thoughtfully.

'Macon Heights was defeated. A compromise; two tracts instead of three. The two tracts were built up right away. You know. We passed through Waterville one afternoon. Nice little place.'

'But no Macon Heights.'

'No. Macon Heights was given up.'

Paine rubbed his jaw. 'That's the story, then.'

'That's the story. Do you realize I lose a whole half-day's pay because of this? You *have* to take me out, tonight. Maybe I should get another fellow. I'm beginning to think you're not such a good bet.'

Paine nodded absently. 'Seven years ago.' All at once a thought came to him. 'The vote! How close was the vote on Macon Heights?'

Laura consulted her notes. 'The project was defeated by a single vote.'

'A single vote. Seven years ago.' Paine moved out into the hall. 'Thanks, honey. Things are beginning to make sense. Lots of sense!'

He caught a cab out front. The cab raced him across the city, toward the train station. Outside, signs and streets flashed by. People and stores and cars.

His hunch had been correct. He *had* heard the name before. Seven years ago. A bitter county debate on a proposed suburban tract. Two towns approved; one defeated and forgotten.

But now the forgotten town was coming into existence – seven years later. The town and an undetermined slice of reality along with it. *Why?* Had something changed in the past? Had an alteration occurred in some past continuum?

That seemed like the explanation. The vote had been close. Macon Heights had *almost* been approved. Maybe certain parts of the past were unstable. Maybe that particular period, seven years ago, had been critical. Maybe it had never completely 'jelled'. An odd thought: the past changing, after it had already happened.

Suddenly Paine's eyes focused. He sat up quickly. Across the street was a store sign, halfway along the block. Over a small, inconspicuous establishment. As the cab moved forward Paine peered to see.

BRADSHAW INSURANCE
[OR]
NOTARY PUBLIC

He pondered. Critchet's place of business. Did it also come and go? Had it always been there? Something about it made him uneasy.

'Hurry it up,' Paine ordered the driver. 'Let's get going.'

When the train slowed down at Macon Heights, Paine got quickly to his feet and made his way up the aisle to the door. The grinding wheels jerked to a halt and Paine leaped down onto the hot gravel siding. He looked around him.

In the afternoon sunlight, Macon Heights glittered and sparkled, its even rows of houses stretching out in all directions. In the center of the town the marquee of the theater rose up.

A theater, even. Paine headed across the track toward the town. Beyond the train station was a parking lot. He stepped up onto the lot and crossed it, following a path past a filling station and onto a sidewalk.

He came out on the main street of the town. A double row of stores stretched out ahead of him. A hardware store. Two drugstores. A dime store. A modern department store.

Paine walked along, hands in his pockets, gazing around him at Macon Heights. An apartment building stuck up, tall and fat. A janitor was washing down the front steps. Everything looked new and modern. The houses, the stores, the pavement and sidewalks. The parking meters. A brown-uniformed cop was giving a car a ticket. Trees, growing at intervals. Neatly clipped and pruned.

He passed a big supermarket. Out in front was a bin of fruit, oranges and grapes. He picked a grape and bit into it.

The grape was real, all right. A big black concord grape, sweet and ripe. Yet twenty-four hours ago there had been nothing here but a barren field.

Paine entered one of the drugstores. He leafed through some magazines and then sat down at the counter. He ordered a cup of coffee from the red-cheeked little waitress.

'This is a nice town,' Paine said, as she brought the coffee.

'Yes, isn't it?'

Paine hesitated. 'How – how long have you been working here?'

'Three months.'

'Three months?' Paine studied the buxom little blonde. 'You live here in Macon Heights?'

'Oh, yes.'

'How long?'

'A couple of years, I guess.' She moved away to wait on a young soldier who had taken a stool down the counter.

Paine sat drinking his coffee and smoking, idly watching the people passing by outside. Ordinary people. Men and women, mostly women. Some had grocery bags and little wire carts. Automobiles drove slowly back and forth. A sleepy little suburban town. Modern, upper middle-class. A quality town. No slums here. Small, attractive houses. Stores with sloping grass fronts and neon signs.

Some high school kids burst into the drugstore, laughing and bumping into each other. Two girls in bright sweaters sat down next to Paine and ordered lime drinks. They chatted gaily, bits of their conversation drifting to him.

He gazed at them, pondering moodily. They were real, all right. Lipstick and red fingernails. Sweaters and armloads of school books. Hundreds of high school kids, crowding eagerly into the drugstore.

Paine rubbed his forehead wearily. It didn't seem possible. Maybe he was out of his mind. The town was *real*. Completely real. It must have always existed. A whole town couldn't rise up out of nothing; out of a cloud of gray haze. Five thousand people, houses and streets and stores.

Stores. Bradshaw Insurance.

Stabbing realization chilled him. Suddenly he understood. It was spreading. Beyond Macon Heights. Into the city. The city was changing, too. Bradshaw Insurance. Crichet's place of business.

Macon Heights couldn't exist without warping the city. They interlocked. The five thousand people came from the city. Their jobs. Their lives. The city was involved.

But how much? How much was the city changing?

Paine threw a quarter on the counter and hurried out of the drugstore, toward the train station. He had to get back to the city. Laura, the change. Was she still there? Was his *own* life safe?

Fear gripped him. Laura, all his possessions, his plans, hopes and dreams. Suddenly Macon Heights was unimportant. His own world was in jeopardy. Only one thing mattered now. He had to make sure of it; make sure his own life was still there.

Untouched by the spreading circle of change that was lapping out from Macon Heights.

'Where to, buddy?' the cabdriver asked, as Paine came rushing out of the train station.

Paine gave him the address of the apartment. The cab roared out into traffic. Paine settled back nervously. Outside the window the streets and office buildings flashed past. White collar workers were already beginning to get off work, swelling out onto the sidewalks to stand in clumps at each corner.

How much had changed? He concentrated on a row of buildings. The big department store. Had that always been there? The little boot-black shop next to it. He had never noticed that before.

NORRIS HOME FURNISHINGS.

He didn't remember *that*. But how could he be sure? He felt confused. How could he tell?

The cab let him off in front of the apartment house. Paine stood for a moment, looking around him. Down at the end of the block the owner of the Italian delicatessen was out putting up the awning. Had he ever noticed a delicatessen there before?

He could not remember.

What had happened to the big meat market across the street? There was nothing but neat little houses; older houses that looked like they'd been there plenty long. Had a meat market ever been there? The houses *looked* solid.

In the next block the striped pole of a barbershop glittered. Had there always been a barbershop there?

Maybe it had always been there. Maybe, and maybe not. Everything was shifting. New things were coming into existence, others going away. The past was altering, and memory was tied to the past. How could he trust his memory? How could he be sure?

Terror gripped him. Laura. His world . . .

Paine raced up the front steps and pushed open the door of the apartment house. He hurried up the carpeted stairs to the second floor. The door of the apartment was unlocked. He pushed it open and entered, his heart in his mouth, praying silently.

The living-room was dark and silent. The shades were half

pulled. He glanced around wildly. The light blue couch, magazines on its arms. The low blond-oak table. The television set.
But the room was empty.

'Laura!' he gasped.

Laura hurried from the kitchen, eyes wide with alarm. 'Bob!
What are you doing home? Is anything the matter?'

Paine relaxed, sagging with relief. 'Hello, honey.' He kissed
her, holding her tight against him. She was warm and substantial; completely real. 'No, nothing's wrong. Everything's fine.'

'Are you sure?'

'I'm sure.' Paine took off his coat shakily and dropped it over
the back of the couch. He wandered around the room, examining things, his confidence returning. His familiar blue couch,
cigarette burns on its arms. His ragged footstool. His desk
where he did his work at night. His fishing rods leaning up
against the wall behind the bookcase.

The big television set he had purchased only last month; that
was safe, too.

Everything, all he owned, was untouched. Safe. Unharmed.

'Dinner won't be ready for half an hour,' Laura murmured
anxiously, unfastening her apron. 'I didn't expect you home so
early. I've just been sitting around all day. I did clean the stove.
Some salesman left a sample of a new cleaner.'

'That's okay.' He examined a favorite Renoir print on the
wall. 'Take your time. It's good to see all these things again.
I – '

From the bedroom a crying sound came. Laura turned
quickly. 'I guess we woke up Jimmy.'

'Jimmy?'

Laura laughed. 'Darling, don't you remember your own
son?'

'Of course,' Paine murmured, annoyed. He followed Laura
slowly into the bedroom. 'Just for a minute everything seemed
strange.' He rubbed his forehead, frowning. 'Strange and
unfamiliar. Sort of out of focus.'

They stood by the crib, gazing down at the baby. Jimmy
glared back up at his mother and dad.

'It must have been the sun,' Laura said. 'It's so terribly hot
outside.'

'That must be it. I'm okay now.' Paine reached down and poked at the baby. He put his arm around his wife, hugging her to him. 'It must have been the sun,' he said. He looked down into her eyes and smiled.

The World She Wanted

Half-dozing, Larry Brewster contemplated the litter of ciga-rette-butts, empty beer-bottles, and twisted match-folders heaped on the table before him. He reached out and adjusted one beer-bottle – thereby achieving just the right effect.

In the back of the *Wind-Up* the small dixieland jazz combo played noisily. The harsh jazz-sound mixed with the murmur of voices, the semi-darkness, the clink of glasses at the bar. Larry Brewster sighed in happy contentment. 'This,' he stated, 'is Nirvana.' He nodded his head slowly, agreeing with the words uttered. 'Or at least the seventh level of zen-buddhist heaven.'

'There aren't seven levels in the zen-buddhist heaven,' a competent female voice corrected, from directly above him.

'That's a fact,' Larry admitted, reflecting on the matter. 'I was speaking metaphorically, not literally.'

'You should be more careful; you should mean exactly what you say.'

'And say exactly what you mean?' Larry peered up. 'Have I had the pleasure of knowing you, young lady?'

The slender, golden-haired girl dropped into the seat across the table from Larry, her eyes sharp and bright in the half-gloom of the bar. She smiled at him, white teeth sparkling. 'No,' she said. 'We've never met; our time has just now arrived.'

'Our – our time?' Larry drew himself up slowly, pulling his lanky frame together. There was something in the girl's bright, competent face that vaguely alarmed him, penetrating his alcoholic haze. Her smile was too calm, too assured. 'Just exactly what do you mean?' Larry murmured. 'What's this all about?'

The girl slipped out of her coat, revealing full, rounded

breasts and supple figure. 'I'll have a martini,' she said. 'And by the way – my name is Allison Holmes.'

'Larry Brewster.' Larry studied the girl intently. 'What did you say you wanted?'

'A martini. Dry.' Allison smiled coolly across at him. 'And get one for yourself, why don't you?'

Larry grunted under his breath. He signaled to the waiter. 'A dry martini, Max.'

'Okay, Mr Brewster.'

A few minutes later Max returned and set a martini glass on the table. When he had gone, Larry leaned toward the blonde-haired girl. 'Now, Miss Holmes – '

'None for you?'

'None for me.' Larry watched her sip her drink. Her hands were small and dainty. She wasn't bad-looking, but he didn't like the self-satisfied calmness in her eyes. 'What's this business about our time having come? Let me in on it.'

'It's very simple. I saw you sitting here and I knew you were the one. In spite of the messy table.' She wrinkled her nose at the litter of bottles and match-folders. 'Why don't you have them clear it off?'

'Because I enjoy it. You knew I was the *one*? Which one?' Larry was getting interested. 'Go on.'

'Larry, this is a very important moment in my life.' Allison gazed around her. 'Who would think I'd find you in a place like this? But that's the way it's always been for me. This is only one link of a great chain going back – well, as far back as I can remember.'

'What chain is that?'

Allison laughed. 'Poor Larry. You don't understand.' She leaned toward him, her lovely eyes dancing. 'You see, Larry, I know something no one else knows – no one else in this world. Something I learned when I was a little girl. Something – '

'Wait a minute. What do you mean by "this world"? You mean there are nicer worlds than this? Better worlds? Like in Plato? This world is only a – '

'Certainly not!' Allison frowned. 'This is the best world, Larry. The best of all possible worlds.'

'Oh. Herbert Spencer.'

'The best of all possible worlds – for me.' She smiled at him, a cold, secret smile.

'Why for you?'

There was something almost predatory in the girl's finely-chiseled face as she answered. 'Because,' she said calmly, 'this is *my* world.'

Larry raised an eyebrow. 'Your world?' Then he grinned good-naturedly. 'Sure it is, baby; it belongs to all of us.' He waved expansively around at the room. 'Your world, my world, the banjo player's world – '

'No.' Allison shook her head firmly. 'No, Larry. My world; it belongs to me. Everything and everybody. All mine.' She moved her chair around until she was close by him. He could smell her perfume, warm and sweet and tantalizing. 'Don't you understand? This is mine. All these things – they're here for me; for my happiness.'

Larry edged away a little. 'Oh? You know, as a philosophical tenet that's a bit hard to maintain. I'll admit Descartes said the world is known to us only through our senses, and our senses reflect our own – '

Allison laid her small hand on his arm. 'I don't mean that. You see, Larry, there are *many* worlds. All kinds of worlds. Millions and millions. As many worlds as there are people. Each person has his own world, Larry, his own private world. A world that exists for him, for his happiness.' She lowered her gaze modestly. 'This happens to be *my* world.'

Larry considered. 'Very interesting, but what about other people? Me, for example.'

'You exist for my happiness, of course; that's what I'm talking about.' The pressure of her small hand increased. 'As soon as I saw you, I knew you were the one. I've been thinking about this for several days now. It's time *he* came along. The man for me. The man intended for me to marry – so my happiness can be complete.'

'Hey!' Larry exclaimed, drawing back.

'What's wrong?'

'What about *me*?' Larry demanded. 'That's not fair! Doesn't *my* happiness count?'

'Yes . . . but not here, not in this world.' She gestured

vaguely. 'You have a world someplace else, a world of your own; in this world you're merely a part of my life. You're not completely real. I'm the only one in this world who's *completely* real. All the rest of you are here for me. You're just – just *partly* real.'

'I see.' Larry sat back slowly, rubbing his jaw. 'Then I sort of exist in a lot of different worlds. A little bit here, a little bit there, according to where I'm needed. Like now, for instance, in this world. I've been wandering around for twenty-five years, just so I could turn up when you needed me.'

'That's right.' Allison's eyes danced merrily; 'you have the idea.' Suddenly she glanced at her wristwatch. 'It's getting late. We better go.'

'Go?'

Allison stood up quickly, picking up her tiny purse and pulling her coat around her. 'I want to do so many things with you, Larry! So many places to see! So much to do!' She took hold of his arm. 'Come on. Hurry up.'

Larry rose slowly. 'Say, listen – '

'We're going to have lots of fun.' Allison steered him toward the door. 'Let's see . . . What would be nice . . .'

Larry halted angrily. 'The check! I can't just walk out.' He fumbled in his pocket. 'I owe about – '

'No check; not tonight. This is my special night.' Allison spun toward Max, cleaning up the vacated table. 'Isn't that right?'

The old waiter looked up slowly. 'What's that, Miss?'

'No check tonight.'

Max shook his head. 'No check tonight, Miss. The boss's birthday; drinks on the house.'

Larry gaped. 'What?'

'Come on.' Allison tugged at him, pulling him through the heavy plush doors, out onto the cold, dark New York sidewalk. 'Come on, Larry – we have so much to do!'

Larry murmured, 'I still don't know where that cab came from.'

The cab drove off, racing away down the street. Larry looked around. Where were they? The dark streets were silent and deserted.

'First,' Allison Holmes said, 'I want a corsage. Larry, don't you think you should present your fiancée with a corsage? I want to go in looking nice.'

'A corsage? At this time of night?' Larry gestured at the dark, silent streets. 'Are you kidding?'

Allison pondered, then she crossed the street, abruptly; Larry followed after her. Allison came up to a closed-up flower shop, its sign off, door locked. She rapped with a coin on the plate glass window.

'Have you gone crazy?' Larry cried. 'There's nobody in there, this time of night!'

In the back of the flower shop somebody stirred. An old man came slowly toward the window, removing his glasses and putting them in his pocket. He bent down and unlocked the door. 'What is it, lady?'

'I want a corsage, the best you have.' Allison pushed into the shop, gazing around at the flowers in awe.

'Forget it, buddy,' Larry murmured; 'don't pay any attention to her. She's – '

'That's all right.' The old man sighed. 'I was going over my income tax; I can use a break. There should be some already made up. I'll open the refrigerator.'

Five minutes later they were out on the street again, Allison gazing ecstatically down at the great orchid pinned to her coat. 'It's beautiful, Larry!' she whispered. She squeezed his arm, gazing up in his face. 'Thanks a lot; now, let's go.'

'Where? Maybe you found an old guy sweating over his tax returns at one o'clock in the morning, but I defy you to find anything else in this god-forsaken graveyard.'

Allison looked around. 'Let's see . . . Over this way. This big old house over here. I wouldn't be a bit surprised – ' She tugged Larry down the sidewalk, her high heels clattering in the night silence.

'All right,' Larry murmured, grinning a little. 'I'll go along with you; this ought to be interesting.'

No light showed in the great square house; all the shades were down. Allison hurried down the walk, feeling her way through the darkness, up onto the porch of the house.

'Hey!' Larry exclaimed, suddenly alarmed. Allison had taken hold of the doorknob; she pushed the door open.

A burst of light struck them, light and sound. The murmur of voices. Past a heavy curtain people moved, an immense room of people. Men and women in evening dress, bending over long tables and counters.

'Oh, oh,' Larry muttered. 'Now you've got us into it; this is no place for us.'

Three tough-looking gorillas come strolling over, their hands in their pockets. 'Okay, mister; let's go.'

Larry started out. 'That's fine by me. I'm an easy-going person.'

'Nonsense.' Allison caught hold of his arm, her eyes glittering with excitement. 'I always wanted to visit a gambling-place. Look at all the tables! What are they doing? What's that over there?'

'For Lord's sake,' Larry gasped desperately. 'Let's get out of here. These people don't know us.'

'You bet we don't,' one of the three hulking bruisers rasped. He nodded to his companions. 'Here we go.' They grabbed hold of Larry and propelled him toward the door.

Allison blinked. 'What are you doing to him? You stop that!' She concentrated, her lips moving. 'Let me – let me talk to *Connie*.'

The three bruisers froze. They turned toward her slowly. 'To *who*? Who did you say, lady?'

Allison smiled up at them. 'To Connie – I think. Isn't that what I said? Connie. Where is he?' She looked around. 'Is that him over there?'

A small dapper man at one of the tables turned resentfully at his name, his face twisting with annoyance.

'Let it go, lady,' one of the bruisers said quickly. 'Don't bother Connie; he don't like to be bothered.' He closed the door, pushing Larry and Allison past the curtain, into the big room. 'You go and play. Enjoy yourselves; have a good time.'

Larry looked down at the girl beside him. He shook his head weakly. 'I could sure use a drink – a stiff one.'

'All right,' Allison said happily, her eyes fastened on the

roulette table. 'You go have your drink. I'm going to start playing!'

After a couple of good stiff scotch-and-waters, Larry slid off the stool and wandered away from the bar, over toward the roulette table in the center of the room.

A big crowd had collected around the table. Larry closed his eyes, steadying himself; he knew already. After he had gathered his strength he pushed his way through the people and up to the table.

'What does this one mean?' Allison was asking the croupier, holding up a blue chip. In front of her was an immense stack of chips – all colors. Everyone was murmuring and talking and looking at her.

Larry made his way over to her. 'How are you getting along? Lost your dowry yet?'

'Not yet. According to this man, I'm ahead.'

'He should know,' Larry sighed wearily; 'he's in the business.'

'Do you want to play, too?' Allison asked, accepting an armload of chips. 'You can have these. I've got more.'

'I see that. But – no, thanks; it's out of my line. Come on.' Larry led her away from the table. 'I think the time has come for you and me to have a little chat. Over in the corner where it's quiet.'

'A chat?'

'I got to thinking about it; this thing has gone far enough.'

Allison trailed after him. Larry strode over to the side of the room. In a huge fireplace, a roaring fire blazed. Larry threw himself down in a deep chair, pointing to the chair next to it. 'Sit,' Larry said.

Allison sat down, crossing her legs and smoothing down her skirt. She leaned back, sighed. 'Isn't this nice? The fire and everything? Just what I always imagined.' She closed her eyes dreamily.

Larry took his cigarettes out and lit up slowly, deep in thought. 'Now look here, Miss Holmes – '

'Allison. After all, we're going to be married.'

'Allison, then. Look here, Allison, this whole thing is absurd.

While I was at the bar I got to thinking it over. It isn't right, this crazy theory of yours.'

'Why not?' Her voice was sleepy, far-off.

Larry gestured angrily. 'I'll tell you why not. You claim I'm only *partly* real. Isn't that right? You're the only one who's completely real.'

Allison nodded. 'That's right.'

'But look! I don't know about all these other people – ' Larry waved at them deprecatingly. 'Maybe you're right about them. Maybe they *are* only phantoms. But not me! You can't say I'm just a phantom.' He banged his fist against the arm of the chair. 'See? You call that just partly real?'

'The chair's only partly real, too.'

Larry groaned. 'Damn it. I've been in this world twenty-five years, and I just met you a few hours ago. Am I supposed to believe I'm not really alive? Not really – not really me? That I'm only a sort of – a hunk of scenery in your world? Part of the fixtures?'

'Larry, darling. You *have* your own world. We each have our own world. But this one happens to be mine, and you're in it for me.' Allison opened her large blue eyes. 'In your real world I may exist a little for you, too. All our worlds overlap, darling; don't you see? You exist for me in my world. Probably I exist for you in yours.' She smiled. 'The Great Designer has to be economical – like all good artists. Many of the worlds are similar, almost the same. But each of them belongs to only one person.'

'And this one is yours.' Larry let his breath out with a sigh. 'Okay, baby. You have your mind made up; I'll play along with you – for a while, at least. I'll string along.' He contemplated the girl leaning back in the deep chair next to him. 'You know, you're not bad-looking, not bad at all.'

'Thank you.'

'Yeah, I'll bite. For a while, at least. Maybe we *are* meant for each other. But you've got to calm down a little; you try your luck too hard. If you're going to be around me, you better take it a little easier.'

'What do you mean, Larry?'

'All this. This place. What if the cops come? Gambling.

Philip K. Dick

Running around.' Larry gazed off into the distance. 'No, this isn't right. This isn't the kind of life I've got pictured. You know what I see in my mind's eye?' Larry's face lit up with wistful pleasure. 'I see a little house, baby. Out in the country. Way out. The farm country. Flat fields. Maybe Kansas. Colorado. A little cabin. With a well. And cows.'

Allison frowned. 'Oh?'

'And you know what else? Me, out in the back. Farming. Or – or feeding the chickens. Ever fed chickens?' Larry shook his head happily. 'A lot of fun, baby. And squirrels. Ever walk in the park and feed squirrels? Gray squirrels, big long tails? Tails as long as the squirrels.'

Allison yawned. Abruptly she got to her feet, picking up her purse. 'I think it's time we ran along.'

Larry got up slowly. 'Yeah, I guess it is.'

'Tomorrow is going to be a busy day. I want to get started early.' Allison made her way through the people, toward the door. 'First of all, I think we should begin looking for – '

Larry stopped her. 'Your chips.'

'What?'

'Your chips. Turn them in.'

'What for?'

'For money – I think they call it now.'

'Oh, bother.' Allison turned to a heavy-set man sitting at the black-jack table. 'Here!' She dumped the chips in the man's lap. 'You take them. All right, Larry. Let's go!'

The cab pulled up in front of Larry's apartment. 'Is this where you live?' Allison asked, gazing up at the building. 'It's not very modern, is it?'

'No.' Larry pushed the door open. 'And the plumbing isn't very good, either. But what the hell.'

'Larry?' Allison stopped him as he started to get out.

'Yes?'

'You won't forget about tomorrow, will you?'

'Tomorrow?'

'We have so much to do. I want you to be up bright and early, ready to go places. So we can get things done.'

'How about six o'clock in the evening? Is that early enough?' Larry yawned. It was late, and cold.

'Oh, no. I'll be by for you at ten A.M.'

'Ten! But my job. I got to work!'

'Not tomorrow. Tomorrow is *our* day.'

'How the hell am I going to live if I don't – '

Allison reached up, putting her slender arms around him. 'Don't worry; it'll be all right. Remember? This is my world.' She pulled him down to her, kissing him on the mouth. Her lips were sweet and cool. She held onto him tightly, her eyes closed.

Larry broke away. 'All right, already.' He straightened his tie, standing up on the pavement.

'Tomorrow, then. And don't worry about your old job. Goodbye, Larry darling.' Allison slammed the door. The cab drove off down the dark street. Larry gazed after it, still dazed. Finally he shrugged and turned toward the apartment house.

Inside, on the table in the hall, was a letter for him. He scooped it up, opening it as he climbed the stairs. The letter was from his office, Bray Insurance Company. The annual vacation schedule for the staff, listing the two weeks doled out to each employee. He didn't even have to find his name to know when *his* began.

'*Don't worry*,' Allison had said.

Larry grinned ruefully, stuffing the letter in his coat pocket. He unlocked his apartment door. Ten o'clock did she say? Well, at least he would have a good night's sleep.

The day was warm and bright. Larry Brewster sat out on the front steps of the apartment building, smoking and thinking while he waited for Allison.

She was doing all right; no doubt about that. A hell of a lot of things seemed to fall like ripe plums into her lap. No wonder she thought it was her world . . . She was getting the breaks, all right. But some people were like that. Lucky. Walked into fortune every time; won on quiz shows; found money in the gutter; bet on the right horse. It happened.

Her world? Larry grinned. Apparently Allison really

believed it. Interesting. Well, he'd string along with her a little
while longer, at least; she was a nice kid.

A horn sounded, and Larry glanced up. A two-tone convert-
ible was parked in front of him, the top down. Allison waved.
'Hi! Come on!'

Larry got up and came over. 'Where did you get this?' He
opened the door and slid in slowly.

'This?' Allison started the car up. It zoomed out into traffic.
'I forget; I think someone gave it to me.'

'You forget!' He stared at her. Then he relaxed against the
soft seat. 'Well? What's first on the list?'

'We're going to look at our new house.'

'Whose new house?'

'Ours. Yours and mine.'

Larry sank down into the seat. 'What! But you – '

Allison spun the car around a corner. 'You'll love it; it's nice.
How big is your apartment?'

'Three rooms.'

Allison laughed merrily. 'This is eleven rooms. Two stories.
Half an acre. Or so they tell me.'

'Haven't you seen it?'

'Not yet. My lawyer just called me this morning.'

'Your lawyer?'

'It's part of an estate left to me.'

Larry pulled himself together slowly. Allison, in a scarlet
two-piece outfit, gazed happily at the road ahead, her small
face blank and contented. 'Let me get all this straight. You've
never seen it; your lawyer just called you; you get it as part of
an estate.'

'That's right. Some old uncle of mine. I forget his name. I
didn't expect him to leave me anything.' She turned toward
Larry, beaming warmly at him. 'But this is such a special time
for me. It's important that *everything* go right. My whole
world . . .'

'Yeah. Your whole world. Well, I hope you like the house
after you see it.'

Allison laughed. 'I will. After all, it exists for me; that's what
it's there for.'

'You've got this worked out like an exact science,' Larry

murmured. 'Everything that happens to you is for the best. You're pleased with everything. So it *must* be your world. Maybe you're just making the best of things – telling yourself you really like the things that happen to you.'

'Do you think so?'

He frowned in thought as they zipped along. 'Tell me,' he said finally, 'how did you learn about these multiple worlds? Why are you so sure this one is yours?'

She smiled at him. 'I worked it out myself,' she said. 'I studied logic and philosophy, and history – and there was always something that puzzled me. Why were there so many vital changes in the fortunes of people and nations that seemed to come about providentially, just at the right moment? Why did it really seem as if my world had to be just the way it was, so that all through history, strange things happened which make it work out that way?

'I'd heard the "This Is the Best of All Possible Worlds" theory, but it didn't make sense the way I read about it. I studied the religions of mankind, and scientific speculations of the existence of a Creator – but something was lacking, something which either couldn't be accounted for, or was just overlooked.'

Larry nodded. 'Well, sure. It's easy; if this is the best of all possible worlds, then why is there so much suffering – unnecessary suffering – in it, if there's a benevolent and all-powerful Creator, as so many millions have believed, do believe, and will believe in the future, no doubt, then how do you account for the existence of evil?' He grinned at her. 'And you worked out the answer to all that, eh – just tossed it off like a martini?'

Allison sniffed. 'You don't have to put it that way . . . Well, it *is* simple and I'm not the only one who's figured it out, although obviously I'm the only one in *this* world . . .'

'Okay,' Larry broke in, 'I'll hold back objections until you've told me how you did it.'

'Thank you, darling,' she said. 'You see, you *are* understanding – even if you don't agree with me right off the bat . . . Well, that would get tiresome, I'm sure. It's much more fun if I have to work to convince you . . . Oh, don't get impatient, I'll come to the point.'

'Thank you,' he said.

'It's simple, like the egg-trick, once you know the angle. The reason why both the benevolent Creator *and* the "Best of All Possible Worlds" theory seem to bog down is because we start out with an unjustified assumption – that this is the *only* world. But suppose we try a different approach: assume a Creator of infinite power; surely, such a being would be capable of creating infinite worlds . . . or at least, so large a number of them to seem infinite to us.

'If you assume *that*, then everything else makes sense. The Creator set forces into motion; He created separate worlds for every single human being in existence; each one exists for that human being alone. He's an artist, but He uses an economy of means, so that there's much duplication of themes and events and motives throughout the worlds.'

'Oh,' Larry replied softly, 'now I begin to see what you're driving at. In some worlds, Napoleon won the battle of Waterloo – although only in his own world did *everything* work out just right for him; in this one he had to lose . . .'

'I'm not sure Napoleon ever existed in my world,' Allison said thoughtfully. 'I think he's just a name in the records, although some such person did exist in other worlds. In my world, Hitler was defeated, Roosevelt died – I'd be sorry about that, only I didn't know him, and he wasn't very real, anyway; they were both just images carried over from other people's worlds . . .'

'All right,' he said. 'And everything worked out wonderfully for you, all your life, huh? You were never really sick, or hurt, or hungry . . .'

'That's about it,' she agreed. 'I've had some hurts and frustrations, but nothing really . . . well, really crippling. And every one has been important toward getting something I really wanted, or getting to understand something important. You see, Larry, the logic is perfect; I deduced it all from the evidence. There's no other answer that will stand up.'

Larry smiled. 'What does it matter what I think? You're not going to change your mind.'

* * *

Larry gazed at the building in sick disgust. 'That's a house?' he muttered at last.

Allison's eyes danced with happiness as she looked up at the great mansion. 'What, darling? What did you say?'

The house was immense – and super-modern, like a pastry-cook's nightmare. Great columns reared up, connected by sloping beams and buttresses. The rooms were set one on top of each other like shoe-boxes, each at its own angle. The whole building was finished in some kind of bright metal shingle, a frightening butter-yellow. In the morning sun the house blazed and sparkled.

'What are – those?' Larry indicated some forlorn plants snaking up the irregular sides of the house. 'Are those supposed to be there?'

Allison blinked, frowning a little. 'What did you say, darling? You mean the bougainvillaea? That's a very exotic plant. It comes from the South Pacific.'

'What's it do? Hold the house together?'

Allison's smile vanished. She raised her eyebrow. 'Darling, are you feeling all right? Is there anything the matter?'

Larry moved back toward the car. 'Let's go back to town. I'm getting hungry for lunch.'

'All right,' Allison said, watching him oddly. 'All right, we'll go back.'

That night, after dinner, Larry seemed moody and unresponsive. 'Let's go to the *Wind-Up*,' he said suddenly. 'I feel like seeing something familiar, for a change.'

'What do you mean?'

Larry nodded at the expensive restaurant they had just left. 'All those fancy lights. And little people in uniforms whispering in your ear. In French.'

'If you expect to order food you should know some French,' Allison stated. Her face twisted into an angry pout. 'Larry, I'm beginning to wonder about you. The way you acted out at the house. The strange things you said.'

Larry shrugged. 'The sight of it drove me temporarily insane.'

'Well, I certainly hope you recover.'

'I'm recovering each minute.'

They came to the *Wind-Up*. Allison started to go inside. Larry stopped for a moment, lighting a cigarette. The good old *Wind-Up*; he felt better already, just standing in front of it. Warm, dark, noisy, the sound of the ragged dixieland combo in the background –

His spirits returned. The peace and contentment of a good run-down bar. He sighed, pushing the door open.

And stopped, stricken.

The *Wind-Up* had changed. It was well-lit. Instead of Max the waiter, there were waitresses in neat white uniforms bustling around. The place was full of well-dressed women, sipping cocktails and chatting. And in the rear was an imitation gypsy orchestra, with a long-haired churl in fake costume, torturing a violin.

Allison turned around. 'Come on!' she snapped impatiently. 'You're attracting attention, standing there in the door.'

Larry gazed for a long time at the imitation gypsy orchestra; at the bustling waitresses; the chatting ladies; the recessed neon lighting. Numbness crept over him. He sagged.

'What's the matter?' Allison caught his arm crossly. 'What's the matter with you?'

'What – what happened?' Larry waved his hand feebly at the interior. 'There been an accident?'

'Oh, this. I forgot to tell you. I spoke to Mr O'Mallery about it. Just before I met you last night.'

'Mr O'Mallery?'

'He owns this building. He's an old friend of mine. I pointed out how – how *dirty* and unattractive his little place was getting. I pointed out what a few improvements would do.'

Larry made his way outside, onto the sidewalk. He ground his cigarette out with his heel and shoved his hands in his pockets.

Allison hurried after him, her cheeks red with indignation. 'Larry! Where are you going?'

'Goodnight.'

'Goodnight?' She stared at him in astonishment. 'What do you mean?'

'I'm going.'

'Going where?'

'Out. Home. To the park. Anywhere.' Larry started off down the sidewalk, hunched over, hands in his pockets.

Allison caught up with him, stepping angrily in front of him. 'Have you gone out of your mind? Do you know what you're saying?'

'Sure. I'm leaving you; we're splitting up. Well, it was nice. See you sometime.'

The two spots in Allison's cheeks glowed like two red coals. 'Just a minute, Mr Brewster. I think you've forgotten something.' Her voice was hard and brittle.

'Forgotten something? Like what?'

'You *can't* leave; you can't walk out on me.'

Larry raised an eyebrow. 'I can't?'

'I think you better reconsider, while you still have time.'

'I don't get your drift.' Larry yawned. 'I think I'll go home to my three room apartment and go to bed. I'm tired.' He started past her.

'Have you forgotten?' Allison snapped. 'Have you forgotten that you're not *completely real*? That you exist only as a part of my world?'

'Lord! Are you going to start *that* again?'

'Better think about it before you walk off. You exist for my benefit, Mr Brewster. This is *my* world; remember that. Maybe in your own world things are different, but this is *my* world. And in my world things do as *I* say.'

'So long,' Larry Brewster said.

'You're – you're still leaving?'

Slowly, Larry Brewster shook his head. 'No,' he said. 'No, as a matter of fact, I'm not; I've changed my mind. You're too much trouble. *You're leaving.*'

And as he spoke a ball of radiant light gently settled over Allison Holmes, engulfing her in a glowing aura of splendor. The ball of light lifted, carrying Miss Holmes up into the air, raising her effortlessly above the level of the buildings, into the evening sky.

Larry Brewster watched calmly, as the ball of light carried Miss Holmes off. He was not surprised to see her gradually fade and grow indistinct – until all at once there was nothing.

Nothing but a faint shimmer in the sky. Allison Holmes was gone.

For a long time Larry Brewster stood, deep in thought, rubbing his jaw reflectively. He would miss Allison Holmes. In some ways he had liked her; for a while, she had been fun. Well, she was off now. In this world, Allison Holmes had not been completely real. What he had known, what Larry had called 'Allison Holmes,' wasn't any more than a partial appearance of her.

Then he paused, remembering: as the ball of radiant light had carried her away, he had seen a glimpse – a glimpse past her into a different world, one which was obviously *her* world, her real world, the world she wanted. The buildings were uncomfortably familiar; he could still remember the house . . .

Then – Allison had been real, after all – existing in Larry's world, until the time came for her to be transported to hers. Would she find another Larry Brewster there – one who saw eye-to-eye with her? He shuddered at the thought.

In fact, the whole experience had been somewhat unnerving.

'I wonder why,' he murmured softly. He thought back to other unpleasant events, remembering how they had led him to greater satisfactions for their having happened – richness of experience he could not have appreciated without them. 'Ah well,' he sighed, 'it's all for the best.'

He started to walk home slowly, hands in his pockets, glancing up at the sky every now and then, as if for confirmation . . .

A Surface Raid

Harl left the third level, catching a tube car going North. The tube car carried him swiftly through one of the big junction bubbles and down to the fifth level. Harl caught an exciting, fugitive glimpse of people and outlets, a complex tangle of mid-period business and milling confusion.

Then the bubble was behind him and he was nearing his destination, the vast industrial fifth level, sprawling below everything else like some gigantic, soot-encrusted octopus of the night's misrule.

The gleaming tube car ejected him and continued on its way, disappearing down the tube. Harl bounded agilely into the receiving strip and slowed to a stop, still on his feet, swaying expertly back and forth.

A few minutes later he reached the entrance to his father's office. Harl raised his hand and the code door slid back. He entered, his heart thumping with excitement. The time had come.

Edward Boynton was in the planning department studying the outline for a new robot bore when he was informed that his son had entered the main office.

'I'll be right back,' Boynton said, making his way past his policy staff and up the ramp into the office.

'Hello, Dad,' Harl exclaimed, squaring his shoulders. Father and son exchanged handclasps. Then Harl sat down slowly. 'How are things?' he asked. 'I guess you expected me.'

Then Edward Boynton seated himself behind his desk. 'What do you want here?' he demanded. 'You know I'm busy.'

Harl smiled thinly across at his father. In his brown industrial-planner uniform, Edward Boynton towered above his young son, a massive man with broad shoulders and thick blond hair. His blue eyes were cold and hard as he returned the young man's level gaze.

'I happened to come into some information.' Harl glanced uneasily around the room. 'Your office isn't tapped, is it?'

'Of course not,' the elder Boynton assured him.

'No screens or ears?' Harl relaxed a little. 'I've learned that you and several others from your department are going up to the surface soon.' Harl leaned eagerly toward his father. 'Up to the surface – on a raid for saps.'

Ed Boynton's face darkened. 'Where did you hear that?' He gazed intently at his son. 'Did anyone in this department – ?'

'No,' Harl said quickly. 'No one informed. I picked up the information on my own, in connection with my educational activities.'

Ed Boynton began to understand. 'I see. You were experimenting with channel taps, cutting across the confidential channels. Like they teach you to do in communications.'

'That's right. I happened to pick up a conversation between you and Robin Turner concerning the raid.'

The atmosphere in the room became easier, more friendly. Ed Boynton relaxed, settling back in his chair. 'Go on,' he urged.

'It was mere chance. I had cut across ten or twelve channels, holding each one for only a second. I was using the Youth League equipment. All at once I recognized your voice. So I stayed on and caught the whole conversation.'

'Then you heard most of it.'

Harl nodded. 'Exactly when are you going up, Dad? Have you set an exact date?'

Ed Boynton frowned. 'No,' he said, 'I haven't. But it will be sometime this week. Almost everything is arranged.'

'How many are going?' Harl asked.

'We're taking up one mother ship and about thirty eggs. All from this department.'

'Thirty eggs? Sixty or seventy men.'

'That's right.' Ed Boynton stared intently at his son. 'It won't be a big raid. Nothing compared to some of the Directorate raids of the past few years.'

'But big enough for a single department.'

Ed Boynton's eyes flickered. 'Be careful, Harl. If such loose talk should get out – '

'I know. I cut the recorder off as soon as I picked up the drift of your talk. I know what would happen if the Directorate found out a department was raiding without authorization – for its own factories.'

'Do you really know? I wonder.'

'One mother ship and thirty eggs,' Harl exclaimed, ignoring the remark. 'You'll be on the surface for about forty hours?'

'About. It depends on what luck we have.'

'How many saps are you after?'

'We need at least two dozen,' the elder Boynton replied.

'Males?'

'For the most part. A few females, but males primarily.'

'For the basic-industry factory units, I assume.' Harl straightened in his chair. 'All right, then. Now that I know more about the raid itself I can get down to business.'

He stared hard at his father.

'Business?' Boynton glanced up sharply. 'Precisely what do you mean?'

'My exact reason for coming down here.' Harl leaned across the desk toward his father, his voice clipped and intense. 'I'm going along with you on the raid. I want to go along – to get some saps for myself.'

For a moment there was an astonished silence. Then Ed Boynton laughed. 'What are you talking about? What do *you* know about saps?'

The inner door slid back, and Robin Turner came quickly into the office. He joined Boynton behind the desk.

'He can't go,' Turner said flatly. 'It would increase the risks tenfold.'

Harl glanced up. 'There *was* an ear in here, then.'

'Of course. Turner always listens in.' Ed Boynton nodded, regarding his son thoughtfully. 'Why do you want to go along?'

'That's my concern,' Harl said, his lips tightening.

Turner rasped: 'Emotional immaturity. A sub-rational adolescent craving for adventure and excitement. There's still a few like him who can't throw the old brain completely off. After two hundred years you'd think – '

'Is that it?' Boynton demanded. 'You have some non-adult desire to go up and see the surface?'

'Perhaps,' Harl admitted, flushing a little.

'You can't come,' Ed Boynton stated emphatically. 'It's far too dangerous. We're not going up there for romantic adventure. It's a job – a grim, hard, exacting job. The saps are getting wary. It's becoming more and more difficult to bring back a full load. We can't spare any of our eggs for whatever romantic foolishness – '

'I know it's getting hard,' Harl interrupted. 'You don't have to convince me that it's almost impossible to round up a whole load.' Harl looked up defiantly at Turner and his father. He chose his words carefully. 'And I know that's why the Directorate considers private raids a major crime against the State.'

Silence.

Finally, Ed Boynton sighed, a reluctant admiration in his stare. He looked his son slowly up and down. 'Okay, Harl,' he said. 'You win.'

Turner said nothing. His face was hard.

Harl got quickly to his feet. 'Then it's all settled. I'll return to my quarters and get prepared. As soon as you're ready to go, notify me at once. I'll join you at the launching stage on the first level.'

The elder Boynton shook his head. 'We're not leaving from the first level. It would be too risky.' His voice was heavy. 'There are too many Directorate guards prowling around. We have the ship down here at fifth level, in one of the warehouses.'

'Where shall I meet you, then?'

Ed Boynton stood up slowly. 'We'll notify you, Harl. It will be soon, I promise you. In a couple of periods, at the most. Be at our vocational quarters.'

'The surface is completely cool, isn't it?' Harl asked. 'There aren't any radioactive areas left?'

'It's been cool for fifty years,' his father assured him.

'Then I won't have to worry about a radiation shield,' Harl said. 'One more thing, Dad. What language will we have to use? Can we speak our regular – '

Ed Boynton shook his head. 'No. The saps never mastered

any of the rational semantic systems. We'll have to revert to the old traditional forms.'

Harl's face fell. 'I don't know any of the traditional forms. They're not being taught anymore.'

Ed Boynton shrugged. 'It doesn't matter.'

'How about their defenses? What sort of weapons should I bring? Will a screen and blast rifle be sufficient?'

'Only the screen is of vital importance,' the elder Boynton said. 'When the saps see us they scatter in all directions. One look at us and off they go.'

'Fine,' Harl said. 'I'll have my screen checked over.' He moved toward the door. 'I'll go back up to the third level. I'll be expecting your signal. I'll have my equipment ready.'

'All right,' Ed Boynton said.

The two men watched the door slide shut after the youth.

'Quite a boy,' Turner muttered.

'Turning out to be something, after all,' Ed Boynton murmured. 'He'll go a long way.' He rubbed his jaw thoughtfully. 'But I wonder how he'll act up on the surface during the raid.'

Harl met with his group leader on the third level, an hour after he left his father's office.

'Then it's all settled?' Fashold asked, looking up from his report spools.

'All settled. They're going to signal me as soon as the ship is ready.'

'By the way.' Fashold put down the spools, pushing the scanner back. 'I've learned something about the saps. As a YL leader I have access to the Directorate files. I've learned something virtually no one else knows.'

'What is it?' asked Harl.

'Harl, the saps are related to us. They're a different species, but they're very closely related to us.'

'Go on,' Harl urged.

'At one time there was only the one species – the saps. Their full name is *homo sapiens*. We grew out of them, developed from them. We're biogenetic mutants. The change occurred during the Third World War, two and a half centuries ago. Up to that time there had never been any *technos*.'

'*Technos?*'

Fashold smiled. 'That's what they called us at first. When they thought of us only as a separate class, and not as a distinct race. *Technos*. That was their name for *us*. That was how they always referred to us.'

'But why? It's a strange name. Why *technos*, Fashold?'

'Because the first mutants appeared among the technocratic classes and gradually spread throughout all other educated classes. They appeared among scientists, scholars, field workers, trained groups, all the various specialized classes.'

'And the saps didn't realize – '

'They thought of us only as a class, as I've just told you. That was during the Third World War and after. It was during the Final War that we fully emerged as recognizably and profoundly different. It became evident that we weren't just another specialized offshoot of *homo sapiens*. Not just another class of men more educated than the rest, with higher intellectual capacities.'

Fashold gazed off into the distance. 'During the Final War we emerged and showed ourselves for what we really were – a superior species supplanting *homo sapiens* in the same way that *homo sapiens* had supplanted Neanderthal man.'

Harl considered what Fashold had said. 'I didn't realize we were so closely related to them. I had no idea we had emerged so lately.'

Fashold nodded. 'It was only two centuries ago, during the war that ravaged the surface of the planet. Most of us were working down in the big underground laboratories and factories under the different mountain ranges – the Urals, the Alps, and the Rockies. We were down underground, under miles of rock and dirt and clay. And on the surface *homo sapiens* slugged it out with the weapons we designed.'

'I'm beginning to understand. We designed the weapons for them to fight the war. They used our weapons without realizing – '

'We designed them and the saps used them to destroy themselves,' Fashold interjected. 'It was Nature's crucible, the elimination of one species and the emergence of another. We gave them the weapons and they destroyed themselves. When the war ended the surface was fused, and nothing but ash and hydroglass and radioactive clouds remained.

'We sent out scouting parties from our underground labs and found nothing but a silent, barren waste. It had been accomplished. They were gone, wiped out. And we had come to take their place.'

'Not all of them could have been wiped out,' Harl pointed out. 'There still a lot of them up there on the surface.'

'True,' Fashold admitted. 'Some survived. Scattered remnants here and there. Gradually, as the surface cooled, they began to reform again, getting together and building little villages and huts. Yes, and even clearing some of the land – planting and growing things. But they're still remnants of a dying race now almost extinct, as the Neanderthal is extinct.'

'So nothing exists now but males and females without homes.'

'There are a few villages here and there – wherever they've managed to clear the surface. But they've descended to utter savagery, and live like animals, wearing skins and hunting with rocks and spears. They've become almost bestial remnants who offer no organized resistance when we go up to raid a few of their villages for our factories.'

'Then we – ' Harl broke off abruptly as a faint bell sounded. He turned in startled apprehension, snapping on the vidphone.

His father's face formed on the screen, hard and stern. 'Okay, Harl,' he said. 'We're ready.'

'So soon? But – '

'We set the time ahead. Come down to my office.' The image on the screen dimmed and vanished.

Harl did not move.

'They must have got worried,' Fashold said, grinning. 'They were apparently afraid you'd pass the information along.'

'I'm all ready,' Harl said. He picked up his blast gun from the table. 'How do I look?'

In his silver communications uniform Harl looked splendid and impressive. He had put on heavy military boots and gloves. In one hand he gripped his blast gun. Around his waist was his screen control-belt.

'What's that?' Fashold asked, as Harl lowered black goggles over his eyes.

'These? Oh, they're for the sun.'

'Of course – the sun. I forgot.'

Harl cradled his gun, balancing it expertly. 'The sun would
blind me. The goggles protect my eyes. I'll be safe up there,
with my screen and gun, and these goggles.'

'I hope so.' Still grinning, Fashold thumped him on the back
as he moved toward the door. 'Bring back a lot of saps. Do a
good job – and don't forget to include a female!'

The mother ship moved slowly from the warehouse, and out
onto the lift stage, a rotund black teardrop emerging from
storage. Its port locks slid back, and ramps climbed to meet the
locks. Immediately supplies and equipment were on their way
up, rising into the bowels of the ship.

'Almost ready,' Turner said, his face twitching with nervous-
ness as he gazed through the observation windows at the
loading ramps outside. 'I hope nothing goes wrong. If the
Directorate should find out – '

'Quit worrying!' Ed Boynton ordered. 'You picked the wrong
time to let your thalamic impulses take over control.'

'Sorry.' Turner tightened his lips and moved away from the
windows. The lift stage was ready to rise.

'Let's get started,' Boynton urged. 'Have you men from the
department at each level?'

'Nobody but department members will be near the stage,'
Turner replied.

'Where is the balance of the crew?' Boynton demanded.

'At the first level. I sent them up during the day.'

'Very well.' Boynton gave the signal, and the stage under the
ship began slowly to rise, lifting them steadily toward the level
above.

Harl peered out the observation windows, watching the fifth
level drop below and the fourth level, the vast commercial
center of the under-surface system, come into view.

'Won't be long,' Ed Boynton said, as the fourth level glided
past. 'So far so good.'

'Where will we finally emerge?' Harl asked.

'In the latter stages of the war our various underground
structures were connected by tunnels. That original network
formed the basis of our present system. We'll emerge at one of

the original entrances, located in the mountain range called "The Alps".'

'The Alps,' Harl murmured.

'Yes, in Europe. We have maps of the surface, showing locations of sap villages in that region. A whole cluster of villages lie to the North and North East in what used to be Denmark and Germany. We've never raided there before. The saps have managed to clear the slag away from several thousand acres in that region, and seem gradually to be reclaiming most of Europe.'

'But why, Dad?' Harl asked.

Ed Boynton shrugged. 'I don't know. They don't seem to have set themselves any organized objective. They show no signs at all, in fact, of emerging from their savage state. All their traditions were lost – books and records, inventions, and techniques. If you ask me – ' He broke off abruptly. 'Here comes the third level. We're almost there.'

The huge mother ship roared slowly along, gliding above the surface of the planet. Harl peered out, awed by what he saw below.

Across the surface of the earth lay a crust of slag, an endless coating of blackened rock. The mineral deposit was unbroken except for occasional hills sharply jutting up, ash-covered, and with a few sparse bushes growing near their tops. Great sheets of sun-darkening ash drifted across the sky, but nothing living stirred. The surface of the earth was dead and barren, without sign of life.

'Is it all like that?' Harl asked.

Ed Boynton shook his head. 'Not all. The saps have reclaimed some of the land.' He gripped his son's arm and pointed. 'See off that way? They've done quite a bit of clearing up there.'

'Just how do they clear the slag?' Harl asked.

'It's hard,' his father replied. 'Fused, like volcanic glass – hydroglass – from the hydrogen bombs. They pick it away bit by bit, year after year. With their hands, with rocks, and with the axes made from the glass itself.'

'Why don't they develop better tools?'

Ed Boynton grinned wryly. 'You know the answer to that.

We made most of their tools for them, their tools and weapons and inventions, for hundreds of years.'

'Here we go,' Turner said. 'We're landing.'

The ship settled down, coming to rest on the surface of the slag. For a moment the blackened rock rumbled under them. Then there was silence.

'We're down,' Turner said.

Ed Boynton studied the surface map, sending it darting through the scanner. 'We'll send out ten eggs as a starter. If we don't have much luck here we'll take the ship farther North. But we should do well. This area has never been raided before.'

'How will the eggs cover?' Turner asked.

'The eggs will fan out in a spectrum, giving each egg a separate area. Our egg will move over toward the right. If we have any success, we'll return to the ship at once. Otherwise, we'll stay out until nightfall.'

'Nightfall?' Harl asked.

Ed Boynton smiled. 'Until dark. Until this side of the planet is turned away from the sun.'

'Let's go,' Turner said impatiently.

The port locks opened. The first eggs scooted out onto the slag, their treads digging into the slippery surface. One by one they emerged from the black hull of the mother ship, tiny spheres with their backs tapering into jet tubes, and their noses blunted into control turrets. They roared off across the slag and disappeared.

'Ours, next,' Ed Boynton said.

Harl nodded and gripped his blast rifle tightly. He lowered his protection goggles over his eyes, and Turner and Boynton did the same. They entered their egg, Boynton seating himself behind the controls.

A moment later they shot out of the ship onto the smooth surface of the planet.

Harl peered out. He could see nothing but slag on all sides. Slag and drifting clouds of ash.

'It's dismal,' he murmured. 'Even with the goggles the sun burns my eyes.'

'Don't look at it then,' Ed Boynton cautioned. 'Look away from it.'

'I can't help it. It's so – so strange.'

Ed Boynton grunted and increased the egg's speed. Far ahead of them something was coming into view. He headed the egg toward it.

'What's that?' Turner asked, alarmed.

'Trees,' Boynton said, reassuringly. 'Trees growing up in a clump. It marks the end of the slag. Then there's ash for a while, and finally fields the saps have planted.'

Boynton drove the egg to the edge of the slag area. He stopped it where the slag ended and the clump of trees began, snapping off the jets and locking the treads. He and Harl and Turner got out cautiously, their guns ready.

Nothing stirred. There was only silence, and the endless surface of slag. Between drifting clouds of ash the sky was a pale robin's-egg blue, and a few moisture clouds drifted with the ash. The air smelled good. It was thin and crisp, and the sun shed a friendly warmth.

'Put your screens on,' Ed Boynton warned. As he spoke he snapped the switch at his belt and his own screen hummed, flashing on around him. Swiftly, Boynton's figure dimmed, wavering and fading. It winked out – and was gone.

Turner quickly followed suit. 'Okay,' his voice came, from a glimmering oval to Harl's right. 'You next.'

Harl turned on his screen. For an instant a strange cold fire enveloped him from head to foot, bathing him in sparks. Then his body too dimmed and vanished. The screens were functioning perfectly.

In Harl's ears a faint clicking sounded, warning him of the presence of the two others. 'I can hear you,' Harl said. 'Your screens are in my earphones.'

'Don't wander off,' Ed Boynton cautioned. 'Keep by us and listen for the clicks. It's dangerous to be separated, up here on the surface.'

Harl advanced carefully. The other two were on his right, a few yards off. They were crossing a dry yellow field overgrown with some kind of plant. The plants had long stalks that broke and crunched underfoot. Behind Harl was a trail of broken vegetation. He could clearly see the similar trails which Turner and his father were leaving.

But now it became necessary for him to separate from Turner and his father. Ahead of Harl the outline of a sap village rose up, its huts fashioned from some kind of plant fiber piled in heaps on top of wooden frames. He could see the shadowy outlines of animals tied to the huts. Trees and plants encircled the village, and he could distinguish the moving forms of people, and hear their voices.

People – saps. His heart beat quickly. With luck he might capture and bring back three or four for the Youth League. He felt suddenly confident and unafraid. Surely it would not be difficult. Planted fields, tied-up animals, rickety huts leaning and tilting –

The smell of dung commingling with the heat of the late afternoon became almost intolerable as Harl advanced. Cries, and other sounds of feverish human activity, drifted to him. The ground was flat and dry, weeds and plants grew up everywhere. He left the yellow field and came onto a narrow footpath, littered with human refuse and animal dung.

And just beyond the road was the village.

The clicks had diminished in his earphones. Now they died out completely. Harl grinned to himself. He had moved away from Turner and Boynton, and was no longer in contact with them. They had no idea where he was.

He turned to the left, circling cautiously around the edge of the village. He passed by a hut, then several in a cluster. Around him green trees and plants grew in great clumps, and directly ahead of him gleamed a narrow stream with sloping, moss-covered banks.

A dozen people were washing at the edge of the stream, the children leaping into the water and scrambling up on the bank.

Harl halted, gazing at them in astonishment. Their skins were dark, almost black. A shiny, coppery black it was – a rich bronze mixed in with the dirt-color. *Was* it dirt?

He suddenly realized that the bathers had been burned black by the constant sun. The hydrogen explosions had thinned the atmosphere, searing off most of the layer of moisture clouds and for two hundred years the sun had beat mercilessly down on them – in sharp contrast to his own race. Under-surface, there was no ultraviolet light to burn the skin, or to raise the pigment level. He and the other *technos* had lost their skin color. There was no need for it in their subterranean world.

But the bathers were incredibly dark, a rich reddish-black color. And they had nothing on at all. They were leaping and jumping eagerly about, splashing through the water and sunning themselves on the bank.

Harl watched them for a time. Children and three or four scrawny, elderly females. Would they do? He shook his head, and warily encircled the stream.

He continued on back among the huts, walking slowly and carefully, gazing alertly around with his gun held ready.

A faint breeze blew against him, rustling through the trees to his right. The sounds of the bathing children mixed with the dung smell, the wind, and the swaying of the trees.

Harl advanced cautiously. He was invisible, but he knew that he might at any moment be discovered and tracked down by his footprints or the sounds he might make. And if someone ran against him –

He stealthily darted past a hut, and emerged into an open place, a flat area of beaten earth. In the shade of the hut a dog lay sleeping with flies crawling over its lean flanks. An old woman was sitting on the porch of the rude dwelling, combing her long gray hair with a bone comb.

Harl passed by her cautiously. In the center of the open place a group of young men were standing. They were gesturing and talking together. Some were cleaning their weapons, long spears and knives of an inconceivable primitiveness. On the ground lay a dead animal, a huge beast with long, gleaming tusks and a thick hide. Blood oozed from its mouth – thick, dark blood. One of the young men turned suddenly – and kicked it with his foot.

Harl came up to the young men, and stopped. They were dressed in cloth clothing, long leg garments and shirts. Their feet were bare on top, for they wore loosely-woven vegetable-fiber sandals instead of shoes. They were clean-shaven, but their skin gleamed almost ebony black. Their sleeves were rolled up, exposing bulging, glistening muscles, dripping with sweat in the hot sun.

Harl could not understand what they were saying, but he was sure they were speaking one of the archaic traditional tongues.

He passed on. At the other side of the open place a group of old men was sitting cross-legged in a circle, weaving rough cloth on crude frames. Harl watched them in silence for a time. Their chatter drifted noisily up to him. Each old man was bent intently over his frame, his eyes glued on his work.

Beyond the row of huts some younger men and women were plowing a field, dragging the plow by ropes securely attached to their waists and shoulders.

Harl wandered on, fascinated. Everyone was engaged in some kind of activity – except the dog asleep under the hut. The young men with their spears, the old woman in front of the hut combing her hair, and weaving.

In one corner a huge woman was teaching a child what appeared to be an adding and subtracting game, using small sticks in lieu of figures. Two men were removing the hide from a small furred animal, stripping the pelt off carefully.

Harl passed a wall of hides, all hung up carefully to dry. The dull stench irritated his nostrils, making him want to sneeze. He passed a group of children pounding grain in a hollowed-out stone, beating the grain into meal. None of them looked up as he passed.

Some animals were tied together in a bunch. Some lay in the shade, big beasts with huge udders. They watched him silently.

Harl came to the edge of the village and stopped. From that point onward deserted fields stretched out. For perhaps a mile beyond the fields were trees and bushes, and beyond that the endless miles of slag.

He turned and walked back. Off to one side, sitting in the shade, a young man was chipping away at a block of hydroslag, cutting it carefully with a few rough tools. He seemed to be fashioning a weapon. Harl watched him, watched the endless, solemn blows descending again and again. The slag was hard. It was a long tedious job.

He walked on. A group of women were mending broken arrows. Their chatter followed him for a time, and he found himself wishing he could understand it. Everyone was busy, working rapidly. Dark, shiny arms rose and fell, and the chattering murmur of voices drifted back and forth.

Activity. Laughter. A child's laughter echoed suddenly through the village, and a few heads turned. Harl bent down, intently studying a man's head at close range.

A strong face he had. His twisted knotted hair was short, and his teeth were even and white. On his arms were copper bracelets, almost matching the rich bronze hue of his skin. His bare chest was marked with tattoos, etched into his flesh with brightly colored pigments.

Harl wandered back the way he had come. He passed the old woman on the porch, and paused again to observe her. She had stopped combing her hair. Now she was fixing a child's hair, braiding it skillfully back into an elaborate pattern. Harl watched her, fascinated. The pattern was intricate, complex, and the task took a long time. The old woman's faded eyes were intent on the child's hair, on the detailed work. Her withered hands flew.

Harl walked on, moving toward the stream. He passed the bathing children again. They had all climbed out on the bank and were drying themselves in the sun. So these were the *saps*. The race that was dying out – the dying race, soon to be extinct. Remnants.

But they did not appear to be a dying race. They were working hard, tirelessly chipping at the hydroslag, fixing their arrows, hunting, plowing, pounding grain, weaving, combing –

He stopped suddenly, rigid, his blast gun at his shoulder. Ahead of him, through the trees by the stream, something moved. Then he heard two voices – a man's voice and a woman's voice, raised in excited conversation.

Harl advanced cautiously. He pushed past a flowering bush, and peered into the gloom between the trees.

A man and woman were sitting at the edge of the water, in the dark shadow of the tree. The man was making bowls, shaping them out of wet clay scooped up from the water. His fingers flew, expertly, rapidly. He spun the bowls, turning them on a revolving platform between his knees.

As the man finished the bowls the woman took them and

painted them with deft, vigorous strokes of a crude brush gleaming with red pigment.

The woman was beautiful. Harl gazed down at her in stunned admiration. She sat almost motionless, resting against a tree, holding each bowl securely as she painted it. Her black hair hung down to her waist, falling across her shoulders and back. Her features were finely cut, each line clear and vivid, her dark eyes immense. She studied each bowl intently, her lips moving a little and Harl noticed that her hands were small and delicately fashioned.

He walked over toward her, moving carefully. The woman did not hear him or look up. In growing wonder he realized that her coppery body was small and beautifully formed, her limbs slender and supple. She did not seem to be aware of him.

Suddenly the man spoke again. The woman glanced up, lowering the bowl to the ground. She rested a minute, cleaning her brush with a leaf. She wore rough leg garments, reaching down to her knees, and tied at her waist with a twisted flaxen rope. She wore no other garment. Her feet and shoulders were bare, and in the afternoon sun her bosom rose and fell quickly as she breathed.

The man said something else. After a moment the woman picked up another bowl and began to paint again. The two of them worked rapidly, silently, both intent on their work.

Harl studied the bowls. They were all of similar design. The man made them rapidly, building them up from coils of clay, and then snaking the coils around and around, higher and higher. He slapped water against the clay, rubbing the surface smooth and firm. Finally he laid them out in rows, to dry in the sun.

The woman selected the bowls that were dry and then painted them.

Harl watched her. He studied her a long time – the way she moved her coppery body, the intense expression on her face, the faint movement of her lips and chin. Her fingers were slender and exquisitely tapered. Her nails were long, coming finally to a point. She held each bowl carefully, turning it with expert care, painting her design with rapid strokes.

He watched her closely. She was painting the same design on

each bowl, painting it again and again. A bird, and then a tree. A line that appeared to represent the ground. A cloud suspended directly above it.

What was the precise significance of that recurrent motif? Harl bent closer, peering intently. Was it really the same? He watched the skillful motion of her hands as she took bowl after bowl, starting the design again and again. The design was basically the same – but each time she made it a little different. No two bowls came out exactly the same.

He was both puzzled, and fascinated. It was the same design, but altered slightly each time. The color of the bird would be altered – or the length of its plume. Less frequently the position of the tree, or the cloud. Once she painted two tiny clouds hovering above the ground. Sometimes she put grass and the outline of hills in the background.

Suddenly the man got to his feet, wiping his hands on his cloth. He spoke to the girl and then hurried off, threading his way through the bushes until he was lost to view.

Harl glanced around excitedly. The girl went right on painting rapidly, calmly. The man had disappeared and the girl remained alone, painting quietly by herself.

Harl was caught in the grip of conflicting and almost overpowering emotions. He wanted to speak to the girl, to ask her about her painting, her design. He wanted to ask her why she changed it each time.

He wanted to sit down and talk to her. To speak to her and hear her talk to him. It was strange. He didn't understand it himself. His vision swam, twisting and blurring, and sweat dripped from his neck and stooping shoulders. The girl continued to paint. She did not look up, or suspect that he was standing directly in front of her. Harl's hand flew to his belt. He took a deep breath, hesitating. Dared he? Should he? The man would be back –

Harl pressed the stud on his belt. Around him the screen hissed, and sparked.

The girl glanced up, startled. Her eyes widened in swift horror.

She screamed.

Harl stepped quickly back, gripping his gun, appalled by what he had done.

The girl scrambled to her feet, sending bowls and paints flying. She gazed at him, her eyes still wide, her mouth open. Slowly she backed away toward the bushes. Then abruptly she turned and fled, crashing through the shrubbery, screaming and shrieking.

Harl straightened in sudden fear. Quickly, he restored his screen. The village was alive with growing sound. He could hear voices raised in excited panic, and the sound of people running, crashing through the bushes – the entire village erupting in a torrent of excited activity.

Harl made his way quickly down the stream, past the bushes and out into the open.

Suddenly he stopped, his heart pounding furiously. A crowd of saps was hurrying toward the stream – men with spears, old women, and shrieking children. At the edge of the bushes they stopped, staring and listening, their faces frozen in a strange, intent expression. Then they were advancing into the bushes, furiously pushing the branches out of the way – *searching for him.*

Abruptly his earphones clicked.

'Harl!' Ed Boynton's voice came clear and sharp. 'Harl, lad!'

Harl jumped, then cried out in desperate gratefulness. 'Dad, I'm here.'

Ed Boynton gripped his arm, yanking him off balance. 'What's the matter with you? Where did you go? What did you do?'

'You got him?' Turner's voice broke in. 'Come on then – both of you! We have to get out of here, fast. They're scattering white powder everywhere.'

Saps were rushing around, throwing the powder into the air in great clouds. It drifted through the air, settling down over everything. It appeared to be a kind of pulverized chalk. Other saps were sprinkling oil from big jars and shouting in high-pitched excitement.

'We better get out,' Boynton agreed grimly. 'We don't want to tangle with them when they're aroused.'

Harl hesitated. 'But – '

'Come on!' his father urged, tugging at his arm. 'Let's go. We haven't a moment to lose.'

Harl gazed back. He could not see the woman, but saps were running everywhere, throwing their sheets of chalk and sprinkling the oil. Saps with iron-tipped spears advanced ominously, kicking at the weeds and bushes as they circled about.

Harl allowed himself to be led by his father. His mind whirled. The woman was gone, and he was sure that he would never see her again. When he had made himself visible she had screamed, and run off.

Why? It didn't make sense. Why had she recoiled from him in blind terror? What had he done?

And what did it matter to him whether he saw her again or not? Why was she important? He did not understand. He did not understand *himself*. There was no rational explanation for what had happened. It was totally incomprehensible.

Harl followed his father and Turner back to the egg, still bewildered and wretched, still trying to understand, to grasp the meaning of what had happened between him and the woman. It did not make sense. He had gone out of his mind and then she had gone out of *her* mind. There had to be some meaning to it – if he could only grasp it.

At the egg Ed Boynton halted, glancing back. 'We were lucky to get away,' he said to Harl, shaking his head. 'When they're aroused they're like beasts. They're animals, Harl. That's what they are. Savage animals.'

'Come on,' Turner said impatiently. 'Let's get out of here – while we still can walk.'

Julie continued to shudder even after she had been carefully bathed and purified in the stream and rubbed down with oil by one of the older women.

She sat in a heap, her arms wrapped around her knees, shaking and trembling uncontrollably. Ken, her brother, stood beside her, grim-faced, his hand on her bare, coppery shoulder.

'What was it?' Julie murmured. 'What was it?' She shuddered. 'It was – horrible. It revolted me, made me ill, just to look at it.'

'What did it look like?' Ken demanded.

'It was – it was like a man. But it couldn't have been a man. It was metallic all over, from head to foot, and it had huge hands and feet. Its face was all pasty white like – like meal. It was – sickly. Hideously sickly. White and metallic, and sickly. Like some kind of root dug up out of the soil.'

Ken turned to the old man sitting behind him, who was listening intently. 'What was it?' he demanded. 'What was it, Mr Stebbins? You know about such things. What did she see?'

Mr Stebbins got slowly to his feet. 'You say it had white skin? Pasty? Like dough? And huge hands and feet?'

Julie nodded. 'And – something else.'

'What?'

'It was *blind*. It had something instead of eyes. Two black spaces. Darkness.' She shuddered and stared toward the stream.

Suddenly Mr Stebbins tensed, his jaw hardening. He nodded. 'I know,' he said. 'I know what it was.'

'What was it?'

Mr Stebbins muttered to himself, frowning. 'It's not possible. But your description – ' He stared off in the distance, his brow wrinkled. 'They live underground,' he said finally, 'under the surface. They emerge from the mountains. They live in the earth, in great tunnels and chambers they have hewn out for themselves. They are not men. They look like men, but they are not. They live under the ground and dig the metal from the earth. They dig and horde the metal. They seldom come up to the surface. They cannot look at the sun.'

'What are they called?' Julie asked.

Mr Stebbins searched his mind, thinking back through the years. Back to the old books and legends he had heard. Things that lived under the ground . . . Like men but not men . . . Things that dug tunnels, that mined metals . . . Things that were blind and had great hands and feet and pasty white skin.

'Goblins,' Mr Stebbins stated. 'What you saw was a goblin.'

Julie nodded, gazing down wide-eyed at the ground, her arms clasped around her knees. 'Yes,' she said. 'That sounds like what it was. It frightened me. I was so afraid. I turned and ran. It seemed so horrible.' She looked up at her brother, smiling a little. 'But I'm better now . . .'

Ken rubbed his big dark hands together, nodding with relief. 'Fine,' he said. 'Now we can get back to work. There's a lot to do. A lot of things to get done.'

Project: Earth

The sound echoed hollowly through the big frame house. It vibrated among the dishes in the kitchen, the gutters along the roof, thumping slowly and evenly like distant thunder. From time to time it ceased, but then it began again, booming through the quiet night, a relentless sound, brutal in its regularity. From the top floor of the big house.

In the bathroom the three children huddled around the chair, nervous and hushed, pushing against each other with curiosity.

'You sure he can't see us?' Tommy rasped.

'How could he see us? Just don't make any noise.' Dave Grant shifted on the chair, his face to the wall. 'Don't talk so loud.' He went on looking, ignoring them both.

'Let me see,' Joan whispered, nudging her brother with a sharp elbow. 'Get out of the way.'

'Shut up.' Dave pushed her back. 'I can see better now.' He turned up the light.

'I want to see,' Tommy said. He pushed Dave off the chair onto the bathroom floor. 'Come on.'

Dave withdrew sullenly. 'It's our house.'

Tommy stepped cautiously up onto the chair. He put his eye to the crack, his face against the wall. For a time he saw nothing. The crack was narrow and the light on the other side was bad. Then, gradually, he began to make out shapes, forms beyond the wall.

Edward Billings was sitting at an immense old-fashioned desk. He had stopped typing and was resting his eyes. From his vest pocket he had taken a round pocket watch. Slowly, carefully, he wound the great watch. Without his glasses his lean, withered face seemed naked and bleak, the features of some elderly bird. Then he put his glasses on again and drew his chair closer to the desk.

He began to type, working with expert fingers the towering mass of metal and parts that reared up before him. Again the ominous booming echoed through the house, resuming its insistent beat.

Mr Billings's room was dark and littered. Books and papers lay everywhere, in piles and stacks, on the desk, on the table, in heaps on the floor. The walls were covered with charts, anatomy charts, maps, astronomy charts, signs of the zodiac. By the windows rows of dust-covered chemical bottles and packages lay stacked. A stuffed bird stood on the top of the bookcase, gray and drooping. On the desk was a huge magnifying glass, Greek and Hebrew dictionaries, a postage stamp box, a bone letter opener. Against the door a curling strip of flypaper moved with the air currents rising from the gas heater.

The remains of a magic lantern lay against one wall. A black satchel with clothes piled on it. Shirts and socks and a long frock coat, faded and threadbare. Heaps of newspapers and magazines, tied with brown cord. A great black umbrella against the table, a pool of sticky water around its metal point. A glass frame of dried butterflies, pressed into yellowing cotton.

And at the desk the huge old man hunched over his ancient typewriter and heaps of notes and papers.

'Gosh,' Tommy said.

Edward Billings was working on his report. The report was open on the desk beside him, an immense book, leather-bound, bulging at its cracked seams. He was transferring material into it from his heaps of notes.

The steady thumping of the great typewriter made the things in the bathroom rattle and shake, the light fixture, the bottles and tubes in the medicine cabinet. Even the floor under the children's feet.

'He's some kind of Communist agent,' Joan said. 'He's drawing maps of the city so he can set off bombs when Moscow gives the word.'

'The heck he is,' Dave said angrily.

'Don't you see all the maps and pencils and papers? Why else would – '

'Be quiet,' Dave snapped. 'He will hear us. He is not a spy. He's too old to be a spy.'

'What is he, then?'

'I don't know. But he isn't a spy. You're sure dumb. Anyhow, spies have beards.'

'Maybe he's a criminal,' Joan said.

'I talked to him once,' Dave said. 'He was coming downstairs. He spoke to me and gave me some candy out of a bag.'

'What kind of candy was it?'

'I don't know. Hard candy. It wasn't any good.'

'What's he do?' Tommy asked, turning from the crack.

'Sits in his room all day. Typing.'

'Doesn't he work?'

Dave sneered. 'That's what he does. He writes on his report. He's an official with a company.'

'What company?'

'I forget.'

'Doesn't he ever go out?'

'He goes out on the roof.'

'On the roof?'

'He has a porch he goes out on. We fixed it. It's part of the apartment. He's got a garden. He comes downstairs and gets dirt from the back yard.'

'Shhh!' Tommy warned. 'He turned around.'

Edward Billings had got to his feet. He was covering the typewriter with a black cloth, pushing it back and gathering up the pencils and erasers. He opened the desk drawer and dropped the pencils into it.

'He's through,' Tommy said. 'He's finished working.'

The old man removed his glasses and put them away in a case. He dabbed at his forehead wearily, loosening his collar and necktie. His neck was long and the cords stood out from yellow, wrinkled skin. His adam's apple bobbed up and down as he sipped some water from a glass.

His eyes were blue and faded, almost without color. For a moment he gazed directly at Tommy, his hawk-like face blank. Then abruptly he left the room, going through a door.

'He's going to bed,' Tommy said.

Mr Billings returned, a towel over his arm. At the desk he stopped and laid the towel over the back of the chair. He lifted the massive report book and carried it from the desk over to the bookcase, holding it tightly with both hands. It was heavy. He laid it down and left the room again.

The report was very close. Tommy could make out the gold letters stamped into the cracked leather binding. He gazed at the letters a long time – until Joan finally pushed him away from the crack, shoving him impatiently off the chair.

Tommy stepped down and moved away, awed and fascinated by what he had seen. The great report book, the huge volume of material on which the old man worked, day after day. In the flickering light from the lamp on the desk he had easily been able to make out the gold-stamped words on the ragged leather binding.

PROJECT B: EARTH.

'Let's go,' Dave said. 'He'll come in here in a couple minutes. He might catch us watching.'

'You're afraid of him,' Joan taunted.

'So are you. So is Mom. So is everybody.' He glanced at Tommy. 'You afraid of him?'

Tommy shook his head. 'I'd sure like to know what's in that book,' he murmured. 'I'd sure like to know what that old man is doing.'

The late afternoon sunlight shone down bright and cold. Edward Billings came slowly down the back steps, an empty pail in one hand, rolled-up newspapers under his arm. He paused a moment, shielding his eyes and gazing around him. Then he disappeared into the back yard, pushing through the thick wet grass.

Tommy stepped out from behind the garage. He raced silently up the steps two at a time. He entered the building, hurrying down the dark corridor.

A moment later he stood before the door of Edward Billings's apartment, his chest rising and falling, listening intently.

There was no sound.

Tommy tried the knob. It turned easily. He pushed. The

door swung open and a musty cloud of warm air drifted past him out into the corridor.

He had little time. The old man would be coming back with his pail of dirt from the yard.

Tommy entered the room and crossed to the bookcase, his heart pounding excitedly. The huge report book lay among heaps of notes and bundles of clippings. He pushed the papers away, sliding them from the book. He opened it quickly, at random, the thick pages crackling and bending.

Denmark.

Figures and facts. Endless facts, pages and columns, row after row. The lines of type danced before his eyes. He could make little out of them. He turned to another section.

New York.

Facts about New York. He struggled to understand the column heads. The number of people. What they did. How they lived. What they earned. How they spent their time. Their beliefs. Politics. Philosophy. Morals. Their age. Health. Intelligence. Graphs and statistics, averages and evaluations.

Evaluations. Appraisals. He shook his head and turned to another section.

California.

Population. Wealth. Activity of the state government. Ports and harbors. Facts, facts, facts –

Facts on everything. Everywhere. He thumbed through the report. On every part of the world. Every city, every state, every country. Any and all possible information.

Tommy closed the report uneasily. He wandered restlessly around the room, examining the heaps of notes and papers, the bundles of clippings and charts. The old man, typing day after day. Gathering facts, facts about the whole world. The earth. A report on the earth, the earth and everything on it. All the people. Everything they did and thought, their actions, deeds, achievements, beliefs, prejudices. A great report of all the information in the whole world.

Tommy picked up the big magnifying glass from the desk. He examined the surface of the desk with it, studying the wood. After a moment he put down the glass and picked up the bone letter knife. He put down the letter knife and examined the broken magic lantern in the corner. The frame of dead butter-flies. The drooping stuffed bird. The bottles of chemicals.

He left the room, going out onto the roof porch. The late afternoon sunlight flickered fitfully; the sun was going down. In the center of the porch was a wooden frame, dirt and grass heaped around it. Along the rail were big earthen jars, sacks of fertilizer, damp packages of seeds. An over-turned spray gun. A dirty trowel. Strips of carpet and a rickety chair. A sprinkling can.

Over the wood frame was a wire netting. Tommy bent down, peering through the netting. He saw plants, small plants in rows. Some moss, growing on the ground. Tangled plants, tiny and very intricate.

At one place some dried grass was heaped up in a pile. Like some sort of cocoon.

Bugs? Insects of some sort? Animals?

He took a straw and poked it through the netting at the dried grass. The grass stirred. Something was in it. There were other cocoons, several of them, here and there among the plants.

Suddenly something scuttled out of one of the cocoons, racing across the grass. It squeaked in fright. A second followed it. Pink, running quickly. A small herd of shrilling pink things, two inches high, running and dashing among the plants.

Tommy leaned closer, squinting excitedly through the netting, trying to see what they were. Hairless. Some kind of hairless animals. But tiny, tiny as grasshoppers. Baby things? His pulse raced wildly. Baby things or maybe –

A sound. He turned quickly, rigid.

Edward Billings stood at the door, gasping for breath. He set down the pail of dirt, sighing and feeling for his handkerchief in the pocket of his dark blue coat. He mopped his forehead silently, gazing at the boy standing by the frame.

'Who are you, young man?' Billings said, after a moment. 'I don't remember seeing you before.'

Tommy shook his head. 'No.'

'What are you doing here?'

'Nothing.'

'Would you like to carry this pail out onto the porch for me? It's heavier than I realized.'

Tommy stood for a moment. Then he came over and picked up the pail. He carried it out onto the roof porch and put it down by the wood frame.

'Thank you,' Billings said. 'I appreciate that.' His keen, faded-blue eyes flickered as he studied the boy, his gaunt face shrewd, yet not unkind. 'You look pretty strong to me. How old are you? About eleven?'

Tommy nodded. He moved back toward the railing. Below, two or three stories down, was the street. Mr Murphy was walking along, coming home from the office. Some kids were playing at the corner. A young woman across the street was watering her lawn, a blue sweater around her slim shoulders. He was fairly safe. If the old man tried to do anything –

'Why did you come here?' Billings asked.

Tommy said nothing. They stood looking at each other, the stooped old man, immense in his dark old-fashioned suit, the young boy in a red sweater and jeans, a beanie cap on his head, tennis shoes and freckles. Presently Tommy glanced toward the wood frame covered with netting, then up at Billings.

'That? You wanted to see that?'

'What's in there? What are they?'

'They?'

'The things. Bugs? I never saw anything like them. What are they?'

Billings walked slowly over. He bent down and unfastened the corner of the netting. 'I'll show you what they are. If you're interested.' He twisted the netting loose and pulled it back.

Tommy came over, his eyes wide.

'Well?' Billings said presently. 'You can see what they are.'

Tommy whistled softly. 'I thought maybe they were.' He straightened up slowly, his face pale. 'I thought maybe – but I wasn't sure. Little tiny men!'

'Not exactly,' Mr Billings said. He sat down heavily in the rickety chair. From his coat he took a pipe and a worn tobacco pouch. He filled the pipe slowly, shaking tobacco into it. 'Not exactly men.'

Tommy continued to gaze down into the frame. The cocoons were tiny huts, put together by the little men. Some of them had come out in the open now. They gazed up at him, standing together. Tiny pink creatures, two inches high. Naked. That was why they were pink.

'Look closer,' Billings murmured. 'Look at their heads. What do you see?'

'They're so small – '

'Go get the glass from the desk. The big magnifying glass.' He watched Tommy hurry into the study and come out quickly with the glass. 'Now tell me what you see.'

Tommy examined the figures through the glass. They seemed to be men, all right. Arms, legs – some were women. Their heads. He squinted.

And then recoiled.

'What's the matter?' Billings grunted.

'They're – they're queer.'

'Queer?' Billings smiled. 'Well, it all depends on what you're used to. They're different – from you. But they're not queer. There's nothing wrong with them. At least, I hope there's nothing wrong.' His smile faded, and he sat sucking on his pipe, deep in silent thought.

'Did you make them?' Tommy asked.

'I?' Billings removed his pipe. 'No, not I.'

'Where did you get them?'

'They were lent to me. A trial group. In fact, *the* trial group. They're new. Very new.'

'You want – you want to sell one of them?'

Billings laughed. 'No, I don't. Sorry. I have to keep them.'

Tommy nodded, resuming his study. Through the glass he could see their heads clearly. They were not quite men. From the front of each forehead antennae sprouted, tiny wire-like projections ending in knobs. Like the vanes of insects he had seen. They were not men, but they were similar to men. Except for the antennae they seemed normal – the antennae and their extreme minuteness.

'Did they come from another planet?' Tommy asked. 'From Mars? Venus?'

'No.'

'Where, then?'

'That's a hard question to answer. The question has no meaning, not in connection with them.'

'What's the report for?'

'The report?'

'In there. The big book with all the facts. The thing you're doing.'

'I've been working on that a long time.'

'How long?'

Billings smiled. 'That can't be answered, either. It has no meaning. But a long time indeed. I'm getting near the end, though.'

'What are you going to do with it? When it's finished.'

'Turn it over to my superiors.'

'Who are they?'

'You wouldn't know them.'

'Where are they? Are they here in town?'

'Yes. And no. There's no way to answer that. Maybe someday you'll – '

'The report's about us,' Tommy said.

Billings turned his head. His keen eyes bored into Tommy. 'Oh?'

'It's about us. The report. The book.'

'How do you know?'

'I looked at it. I saw the title on the back. It's about the earth, isn't it?'

Billings nodded. 'Yes. It's about the earth.'

'You're not from here, are you? You're from someplace else. Outside the system.'

'How – how do you know that?'

Tommmy grinned with superior pride. 'I can tell. I have ways.'

'How much did you see in the report?'

'Not much. What's it for? Why are you making it? What are they going to do with it?'

Billings considered a long time before he answered. At last he spoke. 'That,' he said, 'depends on *those*.' He gestured toward the wood frame. 'What they do with the report depends on how Project C works.'

'Project C?'

'The third project. There've been only two others before. They wait a long time. Each project is planned carefully. New factors are considered at great length before any decision is reached.'

'Two others?'

'Antennae for these. A complete new arrangement of the cognitive faculties. Almost no dependence on innate drives. Greater flexibility. Some decrease in over-all emotional index, but what they lose in libido energy they gain in rational control. I would expect more emphasis on individual experience, rather than dependence on traditional group learning. Less stereo-typed thinking. More rapid advance in situation control.'

Billings's words made little sense. Tommy was lost. 'What were the others like?' he asked.

'The others? Project A was a long time ago. It's dim in my mind. Wings.'

'Wings.'

'They were winged, depending on mobility and possessing considerable individualistic characteristics. In the final analysis we allowed them too much self-dependence. Pride. They had concepts of pride and honor. They were fighters. Each against the others. Divided into atomized antagonistic factions and – '

'What were the rest like?'

Billings knocked his pipe against the railing. He continued, speaking more to himself than to the boy standing in front of him. 'The winged type was our first attempt at high-level organisms. Project A. After it failed we went into conference. Project B was the result. We were certain of success. We eliminated many of the excessive individualistic characteristics and substituted a group orientation process. A herd method of learning and experiencing. We hoped general control over the project would be assured. Our work with the first project convinced us that greater supervision would be necessary if we were to be successful.'

'What did the second kind look like?' Tommy asked, search-ing for a meaningful thread in Billings's dissertation.

'We removed the wings, as I said. The general physiognomy remained the same. Although control was maintained for a short time, this second type also fractured away from the pattern, splintering into self-determined groups beyond our supervision. There is no doubt that surviving members of the initial type A were instrumental in influencing them. We should have exterminated the initial type as soon – '

'Are there any left?'

'Of Project B? Of course.' Billings was irritated. 'You're Project B. That's why I'm down here. As soon as my report is complete the final disposition of your type can be effected. There is no doubt my recommendation will be identical with that regarding Project A. Since your Project has moved out of jurisdiction to such a degree that for all intents and purposes you are no longer functional – '

But Tommy wasn't listening. He was bent over the wood frame, peering down at the tiny figures within. Nine little people, men and women both. Nine – and no more in all the world.

Tommy began to tremble. Excitement rushed through him. A plan was dawning, bursting alive inside him. He held his face rigid, his body tense.

'I guess I'll be going.' He moved from the porch, back into the room toward the hall door.

'Going?' Billings got to his feet. 'But – '

'I have to go. It's getting late. I'll see you later.' He opened the hall door. 'Goodbye.'

'Goodbye,' Mr Billings said, surprised. 'I hope I'll see you again, young man.'

'You will,' Tommy said.

He ran home as fast as he could. He raced up the porch steps and inside the house.

'Just in time for dinner,' his mother said, from the kitchen.

Tommy halted on the stairs. 'I have to go out again.'

'No you don't! You're going to – '

'Just for awhile. I'll be right back.' Tommy hurried up to his room and entered, glancing around.

The bright yellow room. Pennants on the walls. The big dresser and mirror, brush and comb, model airplanes, pictures of baseball players. The paper bag of bottle caps. The small radio with its cracked plastic cabinet. The wooden cigar boxes full of junk, odds and ends, things he had collected.

Tommy grabbed up one of the cigar boxes and dumped its

contents out on the bed. He stuck the box under his jacket and headed out of the room.

'Where are you going?' his father demanded, lowering his evening newspaper and looking up.

'I'll be back.'

'Your mother said it was time for dinner. Didn't you hear her?'

'I'll be back. This is important.' Tommy pushed the front door open. Chill evening air blew in, cold and thin. 'Honest. Real important.'

'Ten minutes.' Vince Jackson looked at his wristwatch. 'No longer. Or you don't get any dinner.'

'Ten minutes.' Tommy slammed the door. He ran down the steps, out into the darkness.

A light showed, flickering under the bottom and through the keyhole of Mr Billings's room.

Tommy hesitated a moment. Then he raised his hand and knocked. For a time there was silence. Then a stirring sound. The sound of heavy footsteps.

The door opened. Mr Billings peered out into the hall.

'Hello,' Tommy said.

'You're back!' Mr Billings opened the door wide and Tommy walked quickly into the room. 'Did you forget something?'

'No.'

Billings closed the door. 'Sit down. Would you like anything? An apple? Some milk?'

'No.' Tommy wandered nervously around the room, touching things here and there, books and papers and bundles of clippings.

Billings watched the boy a moment. Then he returned to his desk, seating himself with a sigh. 'I think I'll continue with my report. I hope to finish very soon.' He tapped a pile of notes beside him. 'The last of them. Then I can leave here and present the report along with my recommendations.'

Billings bent over his immense typewriter, tapping steadily away. The relentless rumble of the ancient machine vibrated through the room. Tommy turned and stepped out of the room, onto the porch.

In the cold evening air the porch was pitch black. He halted, adjusting to the darkness. After a time he made out the sacks of fertilizer, the rickety chair. And in the center, the wood frame with its wire netting over it, heaps of dirt and grass piled around.

Tommy glanced back into the room. Billings was bent over the typewriter, absorbed in his work. He had taken off his dark blue coat and hung it over the chair. He was working in his vest, his sleeves rolled up.

Tommy squatted beside the frame. He slid the cigar box from under his jacket and laid it down, lid open. He grasped the netting and pried it back, loose from the row of nails.

From the frame a few faint apprehensive squeaks sounded. Nervous scuttlings among the dried grass.

Tommy reached down, feeling among the grass and plants. His fingers closed over something, a small thing that squirmed in fright, twisting in wild terror. He dropped it into the cigar box and sought another.

In a moment he had them all. Nine of them, all nine in the wood cigar box.

He closed the lid and slipped it back under his jacket. Quickly he left the porch, returning to the room.

Billings glanced up vaguely from his work, pen in one hand, papers in the other. 'Did you want to talk to me?' he murmured, pushing up his glasses.

Tommy shook his head. 'I have to go.'

'Already? But you just came!'

'I have to go.' Tommy opened the door to the hall. 'Goodnight.'

Billings rubbed his forehead wearily, his face lined with fatigue. 'All right, boy. Perhaps I'll see you again before I leave.' He resumed his work, tapping slowly away at the great typewriter, bent with fatigue.

Tommy shut the door behind him. He ran down the stairs, outside on the porch. Against his chest the cigar box shook and moved. Nine. All nine of them. He had them all. Now they were his. They belonged to him – and there weren't any more of them, anywhere in the world. His plan had worked perfectly.

He hurried down the street toward his own house, as fast as he could run.

He found an old cage out in the garage he had once kept white rats in. He cleaned it and carried it upstairs to his room. He spread papers on the floor of the cage and fixed a water dish and some sand.

When the cage was ready he emptied the contents of the cigar box into it.

The nine tiny figures huddled together in the center of the cage, a little bundle of pink. Tommy shut the door of the cage and fastened it tightly. He carried the cage to the dresser and then drew a chair up by it so he could watch.

The nine little people began to move around hesitantly, exploring the cage. Tommy's heart beat with rapid excitement as he watched them.

He had got them away from Mr Billings. They were his, now. And Mr Billings didn't know where he lived or even his name.

They were talking to each other. Moving their antennae rapidly, the way he had seen ants do. One of the little people came over to the side of the cage. He stood gripping the wire, peering out into the room. He was joined by another, a female. They were naked. Except for the hair on their heads they were pink and smooth.

He wondered what they ate. From the big refrigerator in the kitchen he took some cheese and some hamburger, adding crumbled up bits of bread and lettuce leaves and a little plate of milk.

They liked the milk and bread. But they left the meat alone. The lettuce leaves they used to begin the making of little huts.

Tommy was fascinated. He watched them all the next morning before school, then again at lunch time, and all afternoon until dinner.

'What you got up there?' his Dad demanded, at dinner.

'Nothing.'

'You haven't got a snake, have you?' his Mom asked apprehensively. 'If you have another snake up there, young man – '

'No.' Tommy shook his head, bolting down his meal. 'It's not a snake.'

He finished eating and ran upstairs.

The little creatures had finished fixing their huts out of the lettuce leaves. Some were inside. Others were wandering around the cage, exploring it.

Tommy seated himself before the dresser and watched. They were smart. A lot smarter than the white rats he had owned. And cleaner. They used the sand he had put there for them. They were smart – and quite tame.

After awhile Tommy closed the door of the room. Holding his breath he unfastened the cage, opening one side wide. He reached in his hand and caught one of the little men. He drew him out of the cage and then opened his hand carefully.

The little man clung to his palm, peering over the edge and up at him, antennae waving wildly.

'Don't be afraid,' Tommy said.

The little man got cautiously to his feet. He walked across Tommy's palm, to his wrist. Slowly he climbed Tommy's arm, glancing over the side. He reached Tommy's shoulder and stopped, gazing up into his face.

'You're sure small,' Tommy said. He got another one from the cage and put the two of them on the bed. They walked around the bed for a long time. More had come to the open side of the cage and were staring cautiously out onto the dresser. One found Tommy's comb. He inspected it, tugging at the teeth. A second joined him. The two tiny creatures tugged at the comb, but without success.

'What do you want?' Tommy asked. After a while they gave up. They found a nickel lying on the dresser. One of them managed to turn it up on end. He rolled it. The nickel gained speed, rushing toward the edge of the dresser. The tiny men ran after it in consternation. The nickel fell over the side.

'Be careful,' Tommy warned. He didn't want anything to happen to them. He had too many plans. It would be easy to rig up things for them to do – like fleas he had seen at the circus. Little carts to pull. Swings, slides. Things they could operate. He could train them, and then charge admission.

Maybe he could take them on tour. Maybe he'd even get a write-up in the newspaper. His mind raced. All kinds of things.

Endless possibilities. But he had to start out easy – and be careful.

The next day he took one to school in his pocket, inside a fruit jar. He punched holes in the lid so it could breathe.

At recess he showed it to Dave and Joan Grant. They were fascinated.

'Where did you get it?' Dave demanded.

'That's my business.'

'Want to sell it?'

'It's not *it*. It's him.'

Jean blushed. 'It doesn't have anything on. You better make it put clothes on right away.'

'Can you make clothes for them? I have eight more. Four men and four women.'

Joan was excited. 'I can – if you'll give me one of them.'

'The heck I will. They're mine.'

'Where did they come from? Who made them?'

'None of your business.'

Joan made little clothes for the four women. Little skirts and blouses. Tommy lowered the clothing into the cage. The little people moved around the heap uncertainly, not knowing what to do.

'You better show them,' Joan said.

'Show them? Nuts to you.'

'I'll dress them.' Joan took one of the tiny women from the cage and carefully dressed her in a blouse and skirt. She dropped the figure back in. 'Now let's see what happens.'

The others crowded around the dressed woman, plucking curiously at the clothing. Presently they began to divide up the remaining clothes, some taking blouses, some skirts.

Tommy laughed and laughed. 'You better make pants for the men. So they'll all be dressed.'

He took a couple of them out and let them run up and down his arms.

'Be careful,' Joan warned. 'You'll lose them. They'll get away.'

'They're tame. They won't run away. I'll show you.' Tommy put them down onto the floor. 'We have a game. Watch.'

'A game?'

'They hide and I find them.'

The figures scampered off, looking for places to hide. In a moment none were in sight. Tommy got down on his hands and knees, reaching under the dresser, among the bedcovers. A shrill squeak. He had found one.

'See? They like it.' He carried them back to the cage, one by one. The last one stayed hidden a long time. It had got into one of the dresser drawers, down in a bag of marbles, pulling the marbles over its head.

'They're clever,' Joan said. 'Wouldn't you give me even one of them?'

'No,' Tommy said emphatically. 'They're mine. I'm not letting them get away from me. I'm not giving any of them to *anybody*.'

Tommy met Joan after school the next day. She had made little trousers and shirts for the men.

'Here.' She gave them to him. They walked along the sidewalk. 'I hope they fit.'

'Thanks.' Tommy took the clothes and put them in his pocket. They cut across the vacant lot. At the end of the lot Dave Grant and some kids were sitting around in a circle, playing marbles.

'Who's winning?' Tommy said, stopping.

'I am,' Dave said, not looking up.

'Let me play.' Tommy dropped down. 'Come on.' He held out his hand. 'Give me your agate.'

Dave shook his head. 'Get away.'

Tommy punched him on the arm. 'Come on! Just one shot.' He considered. 'Tell you what – '

A shadow fell over them.

Tommy looked up. And blanched.

Edward Billings gazed down silently at the boy, leaning on his umbrella, its metal point lost in the soft ground. He said nothing. His aged face was lined and hard, his eyes like faded blue stones.

Tommy got slowly to his feet. Silence had fallen over the children. Some of them scrambled away, snatching up their marbles.

'What do you want?' Tommy demanded. His voice was dry and husky, almost inaudible.

Billings's cold eyes bored into him, two keen orbs, without warmth of any kind. 'You took them. I want them back. Right away.' His voice was hard, colorless. He held out his hand. 'Where are they?'

'What are you talking about?' Tommy muttered. He backed away. 'I don't know what you mean.'

'The Project. You stole them from my room. I want them back.'

'The heck I did. What do you mean?'

Billings turned toward Dave Grant. 'He's the one you meant, isn't he?'

Dave nodded. 'I saw them. He has them in his room. He won't let anybody near them.'

'You came and stole them. *Why?*' Billings moved toward Tommy ominously. 'Why did you take them? What do you want with them?'

'You're crazy,' Tommy murmured, but his voice trembled. Dave Grant said nothing. He looked away sheepishly. 'It's a lie,' Tommy said.

Billings grabbed him. Cold, ancient hands gripped him, digging into his shoulders. 'Give them back! I want them. I'm responsible for them.'

'Let go.' Tommy jerked loose. 'I don't have them with me.' He caught his breath. 'I mean – '

'Then you do have them. At home. In your room. Bring them there. Go and get them. All nine.'

Tommy put his hands in his pockets. Some of his courage was returning. 'I don't know,' he said. 'What'll you give me?'

Billings's eyes flashed. 'Give you?' He raised his arm threateningly. 'Why, you little – '

Tommy jumped back. 'You can't make me return them. You don't have any control over us.' He grinned boldly. 'You said so yourself. We're out of your power. I heard you say so.'

Billings's face was like granite. 'I'll take them. They're mine. They belong to me.'

'If you try to take them I'll call the cops. And my Dad'll be there. My Dad and the cops.'

Billings gripped his umbrella. He opened and shut his mouth, his face a dark, ugly red. Neither he nor Tommy spoke. The other kids gazed at the two of them wide-eyed, awed and subdued.

Suddenly a thought twisted across Billings's face. He looked down at the ground, the crude circle and the marbles. His cold eyes flickered. 'Listen to this. I will – I will play against you for them.'

'What?'

'The game. Marbles. If you win you can keep them. If I win I get them back at once. All of them.'

Tommy considered, glancing from Mr Billings down at the circle on the ground. 'If I win you won't ever try to take them? You will let me keep them – for good?'

'Yes.'

'All right.' Tommy moved away. 'It's a deal. If you win you can have them back. But if I win they belong to me. And you don't ever get them back.'

'Bring them here at once.'

'Sure. I'll go get them.' – And my agate, too, he thought to himself. 'I'll be right back.'

'I'll wait here,' Mr Billings said, his huge hands gripping the umbrella.

Tommy ran down the porch steps, two at a time.

His mother came to the door. 'You shouldn't be going out again so late. If you're not home in half an hour you don't get any dinner.'

'Half an hour,' Tommy cried, running down the dark sidewalk, his hands pressed against the bulge in his jacket. Against the wood cigar box that moved and squirmed. He ran and ran, gasping for breath.

Mr Billings was still standing by the edge of the lot, waiting silently. The sun had set. Evening was coming. The children had gone home. As Tommy stepped onto the vacant lot a chill, hostile wind moved among the weeds and grass, flapping against his pants legs.

'Did you bring them?' Mr Billings demanded.

'Sure.' Tommy halted, his chest rising and falling. He

reached slowly under his jacket and brought out the heavy wood cigar box. He slipped the rubber band off it, lifting the lid a crack. 'In here.'

Mr Billings came close, breathing hoarsely. Tommy snapped the lid shut and restored the rubber band. 'We have to play.' He put the box down on the ground. 'They're mine – unless you win them back.'

Billings subsided. 'All right. Let's begin, then.'

Tommy searched his pockets. He brought out his agate, holding it carefully. In the fading light the big red-black marble gleamed, rings of sand and white. Like Jupiter. An immense, hard marble.

'Here we go,' Tommy said. He knelt down, sketching a rough circle on the ground. He emptied out a sack of marbles into the ring. 'You got any?'

'Any?'

'Marbles. What are you going to shoot with?'

'One of yours.'

'Sure.' Tommy took a marble from the ring and tossed it to him. 'Want me to shoot first?'

Billings nodded.

'Fine.' Tommy grinned. He took aim carefully, closing one eye. For a moment his body was rigid, set in an intense, hard arc. Then he shot. Marbles rattled and clinked, rolling out of the circle and into the grass and weeds beyond. He had done well. He gathered up his winnings, collecting them back in the cloth sack.

'Is it my turn?' Billings asked.

'No. My agate's still in the ring.' Tommy squatted down again. 'I get another shot.'

He shot. This time he collected three marbles. Again his agate was within the circle.

'Another shot,' Tommy said, grinning. He had almost half. He knelt and aimed, holding his breath. Twenty-four marbles remained. If he could get four more he would have won. Four more –

He shot. Two marbles left the circle. And his agate. The agate rolled out, bouncing into the weeds.

Tommy collected the two marbles and the agate. He had nineteen in all. Twenty-two remained in the ring.

'Okay,' he murmured reluctantly. 'It's your shot this time. Go ahead.'

Edward Billings knelt down stiffly, gasping and tottering. His face was gray. He turned his marble around in his hand uncertainly.

'Haven't you ever played before?' Tommy demanded. 'You don't know how to hold it, do you?'

Billings shook his head. 'No.'

'You have to get it between your first finger and your thumb.' Tommy watched the stiff old fingers with the marble. Billings dropped it once and picked it quickly up again. 'Your thumb makes it go. Like this. Here, I'll show you.'

Tommy took hold of the ancient fingers and bent them around the marble. Finally he had them in place. 'Go ahead.' Tommy straightened up. 'Let's see how you do.'

The old man took a long time. He gazed at the marbles in the ring, his hand shaking. Tommy could hear his breathing, the hoarse, deep panting, in the damp evening air.

The old man glanced at the cigar box resting in the shadows. Then back at the circle. His fingers moved –

There was a flash. A blinding flash. Tommy gave a cry, wiping at his eyes. Everything spun, lashing and tilting. He stumbled and fell, sinking into the wet weeds. His head throbbed. He sat on the ground, rubbing his eyes, shaking his head, trying to see.

At last the drifting sparks cleared. He looked around him, blinking.

The circle was empty. There were no marbles in the ring. Billings had got them all.

Tommy reached out. His fingers touched something hot. He jumped. It was a fragment of glass, a glowing red fragment of molten glass. All round him, in the damp weeds and grass, fragments of glass gleamed, cooling slowly into darkness. A thousand splinters of stars, glowing and fading around him.

Edward Billings stood up slowly, rubbing his hands together. 'I'm glad that's over,' he gasped. 'I'm too old to bend down like that.'

His eyes made out the cigar box, lying on the ground.

'Now they can go back. And I can continue with my work.' He picked up the wood box, putting it under his arm. He gathered up his umbrella and shuffled away, toward the sidewalk beyond the lot.

'Goodbye,' Billings said, stopping for a moment. Tommy said nothing.

Billings hurried off down the sidewalk, the cigar box clutched tightly.

He entered his apartment, breathing rapidly. He tossed his black umbrella into the corner and sat down before the desk, laying the cigar box in front of him. For a moment he sat, breathing deeply and gazing down at the brown and white square of wood and cardboard.

He had won. He had got them back. They were his, again. And just in time. The filing date for the report was practically upon him.

Billings slid out of his coat and vest. He rolled up his sleeves, trembling a little. He had been lucky. Control over the B type was extremely limited. They were virtually out of jurisdiction. That, of course, was the problem itself. Both the A and B types had managed to escape supervision. They had rebelled, disobeying orders and therefore putting themselves outside the limit of the plan.

But these – the new type, Project C. Everything depended on them. They had left his hands, but now they were back again. Under control, as intended. Within the periphery of supervisory instruction.

Billings slid the rubber band from the box. He raised the lid, slowly and carefully.

Out they swarmed – fast. Some headed to the right, some to the left. Two columns of tiny figures racing off, head down. One reached the edge of the desk and leaped. He landed on the rug, rolling and falling. A second jumped after him, then a third.

Billings broke out of his paralysis. He grabbed frantically, wildly. Only two remained. He swiped at one and missed. The other –

He grabbed it, squeezing it tight between his clenched fingers. Its companion wheeled. It had something in its hand. A splinter. A splinter of wood, torn from the inside of the cigar box.

It ran up and stuck the end of the splinter into Billings's finger.

Billings gasped in pain. His fingers flew open. The captive tumbled out, rolling on its back. Its companion helped it up, half-dragging it to the edge of the desk. Together the two of them leaped.

Billings bent down, groping for them. They scampered rapidly, toward the door to the porch. One of them was at the lamp plug. It tugged. A second joined it and the two tiny figures pulled together. The lamp cord came out of the wall. The room plunged into darkness.

Billings found the desk drawer. He yanked it open, spilling its contents onto the floor. He found some big sulphur matches and lit one.

They were gone – out onto the porch.

Billings hurried after them. The match blew out. He lit another, shielding it with his hand.

The creatures had got to the railing. They were going over the edge, catching hold of the ivy and swinging down into the darkness.

He got to the edge too late. They were gone, all of them. All nine, over the side of the roof, into the blackness of the night.

Billings ran downstairs and out onto the back porch. He reached the ground, hurrying around the side of the house, where the ivy grew up the side.

Nothing moved. Nothing stirred. Silence. No sign of them anywhere.

They had escaped. They were gone. They had worked out a plan of escape and put it into operation. Two columns, going in opposite directions, as soon as the lid was lifted. Perfectly timed and executed.

Slowly Billings climbed the stairs to his room. He pushed the door open and stood, breathing deeply, dazed from the shock.

They were gone. Project C was already over. It had gone like the others. The same way. Rebellion and independence.

Out of supervision. Beyond control. Project A had influenced Project B – and now, in the same way, the contamination had spread to C.

Billings sat down heavily at his desk. For a long time he sat immobile, silent and thoughtful, gradual comprehension coming to him. It was not his fault. It had happened before – twice before. And it would happen again. Each Project would carry the discontent to the next. It would never end, no matter how many Projects were conceived and put into operation. The rebellion and escape. The evasion of the plan.

After a time, Billings reached out and pulled his big report book to him. Slowly he opened it to the place he had left off. From the report he removed the entire last section. The summary. There was no use scrapping the current Project. One Project was as good as any other. They would all be equal – equal failures.

He had known as soon as he saw them. As soon as he had raised the lid. They had clothes on. Little suits of clothing. Like the others, a long time before.

The Trouble with Bubbles

Nathan Hull left his surface car and crossed the pavement on foot, sniffing the chill morning air. Robot work-trucks were starting to rumble past. A gutter slot sucked night debris greedily. A vanishing headline caught his eye momentarily:

PACIFIC TUBE COMPLETED;
ASIAN LAND MASS LINKED

He passed on away from the corner, hands in his pockets, looking for Farley's house.

Past the usual Worldcraft Store with its conspicuous motto: 'Own Your Own World!' Down a short grass-lined walk and onto a sloping tilt-front porch. Up three imitation marble stairs. Then Hull flicked his hand before the code beam and the door melted away.

The house was still. Hull found the ascent tube to the second floor and peered up. No sound. Warm air blew around him, tinged with faint smells – smells of food and people and familiar objects. Had they gone? No. It was only the third day; they'd be around someplace, maybe up on the roof terrace.

He ascended to the second floor and found it also vacant. But distant sounds drifted to his ears. A tinkle of laughter, a man's voice. A woman's – perhaps Julia's. He hoped so – hoped she were still conscious.

He tried a door at random, steeling himself. Sometimes during the third and fourth days the Contest Parties got a little rough. The door melted, but the room was empty. Couches, empty glasses, ashtrays, exhausted stimulant tubes, articles of clothing strewn everywhere –

Abruptly Julia Marlow and Max Farley appeared, arm in

arm, followed by several others, pushing forward in a group, excited and red-cheeked, eyes bright, almost feverish. They entered the room and halted.

'Nat!' Julia broke away from Farley and came breathlessly up to him. 'Is it that late already?'

'Third day,' Hull said. 'Hello, Max.'

'Hello, Hull. Sit down and make yourself comfortable. Can I get you something?'

'Nothing. Can't stay. Julia – '

Farley waved a robant over, sweeping two drinks from its chest tray. 'Here, Hull. You can stay long enough for one drink.'

Bart Longstreet and a slender blonde appeared through a door. 'Hull! You here? So soon?'

'Third day. I'm picking Julia up. If she still wants to leave.'

'Don't take her away,' the slim blonde protested. She wore a *sideglance* robe, invisible out of the corner of the eye, but an opaque fountain when looked at directly. 'They're judging right now. In the lounge. Stick around. The fun's just beginning.' She winked at him with heavy blue-lidded eyes, glazed and sleep-drugged.

Hull turned to Julia. 'If you want to stay . . .'

Julia put her hand nervously on his arm, standing close to him. Not losing her fixed smile she grated in his ear: 'Nat, for God's sake, get me out of here. I can't stand it. Please!'

Hull caught her intense appeal, her eyes bright with desperation. He could feel the mute urgency quivering through her body, tense and strained. 'Okay, Julia. We'll take off. Maybe get some breakfast. When did you last eat?'

'Two days. I think. I don't know.' Her voice trembled. 'They're judging right now. God, Nat, you should have seen – '

'Can't go until the judging's over,' Farley rumbled. 'I think they're almost through. You didn't enter, Hull? No entry for you?'

'No entry.'

'Surely you're an owner – '

'Nope. Sorry.' Hull's voice was faintly ironic. 'No world of my own, Max. Can't see it.'

'You're missing something.' Max beamed dopily, rocking back on his heels. 'Quite a time – best Contest Party for weeks. And the real fun begins *after* the judging. All this is just preliminary.'

'I know.' Hull moved Julia rapidly toward the descent tube. 'We'll see you. So long, Bart. Give me a call when you're out of here.'

'Hold it!' Bart murmured suddenly, cocking his head. 'The judging's over. The winner is going to be announced.' He pushed toward the lounge, the others excitedly behind. 'You coming, Hull? Julia?'

Hull glanced at the girl. 'All right.' They followed reluctantly. 'For a minute, maybe.'

A wall of sound struck them. The lounge was a seething chaos of milling men and women.

'I won!' Lora Becker shouted in ecstasy. People pushed and shoved around her, toward the Contest table, grabbing up their entries. Their voices grew in volume, an ominous rumble of discordant sound. Robants calmly moved furniture and fixtures back out of the way, clearing the floor rapidly. An unleashed frenzy of mounting hysteria was beginning to fill the big room.

'I knew it!' Julia's fingers tightened around Hull's arm. 'Come on. Let's get out before they start.'

'Start?'

'Listen to them!' Julia's eyes flickered with fear. 'Come on, Nat! I've had enough. I can't stand any more of this.'

'I told you before you came.'

'You did, didn't you?' Julia smiled briefly, grabbing her coat from a robant. She fastened the coat rapidly around her breasts and shoulders. 'I admit it. You told me. Now let's go, for God's sake.' She turned, making her way through the surging mass of people toward the descent tube. 'Let's get out of here. We'll have breakfast. You were right. These things aren't for us.'

Lora Becker, plump and middle-aged, was making her way up onto the stand beside the judges, her entry clasped in her arms. Hull paused a moment, watching the immense woman struggle up, her chemically corrected features gray and sagging in the unwinking overhead lights. The third day – a lot of old-timers were beginning to show the effects, even through their artificial masks.

Lora reached the stand. 'Look!' she shouted, holding up her entry. The Worldcraft bubble glittered, catching the light. In spite of himself Hull had to admire the thing. If the actual world inside was as good as the exterior . . .

Lora turned on the bubble. It glowed, winking into brilliance. The roomful of people became silent, gazing up at the winning entry, the world that had taken the prize over all other comers.

Lora Becker's entry was masterful. Even Hull had to admit it. She increased the magnification, bringing the microscopic central planet into focus. A murmur of admiration swept the room.

Again Lora increased the magnification. The central planet grew, showing a pale green ocean lapping faintly at a low shoreline. A city came into view, towers and broad streets, fine ribbons of gold and steel. Above, twin suns beamed down, warming the city. Myriads of inhabitants swarmed about their activities.

'Wonderful,' Bart Longstreet said softly, coming over beside Hull. 'But the old hag has been at it sixty years. No wonder she won. She's entered every Contest I can remember.'

'It's nice,' Julia admitted in a clipped voice.

'You don't care for it?' Longstreet asked.

'I don't care for any of this!'

'She wants to go,' Hull explained, moving toward the descent tube. 'We'll see you later, Bart.'

Bart Longstreet nodded. 'I know what you mean. In many ways I agree. You mind if I – '

'Watch!' Lora Becker shouted, her face flushed. She increased the magnification to maximum focus, showing details of the minute city. 'See them? *See?*'

The inhabitants of the city came into sharp view. They hurried about their business, endless thousands of them. In cars and on foot. Across spidery spans between buildings, breathtakingly beautiful.

Lora held the Worldcraft bubble up high, breathing rapidly. She gazed around the room, her eyes bright and inflamed,

252 Philip K. Dick

glittering unhealthily. The murmurings rose, sweeping up in excitement. Numerous Worldcraft bubbles came up, chest-high, gripped in eager, impassioned hands.

Lora's mouth opened. Saliva dribbled down the creases of her sagging face. Her lips twitched. She raised her bubble up over her head, her doughy chest swelling convulsively. Suddenly her face jerked, features twisting wildly. Her thick body swayed grotesquely – and from her hands the Worldcraft bubble flew, crashing to the stand in front of her.

The bubble smashed, bursting into a thousand pieces. Metal and glass, plastic parts, gears, struts, tubes, the vital machinery of the bubble, splattered in all directions.

Pandemonium broke loose. All around the room other owners were smashing their worlds, breaking them and crushing them, stamping on them, grinding the delicate control mechanisms underfoot. Men and women in a frenzy of abandon, released by Lora Becker's signal, quivering in an orgy of Dionysian lust. Crushing and breaking their carefully constructed worlds, one after another.

'God,' Julia gasped, struggling to get away, Longstreet and Hull beside her.

Faces gleamed with sweat, eyes feverish and bright. Mouths gaped foolishly, muttering meaningless sounds. Clothes were torn, ripped off. A girl went down, sliding underfoot, her shrieks lost in the general din. Another followed, dragged down into the milling mass. Men and women struggled in a blur of abandon, cries and gasps. And on all sides the hideous sounds of smashing metal and glass, the unending noise of worlds being destroyed one after another.

Julia dragged Hull from the lounge, her face white. She shuddered, closing her eyes. 'I knew it was coming. Three days, building up to this. Smashed – they're smashing them all. All the worlds.'

Bart Longstreet made his way out after Hull and Julia. 'Lunatics.' He lit a cigarette shakily. 'What the hell gets into them? This has happened before. They start breaking, smashing their worlds up. It doesn't make sense.'

Hull reached the descent tube. 'Come along with us, Bart.

We'll have breakfast – and I'll give you my theory, for what it's worth.'

'Just a second.' Bart Longstreet scooped up his Worldcraft bubble from the arms of a robant. 'My Contest entry. Don't want to lose it.'

He hurried after Julia and Hull.

'More coffee?' Hull asked, looking around.

'None for me,' Julia murmured. She settled back in her chair, sighing. 'I'm perfectly happy.'

'I'll take some.' Bart pushed his cup toward the coffee dispenser. It filled the cup and returned it. 'You've got a nice little place here, Hull.'

'Haven't you seen it before?'

'I don't get up this way. I haven't been in Canada in years.'

'Let's hear your theory,' Julia murmured.

'Go ahead,' Bart said. 'We're waiting.'

Hull was silent for a moment. He gazed moodily across the table, past the dishes, at the thing sitting on the window ledge. Bart's Contest entry, his Worldcraft bubble.

'"Own Your Own World",' Hull quoted ironically. 'Quite a slogan.'

'Packman thought it up himself,' Bart said. 'When he was young. Almost a century ago.'

'That long?'

'Packman takes treatments. A man in his position can afford them.'

'Of course.' Hull got slowly to his feet. He crossed the room and returned with the bubble. 'Mind?' he asked Bart.

'Go ahead.'

Hull adjusted the controls mounted on the bubble's surface. The interior scene flickered into focus. A miniature planet, revolving slowly. A tiny blue-white sun. He increased the magnification, bringing the planet up in size.

'Not bad,' Hull admitted presently.

'Primitive. Late Jurassic. I don't have the knack. I can't seem to get them into the mammal stage. This is my sixteenth try. I never can get any farther than this.'

The scene was a dense jungle, steaming with fetid rot. Great shapes stirred fitfully among the decaying ferns and marshes. Coiled, gleaming, reptilian bodies, smoking shapes rising up from the thick mud –

'Turn it off,' Julia murmured. 'I've seen enough of them. We viewed hundreds for the Contest.'

'I didn't have a chance.' Bart retrieved his bubble, snapping it off. 'You have to do better than the Jurassic, to win. Competition is keen. Half the people there had their bubbles into the Eocene – and at least ten into the Pliocene. Lora's entry wasn't much ahead. I counted several city-building civilizations. But hers was almost as advanced as we are.'

'Sixty years,' Julia said.

'She's been trying a long time. She's worked hard. One of those to whom it's not a game but a real passion. A way of life.'

'And then she smashes it,' Hull said thoughtfully. 'Smashes the bubble to bits. A world she's been working on for years. Guiding it through period after period. Higher and higher. Smashes it into a million pieces.'

'Why?' Julia asked. 'Why, Nat? Why do they do it? They get so far, building it up – and then they tear it all down again.'

Hull leaned back in his chair. 'It began,' he stated, 'when we failed to find life on any of the other planets. When our exploring parties came back empty-handed. Eight dead orbs – lifeless. Good for nothing. Not even lichen. Rock and sand. Endless deserts. One after the other, all the way out to Pluto.'

'It was a hard realization,' Bart said. 'Of course, that was before our time.'

'Not much before. Packman remembers it. A century ago. We waited a long time for rocket travel, flight to other planets. And then to find nothing . . .'

'Like Columbus finding the world really was flat,' Julia said. 'With an edge and a void.'

'Worse. Columbus was looking for a short route to China. They *could* have continued the long way. But when we explored the system and found nothing we were in for trouble. People had counted on new worlds, new lands in the sky. Colonization. Contact with a variety of races. Trade. Minerals and cultural products to exchange. But most of all the thrill of landing on planets with amazing life-forms.'

'And instead of that . . .'

'Nothing but dead rock and waste. Nothing that could support life – our own or any other kind. A vast disappointment set in on all levels of society.'

'And then Packman brought out the Worldcraft bubble,' Bart murmured. '"Own Your Own World." There was no place to go, outside of Terra. No other worlds to visit. You couldn't leave here and go to another world. So instead, you – '

'Instead you stayed home and put together your own world.' Hull smiled wryly. 'You know, he has a child's version out, now. A sort of preparation kit. So the child can cover the basic problems of world-building before he even has a bubble.'

'But look, Nat,' Bart said. 'The bubbles seemed like a good idea, at first. We couldn't leave Terra so we built our own worlds right here. Sub-atomic worlds, in controlled containers. We start life going on a sub-atomic world, feed it problems to make it evolve, try to raise it higher and higher. In theory there's nothing wrong with the idea. It's certainly a creative pastime. Not a merely passive viewing like television. In fact, world-building is the ultimate art form. It takes the place of all entertainments, all the passive sports as well as music and painting – '

'But something went wrong.'

'Not at first,' Bart objected. 'At first it was creative. Everybody bought a Worldcraft bubble and built his own world. Evolved life farther and farther. Molded life. Controlled it. Competed with others to see who could achieve the most advanced world.'

'And it solved another problem,' Julia added. 'The problem of leisure. With robots to work for us and robants to serve us and take care of our needs – '

'Yes, that was a problem,' Hull admitted. 'Too much leisure. Nothing to do. That, and the disappointment of finding our planet the only habitable planet in the system.

'Packman's bubbles seemed to solve both problems. But something went wrong. A change came. I noticed it right away.' Hull stubbed out his cigarette and lit another. 'The change began ten years ago – and it's been growing worse.'

'But why?' Julie demanded. 'Explain to me why everyone stopped building their worlds creatively and began to destroy.'

'Ever seen a child pull wings off a fly?'

'Certainly. But – '

'The same thing. Sadism? No, not exactly. More a sort of curiosity. Power. Why does a child break things? Power, again. We must never forget something. These world bubbles are *substitutes*. They take the place of something else, of finding genuine life on our own planets. And they're just too damn small to do that.

'These worlds are like toy boats in a bath tub. Or model rocketships you see kids playing with. They're surrogates, not the actual thing. These people who operate them – why do they want them? Because they can't explore real planets, big planets. They have a lot of energy dammed up inside them. Energy they can't express.

'And bottled-up energy sours. It becomes aggressive. People work with their little worlds for a time, building them up. But finally they reach a point where their latent hostility, their sense of being deprived, their – '

'It can be explained more easily,' Bart said calmly. 'Your theory is too elaborate.'

'How do you explain it?'

'Man's innate destructive tendencies. His natural desire to kill and spread ruin.'

'There's no such thing,' Hull said flatly. 'Man isn't an ant. He has no fixed direction to his drives. He has no instinctive "desire to destroy" any more than he had an instinctive desire to carve ivory letter-openers. He has *energy* – and the outlet it takes depends on the opportunities available.

'That's what's wrong. All of us have energy, the desire to move, act, do. But we're bottled up here, sealed off, on one planet. So we buy Worldcraft bubbles and make little worlds of our own. But microscopic worlds aren't enough. They're as satisfactory as a toy sailboat is to a man who wants to go sailing.'

Bart considered a long time, deep in thought. 'You may be

right,' he admitted finally. 'It sounds reasonable. But what's your suggestion? If the other eight planets are dead – '

'Keep exploring. Beyond the system.'

'We're doing that.'

'Try to find outlets that aren't so artificial.'

Bart grinned. 'You feel this way because you never caught the hang of it.' He thumped his bubble fondly. 'I don't find it artificial.'

'But most people do,' Julia put in. 'Most people aren't satisfied. That's why we left the Contest Party.'

Bart grunted. 'It's turning sour, all right. Quite a scene, wasn't it?' He reflected, frowning. 'But the bubbles are better than nothing. What do you suggest? Give up our bubbles? What should we do instead? Just sit around and talk?'

'Nat loves to talk,' Julia murmured.

'Like all intellectuals.' Bart tapped Hull's sleeve. 'When you sit in your seat in the Directorate you're with the Intellectual and Professional class – gray stripe.'

'And you?'

'Blue stripe. Industrial. You know that.'

Hull nodded. 'That's right. You're with Terran Spaceways. The ever-hopeful company.'

'So you want us to give up our bubbles and just sit around. Quite a solution to the problem.'

'You're going to *have* to give them up.' Hull's face flushed. 'What you do after that is your affair.'

'What do you mean?'

Hull turned toward Longstreet, eyes blazing. 'I've introduced a bill in the Directorate. A bill that will outlaw Worldcraft.'

Bart's mouth fell open. 'You *what*?'

'On what grounds?' Julia asked, waking up.

'On moral grounds,' Hull stated calmly. 'And I think I can get it through.'

The Directorate hall buzzed with murmuring echoes, its vast reaches alive with moving shadows, men taking their places and preparing for the session's business.

Eldon von Stern, Directorate Floor Leader, stood with Hull off to one side behind the platform. 'Let's get this straight,' von

Stern said nervously, running his fingers through his iron-gray hair. 'You intend to *speak* for this bill of yours? You want to defend it yourself?'

Hull nodded. 'That's right. Why not?'

'The analytical machines can break the bill down and present an impartial report for the members. Spellbinding has gone out of style. If you present an emotional harangue you can be certain of losing. The members won't – '

'I'll take the chance. It's too important to leave to the machines.'

Hull gazed out over the immense room that was slowly quieting. Representatives from all over the world were in their places. White-clad property owners. Blue-clad financial and industrial magnates. The red shirts of leaders from factory cooperatives and communal farms. The green-clad men and women representing the middle-class consumer group. His own gray-striped body, at the extreme right, the doctors, lawyers, scientists, educators, intellectuals and professionals of all kinds.

'I'll take the chance,' Hull repeated. 'I want to see the bill passed. It's time the issues were made clear.'

Von Stern shrugged. 'Suit yourself.' He eyed Hull curiously. 'What do you have against Worldcraft? It's too powerful a combine to buck. Packman himself is here, someplace. I'm surprised you – '

The robot chair flashed a signal. Von Stern moved away from Hull, up onto the platform.

'Are you sure you want to speak for the bill?' Julia said, standing beside Hull in the shadows. 'Maybe he's right. Let the machines analyze the bill.'

Hull was gazing out across the sea of faces, trying to locate Packman. The owner of Worldcraft was sitting out there. Forrest Packman, in his immaculate white shirt, like an ancient, withered angel. Packman preferred to sit with the property group, considering Worldcraft real estate instead of industry. Property still had the edge on prestige.

Von Stern touched Hull's arm. 'All right. Take the chair and explain your proposal.'

Hull stepped out onto the platform and seated himself in the big marble chair. The endless rows of faces before him were carefully devoid of expression.

'You've read the terms of the proposal I'm speaking for,' Hull began, his voice magnified by the speakers on each member's desk. 'I propose we should declare Worldcraft Industries a public menace and the real property the possession of the State. I can state my grounds in a few sentences.

'The theory and construction of the Worldcraft product, the sub-atomic universe system, is known to you. An infinite number of sub-atomic worlds exist, microscopic counterparts of our own spatial coordinate. Worldcraft developed, almost a century ago, a method of controlling to thirty decimals the forces and stresses involved on these micro-coordinate planes, and a fairly simplified machine which could be manipulated by an adult person.

'These machines for controlling specific areas of sub-atomic coordinates have been manufactured and sold to the general public with the slogan: "Own Your Own World." The idea is that the owner of the machine becomes literally a world owner, since the machine controls forces that govern a sub-atomic universe that is directly analogous to our own.

'By purchasing one of these Worldcraft machines, or bubbles, the person finds himself in possession of a virtual universe, to do with as he sees fit. Instruction manuals supplied by the Company show him how to control these minute worlds so that life forms appear and rapidly evolve, giving rise to higher and higher forms until at last – assuming the owner is sufficiently skillful – he has in his personal possession a civilization of beings on a cultural par with our own.

'During the last few years we have seen the sale of these machines grow until now almost everyone possesses one or more sub-atomic worlds, complete with civilizations, and these years have also seen many of us take our private universes and grind the inhabitants and planets into dust.

'There is no law which prevents us from building up elaborate civilizations, evolved at an incredible rate of speed, and then crushing them out of existence. That is why my proposal has been presented. These minute civilizations are not dreams.

They are real. They actually exist. The microscopic inhabitants are – '

A restless stir moved through the vast hall. There were murmurs and coughs. Some members had switched off their speakers. Hull hesitated. A chill touched him. The faces below were blank, cold, uninterested. He continued rapidly.

'The inhabitants are, at present, subject to the slightest whim their owner may feel. If we wish to reach down and crush their world, turn on tidal waves, earthquakes, tornados, fire, volcanic action – if we wish to destroy them utterly, there is nothing they can do.

'Our position in relation to these minute civilizations is godlike. We can, with a wave of the hand, obliterate countless millions. We can send the lightning down, level their cities, squash their tiny buildings like ant hills. We can toss them about like toys, playthings, victims of our every whim.'

Hull stopped, rigid with apprehension. Some of the members had risen and strolled out. Von Stern's face twisted with ironic amusement.

Hull continued lamely. 'I want to see Worldcraft bubbles outlawed. We owe it to these civilizations on humanitarian grounds, on moral grounds – '

He went on, finishing as best he could. When he got to his feet there was a faint ripple of applause from the gray-striped professional group. But the white-clad property owners were utterly silent. And the blue industrialists. The red shirts and the green-clad consumer representatives were silent, impassive, even a little amused.

Hull returned to the wings, cold with the stark realization of defeat. 'We've lost,' he muttered, dazed. 'I don't understand.'

Julia took his arm. 'Maybe an appeal on some other grounds . . . Maybe the machines can still – '

Bart Longstreet came out of the shadows. 'No good, Nat. Won't work.'

Hull nodded. 'I know.'

'You can't moralize Worldcraft away. That's not the solution.'

Von Stern had given the signal. The members began to cast their votes, the tabulation machines whirring to life. Hull stood staring silently out at the murmuring room, crushed and bewildered.

Suddenly a shape appeared in front of him, cutting off his view. Impatiently he moved to one side – but a rasping voice stopped him.

'Too bad, Mr Hull. Better luck next time.'

Hull stiffened. 'Packman!' he muttered. 'What do you want?'

Forrest Packman came out of the shadows, moving toward him slowly, feeling his way blindly along.

Bart Longstreet stared at the old man with unconcealed hostility. 'I'll see you later, Nat.' He turned abruptly and started off.

Julia stopped him. 'Bart, do you have to – '

'Important business. I'll be back later.' He moved off down the aisle, toward the industrial section of the hall.

Hull faced Packman. He had never seen the old man so close before. He studied him as he advanced slowly, feeling his way along on the arm of his robant.

Forrest Packman was old – a hundred and seven years. Preserved by hormones and blood transfusions, elaborate washing and rejuvenating processes that maintained life in his ancient, withered body. His eyes, deep-sunk, peered up at Hull as he came near, shrunken hands clutching the arm of his robant, breath coming hoarse and dry.

'Hull? You don't mind if I chat with you as the voting goes on? I won't be long.' He peered blindly past Hull. 'Who left? I couldn't see – '

'Bart Longstreet. Spaceways.'

'Oh, yes. I know him. Your speech was quite interesting, Hull. It reminded me of the old days. These people don't remember how it was. Times have changed.' He stopped, letting the robant wipe his mouth and chin. 'I used to be interested in rhetoric. Some of the old masters . . .'

The old man rambled on. Hull studied him curiously. Was this frail withered old man really the power behind Worldcraft? It didn't seem possible.

'Bryan,' Packman whispered, voice dry as ashes. 'William Jennings Bryan. I never heard him, of course. But they say he was the greatest. Your speech wasn't bad. But you don't

understand. I listened carefully. You have some good ideas.
But what you're trying to do is absurd. You don't know enough
about people. Nobody's really interested in – '

He broke off, coughing feebly, his robant gripping him with
metal supports.

Hull pushed impatiently past. 'The voting is almost finished.
I want to hear. If you have anything to say to me you can file a
regular memo plate.'

Packman's robant stepped out, barring his way. Packman
went on slowly, shakily. 'Nobody is really interested in such
appeals, Hull. You made a good speech but you don't have the
idea. Not yet, at least. But you talk well, better than I've heard
for a long time. These young fellows, faces all washed, running
around like office boys – '

Hull strained, listening to the vote. The impassive robant
body cut off his view, but over Packman's dry rasp he could
hear the results. Von Stern had risen and was reading the
totals, group by group.

'Four hundred against, thirty-five in favor,' von Stern stated.
'The proposal has been defeated.' He tossed the tabulation
cards down and picked up his agenda. 'We'll continue with the
next business.'

Behind Hull, Packman broke off suddenly, his skull-like
head cocked on one side. His deep-sunk eyes glittered and the
trace of a smile twitched across his lips. 'Defeated? Not even
all the grays voted for you, Hull. Now maybe you'll listen to
what I have to say.'

Hull turned away from the hall. The robant lowered its arm.
'It's over,' Hull said.

'Come on.' Julia moved uneasily away from Packman. 'Let's
get out of here.'

'You see,' Packman continued relentlessly, 'you have poten-
tials that could be developed into something. When I was your
age I had the same idea you have. I thought if people could see
the moral issues involved, they would respond. But people
aren't like that. You have to be realistic, if you want to get
somewhere. People . . .'

Hull scarcely heard the dry, raspy voice whispering away.
Defeat. Worldcraft, the world bubbles, would continue. The

Contest Parties: bored, restless men and women with too much time, drinking and dancing, comparing worlds, building up to the climax – then the orgy of breaking and smashing. Over and over. Endlessly.

'Nobody can buck Worldcraft,' Julia said. 'It's too big. We'll have to accept the bubbles as part of our lives. As Bart says, unless we have something else to offer in their place . . .'

Bart Longstreet came rapidly out of the shadows. 'You still here?' he said to Packman.

'I lost,' Hull said. 'The vote – '

'I know. I heard it. But it doesn't matter.' Longstreet pushed past Packman and his robant. 'Stay here. I'll join you in a second. I have to see von Stern.'

Something in Longstreet's voice made Hull look up sharply. 'What is it? What's happened?'

'Why doesn't it matter?' Julia demanded.

Longstreet stepped up on the platform and made his way to von Stern. He handed him a message plate and then retired to the shadows.

Von Stern glanced at the plate –

And stopped talking. He got to his feet slowly, the plate gripped tightly. 'I have an announcement to make.' Von Stern's voice was shaking, almost inaudible. 'A dispatch from Spaceways' check station on Proxima Centauri.'

An excited murmur rushed through the hall.

'Exploring ships in the Proxima system have contacted trading scouts from an extra-galactic civilization. An exchange of messages has already occurred. Spaceways ships are moving toward the Arcturan system with the expectation of finding – '

Shouts, a bedlam of sound. Men and women on their feet, screaming in wild joy. Von Stern stopped reading and stood, his arms folded, his gray face calm, waiting for them to quiet.

Forrest Packman stood unmoving, his withered hands pressed together, his eyes shut. His robant sent support braces around him, catching him in a shield of protecting metal.

'Well?' Longstreet shouted, pushing back to them. He glanced at the frail, withered figure held up by the robant's supports, then at Hull and Julia. 'What do you say, Hull? Let's get out of here – so we can celebrate.'

'I'll fly you home,' Hull said to Julia. He looked around for an inter-continental cruiser. 'Too bad you live so far away. Hong Kong is so damn out of the way.'

Julia caught his arm. 'You can drive me yourself. Remember? The Pacific Tube is open. We're connected with Asia now.'

'That's right.' Hull opened the door of his surface car and Julia slid in. Hull got behind the wheel and slammed the door. 'I forgot, with all these other things on my mind. Maybe we can see each other more often. I wouldn't mind spending a few days' vacation in Hong Kong. Maybe you'll invite me.'

He sent the car out into traffic, moving with the remote-controlled beam. 'Tell me more,' Julia asked. 'I want to know all Bart said.'

'Not much more. They've known for some time that something was up. That's why he wasn't too worried about World-craft. He knew the bottom would fall out as soon as the announcement was made.'

'Why didn't he tell you?'

Hull grinned wryly. 'How could he? Suppose the first reports were wrong? He wanted to wait until they were sure. He knew what the results would be.' Hull gestured. 'Look.'

On both sides of the strip a tide of men and women poured out of buildings, up from the underground factories, a seething mass milling everywhere in disordered confusion, shouting and cheering, throwing things in the air, tossing paper out of windows, carrying each other on their shoulders.

'They're working it off,' Hull said. 'The way it should be. Bart says Arcturus is supposed to have seven or eight fertile planets, some of them inhabited, some just forests and oceans. The extra-galactic traders say that most systems have at least one usable planet. They visited our system a long time ago. Our early ancestors may have traded with them.'

'Then there's plenty of life in the galaxy?'

Hull laughed. 'If what they say is true. And the fact that *they* exist is proof enough.'

'No more Worldcraft.'

'No.' Hull shook his head. No more Worldcraft. Stock was already being dumped. Worthless. Probably the State would absorb the bubbles already in existence and seal them off, leaving the inhabitants free to determine their own futures.

The neurotic smashing of laboriously achieved cultures was a thing of the past. The buildings of living creatures would no longer be pushed over to amuse some god suffering from *ennui* and frustration.

Julia laughed, leaning against Hull. 'Now we can take it easy. Sure, you're invited to stay. We can take out permanent cohabitation papers if you want to – '

Hull leaned forward suddenly, his body rigid. 'Where's the Tube?' he demanded. 'The strip should be hitting it any minute.'

Julia peered ahead, frowning. 'Something's wrong. Slow down.'

Hull slowed the car. An obstruction signal was flashing ahead. Cars were stopping on all sides, shifting into emergency retard lanes.

He ground the car to a halt. Rocket cruisers were sweeping overhead, exhaust tubes shattering the evening silence. A dozen uniformed men ran across a field, directing a rumbling robot derrick.

'What the hell – ' Hull muttered. A soldier stepped up to the car, swinging a communication flare.

'Turn around. We need the whole strip.'

'But – '

'What happened?' Julia asked.

'The Tube. Earthquake, someplace halfway out. Broke the Tube in ten sections.' The soldier hurried off. Construction robots rushed past in a hand cart, assembling equipment as they went.

Julia and Hull stared at each other wide-eyed. 'Good Lord,' Hull muttered. 'Ten places. And the Tube must have been full of cars.'

A Red Cross ship landed, its ports grating open. Dollies shuttled across to it, loading injured men.

Two relief workers appeared. They opened the door to Hull's car, getting in the back. 'Drive us to town.' They sank down, exhausted. 'We got to get more help. Hurry it.'

'Sure.' Hull started the car again, gained speed.

'How did it happen?' Julia asked one of the grim-faced exhausted men, who dabbed automatically at the cuts on his face and neck.

'Earthquake.'

'But why? Didn't they build it so – '

'Big quake.' The man shook his head wearily. 'Nobody expected. Total loss. Thousands of cars. Tens of thousands of people.'

The other worker grunted. 'An act of God.'

Hull stiffened suddenly. His eyes flickered.

'What is it?' Julia asked him.

'Nothing.'

'Are you sure? Is something wrong?'

Hull said nothing. He was deep in thought, his face a mask of startled, growing horror.

Breakfast at Twilight

'Dad?' Earl asked, hurrying out of the bathroom, 'you going to drive us to school today?'

Tim McLean poured himself a second cup of coffee. 'You kids can walk for a change. The car's in the garage.'

Judy pouted. 'It's raining.'

'No it isn't,' Virginia corrected her sister. She drew the shade back. 'It's all foggy, but it isn't raining.'

'Let me look.' Mary McLean dried her hands and came over from the sink. 'What an odd day. Is that fog? It looks more like smoke. I can't make out a thing. What did the weatherman say?'

'I couldn't get anything on the radio,' Earl said. 'Nothing but static.'

Tim stirred angrily. 'That darn thing on the blink again? Seems like I just had it fixed.' He got up and moved sleepily over to the radio. He fiddled idly with the dials. The three children hurried back and forth, getting ready for school. 'Strange,' Tim said.

'I'm going.' Earl opened the front door.

'Wait for your sisters,' Mary ordered absently.

'I'm ready,' Virginia said. 'Do I look all right?'

'You look fine,' Mary said, kissing her.

'I'll call the radio repair place from the office,' Tim said.

He broke off. Earl stood at the kitchen door, pale and silent, his eyes wide with terror.

'What is it?'

'I – I came back.'

'What is it? Are you sick?'

'I can't go to school.'

They stared at him. 'What is wrong?' Tim grabbed his son's arm. 'Why can't you go to school?'

'They – they won't let me.'

'*Who?*'

'The soldiers.' It came tumbling out with a rush. 'They're all over. Soldiers and guns. And they're coming here.'

'Coming? Coming here?' Tim echoed, dazed.

'They're coming here and they're going to – ' Earl broke off, terrified. From the front porch came the sound of heavy boots. A crash. Splintering wood. Voices.

'Good Lord,' Mary gasped. 'What is it, Tim?'

Tim entered the living-room, his heart laboring painfully. Three men stood inside the door. Men in gray-green uniforms, weighted with guns and complex tangles of equipment. Tubes and hoses. Meters on thick cords. Boxes and leather straps and antennae. Elaborate masks locked over their heads. Behind the masks Tim saw tired, whisker-stubbled faces, red-rimmed eyes that gazed at him in brutal displeasure.

One of the soldiers jerked up his gun, aiming at McLean's middle. Tim peered at it dumbly. *The gun.* Long and thin. Like a needle. Attached to a coil of tubes.

'What in the name of – ' he began, but the soldier cut him off savagely.

'Who are you?' His voice was harsh, guttural. 'What are you doing here?' He pushed his mask aside. His skin was dirty. Cuts and pocks lined his sallow flesh. His teeth were broken and missing.

'Answer!' a second soldier demanded. 'What are you doing here?'

'Show your blue card,' the third said. 'Let's see your Sector number.' His eyes strayed to the children and Mary standing mutely at the dining-room door. His mouth fell open.

'*A woman!*'

The three soldiers gazed in disbelief.

'What the hell is this?' the first demanded. 'How long has this woman been here?'

Tim found his voice. 'She's my wife. What is this? What – '

'Your *wife*?' They were incredulous.

'My wife and children. For God's sake – '

'Your wife? And you'd bring her here? You must be out of your head!'

'He's got ash sickness,' one said. He lowered his gun and strode across the living-room to Mary. 'Come on, sister. You're coming with us.'

Tim lunged.

A wall of force hit him. He sprawled, clouds of darkness rolling around him. His ears sang. His head throbbed. Everything receded. Dimly, he was aware of shapes moving. Voices. The room. He concentrated.

The soldiers were herding the children back. One of them grabbed Mary by the arm. He tore her dress away, ripping it from her shoulders. 'Gee,' he snarled. 'He'd bring her here, and she's not even strung!'

'Take her along.'

'Okay, Captain.' The soldier dragged Mary toward the front door. 'We'll do what we can with her.'

'The kids.' The captain waved the other soldier over with the children. 'Take them along. I don't get it. No masks. No cards. How'd this house miss getting hit? Last night was the worst in months!'

Tim struggled painfully to his feet. His mouth was bleeding. His vision blurred. He hung on tight to the wall. 'Look,' he muttered. 'For God's sake – '

The captain was staring into the kitchen. 'Is that – is that *food*?' He advanced slowly through the dining-room. 'Look!'

The other soldiers came after him, Mary and the children forgotten. They stood around the table, amazed.

'Look at it!'

'Coffee.' One grabbed up the pot and drank it greedily down. He choked, black coffee dripping down his tunic. 'Hot. Jeez. Hot coffee.'

'Cream!' Another soldier tore open the refrigerator. 'Look. Milk. Eggs. Butter. Meat.' His voice broke. 'It's full of food.'

The captain disappeared into the pantry. He came out, lugging a case of canned peas. 'Get the rest. Get it all. We'll load it in the snake.'

He dropped the case on the table with a crash. Watching Tim intently, he fumbled in his dirty tunic until he found a cigarette.

He lit it slowly, not taking his eyes from Tim. 'All right,' he said. 'Let's hear what you have to say.'

Tim's mouth opened and closed. No words came. His mind was blank. Dead. He couldn't think.

'This food. Where'd you get it? And these things.' The captain waved around the kitchen. 'Dishes. Furniture. How come this house hasn't been hit? How did you survive last night's attack?'

'I – ' Tim gasped.

The captain came toward him ominously. 'The woman. And the kids. All of you. What are you doing here?' His voice was hard. 'You better be able to explain, mister. You better be able to explain what you're doing here – or we'll have to burn the whole damn lot of you.'

Tim sat down at the table. He took a deep, shuddering breath, trying to focus his mind. His body ached. He rubbed blood from his mouth, conscious of a broken molar and bits of loose tooth. He got out a handkerchief and spat the bits into it. His hands were shaking.

'Come on,' the captain said.

Mary and the children slipped into the room. Judy was crying. Virginia's face was blank with shock. Earl stared wide-eyed at the soldiers, his face white.

'Tim,' Mary said, putting her hand on his arm. 'Are you all right?'

Tim nodded. 'I'm all right.'

Mary pulled her dress around her. 'Tim, they can't get away with it. Somebody'll come. The mailman. The neighbors. They can't just – '

'Shut up,' the captain snapped. His eyes flickered oddly. 'The mailman? What are you talking about?' He held out his hand. 'Let's see your yellow slip, sister.'

'Yellow slip?' Mary faltered.

The captain rubbed his jaw. 'No yellow slip. No masks. No cards.'

'They're geeps,' a soldier said.

'Maybe. And maybe not.'

'They're geeps, Captain. We better burn 'em. We can't take any chances.'

'There's something funny going on here,' the captain said. He plucked at his neck, lifting up a small box on a cord. 'I'm getting a polic here.'

'A polic?' A shiver moved through the soldiers. 'Wait, Captain. We can handle this. Don't get a polic. He'll put us on 4 and then we'll never – '

The captain spoke into the box. 'Give me Web B.'

Tim looked up at Mary. 'Listen, honey. I – '

'Shut up.' A soldier prodded him. Tim lapsed into silence.

The box squawked. 'Web B.'

'Can you spare a polic? We've run into something strange. Group of five. Man, woman, three kids. No masks, no cards, the woman not strung, dwelling completely intact. Furniture, fixtures, about two hundred pounds of food.'

The box hesitated. 'All right. Polic on the way. Stay there. Don't let them escape.'

'I won't.' The captain dropped the box back in his shirt. 'A polic will be here any minute. Meanwhile, let's get the food loaded.'

From outside came a deep thundering roar. It shook the house, rattling the dishes in the cupboard.

'Jeez,' a soldier said. 'That was close.'

'I hope the screens hold until nightfall.' The captain grabbed up the case of canned peas. 'Get the rest. We want it loaded before the polic comes.'

The two soldiers filled their arms and followed him through the house, out the front door. Their voices diminished as they strode down the path.

Tim got to his feet. 'Stay here,' he said thickly.

'What are you doing?' Mary asked nervously.

'Maybe I can get out.' He ran to the back door and unlatched it, hands shaking. He pulled the door wide and stepped out on the back porch. 'I don't see any of them. If we can only . . .'

He stopped.

Around him gray clouds blew. Gray ash, billowing as far as he could see. Dim shapes were visible. Broken shapes, silent and unmoving in the grayness.

Ruins.

Ruined buildings. Heaps of rubble. Debris everywhere. He

walked slowly down the back steps. The concrete walk ended abruptly. Beyond it, slag and heaps of rubble were strewn. Nothing else. Nothing as far as the eye could see.

Nothing stirred. Nothing moved. In the gray silence there was no life. No motion. Only the clouds of drifting ash. The slag and the endless heaps.

The city was gone. The buildings were destroyed. Nothing remained. No people. No life. Jagged walls, empty and gaping. A few dark weeds growing among the debris. Tim bent down, touching a weed. Rough, thick stalk. And the slag. It was a metal slag. Melted metal. He straightened up –

'Come back inside,' a crisp voice said.

He turned numbly. A man stood on the porch, behind him, hands on his hips. A small man, hollow-cheeked. Eyes small and bright, like two black coals. He wore a uniform different from the soldiers'. His mask was pushed back, away from his face. His skin was yellow, faintly luminous, clinging to his cheekbones. A sick face, ravaged by fever and fatigue.

'Who are you?' Tim said.

'Douglas. Political Commissioner Douglas.'

'You're – you're the police,' Tim said.

'That's right. Now come inside. I expect to hear some answers from you. I have quite a few questions.

'The first thing I want to know,' Commissioner Douglas said, 'is how this house escaped destruction.'

Tim and Mary and the children sat together on the couch, silent and unmoving, faces blank with shock.

'Well?' Douglas demanded.

Tim found his voice. 'Look,' he said. 'I don't know. I don't know anything. We woke up this morning like every other morning. We dressed and ate breakfast – '

'It was foggy out,' Virginia said. 'We looked out and saw the fog.'

'And the radio wouldn't work,' Earl said.

'The radio?' Douglas's thin face twisted. 'There haven't been any audio signals in months. Except for government purposes. This house. All of you. I don't understand. If you were geeps – '

'Geeps. What does that mean?' Mary murmured.

'Soviet general-purpose troops.'

'Then the war has begun.'

'North America was attacked two years ago,' Douglas said. 'In 1978.'

Tim sagged. '1978. Then this is 1980.' He reached suddenly into his pocket. He pulled out his wallet and tossed it to Douglas. 'Look in there.'

Douglas opened the wallet suspiciously. 'Why?'

'The library card. The parcel receipts. Look at the dates.' Tim turned to Mary. 'I'm beginning to understand now. I had an idea when I saw the ruins.'

'Are we winning?' Earl piped.

Douglas studied Tim's wallet intently. 'Very interesting. These are all old. Seven and eight years.' His eyes flickered. 'What are you trying to say? That you came from the past? That you're time travelers?'

The captain came back inside. 'The snake is all loaded, sir.'

Douglas nodded curtly. 'All right. You can take off with your patrol.'

The captain glanced at Tim. 'Will you be – '

'I'll handle them.'

The captain saluted. 'Fine, sir.' He quickly disappeared through the door. Outside, he and his men climbed aboard a long thin truck, like a pipe mounted on treads. With a faint hum the truck leaped forward.

In a moment only gray clouds and the dim outline of ruined buildings remained.

Douglas paced back and forth, examining the living-room, the wallpaper, the light fixture and chairs. He picked up some magazines and thumbed through them. 'From the past. But not far in the past.'

'Seven years?'

'Could it be? I suppose. A lot of things have happened in the last few months. Time travel.' Douglas grinned ironically. 'You picked a bad spot, McLean. You should have gone farther on.'

'I didn't pick it. It just happened.'

'You must have done *something*.'

Tim shook his head. 'No. Nothing. We got up. And we were – here.'

Douglas was deep in thought. 'Here. Seven years in the future. Moved forward through time. We know nothing about time travel. No work has been done with it. There seem to be evident military possibilities.'

'How did the war begin?' Mary asked faintly.

'Begin? It didn't begin. You remember. There was war seven years ago.'

'The real war. This.'

'There wasn't any point when it became – this. We fought in Korea. We fought in China. In Germany and Yugoslavia and Iran. It spread, farther and farther. Finally the bombs were falling here. It came like the plague. The war *grew*. It didn't begin.' Abruptly he put his notebook away. 'A report on you would be suspect. They might think that I had the ash sickness.'

'What's that?' Virginia asked.

'Radioactive particles in the air. Carried to the brain. Causes insanity. Everybody has a touch of it, even with the masks.'

'I'd sure like to know who's winning,' Earl repeated. 'What was that outside? That truck. Was it rocket propelled?'

'The snake? No. Turbines. Boring snout. Cuts through the debris.'

'Seven years,' Mary said. 'So much has changed. It doesn't seem possible.'

'So much?' Douglas shrugged. 'I suppose so. I remember what I was doing seven years ago. I was still in school. Learning. I had an apartment and a car. I went out dancing. I bought a TV set. But these things were there. The twilight. This. Only I didn't know. None of us knew. But they were there.'

'You're a Political Commissioner?' Tim asked.

'I supervise the troops. Watch for political deviation. In a total war we have to keep people under constant surveillance. One Commie down in the Webs could wreck the whole business. We can't take chances.'

Tim nodded. 'Yes. It was there. The twilight. Only we didn't understand it.'

Douglas examined the books in the bookcase. 'I'll take a couple of these along. I haven't seen fiction in months. Most of it disappeared. Burned back in '77.'

'Burned?'

Douglas helped himself. 'Shakespeare. Milton. Dryden. I'll take the old stuff. It's safer. None of the Steinbeck and Dos Passos. Even a polic can get in trouble. If you stay here, you better get rid of *that*.' He tapped a volume of Dostoevski, *The Brothers Karamazov*.

'If we stay! What else can we do?'

'You want to stay?'

'No,' Mary said quietly.

Douglas shot her a quick glance. 'No, I suppose not. If you stay you'll be separated, of course. Children to the Canadian Relocation Centers. Women are situated down in the under-surface factory-labor camps. Men are automatically a part of Military.'

'Like those there who left,' Tim said.

'Unless you can qualify for the id block.'

'What's that?'

'Industrial Designing and Technology. What training have you had? Anything along scientific lines?'

'No. Accounting.'

Douglas shrugged. 'Well, you'll be given a standard test. If your IQ is high enough you could go in the Political Service. We use a lot of men.' He paused thoughtfully, his arms loaded with books. 'You better go back, McLean. You'll have trouble getting accustomed to this. I'd go back, if I could. But I can't.'

'Back?' Mary echoed. 'How?'

'The way you came.'

'We just came.'

Douglas halted at the front door. 'Last night was the worst rom attack so far. They hit this whole area.'

'Rom?'

'Robot operated missiles. The Soviets are systematically destroying continental America, mile by mile. Roms are cheap. They make them by the million and fire them off. The whole process is automatic. Robot factories turn them out and fire them at us. Last night they came over here – waves of them. This morning the patrol came in and found nothing. Except you, of course.'

Tim nodded slowly. 'I'm beginning to see.'

'The concentrated energy must have tipped some unstable time fault. Like a rock fault. We're always starting earthquakes. But a *time quake* . . . Interesting. That's what happened, I think. The release of energy, the destruction of matter, sucked your house into the future. Carried the house seven years ahead. This street, everything here, this very spot, was pulverized. Your house, seven years back, was caught in the undertow. The blast must have lashed back through time.'

'Sucked into the future,' Tim said. 'During the night. While we were asleep.'

Douglas watched him carefully. 'Tonight,' he said, 'there will be another rom attack. It should finish off what is left.' He looked at his watch. 'It is now four in the afternoon. The attack will begin in a few hours. You should be undersurface. Nothing will survive up here. I can take you down with me, if you want. But if you want to take a chance, if you want to stay here – '

'You think it might tip us back?'

'Maybe. I don't know. It's a gamble. It might tip you back to your own time, or it might not. If not – '

'If not we wouldn't have a chance of survival.'

Douglas flicked out a pocket map and spread it open on the couch. 'A patrol will remain in this area another half-hour. If you decide to come undersurface with us, go down the street this way.' He traced a line on the map. 'To this open field here. The patrol is a Political unit. They'll take you the rest of the way down. You think you can find the field?'

'I think so,' Tim said, looking at the map. His lips twisted. 'That open field used to be the grammar school my kids went to. That's where they were going when the troops stopped them. Just a little while ago.'

'Seven years ago,' Douglas corrected. He snapped the map shut and restored it to his pocket. He pulled his mask down and moved out the front door onto the porch. 'Maybe I'll see you again. Maybe not. It's your decision. You'll have to decide one way or the other. In any case – good luck.'

He turned and walked briskly from the house.

'Dad,' Earl shouted, 'are you going in the Army? Are you going to wear a mask and shoot one of those guns?' His eyes sparkled with excitement. 'Are you going to drive a *snake*?'

Tim McLean squatted down and pulled his son to him. 'You want that? *You want to stay here?* If I'm going to wear a mask and shoot one of those guns we can't go back.'

Earl looked doubtful. 'Couldn't we go back later?'

Tim shook his head. 'Afraid not. We've got to decide now, whether we're going back or not.'

'You heard Mr Douglas,' Virginia said disgustedly. 'The attack's going to start in a couple hours.'

Tim got to his feet and paced back and forth. 'If we stay in the house we'll get blown to bits. Let's face it. There's only a faint chance we'll be tipped back to our own time. A slim possibility – a long shot. Do we want to stay here with roms falling all around us, knowing any second it may be the end – hearing them come closer, hitting nearer – lying on the floor, waiting, listening – '

'Do you really want to go back?' Mary demanded.

'Of course, but the risk – '

'I'm not asking you about the risk. I'm asking you if you really want to go back. Maybe you want to stay here. Maybe Earl's right. You in a uniform and a mask, with one of those needle guns. Driving a snake.'

'With you in a factory-labor camp! And the kids in a Government Relocation Center! How do you think that would be? What do you think they'd teach them? What do you think they'd grow up like? And believe . . .'

'They'd probably teach them to be very useful.'

'Useful! To what? To themselves? To mankind? Or to the war effort . . .?'

'They'd be alive,' Mary said. 'They'd be safe. This way, if we stay in the house, wait for the attack to come – '

'Sure,' Tim grated. 'They would be alive. Probably quite healthy. Well fed. Well clothed and cared for.' He looked down at his children, his face hard. 'They'd stay alive, all right. They'd live to grow up and become adults. But what kind of adults? You heard what he said! Book burnings in '77. What'll they be taught from? What kind of ideas are left, since '77? What kind of beliefs can they get from a Government Reloca-tion Center? What kind of values will they have?'

'There's the id block,' Mary suggested.

'Industrial Designing and Technology. For the bright ones. The clever ones with imagination. Busy slide rules and pencils. Drawing and planning and making discoveries. The girls could go into that. They could design the guns. Earl could go into the Political Service. He could make sure the guns were used. If any of the troops deviated, didn't want to shoot, Earl could report them and have them hauled off for reeducation. To have their political faith strengthened – in a world where those *with* brains design weapons and those *without* brains fire them.'

'But they'd be alive,' Mary repeated.

'You've got a strange idea of what being alive is! You call that alive? Maybe it is.' Tim shook his head wearily. 'Maybe you're right. Maybe we should go undersurface with Douglas. Stay in this world. Stay alive.'

'I didn't say that,' Mary said softly. 'Tim, I had to find out if you *really* understood why it's worth it. Worth staying in the house, taking the chance we won't be tipped back.'

'Then you want to take the chance?'

'Of course! We *have* to. We can't turn our children over to them – to the Relocation Center. To be taught how to hate and kill and destroy.' Mary smiled up wanly. 'Anyhow, they've always gone to the Jefferson School. And here, in this world, it's only an open field.'

'Are we going back?' Judy piped. She caught hold of Tim's sleeve imploringly. 'Are we going back now?'

Tim disengaged her arm. 'Very soon, honey.'

Mary opened the supply cupboards and rooted in them. 'Everything's here. What did they take?'

'The case of canned peas. Everything we had in the refrigerator. And they smashed the front door.'

'I'll bet we're beating them!' Earl shouted. He ran to the window and peered out. The sight of the rolling ash disappointed him. 'I can't see anything! Just the fog!' He turned questioningly to Tim. 'Is it always like this, here?'

'Yes,' Tim answered.

Earl's face fell. 'Just fog? Nothing else. Doesn't the sun shine ever?'

'I'll fix some coffee,' Mary said.

'Good.' Tim went into the bathroom and examined himself

in the mirror. His mouth was cut, caked with dried blood. His head ached. He felt sick at his stomach.

'It doesn't seem possible,' Mary said, as they sat down at the kitchen table.

Tim sipped his coffee. 'No. It doesn't.' Where he sat he could see out the window. The clouds of ash. The dim, jagged outline of ruined buildings.

'Is the man coming back?' Judy piped. 'He was all thin and funny-looking. He isn't coming back, is he?'

Tim looked at his watch. It read ten o'clock. He reset it, moving the hands to four-fifteen. 'Douglas said it would begin at nightfall. That won't be long.'

'Then we're really staying in the house,' Mary said.

'That's right.'

'Even though there's only a little chance?'

'Even though there's only a little chance we'll get back. Are you glad?'

'I'm glad,' Mary said, her eyes bright. 'It's worth it, Tim. You know it is. Anything's worth it, any chance. *To get back.* And something else. We'll all be here together . . . We can't be – broken up. Separated.'

Tim poured himself more coffee. 'We might as well make ourselves comfortable. We have maybe three hours to wait. We might as well try to enjoy them.'

At six-thirty the first rom fell. They felt the shock, a deep rolling wave of force that lapped over the house.

Judy came running in from the dining-room, face white with fear. 'Daddy! What is it?'

'Nothing. Don't worry.'

'Come on back,' Virginia called impatiently. 'It's your turn.' They were playing Monopoly.

Earl leaped to his feet. 'I want to see.' He ran excitedly to the window. 'I can see where it hit!'

Tim lifted the shade and looked out. Far off, in the distance, a white glare burned fitfully. A towering column of luminous smoke rose from it.

A second shudder vibrated through the house. A dish crashed from the shelf, into the sink.

It was almost dark outside. Except for the two spots of white

Tim could make out nothing. The clouds of ash were lost in the gloom. The ash and the ragged remains of buildings.

'That was closer,' Mary said.

A third rom fell. In the living-room windows burst, showering glass across the rug.

'We better get back,' Tim said.

'Where?'

'Down in the basement. Come on.' Tim unlocked the basement door and they trooped nervously downstairs.

'Food,' Mary said. 'We better bring the food that's left.'

'Good idea. You kids go on down. We'll come along in a minute.'

'I can carry something,' Earl said.

'Go on down.' The fourth rom hit, farther off than the last. 'And stay away from the window.'

'I'll move something over the window,' Earl said. 'The big piece of plywood we used for my train.'

'Good idea.' Tim and Mary returned to the kitchen. 'Food. Dishes. What else?'

'Books.' Mary looked nervously around. 'I don't know. Nothing else. Come on.'

A shattering roar drowned out her words. The kitchen window gave, showering glass over them. The dishes over the sink tumbled down in a torrent of breaking china. Tim grabbed Mary and pulled her down.

From the broken window rolling clouds of ominous gray drifted into the room. The evening air stank, a sour, rotten smell. Tim shuddered.

'Forget the food. Let's get back down.'

'But – '

'Forget it.' He grabbed her and pulled her down the basement stairs. They tumbled in a heap, Tim slamming the door after them.

'Where's the food?' Virginia demanded.

Tim wiped his forehead shakily. 'Forget it. We won't need it.'

'Help me,' Earl gasped. Tim helped him move the sheet of plywood over the window above the laundry tubs. The basement was cold and silent. The cement floor under them was faintly moist.

Two roms struck at once. Tim was hurled to the floor. The concrete hit him and he grunted. For a moment blackness swirled around him. Then he was on his knees, groping his way up.

'Everybody all right?' he muttered.

'I'm all right,' Mary said. Judy began to whimper. Earl was feeling his way across the room.

'I'm all right,' Virginia said. 'I guess.'

The lights flickered and dimmed. Abruptly they went out. The basement was pitch-black.

'Well,' Tim said. 'There they go.'

'I have my flashlight.' Earl winked the flashlight on. 'How's that?'

'Fine,' Tim said.

More roms hit. The ground leaped under them, bucking and heaving. A wave of force shuddering the whole house.

'We better lie down,' Mary said.

'Yes. Lie down.' Tim stretched himself out awkwardly. A few bits of plaster rained down around them.

'When will it stop?' Earl asked uneasily.

'Soon,' Tim said.

'Then we'll be back?'

'Yes. We'll be back.'

The next blast hit them almost at once. Tim felt the concrete rise under him. It grew, swelling higher and higher. He was going up. He shut his eyes, holding on tight. Higher and higher he went, carried up by the ballooning concrete. Around him beams and timbers cracked. Plaster poured down. He could hear glass breaking. And a long way off, the licking crackles of fire.

'Tim,' Mary's voice came faintly.

'Yes.'

'We're not going to – to make it.'

'I don't know.'

'We're not. I can tell.'

'Maybe not.' He grunted in pain as a board struck his back, settling over him. Boards and plaster, covering him, burying him. He could smell the sour smell, the night air and ash. It drifted and rolled into the cellar, through the broken window.

'Daddy,' Judy's voice came faintly.

'What?'

'Aren't we going back?'

He opened his mouth to answer. A shattering roar cut his words off. He jerked, tossed by the blast. Everything was moving around him. A vast wind tugged at him, a hot wind, licking at him, gnawing at him. He held on tight. The wind pulled, dragging him with it. He cried out as it seared his hands and face.

'Mary – '

Then silence. Only blackness and silence.

Cars.

Cars were stopping nearby. Then voices. And the noise of footsteps. Tim stirred, pushing the boards from him. He struggled to his feet.

'Mary.' He looked around. 'We're back.'

The basement was in ruins. The walls were broken and sagging. Great gaping holes showed a green line of grass beyond. A concrete walk. The small rose garden. The white stucco house next door.

Lines of telephone poles. Roofs. Houses. The city. As it had always been. Every morning.

'We're back!' Wild joy leaped through him. *Back*. Safe. It was over. Tim pushed quickly through the debris of his ruined house. 'Mary, are you all right?'

'Here.' Mary sat up, plaster dust raining from her. She was white all over, her hair, her skin, her clothing. Her face was cut and scratched. Her dress was torn. 'Are we really back?'

'Mr McLean! You all right?'

A blue-clad policeman leaped down into the cellar. Behind him two white-clad figures jumped. A group of neighbors collected outside, peering anxiously to see.

'I'm okay,' Tim said. He helped Judy and Virginia up. 'I think we're all okay.'

'What happened?' The policeman pushed boards aside, coming over. 'A bomb? Some kind of a bomb?'

'The house is a shambles,' one of the white-clad interns said. 'You sure nobody's hurt?'

'We were down here. In the basement.'

'You all right, Tim?' Mrs Hendricks called, stepping down gingerly into the cellar.

'What happened?' Frank Foley shouted. He leaped down with a crash. 'God, Tim! What the hell were you doing?'

The two white-clad interns poked suspiciously around the ruins. 'You're lucky, mister. Damn lucky. There's nothing left upstairs.'

Foley came over beside Tim. 'Damn it man! I *told* you to have that hot water heater looked at!'

'What?' Tim muttered.

'The hot water heater! I told you there was something wrong with the cut-off. It must've kept heating up, not turned off . . .' Foley winked nervously. 'But I won't say anything, Tim. The insurance. You can count on me.'

Tim opened his mouth. But the words didn't come. What could he say? – No, it wasn't a defective hot water heater that I forgot to have repaired. No, it wasn't a faulty connection in the stove. It wasn't any of those things. It wasn't a leaky gas line, it wasn't a plugged furnace, it wasn't a pressure cooker we forgot to turn off.

It's war. Total war. And not just war for me. For my family. For my house.

It's for your house, too. Your house and my house and all the houses. Here and in the next block, in the next town, the next state and country and continent. The whole world, like this. Shambles and ruins. Fog and dank weeds growing in the rusting slag. War for all of us. For everybody crowding down into the basement, white-faced, frightened, somehow sensing something terrible.

And when it really came, when the five years were up, there'd be no escape. No going back, tipping back into the past, away from it. When it came for them all, it would have them for eternity; there would be no one climbing back out, as he had.

Mary was watching him. The policeman, the neighbors, the white-clad interns – all of them were watching him. Waiting for him to explain. To tell them what it was.

'Was it the hot water heater?' Mrs Hendricks asked timidly.

'That was it, wasn't it, Tim? Things like that do happen. You can't be sure . . .'

'Maybe it was home brew,' a neighbor suggested, in a feeble attempt at humor. 'Was that it?'

He couldn't tell them. They wouldn't understand, because they didn't want to understand. They didn't want to know. They needed reassurance. He could see it in their eyes. Pitiful, pathetic fear. They sensed something terrible – and they were afraid. They were searching his face, seeking his help. Words of comfort. Words to banish their fear.

'Yeah,' Tim said heavily. 'It was the hot water heater.'

'I thought so!' Foley breathed. A sigh of relief swept through them all. Murmurs, shaky laughs. Nods, grins.

'I should have got it fixed,' Tim went on. 'I should have had it looked at a long time ago. Before it got in such bad shape.' Tim looked around at the circle of anxious people, hanging on his words. 'I should have had it looked at. Before it was too late.'

A Present for Pat

'What is it?' Patricia Blake demanded eagerly.

'What's what?' Eric Blake murmured.

'What did you bring? I *know* you brought me something!' Her bosom rose and fell excitedly under her mesh blouse. 'You brought me a present. I can tell!'

'Honey, I went to Ganymede for Terran Metals, not to find you curios. Now let me unpack my things. Bradshaw says I have to report to the office early tomorrow. He says I better report some good ore deposits.'

Pat snatched up a small box, heaped with all the other luggage the robot porter had deposited at the door. 'Is it jewelry? No, it's too big for jewelry.' She began to tear the cord from the box with her sharp fingernails.

Eric frowned uneasily. 'Don't be disappointed, honey. It's sort of strange. Not what you expect.' He watched apprehensively. 'Don't get mad at me. I'll explain all about it.'

Pat's mouth fell open. She turned pale. She dropped the box quickly on the table, eyes wide with horror. 'Good Lord! What *is* it?'

Eric twisted nervously. 'I got a good buy on it, honey. You can't usually pick one of them up. The Ganymedeans don't like to sell them, and I – '

'*What is it?*'

'It's a god,' Eric muttered. 'A minor Ganymedean deity. I got it practically at cost.'

Pat gazed down at the box with fear and growing disgust. 'That? That's a – a *god*?'

In the box was a small, motionless figure, perhaps ten inches high. It was old, terribly old. Its tiny clawlike hands were pressed against its scaly breast. Its insect face was twisted in a

scowl of anger – mixed with cynical lust. Instead of legs it
rested on a tangle of tentacles. The lower portion of its face
dissolved in a complex beak, mandibles of some hard substance. There was an odor to it, as of manure and stale beer. It
appeared to be bisexual.

Eric had thoughtfully put a little waterdish and some straw
in the box. He had punched air holes in the lid and crumpled
up newspaper fragments.

'You mean it's an idol.' Pat regained her poise slowly. 'An
idol of a deity.'

'No.' Eric shook his head stubbornly. 'This is a genuine
deity. There's a warranty, or something.'

'Is it – dead?'

'Not at all.'

'Then why doesn't it move?'

'You have to arouse it.' The bottom of the figure's belly
cupped outward in a hollow bowl. Eric tapped the bowl. 'Place
an offering here and it comes to life. I'll show you.'

Pat retreated. 'No thanks.'

'Come on! It's interesting to talk to. Its name is – ' He
glanced at some writing on the box. 'Its name is Tinokuknoi
Arevulopapo. We talked most of the way back from Ganymede. It was glad of the opportunity. And I learned quite a
few things about gods.'

Eric searched his pockets and brought out the remains of a
ham sandwich. He wadded up a bit of the ham and stuffed it
into the protruding belly-cup of the god.

'I'm going in the other room,' Pat said.

'Stick around.' Eric caught her arm. 'It only takes a second.
It begins to digest right away.'

The belly-cup quivered. The god's scaly flesh rippled. Presently the cup filled with a sluggish dark-colored substance. The
ham began to dissolve.

Pat snorted in disgust. 'Doesn't it even use its mouth?'

'Not for eating. Only for talking. It's a lot different from
usual life-forms.'

The tiny eye of the god was focused on them now. A single,
unwinking orb of icy malevolence. The mandibles twitched.

'Greetings,' the god said.

'Hi.' Eric nudged Pat forward. 'This is my wife. Mrs Blake. Patricia.'

'How do you do,' the god grated.

Pat gave a squeal of dismay. 'It talks English.'

The god turned to Eric in disgust. 'You were right. She *is* stupid.'

Eric colored. 'Gods can do anything they want, honey. They're omnipotent.'

The god nodded. 'That is so. This is Terra, I presume.'

'Yes. How does it look?'

'As I expected. I have already heard reports. Certain reports about Terra.'

'Eric, are you sure it's safe?' Pat whispered uneasily. 'I don't like its looks. And there's something about the way it talks.' Her bosom quivered nervously.

'Don't worry, honey,' Eric said carelessly. 'It's a nice god. I checked before I left Ganymede.'

'I'm benevolent,' the god explained matter-of-factly. 'My capacity has been that of Weather Deity to the Ganymedean aborigines. I have produced rain and allied phenomena when the occasion demanded.'

'But that's all in the past,' Eric added.

'Correct. I have been a Weather Deity for ten thousand years. There is a limit to even a god's patience. I craved new surroundings.' A peculiar gleam flickered across the loathsome face. 'That is why I arranged to be sold and brought to Terra.'

'You see,' Eric said, 'the Ganymedeans didn't want to sell it. But it whipped up a thunderstorm and they sort of had to. That's partly why it was so cheap.'

'Your husband made a good purchase,' the god said. Its single eye roved around curiously. 'This is your dwelling? You eat and sleep here?'

'That's right,' Eric said. 'Pat and I both – '

The front door chimed. 'Thomas Matson stands on the threshold,' the door stated. 'He wishes admission.'

'Golly,' Eric said. 'Good old Tom. I'll go let him in.'

Pat indicated the god. 'Hadn't you better – '

'Oh, no. I want Tom to see it.' Eric stepped to the door and opened it.

'Hello,' Tom said, striding in. 'Hi, Pat. Nice day.' He and Eric shook hands. 'The Lab has been wondering when you'd get back. Old Bradshaw is leaping up and down to hear your report.' Matson's bean-pole body bent forward in sudden interest. 'Say, what's in the box?'

'That's my god,' Eric said modestly.

'Really? But God is an unscientific concept.'

'This is a different god. I didn't invent it. I bought it. On Ganymede. It's a Ganymedean Weather Deity.'

'Say something,' Pat said to the god. 'So he'll believe your owner.'

'Let's debate my existence,' the god said sneeringly. 'You take the negative. Agreed?'

Matson grinned. 'What is this, Eric? A little robot? Sort of hideous looking.'

'Honest. It's a god. On the way it did a couple of miracles for me. Not big miracles, of course, but enough to convince me.'

'Hearsay,' Matson said. But he was interested. 'Pass a miracle, god. I'm all ears.'

'I am not a vulgar showpiece,' the god growled.

'Don't get it angry,' Eric cautioned. 'There's no limit to its powers, once aroused.'

'How does a god come into being?' Tom asked. 'Does a god create itself? If it's dependent on something prior then there must be a more ultimate order of being which – '

'Gods,' the tiny figure stated, 'are inhabitants of a higher level, a greater plane of reality. A more advanced dimension. There are a number of planes of existence. Dimensional continuums, arranged in a hierarchy. Mine is one above yours.'

'What are you doing here?'

'Occasionally beings pass from one dimensional continuum to another. When they pass from a superior continuum to an inferior – as I have done – they are worshipped as gods.'

Tom was disappointed. 'You're not a god at all. You're just a life-form of a slightly different dimensional order that's changed phase and entered our vector.'

The little figure glowered. 'You make it sound simple. Actually, such a transformation requires great cunning and is seldom done. I came here because a member of my race, a certain malodorous Nar Dolk, committed a heinous crime and escaped into this continuum. Our law obliged me to follow in hot pursuit. In the process this flotsam, this spawn of dampness, escaped and assumed some disguise or other. I continually search, but he has not yet been apprehended.' The small god broke off suddenly. 'Your curiosity is idle. It annoys me.'

Tom turned his back on the god. 'Pretty weak stuff. We do more down at the Terran Metals Lab than this character ever – '

The air crackled, ozone flashing. Tom Matson shrieked. Invisible hands lifted him bodily and propelled him to the door. The door swung open and Matson sailed down the walk, tumbling in a heap among the rose bushes, arms and legs flailing wildly.

'Help!' Matson yelled, struggling to get up.

'Oh, dear,' Pat gasped.

'Golly.' Eric shot a glance at the tiny figure. 'You did that?'

'Help him,' Pat urged, white-faced. 'I think he's hurt. He looks funny.'

Eric hurried outside and helped Matson to his feet. 'You okay? It's your own fault. I told you if you kept annoying it something might happen.'

Matson's face was ablaze with rage. 'No little pipsqueak god is going to treat me like this!' He pushed Eric aside, heading back for the house. 'I'll take it down to the Lab and pop it in a bottle of formaldehyde. I'll dissect it and skin it and hang it up on the wall. I'll have the first specimen of a god known to – '

A ball of light glowed around Matson. The ball enveloped him, settling in place around his lean body so that he looked like a filament in an incandescent light.

'What the hell!' Matson muttered. Suddenly he jerked. His body faded. He began to shrink. With a faint whoosh he diminished rapidly. Smaller and smaller he dwindled. His body shuddered, altering strangely.

The light winked out. Sitting stupidly on the walk was a small green toad.

'See?' Eric said wildly. 'I told you to keep quiet! Now look what it's done!'

290 *Philip K. Dick*

The toad hopped feebly toward the house. At the porch it sagged into immobility, defeated by the steps. It uttered a pathetic, hopeless *chug*.

Pat's voice rose in a wail of anguish. 'Oh, Eric! Look what it's done! Poor Tom!'

'His own fault,' Eric said. 'He deserves it.' But he was beginning to get nervous. 'Look here,' he said to the god. 'That's not a very nice thing to do to a grown man. What'll his wife and kids think?'

'What'll Mr Bradshaw think?' Pat cried. 'He can't go to work like that!'

'True,' Eric admitted. He appealed to the god. 'I think he's learned his lesson. How about turning him back? Okay?'

'You just better undo him!' Pat shrieked, clenching her small fists. 'If you don't undo him you'll have Terran Metals after you. Even a god can't stand up to Horace Bradshaw.'

'Better change him back,' Eric said.

'It'll do him good,' the god said. 'I'll leave him that way for a couple of centuries – '

'Centuries!' Pat exploded. 'Why, you little blob of slime!' She advanced ominously toward the box, shaking with wrath. 'See here! You turn him back or I'll take you out of your box and drop you into the garbage disposal unit!'

'Make her be still,' the god said to Eric.

'Calm down, Pat,' Eric implored.

'I will not calm down! Who does it think it is? A present! How *dare* you bring this moldy bit of refuse into our house? Is this your idea of a – '

Her voice ceased abruptly.

Eric turned apprehensively. Pat stood rigid, her mouth open, a word still on her lips. She did not move. She was white all over. A solid gray-white that made cold chills leap up Eric's spine. 'Good Lord,' he said.

'I turned her to stone,' the god explained. 'She made too much noise.' It yawned. 'Now, I think I'll retire. I'm a little tired, after my trip.'

'I can't believe it,' Eric Blake said. He shook his head numbly. 'My best friend a toad. My wife turned to stone.'

'It's true,' the god said. 'We deal out justice according to how people act. They both got what they deserved.'

'Can – can she hear me?'

'I suppose.'

Eric went over to the statue. 'Pat,' he begged imploringly. 'Please don't be mad. It isn't my fault.' He gripped her ice-cold shoulders. 'Don't blame me! I didn't do it.' The granite was hard and smooth under his fingers. Pat stared blankly ahead.

'Terran Metals indeed,' the god grumbled sourly. Its single eye studied Eric intently. 'Who is this Horace Bradshaw? Some local deity, perhaps?'

'Horace Bradshaw owns Terran Metals,' Eric said gloomily. He sat down and shakily lit a cigarette. 'He's about the biggest man on Terra. Terran Metals owns half the planets in the system.'

'Kingdoms of this world do not interest me,' the god said noncommittally, subsiding and shutting its eye. 'I will retire now. I wish to contemplate certain matters. You may wake me later, if you wish. We can converse on theological subjects, as we did on the ship coming here.'

'Theological subjects,' Eric said bitterly. 'My wife a stone block and it wants to talk about religion.'

But the god was already withdrawn, retired into itself.

'A lot you care,' Eric muttered. Anger flickered in him. 'This is the thanks I get for taking you off Ganymede. Ruin my household and my social life. Fine god you are!'

No response.

Eric concentrated desperately. Maybe when the god awoke it would be in a better mood. Maybe he could persuade it to turn Matson and Pat back to their usual forms. Faint hope stirred. He could appeal to the god's better side. After it had rested and slept for a few hours . . .

If nobody came looking for Matson.

The toad sat disconsolately on the walk, drooping with misery. Eric leaned toward it. 'Hey, Matson!'

The toad looked slowly up.

'Don't worry, old man. I'll get it to turn you back. It's a cinch.' The toad didn't stir. 'A lead-pipe cinch,' Eric repeated nervously.

The toad drooped a little more. Eric looked at his watch. It was late afternoon, almost four. Tom's shift at Terran began in half an hour. Sweat came out on his forehead. If the god went on sleeping and didn't wake up in half an hour –

A buzz. The vidphone.

Eric's heart sank. He hurried over and clicked the screen on, steeling himself. Horace Bradshaw's sharp, dignified features faded into focus. His keen glance bored into Eric, penetrating his depths.

'Blake,' he grunted. 'Back from Ganymede, I see.'

'Yes, sir.' Eric's mind raced frantically. He moved in front of the screen, cutting off Bradshaw's view of the room. 'I'm just starting to unpack.'

'Forget that and get over here! We're waiting to hear your report.'

'Right now? Gosh, Mr Bradshaw. Give me a chance to get my things away.' He fought desperately for time. 'I'll be over tomorrow morning bright and early.'

'Is Matson there with you?'

Eric swallowed. 'Yes, sir. But – '

'Put him on. I want to talk to him.'

'He – he can't talk to you right now, sir.'

'What? Why not?'

'He's in no shape to – that is, he – '

Bradshaw snarled impatiently. 'Then bring him along with you. And he better be sober when he gets here. I'll see you at my office in ten minutes.' He broke the circuit. The screen faded abruptly.

Eric sank wearily down in a chair. His mind reeled. Ten minutes! He shook his head, stunned.

The toad hopped a little, stirring on the walk. It emitted a faint, despondent sound.

Eric got heavily to his feet. 'I guess we have to face the music,' he murmured. He bent down and picked up the toad, putting it gingerly in his coat pocket. 'I guess you heard. That was Bradshaw. We're going down to the lab.'

The toad stirred uneasily.

'I wonder what Bradshaw is going to say when he sees you.' Eric kissed his wife's cold granite cheek. 'Good-bye, honey.'

He moved numbly down the walk to the street. A moment later he hailed a robot cab and entered it. 'I have a feeling this is going to be hard to explain.' The cab zipped off down the street. 'Hard as hell to explain.'

Horace Bradshaw stared in dumbfounded amazement. He removed his steel-rimmed glasses and wiped them slowly. He fitted them back on his hard, hawklike face and peered down. The toad rested silently in the center of the immense mahogany desk.

Bradshaw pointed shakily at the toad. 'This – this is Thomas Matson?'

'Yes, sir,' Eric said.

Bradshaw blinked in wonder. 'Matson! What in the world has happened to you?'

'He's a toad,' Eric explained.

'So I see. Incredible.' Bradshaw pressed a stud on his desk. 'Send in Jennings from the Biology Lab,' he ordered. 'A toad.' He poked the toad with his pencil. 'Is that really you, Matson?'

The toad *chugged*.

'Good Lord.' Bradshaw sat back, wiping his forehead. His grim expression faded into sympathetic concern. He shook his head sadly. 'I can't believe it. Some kind of bacterial blight, I suppose. Matson was always experimenting on himself. He took his work seriously. A brave man. A good worker. He did much for Terran Metals. Too bad he had to end this way. We'll extend full pension to him, of course.'

Jennings entered the office. 'You wanted me, sir?'

'Come in.' Bradshaw beckoned him impatiently in. 'We have a problem for your department. You know Eric Blake here.'

'Hi, Blake.'

'And Thomas Matson.' Bradshaw indicated the toad. 'From the Nonferrous Lab.'

'I know Matson,' Jennings said slowly. 'That is, I know a Matson from Nonferrous. But I don't recall – that is, he was taller than this. Almost six feet.'

'This is him,' Eric said gloomily. 'He's a toad now.'

'What happened?' Jennings's scientific curiosity was aroused. 'What's the lowdown?'

'It's a long story,' Eric said evasively.

'Can't you tell it?' Jennings scrutinized the toad professionally. 'Looks like a regular type of toad. You're sure this is Tom Matson? Come clean, Blake. You must know more than you're telling!'

Bradshaw studied Eric intently. 'Yes, what *did* happen, Blake? You have a strange, shifty look. Are you responsible for this?' Bradshaw half rose from his chair, his grim face bleak. 'See here. If it's your fault one of my best men has been incapacitated for further work – '

'Take it easy,' Eric protested, his mind racing frantically. He patted the toad nervously. 'Matson is perfectly safe – as long as nobody steps on him. We can rig up some sort of protective shield and an automatic communication system that'll enable him to spell out words. He can continue his work. With a few adjustments here and there everything should speed along perfectly.'

'Answer me!' Bradshaw roared. 'Are you responsible for this? Is this *your* doing?'

Eric squirmed helplessly. 'In a way, I suppose. Not exactly. Not *directly*.' His voice wavered. 'But I guess you'd say if it hadn't been for me . . .'

Bradshaw's face set in a rigid mask of rage. 'Blake, you're fired.' He yanked a heap of forms from his desk dispenser. 'Get out of here and never come back. And get your hand off that toad. It belongs to Terran Metals.' He shoved a paper across the desk. 'Here's your paycheck. And don't bother looking for work elsewhere. I'm listing you on the inter-system blacklist. Good day.'

'But, Mr Bradshaw – '

'Don't plead.' Bradshaw waved his hand. 'Just go. Jennings, get your biology staff busy at once. This problem must be licked. I want you to rearrange this toad back to its original shape. Matson is a vital part of Terran Metals. There's work to be done, work only Matson can do. We can't have this sort of thing holding up our research.'

'Mr Bradshaw,' Eric begged desperately. 'Please listen. I want to see Tom back as he was. But there's only one way we can get him back his original shape. We – '

Bradshaw's eyes were cold with hostility. 'You still here, Blake? Must I call my guards and have you dismembered? I'm giving you one minute to be off Company land. Understand?'

Eric nodded miserably. 'I understand.' He turned and shuffled unhappily toward the door. 'So long, Jennings. So long, Tom. I'll be home if you want me, Mr Bradshaw.'

'Sorcerer,' Bradshaw snapped. 'Good riddance.'

'What would you do,' Eric asked the robot cabdriver, 'if your wife had turned to stone, your best friend were a toad, and you had lost your job?'

'Robots have no wives,' the driver said. 'They are nonsexual. Robots have no friends, either. They are incapable of emotional relationships.'

'Can robots be fired?'

'Sometimes.' The robot drew his cab up before Eric's modest six-room bungalow. 'But consider. Robots are frequently melted down and new robots made from the remains. Recall Ibsen's *Peer Gynt*, the section concerning the Button Molder. The lines clearly anticipate in symbolic form the trauma of robots to come.'

'Yeah.' The door opened and Eric got out. 'I guess we all have our problems.'

'Robots have worse problems than anybody.' The door shut and the cab zipped off, back down the hill.

Worse? Hardly. Eric entered his home slowly, the front door automatically opening for him.

'Welcome, Mr Blake,' the door greeted him.

'I suppose Pat's still here.'

'Mrs Blake is here, but she is in a cataleptic state, or some similar condition.'

'She's been turned to stone.' Eric kissed the cold lips of the statue gloomily. 'Hi, honey.'

He got some meat from the refrigerator and crumbled it into the belly-cup of the god. Presently digestive fluid rose and covered the food. In a short time the single eye of the god opened, blinked a few times, and focused on Eric.

'Have a good sleep?' Eric inquired icily.

'I wasn't asleep. My mind was turned toward matters of

cosmic import. I detect a hostile quality in your voice. Has something unfavorable occurred?'

'Nothing. Nothing at all. I just lost my job, on top of everything else.'

'Lost your job? Interesting. What else do you refer to?'

Eric exploded in rage. 'You've messed up my whole life, damn you!' He jabbed at the silent, unmoving figure of his wife. 'Look! My wife! Turned to granite. And my best friend, a toad!'

Tinokuknoi Arevulopapo yawned. 'So?'

'*Why?* What did I ever do to you? Why do you treat me this way? Look at all I've done for you. I only brought you here to Terra. Fed you. Fixed you up a box with straw and water and newspapers. That's all.'

'True. You did bring me to Terra.' Again an odd gleam flickered across the god's dark face. 'All right. I'll restore your wife.'

'You will?' Pathetic joy surged through Eric. Tears came to his eyes. He was too relieved to ask any questions. 'Gosh, I sure would appreciate it!'

The god concentrated. 'Stand out of the way. It's easier to distort the molecular arrangement of a body than to restore the original configuration. I hope I can get it exactly as it was.' It made a faint motion.

Around Pat's silent figure the air stirred. The pale granite shuddered. Slowly, color seeped back into her features. She gasped sharply, her dark eyes flashing with fear. Color filled her arms, shoulders, breasts, spreading through her trim body. She cried out, tottering unsteadily. '*Eric!*'

Eric caught her, hugging her tight. 'Gosh, honey. I'm sure glad you're all right.' He crushed her against him, feeling her heart thump with terror. He kissed her soft lips again and again. 'Welcome back.'

Pat pulled abruptly away. 'That little snake. That miserable particle of waste. Wait until I get my hands on it.' She advanced toward the god, eyes blazing. 'Listen, you. What's the idea? How *dare* you!'

'See?' the god said. 'They never change.'

Eric pulled his wife back. 'You better shut up or you'll be granite again. Understand?'

Pat caught the urgent rasp in his voice. She subsided reluctantly. 'All right, Eric, I give up.'

'Listen,' Eric said to the god. 'How about Tom? How about restoring him?'

'The toad? Where is he?'

'In the Biology Lab. Jennings and his staff are working on him.'

The god considered. 'I don't like the sound of that. The Biology Lab? Where is that? How far away?'

'Terran Metals. Main Building.' Eric was impatient. 'Maybe five miles. How about it? Maybe if you restore him Bradshaw will give me my job back. You owe it to me. Set things back the way they were.'

'I can't.'

'You *can't*! Why the hell not?'

'I thought gods were omnipotent,' Pat sniffed petulantly.

'I can do anything – at short range. The Terran Metals Biology Lab is too far. Five miles is beyond my limit. I can distort molecular arrangements within a limited circle only.'

Eric was incredulous. 'What? You mean you can't turn Tom back?'

'That's the way it is. You shouldn't have taken him out of the house. Gods are subject to natural law just as you are. Our laws are different, but they are still laws.'

'I see,' Eric murmured. 'You should have said.'

'As far as your job goes, don't worry about that. Here, I'll create some gold.' The god made a motion with its scaly hands. A section of curtain flashed suddenly yellow and crashed to the floor with a metallic tinkle. 'Solid gold. That ought to keep you a few days.'

'We're no longer on the gold standard.'

'Well, whatever you need. I can do anything.'

'Except turn Tom back into a human being,' Pat said. 'Fine god you are.'

'Shut up, Pat,' Eric muttered, deep in thought.

'If there was some way I could be closer to him,' the god said cautiously. 'If he were within range . . .'

'Bradshaw will never let him go. And I can't set foot around there. The guards will tear me to bits.'

'How about some platinum?' The god made a pass and a section of the wall glowed white. 'Solid platinum. A simple change of atomic weight. Will that help?'

'No!' Eric paced back and forth. 'We've got to get that toad away from Bradshaw. If we can get him back here – '

'I have an idea,' the god said.

'What?'

'Perhaps you could get me in there. Perhaps if I could get onto the Company grounds, within range of the Biology Lab . . .'

'It's worth a try,' Pat said, putting her hand on Eric's shoulder. 'After all, Tom's your best friend. It's a shame to treat him this way. It's – it's un-Terran.'

Eric grabbed his coat. 'It's settled. I'll drive as close as I can to the Company grounds. I ought to be able to get near enough before the guards catch sight of me to – '

A crash. The front door collapsed abruptly in a heap of ash. Teams of robot police surged into the room, blastguns ready.

'All right,' Jennings said. 'That's him.' He strode quickly into the house. 'Get him. And get that thing in the box.'

'Jennings!' Eric swallowed in alarm. 'What the hell is this?'

Jennings's lip curled. 'Cut out the pretense, Blake. You're not fooling me.' He tapped a small metal case under his arm. 'The toad revealed all. So you've got a non-Terrestrial in this house, have you?' He laughed coldly. 'There's a law against bringing non-Terrans to Earth. You're under arrest, Blake. You'll probably get life.'

'Tinokuknoi Arevulopapo!' Eric Blake squeaked. 'Don't forsake me at a time like this!'

'I'm coming,' the god grunted. It heaved violently. 'How's this?'

The robot police jerked as a torrent of force erupted from the box. Abruptly they disappeared, winking out of existence. Where they had stood a horde of mechanical mice milled aimlessly, spilling frantically through the doorway, out into the yard.

Jennings's face showed astonishment and then panic. He

retreated, waving his blaster menacingly. 'See here, Blake. Don't think you can scare me. We've got this house surrounded.'

A bolt of force hit him in the stomach. The bolt lifted him and shook him like a rag doll. His blaster skidded from his fingers, falling to the floor. Jennings groped for it desperately. The blaster turned into a spider and crawled rapidly off, out of his reach.

'Set him down,' Eric urged.

'All right.' The god released Jennings. He crashed to the floor, stunned and frightened. He scrambled wildly to his feet and ran from the house, down the path to the sidewalk.

'Oh dear,' Pat said.

'What is it?'

'Look.'

Pulled up in a circle around the house was a solid line of atomic cannon. Their snouts gleamed wickedly in the late afternoon sunlight. Groups of robot police stood around each cannon, waiting alertly for instructions.

Eric groaned. 'We're sunk. One blast and we're finished.'

'Do something!' Pat gasped. She prodded the box. 'Enchant them. Don't just sit there.'

'They are out of range,' the god replied. 'As I explained, my power is limited by distance.'

'You in there!' a voice came, magnified by a hundred loudspeakers. 'Come out with your hands up. Or we open fire!'

'Bradshaw,' Eric groaned. 'He's out there. We're trapped. You sure you can't do something?'

'Sorry,' the god said. 'I can put up a shield against the cannon.' It concentrated. Outside the house a dull surface formed, a globe rapidly hardening around them.

'All right,' Bradshaw's magnified voice came, muffled by the shield. 'You asked for it.'

The first shell hit. Eric found himself lying on the floor, his ears ringing, everything going around and around. Pat lay beside him, dazed and frightened. The house was a shambles. Walls, chairs, furniture, all was in ruins.

'Fine shield,' Pat gasped.

'The concussion,' the god protested. Its box lay in the corner on its side. 'The shield stops the shells, but the concussion – '

A second shell struck. A wall of pressure rolled over Eric, stunning him. He skidded, tossed by a violent wind, crashing against heaps of debris that had been his house.

'We can't last,' Pat said faintly. 'Tell them to stop, Eric. Please!'

'Your wife is right,' the god's calm voice came up, from its overturned box. 'Surrender, Eric. Give yourself up.'

'I guess I better.' Eric pulled himself up on his knees. 'But golly, I don't want to spend the rest of my life in prison. I knew I was breaking the law when I smuggled the damn thing in here, but I never thought – '

A third shell hit. Eric tumbled down, his chin smacking the floor. Plaster and rubble rained down on him, choking and blinding him. He fought his way up, grabbing hold of a jutting beam.

'Stop!' he shouted.

There was sudden silence.

'Are you willing to surrender?' the magnified voice boomed.

'Surrender,' the god murmured.

Eric's mind raced desperately. 'I – I have a deal. A compromise.' He thought fast, his brain in high gear. 'I have a proposal.'

There was a long pause. 'What's the proposal?'

Eric stepped warily through the rubble to the edge of the shield. The shield was almost gone. Only a shimmering haze remained, through which the circle of atomic cannon was visible, the cannon and the robot police.

'Matson,' Eric gasped, getting his breath. 'The toad. We'll make the following deal. We'll restore Matson to his original shape. We'll return the non-Terrestrial to Ganymede. In return, you waive prosecution and I get my job back.'

'Absurd! My labs can easily restore Matson without your help.'

'Oh yeah? Ask Matson. He'll tell you. If you don't agree, Matson will be a toad for the next two hundred years – at least!'

A long silence followed. Eric could see figures moving back and forth, conferring behind the guns.

'All right,' Bradshaw's voice came at last. 'We agree. Drop the shield and come forward. I'll send Jennings with the toad. No tricks, Blake!'

'No tricks.' Eric sagged with relief. 'Come along,' he said to the god, picking up the dented box. 'Drop the shield and let's get this over with. Those cannon make me nervous.'

The god relaxed. The shield – what was left of it – wavered and faded, blinking off.

'Here I come.' Eric advanced warily, the box in his hands. 'Where's Matson?'

Jennings came toward him. 'I have him.' His curiosity overcame his suspicion. 'This ought to be interesting. We should make a close study of all extra-dimensional life. Apparently they possess science much in advance of our own.'

Jennings squatted down, placing the small green toad carefully on the grass.

'There he is,' Eric said to the god.

'Is this close enough?' Pat asked icily.

'This is sufficient,' the god said. 'This is exactly right.' It turned its single eye on the toad and made a few brief motions with its scaly claws.

A shimmer hovered over the toad. Extra-dimensional forces were at work, fingering and plucking at the toad molecules. Abruptly the toad twitched. For a second it shuddered, an insistent vibration lapped over it. Then –

Matson ballooned into existence, the familiar bean-pole figure, towering over Eric and Jennings and Pat.

'Lord,' Matson breathed shakily. He got out his handkerchief and wiped his face. 'I'm glad that's over. Wouldn't want to go through that again.'

Jennings retreated hurriedly toward the circle of cannon. Matson turned and headed after him. Eric and his wife and god were suddenly alone in the center of the lawn.

'Hey!' Eric demanded, cold alarm plucking at him. 'What is this? What the hell's going on?'

'Sorry, Blake,' Bradshaw's voice came. 'It was essential to restore Matson. But we can't alter the law. The law is above any man, even me. You're under arrest.'

Robot police swarmed forward, grimly surrounding Eric and Pat. 'You skunk,' Eric choked, struggling feebly.

Bradshaw came out from behind the cannon, hands in his pockets, grinning calmly. 'Sorry, Blake. You should be out of jail in ten or fifteen years, though. Your job will be waiting for you – I promise. As for this extra-dimensional being, I'm quite interested in seeing it. I've heard of such things.' He peered toward the box. 'I'm happy to take charge of it. Our labs will perform experiments and tests on it which will . . .'

Bradshaw's words died. His face turned a sickly hue. His mouth opened and closed, but no sounds came.

From the box came a swelling, frenzied buzz of rage. '*Nar Dolk!* I knew I'd find you!'

Bradshaw retreated, trembling violently. 'Why, of all persons. Tinokuknoi Arevulopapo! What are you doing on Terra?' He stumbled, half falling. 'How did you, that is, after so long, how could – '

Then Bradshaw was running, scattering robot police in all directions, rushing wildly past the atomic cannon.

'Nar Dolk!' the god screamed, swelling with fury. 'Scourge of the Seven Temples! Flotsam of Space! I knew you were on this miserable planet! Come back and take your punishment!'

The god burst upward, flashing into the air. It raced past Eric and Pat, growing as it flew. A sickening, nauseous wind, warm and damp, lapped at their faces, as the god gained speed.

Bradshaw – Nar Dolk – ran frantically. And as he ran he *changed*. Immense wings sprouted from him. Great leathery wings, beating the air in frantic haste. His body oozed and altered. Tentacles replaced his legs. Scaly claws replaced arms. Gray hide rippled as he flew up, wings flapping noisily.

Tinokuknoi Arevulopapo struck. For a brief moment the two locked together, twisting and rolling in the air, wings and claws raking and flapping.

Then Nar Dolk broke away, fluttering up. A blazing flash, a pop, and he was gone.

For a moment Tinokuknoi Arevulopapo hovered in the air. The scaly head turned, the single eye glancing back and down at Eric and Pat. It nodded briefly. Then, with a curious shimmy, it vanished.

The sky was empty except for a few feathers and the dull stench of burning scales.

Eric was the first to speak. 'Well,' he said. 'So that's why it wanted to come to Terra. I guess I was sort of exploited.' He grinned sheepishly. 'The first Terran ever to be exploited.'

Matson gawked, still peering up. 'They're gone. Both of them. Back to their own dimension, I guess.'

A robot policeman plucked at Jennings's sleeve. 'Shall we arrest anyone, sir? With Mr Bradshaw gone you are next in charge.'

Jennings glanced at Eric and Pat. 'I suppose not. The evidence has departed. It seems somewhat silly, anyhow.' He shook his head. 'Bradshaw. Imagine! And we worked for him for years. Damn strange business.'

Eric put his arm around his wife. He pulled her against him, hugging her tight. 'I'm sorry, honey,' he said softly.

'Sorry?'

'Your present. It's gone. I guess I'll have to get you something else.'

Pat laughed, pressing against him. 'That's all right. I'll let you in on a secret.'

'What?'

Pat kissed him, her lips warm against his cheek. 'As a matter of fact – I'm just as glad.'

The Hood Maker

'A hood!'

'Somebody with a hood!'

Workers and shoppers hurried down the sidewalk, joining the forming crowd. A sallow-faced youth dropped his bike and raced over. The crowd grew, businessmen in gray coats, tired-faced secretaries, clerks and workmen.

'Get him!' the crowd swarmed forward. 'The old man!'

The sallow-faced youth scooped up a rock from the gutter and hurled it. The rock missed the old man, crashing against a store front.

'He's got a hood, all right!'

'Take it away!'

More rocks fell. The old man gasped in fear, trying to push past two soldiers blocking his way. A rock struck him on the back.

'What you got to hide?' The sallow-faced youth ran up in front of him. 'Why you afraid of a probe?'

'He's got something to hide!' A worker grabbed the old man's hat. Eager hands groped for the thin metal band around his head.

'Nobody's got a right to hide!'

The old man fell, sprawling to his hands and knees, umbrella rolling. A clerk caught hold of the hood and tugged. The crowd surged, struggling to get to the metal band. Suddenly the youth gave a cry. He backed off, the hood held up. 'I got it! I got it!' He ran to his bike and pedaled off rapidly, gripping the bent hood.

A robot police car pulled up to the curb, siren screaming. Robot cops leaped out, clearing the mob away.

'You hurt?' They helped the old man up.

The old man shook his head, dazed. His glasses hung from one ear. Blood and saliva streaked his face.

'All right.' The cop's metal fingers released. 'Better get off the street. Inside someplace. For your own good.'

Clearance Director Ross pushed the memo plate away. 'Another one. I'll be glad when the Anti-Immunity Bill is passed.'

Peters glanced up. 'Another?'

'Another person wearing a hood – a probe shield. That makes ten in the last forty-eight hours. They're mailing more out all the time.'

'Mailed, slipped under doors, in pockets, left at desks – countless ways of distribution.'

'If more of them notified us – '

Peters grinned crookedly. 'It's a wonder any of them do. There's a reason why hoods are sent to these people. They're not picked out at random.'

'Why are they picked?'

'They have something to hide. Why else would hoods be sent to them?'

'What about those who *do* notify us?'

'They're afraid to wear them. They pass the hoods on to us – to avoid suspicion.'

Ross reflected moodily. 'I suppose so.'

'An innocent man has no reason to conceal his thoughts. Ninety-nine per cent of the population is glad to have its mind scanned. Most people *want* to prove their loyalty. But this one per cent is guilty of something.'

Ross opened a manila folder and took out a bent metal band. He studied it intently. 'Look at it. Just a strip of some alloy. But it effectively cuts off all probes. The teeps go crazy. It buzzes them when they try to get past. Like a shock.'

'You've sent samples to the lab, of course.'

'No. I don't want any of the lab workers turning out their own hoods. We have trouble enough!'

'Who was this taken from?'

Ross stabbed a button on his desk. 'We'll find out. I'll have the teep make a report.'

The door melted and a lank sallow-faced youth came into the room. He saw the metal band in Ross's hand and smiled, a thin, alert smile. 'You wanted me?'

Ross studied the youth. Blond hair, blue eyes. An ordinary-looking kid, maybe a college sophomore. But Ross knew better. Ernest Abbud was a telepathic mutant – a teep. One of several hundred employed by Clearance for its loyalty probes.

Before the teeps, loyalty probes had been haphazard. Oaths, examinations, wire-tappings, were not enough. The theory that each person had to prove his loyalty was fine – as a theory. In practice few people could do it. It looked as if the concept of guilty until proved innocent might have to be abandoned and the Roman law restored.

The problem, apparently insoluble, had found its answer in the Madagascar Blast of 2004. Waves of hard radiation had lapped over several thousand troops stationed in the area. Of those who lived, few produced subsequent progeny. But of the several hundred children born to the survivors of the blast, many showed neural characteristics of a radically new kind. A human mutant had come into being – for the first time in thousands of years.

The teeps appeared by accident. But they solved the most pressing problem the Free Union faced: the detection and punishment of disloyalty. The teeps were invaluable to the Government of the Free Union – and the teeps knew it.

'You got this?' Ross asked, tapping the hood.

Abbud nodded. 'Yes.'

The youth was following his thoughts, not his spoken words. Ross flushed angrily. 'What was the man like?' he demanded harshly. 'The memo plate gives no details.'

'Doctor Franklin is his name. Director of the Federal Resources Commission. Sixty-seven years of age. Here on a visit to a relative.'

'Walter Franklin! I've heard of him.' Ross stared up at Abbud. 'Then you already –'

'As soon as I removed the hood I was able to scan him.'

'Where did Franklin go after the assault?'

'Indoors. Instructed by the police.'

'They arrived?'

'After the hood had been taken, of course. It went perfectly. Franklin was spotted by another telepath, not myself. I was informed Franklin was coming my way. When he reached me I shouted that he was wearing a hood. A crowd collected and others took up the shout. The other telepath arrived and we manipulated the crowd until we were near him. I took the hood myself – and you know the rest.'

Ross was silent for a moment. 'Do you know how he got the hood? Did you scan that?'

'He received it by mail.'

'Does he – '

'He has no idea who sent it or where it came from.'

Ross frowned. 'Then he can't give us any information about them. The senders.'

'The Hood Makers,' Abbud said icily.

Ross glanced quickly up. 'What?'

'The Hood Makers. *Somebody* makes them.' Abbud's face was hard. '*Somebody* is making probe screens to keep us out.'

'And you're sure – '

'Franklin knows nothing! He arrived in the city last night. This morning his mail machine brought the hood. For a time he deliberated. Then he purchased a hat and put it on over the hood. He set out on foot toward his niece's house. We spotted him several minutes later, when he entered range.'

'There seem to be more of them, these days. More hoods being sent out. But you know that.' Ross set his jaw. 'We've got to locate the senders.'

'It'll take time. They apparently wear hoods constantly.' Abbud's face twisted. 'We have to get so damn close! Our scanning range is extremely limited. But sooner or later we'll locate one of them. Sooner or later we'll tear a hood off somebody – and find *him* . . .'

'In the last year five thousand hood-wearers have been detected,' Ross stated. 'Five thousand – and not one of them knows anything. Where the hoods come from or who makes them.'

'When there are more of us, we'll have a better chance,' Abbud said grimly. 'Right now there are too few of us. But eventually – '

308 *Philip K. Dick*

'You're going to have Franklin probed, aren't you?' Peters said to Ross. 'As a matter of course.'

'I suppose so.' Ross nodded to Abbud. 'You might as well go ahead on him. Have one of your group run the regular total probe and see if there's anything of interest buried down in his non-conscious neural area. Report the results to me in the usual way.'

Abbud reached into his coat. He brought out a tape spool and tossed it down on the desk in front of Ross. 'Here you are.'

'What's this?'

'The total probe on Franklin. All levels – completely searched and recorded.'

Ross stared up at the youth. 'You –'

'We went ahead with it.' Abbud moved toward the door. 'It's a good job. Cummings did it. We found considerable disloyalty. Mostly ideological rather than overt. You'll probably want to pick him up. When he was twenty-four he found some old books and musical records. He was strongly influenced. The latter part of the tape discusses fully our evaluation of his deviation.'

The door melted and Abbud left.

Ross and Peters stared after him. Finally Ross took the tape spool and put it with the bent metal hood.

'I'll be damned,' Peters said. 'They went ahead with the probe.'

Ross nodded, deep in thought. 'Yeah. And I'm not sure I like it.'

The two men glanced at each other – and knew, as they did so, that outside the office Ernest Abbud was scanning their thoughts.

'Damn it!' Ross said futilely. 'Damn it!'

Walter Franklin breathed rapidly, peering around him. He wiped nervous sweat from his lined face with a trembling hand.

Down the corridor the echoing clang of Clearance agents sounded, growing louder.

He had got away from the mob – spared for a while. That was four hours ago. Now the sun had set and evening was settling over greater New York. He had managed to make his way half across the city, almost to the outskirts – and now a public alarm was out for his arrest.

Why? He had worked for the Free Union Government all his life. He had done nothing disloyal. Nothing, except open the morning mail, find the hood, deliberate about it, and finally put it on. He remembered the small instruction tag:

GREETINGS!
This probe screen is sent to you with the compliments of the maker and the earnest hope that it will be of some value to you. Thank you.

Nothing else. No other information. For a long time he had pondered. Should he wear it? He had never done anything. He had nothing to hide – nothing disloyal to the Union. But the thought fascinated him. If he wore the hood his mind would be his own. Nobody could look into it. His mind would belong to him again, private, secret, to think as he wished, endless thoughts for no one else's consumption but his own.

Finally he had made up his mind and put on the hood, fitting his old Homburg over it. He had gone outside – and within ten minutes a mob was screaming and yelling around him. And now a general alarm was out for his arrest.

Franklin wracked his brain desperately. What could he do? They could bring him up before a Clearance Board. No accusation would be brought: it would be up to him to clear himself, to prove he was loyal. *Had* he ever done anything wrong? Was there something he had done he was forgetting? He had put on the hood. Maybe that was it. There was some sort of an Anti-Immunity bill up in Congress to make wearing of a probe screen a felony, but it hadn't been passed yet –

The Clearance agents were near, almost on him. He retreated down the corridor of the hotel, glancing desperately around him. A red sign glowed: EXIT. He hurried toward it and down a flight of basement stairs, out onto a dark street. It was bad to be outside, where the mobs were. He had tried to remain indoors as much as possible. But now there was no choice.

Behind him a voice shrilled loudly. Something cut past him, smoking away a section of the pavement. A Slem-ray. Franklin ran, gasping for breath, around a corner and down a side street. People glanced at him curiously as he rushed past.

He crossed a busy street and moved with a surging group of theater goers. Had the agents seen him? He peered nervously around. None in sight.

At the corner he crossed with the lights. He reached the safety zone in the center, watching a sleek Clearance car cruising toward him. Had it seen him go out to the safety zone? He left the zone, heading toward the curb on the far side. The Clearance car shot suddenly forward, gaining speed. Another appeared, coming the other way.

Franklin reached the curb.

The first car ground to a halt. Clearance agents piled out, swarming up onto the sidewalk.

He was trapped. There was no place to hide. Around him tired shoppers and office workers gazed curiously, their faces devoid of sympathy. A few grinned at him in vacant amusement. Franklin peered frantically around. No place, no door, no person –

A car pulled up in front of him, its doors sliding open. 'Get in.' A young girl leaned toward him, her pretty face urgent. 'Get in, damn it!'

He got in. The girl slammed the doors and the car picked up speed. A Clearance car swung in ahead of them, its sleek bulk blocking the street. A second Clearance car moved in behind them.

The girl leaned forward, gripping the controls. Abruptly the car lifted. It left the street, clearing the cars ahead, gaining altitude rapidly. A flash of violet lit up the sky behind them.

'Get down!' the girl snapped. Franklin sank down in his seat. The car moved in a wide arc, passing beyond the protective columns of a row of buildings. On the ground, the Clearance cars gave up and turned back.

Franklin settled back, mopping his forehead shakily. 'Thanks,' he muttered.

'Don't mention it.' The girl increased the car's speed. They were leaving the business section of the city, moving above the residential outskirts. She steered silently, intent on the sky ahead.

'Who are you?' Franklin asked.

The girl tossed something back to him. 'Put that on.'

A hood. Franklin unfastened it and slipped it awkwardly over his head. 'It's in place.'

'Otherwise they'll get us with a teep scan. We have to be careful all the time.'

'Where are we going?'

The girl turned to him, studying him with calm gray eyes, one hand resting on the wheel. 'We're going to the Hood Maker,' she said. 'The public alarm for you is top priority. If I let you off you won't last an hour.'

'But I don't understand.' Franklin shook his head, dazed. 'Why do they want me? What have I done?'

'You're being framed.' The girl brought the car around in a wide arc, wind whistling shrilly through its struts and fenders. 'Framed by the teeps. Things are happening fast. There's no time to lose.'

The little bald-headed man removed his glasses and held out his hand to Franklin, peering near-sightedly. 'I'm glad to meet you, Doctor. I've followed your work at the Board with great interest.'

'Who are you?' Franklin demanded.

The little man grinned self-consciously. 'I'm James Cutter. The Hood Maker, as the teeps call me. This is our factory.' He waved around the room. 'Take a look at it.'

Franklin gazed around him. He was in a warehouse, an ancient wooden building of the last century. Giant worm-scored beams rose up, dry and cracking. The floor was concrete. Old-fashioned fluorescent lights glinted and flickered from the roof. The walls were streaked with water stains and bulging pipes.

Franklin moved across the room, Cutter beside him. He was bewildered. Everything had happened fast. He seemed to be outside New York, in some dilapidated industrial suburb. Men were working on all sides of him, bent over stampers and molds. The air was hot. An archaic fan whirred. The warehouse echoed and vibrated with a constant din.

'This – ' Franklin murmured. 'This is – '

'This is where we make the hoods. Not very impressive, is it? Later on we hope to move to new quarters. Come along and I'll show you the rest.'

Cutter pushed a side door open and they entered a small laboratory, bottles and retorts everywhere in cluttered confusion. 'We do our research in here. Pure and applied. We've learned a few things. Some we may use, some we hope won't be needed. And it keeps our refugees busy.'

'Refugees?'

Cutter pushed some equipment back and seated himself on a lab table. 'Most of the others are here for the same reason as you. Framed by the teeps. Accused of deviation. But we got to them first.'

'But why – '

'Why were you framed? Because of your position. Director of a Government Department. All these men were prominent – and all were framed by teep probes.' Cutter lit a cigarette, leaning back against the water-stained wall. 'We exist because of a discovery made ten years ago in a Government lab.' He tapped his hood. 'This alloy – opaque to probes. Discovered by accident, by one of these men. Teeps came after him instantly, but he escaped. He made a number of hoods and passed them to other workers in his field. That's how we got started.'

'How many are here?'

Cutter laughed. 'Can't tell you that. Enough to turn out hoods and keep them circulating. To people prominent in Government. People holding positions of authority. Scientists, officials, educators – '

'Why?'

'Because we want to get them first, before the teeps. We got to you too late. A total probe report had *already* been made out on you, before the hood was even in the mail.

'The teeps are gradually getting a stranglehold over the Government. They're picking off the best men, denouncing them and getting them arrested. If a teep says a man is disloyal Clearance has to haul him in. We tried to get a hood to you in time. The report couldn't be passed on to Clearance if you were wearing a hood. But they outsmarted us. They got a mob after you and snatched the hood. As soon as it was off they served the report to Clearance.'

'So that's why they wanted it off.'

'The teeps can't file a framed report on a man whose mind is opaque to probes. Clearance isn't that stupid. The teeps have to get the hoods off. Every man wearing a hood is a man out of bounds. They've managed so far by stirring up mobs – but that's ineffectual. Now they're working on this bill in Congress. Senator Waldo's Anti-Immunity Bill. It would outlaw wearing hoods.' Cutter grinned ironically. 'If a man is innocent why shouldn't he want his mind probed? The bill makes wearing a probe shield a felony. People who receive hoods will turn them over to Clearance. There won't be a man in ten thousand who'll keep his hood, if it means prison and confiscation of property.'

'I met Waldo, once. I can't believe he understands what his bill would do. If he could be made to see – '

'Exactly! If he could be made to see. This bill has to be stopped. If it goes through we're licked. And the teeps are in. Somebody has to talk to Waldo and make him see the situation.' Cutter's eyes were bright. 'You know the man. He'll remember you.'

'What do you mean?'

'Franklin, we're sending you back again – to meet Waldo. It's our only chance to stop the bill. And it has to be stopped.'

The cruiser roared over the Rockies, brush and tangled forest flashing by below. 'There's a level pasture over to the right,' Cutter said. 'I'll set her down, if I can find it.'

He snapped off the jets. The roar died into silence. They were coasting above the hills.

'To the right,' Franklin said.

Cutter brought the cruiser down in a sweeping glide. 'This will put us within walking distance of Waldo's estate. We'll go the rest of the way on foot.' A shuddering growl shook them as the landing fins dug into the ground – and they were at rest.

Around them tall trees moved faintly with the wind. It was mid-morning. The air was cool and thin. They were high up, still in the mountains, on the Colorado side.

'What are the chances of our reaching him?' Franklin asked.

'Not very good.'

Franklin started. 'Why? Why not?'

Cutter pushed the cruiser door back and leaped out onto the ground. 'Come on.' He helped Franklin out and slammed the door after him. 'Waldo is guarded. He's got a wall of robots around him. That's why we've never tried before. If it weren't crucial we wouldn't be trying now.'

They left the pasture, making their way down the hill along a narrow weed-covered path. 'What are they doing it for?' Franklin asked. 'The teeps. Why do they want to get power?'

'Human nature, I suppose.'

'*Human* nature?'

'The teeps are no different from the Jacobins, the Round-heads, the Nazis, the Bolsheviks. There's always some group that wants to lead mankind – for its own good, of course.'

'Do the teeps believe that?'

'Most teeps believe they're the natural leaders of mankind. Non-telepathic humans are an inferior species. Teeps are the next step, *homo superior*. And because they're superior, it's natural they should lead. Make all the decisions for us.'

'And you don't agree,' Franklin said.

'The teeps are different from us – but that doesn't mean they're superior. A telepathic faculty doesn't imply general superiority. The teeps aren't a superior race. They're human beings with a special ability. But that doesn't give them a right to tell us what to do. It's not a new problem.'

'Who should lead mankind, then?' Franklin asked. 'Who should be the leaders?'

'*Nobody* should lead mankind. It should lead itself.' Cutter leaned forward suddenly, body tense.

'We're almost there. Waldo's estate is directly ahead. Get ready. Everything depends on the next few minutes.'

'A few robot guards.' Cutter lowered his binoculars. 'But that's not what's worrying me. If Waldo has a teep nearby, he'll detect our hoods.'

'And we can't take them off.'

'No. The whole thing would be out, passed from teep to teep.' Cutter moved cautiously forwards. 'The robots will stop us and demand identification. We'll have to count on your Director's clip.'

They left the bushes, crossing the open field toward the buildings that made up Senator Waldo's estate. They came onto a dirt road and followed it, neither of them speaking, watching the landscape ahead.

'Halt!' A robot guard appeared, streaking toward them across the field. 'Identify yourselves!'

Franklin showed his clip. 'I'm Director level. We're here to see the Senator. I'm an old friend.'

Automatic relays clicked as the robot studied the identification clip. 'From the Director level?'

'That's right,' Franklin said, becoming uneasy.

'Get out of the way,' Cutter said impatiently. 'We don't have any time to waste.'

The robot withdrew uncertainly. 'Sorry to have stopped you, sir. The Senator is inside the main building. Directly ahead.'

'All right.' Cutter and Franklin advanced past the robot. Sweat stood out on Cutter's round face. 'We made it,' he murmured. 'Now let's hope there aren't any teeps inside.'

Franklin reached the porch. He stepped slowly up, Cutter behind him. At the door he halted, glancing at the smaller man. 'Shall I – '

'Go ahead.' Cutter was tense. 'Let's get right inside. It's safer.'

Franklin raised his hand. The door clicked sharply as its lens photographed him and checked his image. Franklin prayed silently. If the Clearance alarm had been sent out this far –

The door melted.

'Inside,' Cutter said quickly.

Franklin entered, looking around in the semi-darkness. He blinked, adjusting to the dim light of the hall. Somebody was coming toward him. A shape, a small shape, coming rapidly, lithely. Was it Waldo?

A lank, sallow-faced youth entered the hall, a fixed smile on his face. 'Good morning, Doctor Franklin,' he said. He raised his Slem-gun and fired.

Cutter and Ernest Abbud stared down at the oozing mass that had been Doctor Franklin. Neither of them spoke. Finally Cutter raised his hand, his face drained of color.

'Was that necessary?'

Abbud shifted, suddenly conscious of him. 'Why not?' He

shrugged, the Slem-gun pointed at Cutter's stomach. 'He was an old man. He wouldn't have lasted long in the protective-custody camp.'

Cutter took out his package of cigarettes and lit up slowly, his eyes on the youth's face. He had never seen Ernest Abbud before. But he knew who he was. He watched the sallow-faced youth kick idly at the remains on the floor.

'Then Waldo is a teep,' Cutter said.

'Yes.'

'Franklin was wrong. He *does* have full understanding of his bill.'

'Of course! The Anti-Immunity Bill is an integral part of our activity.' Abbud waved the snout of the Slem-gun. 'Remove your hood. I can't scan you – and it makes me uneasy.'

Cutter hesitated. He dropped his cigarette thoughtfully to the floor and crushed it underfoot. 'What are you doing here? You usually hang out in New York. This is a long way out here.'

Abbud smiled. 'We picked up Doctor Franklin's thoughts as he entered the girl's car – before she gave him the hood. She waited too long. We got a distinct visual image of her, seen from the back seat, of course. But she turned around to give him the hood. Two hours ago Clearance picked her up. She knew a great deal – our first real contact. We were able to locate the factory and round up most of the workers.'

'Oh?' Cutter murmured.

'They're in protective custody. Their hoods are gone – and the supply stored for distribution. The stampers have been dismantled. As far as I know we have all the group. You're the last one.'

'Then does it matter if I keep my hood?'

Abbud's eyes flickered. 'Take it off. I want to scan you – Mister Hood Maker.'

Cutter grunted. 'What do you mean?'

'Several of your men gave us images of you – and details of your trip here. I came out personally, notifying Waldo through our relay system in advance. I wanted to be here myself.'

'Why?'

'It's an occasion. A great occasion.'

'What position do *you* hold?' Cutter demanded.

Abbud's sallow face turned ugly. 'Come on! Off with the hood! I could blast you now. But I want to scan you first.'

'All right. I'll take it off. You can scan me, if you want. Probe all the way down.' Cutter paused, reflecting soberly. 'It's your funeral.'

'What do you mean?'

Cutter removed his hood, tossing it onto a table by the door. 'Well? What do you see? What do I know – *that none of the others knew*?'

For a moment Abbud was silent.

Suddenly his face twitched, his mouth working. The Slem-gun swayed. Abbud staggered, a violent shudder leaping through his lank frame. He gaped at Cutter in rising horror.

'I learned it only recently,' Cutter said. 'In our lab. I didn't want to use it – but you forced me to take off my hood. I always considered the alloy my most important discovery – until this. In some ways, this is even more important. Don't you agree?'

Abbud said nothing. His face was a sickly gray. His lips moved but no sound came.

'I had a hunch – and I played it for all it was worth. I knew you telepaths were born from a single group, resulting from an accident – the Madagascar hydrogen explosion. That made me think. Most mutants, that we know of, are thrown off universally by the species that's reached the mutation stage. Not a single group in one area. The whole world, wherever the species exists.

'Damage to the germ plasma of a specific group of humans is the cause of your existence. You weren't a mutant in the sense that you represented a natural development of the evolutionary process. In no sense could it be said that homo sapiens had reached the mutation stage. So perhaps you weren't a mutant.

'I began to make studies, some biological, some merely statistical. Sociological research. We began correlating facts on you, on each member of your group we could locate. How old you were. What you were doing for a living. How many were married. Number of children. After a while I came across the facts you're scanning right now.'

Cutter leaned toward Abbud, watching the youth intently.

'You're not a true mutant, Abbud. Your group exists because of a chance explosion. You're different from us because of damage to the reproductive apparatus of your parents. You lack one specific characteristic that true mutants possess.' A faint smile twitched across Cutter's features. 'A lot of you are married. But not one birth has been reported. Not one birth! Not a single teep child! You can't reproduce, Abbud. You're *sterile*, the whole lot of you. When you die there won't be any more.

'You're not mutants. You're freaks!'

Abbud grunted hoarsely, his body trembling. 'I see this, in your mind.' He pulled himself together with an effort. 'And you've kept this secret, have you? You're the only one who knows?'

'Somebody else knows,' Cutter said.

'Who?'

'*You* know. You scanned me. And since you're a teep, all the others – '

Abbud fired, the Slem-gun digging frantically into his own middle. He dissolved, showering in a rain of fragments. Cutter moved back, his hands over his face. He closed his eyes, holding his breath.

When he looked again there was nothing.

Cutter shook his head. 'Too late, Abbud. Not fast enough. Scanning is instant – and Waldo is within range. The relay system . . . And even if they missed *you*, they can't avoid picking me up.'

A sound. Cutter turned. Clearance agents were moving rapidly into the hall, glancing down at the remains on the floor and up at Cutter.

Director Ross covered Cutter uncertainly, confused and shaken. 'What happened here? Where – '

'Scan him!' Peters snapped. 'Get a teep in here quick. Bring Waldo in. Find out what happened.'

Cutter grinned ironically. 'Sure,' he said, nodding shakily. He sagged with relief. 'Scan me. I have nothing to hide. Get a teep in here for a probe – if you can find any . . .'

Of Withered Apples

Something was tapping on the window. Blowing up against the pane, again and again. Carried by the wind. Tapping faintly, insistently.

Lori, sitting on the couch, pretended not to hear. She gripped her book tightly and turned a page. The tapping came again, louder and more imperative. It could not be ignored.

'Darn!' Lori said, throwing her book down on the coffee table and hurrying to the window. She grasped the heavy brass handles and lifted.

For a moment the window resisted. Then, with a protesting groan, it reluctantly rose. Cold autumn air rushed into the room. The bit of leaf ceased tapping and swirled against the woman's throat, dancing to the floor.

Lori picked the leaf up. It was old and brown. Her heart skipped a beat as she slipped the leaf into the pocket of her jeans. Against her loins the leaf cut and tingled, a little hard point piercing her smooth skin and sending exciting shivers up and down her spine. She stood at the open window a moment, sniffing the air. The air was full of the presence of trees and rocks, of great boulders and remote places. It was time – time to go again. She touched the leaf. She was *wanted*.

Quickly Lori left the big living-room, hurrying through the hall into the dining-room. The dining-room was empty. A few chords of laughter drifted from the kitchen. Lori pushed the kitchen door open. 'Steve?'

Her husband and his father were sitting around the kitchen table, smoking their cigars and drinking steaming black coffee. 'What is it?' Steve demanded, frowning at his young wife. 'Ed and I are in the middle of business.'

'I – I want to ask you something.'

The two men gazed at her, brown-haired Steven, his dark eyes full of the stubborn dignity of New England men, and his father, silent and withdrawn in *her* presence. Ed Patterson scarcely noticed her. He rustled through a sheaf of feed bills, his broad back turned toward her.

'What is it?' Steve demanded impatiently. 'What do you want? Can't it wait?'

'I have to go,' Lori blurted.

'Go where?'

'Outside.' Anxiety flooded over her. 'This is the last time. I promise. I won't go again, after this. Okay?' She tried to smile, but her heart was pounding too hard. 'Please let me, Steve.'

'Where does she go?' Ed rumbled.

Steve grunted in annoyance. 'Up in the hills. Some old abandoned place up there.'

Ed's gray eyes flickered. 'Abandoned farm?'

'Yes. You know it?'

'The old Rickley farm. Rickley moved away years ago. Couldn't get anything to grow, not up there. Ground's all rocks. Bad soil. A lot of clay and stones. The place is all overgrown, tumbled down.'

'What kind of farm was it?'

'Orchard. Fruit orchard. Never yielded a damn thing. Thin old trees. Waste of effort.'

Steve looked at his pocket watch. 'You'll be back in time to fix dinner?'

'Yes!' Lori moved toward the door. 'Then I can go?'

Steve's face twisted as he made up his mind. Lori waited impatiently, scarcely breathing. She had never got used to Vermont men and their slow, deliberate way. Boston people were quite different. And her group had been more the college youths, dances and talk, and late laughter.

'Why do you go up there?' Steve grumbled.

'Don't ask me, Steve. Just let me go. This is the last time.' She writhed in agony. She clenched her fists. 'Please!'

Steve looked out the window. The cold autumn wind swirled through the trees. 'All right. But it's going to snow. I don't see why you want to – '

Lori ran to get her coat from the closet. 'I'll be back to fix dinner!' she shouted joyfully. She hurried to the front porch, buttoning her coat, her heart racing. Her cheeks were flushed a deep, excited red as she closed the door behind her, her blood pounding in her veins.

Cold wind whipped against her, rumpling her hair, plucking at her body. She took a deep breath of the wind and started down the steps.

She walked rapidly onto the field, toward the bleak line of hills beyond. Except for the wind there was no sound. She patted her pocket. The dry leaf broke and dug hungrily into her.

'I'm coming . . .' she whispered, a little awed and frightened. 'I'm on my way . . .'

Higher and higher the woman climbed. She passed through a deep cleft between two rocky ridges. Huge roots from old stumps spurted out on all sides. She followed a dried-up creek bed, winding and turning.

After a time low mists began to blow about her. At the top of the ridge she halted, breathing deeply, looking back the way she had come.

A few drops of rain stirred the leaves around her. Again the wind moved through the great dead trees along the ridge. Lori turned and started on, her head down, hands in her coat pockets.

She was on a rocky field, overgrown with weeds and dead grass. After a time she came to a ruined fence, broken and rotting. She stepped over it. She passed a tumbled-down well, half filled with stones and earth.

Her heart beat quickly, fluttering with nervous excitement. She was almost there. She passed the remains of a building, sagging timbers and broken glass, a few ruined pieces of furniture strewn nearby. An old automobile tire caked and cracked. Some damp rags heaped over rusty, bent bedsprings.

And there it was – directly ahead.

Along the edge of the field was a grove of ancient trees. Lifeless trees, withered and dead, their thin, blackened stalks rising up leaflessly. Broken sticks stuck in the hard ground.

Row after row of dead trees, some bent and leaning, torn loose from the rocky soil by the unending wind.

Lori crossed the field to the trees, her lungs laboring painfully. The wind surged against her without respite, whipping the foul-smelling mists into her nostrils and face. Her smooth skin was damp and shiny with the mist. She coughed and hurried on, stepping over the rocks and clods of earth, trembling with fear and anticipation.

She circled around the grove of trees, almost to the edge of the ridge. Carefully, she stepped among the sliding heaps of rocks. Then –

She stopped, rigid. Her chest rose and fell with the effort of breathing. 'I came,' she gasped.

For a long time she gazed at the withered old apple tree. She could not take her eyes from it. The sight of the ancient tree fascinated and repelled her. It was the only one alive, the only tree of all the grove still living. All the others were dead, dried-up. They had lost the struggle. But this tree still clung to life.

The tree was hard and barren. Only a few dark leaves hung from it – and some withered apples, dried and seasoned by the wind and mists. They had stayed there, on the branches, forgotten and abandoned. The ground around the tree was cracked and bleak. Stones and decayed heaps of old leaves in ragged clumps.

'I came,' Lori said again. She took the leaf from her pocket and held it cautiously out. 'This tapped at the window. I knew when I heard it.' She smiled mischievously, her red lips curling. 'It tapped and tapped, trying to get in. I ignored it. It was so – so impetuous. It annoyed me.'

The tree swayed ominously. Its gnarled branches rubbed together. Something in the sound made Lori pull away. Terror rushed through her. She hurried back along the ridge, scrambling frantically out of reach.

'Don't,' she whispered. '*Please.*'

The wind ceased. The tree became silent. For a long time Lori watched it apprehensively.

Night was coming. The sky was darkening rapidly. A burst of frigid wind struck her, half turning her around. She shuddered, bracing herself against it, pulling her long coat around her. Far below, the floor of the valley was disappearing into shadow, into the vast cloud of night.

In the darkening mists the tree was stern and menacing, more ominous than usual. A few leaves blew from it, drifting and swirling with the wind. A leaf blew past her and she tried to catch it. The leaf escaped, dancing back toward the tree. Lori followed a little way and then stopped, gasping and laughing.

'No,' she said firmly, her hands on her hips. 'I won't.'

There was silence. Suddenly the heaps of decayed leaves blew up in a furious circle around the tree. They quieted down, settling back.

'No,' Lori said. 'I'm not afraid of you. You can't hurt me.' But her heart was hammering with fear. She moved back farther away.

The tree remained silent. Its wiry branches were motionless.

Lori regained her courage. 'This is the last time I can come,' she said. 'Steve says I can't come any more. He doesn't like it.'

She waited, but the tree did not respond.

'They're sitting in the kitchen. The two of them. Smoking cigars and drinking coffee. Adding up feed bills.' She wrinkled her nose. 'That's all they ever do. Add and subtract feed bills. Figure and figure. Profit and loss. Government taxes. Depreciation on the equipment.'

The tree did not stir.

Lori shivered. A little more rain fell, big icy drops that slid down her cheeks, down the back of her neck and inside her heavy coat.

She moved closer to the tree. 'I won't be back. I won't see you again. This is the last time. I wanted to tell you . . .'

The tree moved. Its branches whipped into sudden life. Lori felt something hard and thin cut across her shoulder. Something caught her around the waist, tugging her forward.

She struggled desperately, trying to pull herself free. Suddenly the tree released her. She stumbled back, laughing and trembling with fear. 'No!' she gasped. 'You can't have me!' She hurried to the edge of the ridge. 'You'll never get me again. Understand? And I'm not afraid of you!'

She stood, waiting and watching, trembling with cold and

324 Philip K. Dick

fear. Suddenly she turned and fled, down the side of the ridge, sliding and falling on the loose stones. Blind terror gripped her. She ran on and on, down the steep slope, grabbing at roots and weeds –

Something rolled beside her shoe. Something small and hard. She bent down and picked it up.

It was a little dried apple.

Lori gazed back up the slope at the tree. The tree was almost lost in the swirling mists. It stood, jutting up against the black sky, a hard unmoving pillar.

Lori put the apple in her coat pocket and continued down the side of the hill. When she reached the floor of the valley she took the apple out of her pocket.

It was late. A deep hunger began to gnaw inside her. She thought suddenly of dinner, the warm kitchen, the white tablecloth. Steaming stew and biscuits.

As she walked she nibbled on the little apple.

Lori sat up in bed, the covers falling away from her. The house was dark and silent. A few night noises sounded faintly, far off. It was past midnight. Beside her Steven slept quietly, turned over on his side.

What had wakened her? Lori pushed her dark hair back out of her eyes, shaking her head. What –

A spasm of pain burst loose inside her. She gasped and put her hand to her stomach. For a time she wrestled silently, jaws locked, swaying back and forth.

The pain went away. Lori sank back. She cried out, a faint, thin cry. 'Steve – '

Steven stirred. He turned over a little, grunting in his sleep.

The pain came again. Harder. She fell forward on her face, writhing in agony. The pain ripped at her, tearing at her belly. She screamed, a shrill wail of fear and pain.

Steve sat up. 'For God's sake – ' He rubbed his eyes and snapped on the lamp. 'What the hell – '

Lori lay on her side, gasping and moaning, her eyes staring, knotted fists pressed into her stomach. The pain twisted and seared, devouring her, eating into her.

'Lori!' Steven grated. 'What is it?'

She screamed. Again and again. Until the house rocked with echoes. She slid from the bed, onto the floor, her body writhing and jerking, her face unrecognizable.

Ed came hurrying into the room, pulling his bathrobe around him. 'What's going on?'

The two men stared helplessly down at the woman on the floor.

'Good God,' Ed said. He closed his eyes.

The day was cold and dark. Snow fell silently over the streets and houses, over the red brick county hospital building. Doctor Blair walked slowly up the gravel path to his Ford car. He slid inside and turned the ignition key. The motor leaped alive, and he let the brake out.

'I'll call you later,' Doctor Blair said. 'There are certain particulars.'

'I know,' Steve muttered. He was still dazed. His face was gray and puffy from lack of sleep.

'I left some sedatives for you. Try to get a little rest.'

'You think,' Steve asked suddenly, 'if we had called you earlier – '

'No.' Blair glanced up at him sympathetically. 'I don't. In a thing like that, there's not much chance. Not after it's burst.'

'Then it *was* appendicitis?'

Blair nodded. 'Yes.'

'If we hadn't been so damn far out,' Steve said bitterly. 'Stuck out in the country. No hospital. Nothing. Miles from town. And we didn't realize at first – '

'Well, it's over now.' The upright Ford moved forward a little. All at once a thought came to the doctor. 'One more thing.'

'What is it?' Steve said dully.

Blair hesitated. 'Post mortems – very unfortunate. I don't think there's any reason for one in this case. I'm certain in my own mind . . . But I wanted to ask – '

'What is it?'

'Is there anything the girl might have swallowed? Did she put things in her mouth? Needles – while she was sewing? Pins, coins, anything like that? Seeds? Did she ever eat watermelon? Sometimes the appendix – '

'No.'

Steve shook his head wearily. 'I don't know.'

'It was just a thought.' Doctor Blair drove slowly off down the narrow tree-lined street, leaving two dark streaks, two soiled lines that marred the packed, glistening snow.

Spring came, warm and sunny. The ground turned black and rich. Overhead the sun shone, a hot white orb, full of strength.

'Stop here,' Steve murmured.

Ed Patterson brought the car to a halt at the side of the street. He turned off the motor. The two men sat in silence, neither of them speaking.

At the end of the street children were playing. A high school boy was mowing a lawn, pushing the machine over wet grass. The street was dark in the shade of the great trees growing along each side.

'Nice,' Ed said.

Steve nodded without answering. Moodily, he watched a young girl walking by, a shopping bag under her arm. The girl climbed the stairs of a porch and disappeared into an old-fashioned yellow house.

Steve pushed the car door open. 'Come on. Let's get it over with.'

Ed lifted the wreath of flowers from the back seat and put them in his son's lap. 'You'll have to carry it. It's your job.'

'All right.' Steve grabbed the flowers and stepped out onto the pavement.

The two men walked up the street together, silent and thoughtful.

'It's been seven or eight months, now,' Steve said abruptly.

'At least.' Ed lit a cigar as they walked along, puffing clouds of gray smoke around them. 'Maybe a little more.'

'I never should have brought her up here. She lived in town all her life. She didn't know anything about the country.'

'It would have happened anyhow.'

'If we had been closer to a hospital – '

'The doctor said it wouldn't have made any difference. Even

if we'd called him right away instead of waiting until morning.' They came to the corner and turned. 'And as you know – '

'Forget it,' Steve said, suddenly tense.

The sounds of the children had fallen behind them. The houses had thinned out. Their footsteps rang out against the pavement as they walked along.

'We're almost there,' Steve said.

They came to a rise. Beyond the rise was a heavy brass fence, running the length of a small field. A green field, neat and even. With carefully placed plaques of white marble criss-crossing it.

'Here we are,' Steve said tightly.

'They keep it nice.'

'Can we get in from this side?'

'We can try.' Ed started along the brass fence, looking for a gate.

Suddenly Steve halted, grunting. He stared across the field, his face white. '*Look*.'

'What is it?' Ed took off his glasses to see. 'What are you looking at?'

'I was right.' Steve's voice was low and indistinct. 'I thought there was something. Last time we were here . . . I saw . . . You see it?'

'I'm not sure. I see the tree, if that's what you mean.'

In the center of the neat green field the little apple tree rose proudly. Its bright leaves sparkled in the warm sunlight. The young tree was strong and very healthy. It swayed confidently with the wind, its supple trunk moist with sweet spring sap.

'They're *red*,' Steve said softly. 'They're already red. How the hell can they be red? It's only April. How the hell can they be red so soon?'

'I don't know,' Ed said. 'I don't know anything about apples.' A strange chill moved through him. But graveyards always made him uncomfortable. 'Maybe we ought to go.'

'Her cheeks were that color,' Steve said, his voice low. 'When she had been running. Remember?'

The two men gazed uneasily at the little apple tree, its shiny red fruit glistening in the spring sunlight, branches moving gently with the wind.

'I remember, all right,' Ed said grimly. 'Come on.' He took his son's arm insistently, the wreath of flowers forgotten. 'Come on, Steve. Let's get out of here.'

Human Is

Jill Herrick's blue eyes filled with tears. She gazed at her husband in unspeakable horror. 'You're – you're hideous!' she wailed.

Lester Herrick continued working, arranging heaps of notes and graphs in precise piles.

'Hideous,' he stated, 'is a value judgment. It contains no factual information.' He sent a report tape on Centauran parasitic life whizzing through the desk scanner. 'Merely an opinion. An expression of emotion, nothing more.'

Jill stumbled back to the kitchen. Listlessly, she waved her hand to trip the stove into activity. Conveyor belts in the wall hummed to life, hurrying the food from the underground storage lockers for the evening meal.

She turned to face her husband one last time. 'Not even a *little* while?' she begged. 'Not even – '

'Not even for a month. When he comes you can tell him. If you haven't the courage, I'll do it. I can't have a child running around here. I have too much work to do. This report on Betelgeuse XI is due in ten days.' Lester dropped a spool on Fomalhautan fossil implements into the scanner. 'What's the matter with your brother? Why can't he take care of his own child?'

Jill dabbed at swollen eyes. 'Don't you understand? I *want* Gus here! I begged Frank to let him come. And now you – '

'I'll be glad when he's old enough to be turned over to the Government.' Lester's thin face twisted in annoyance. 'Damn it, Jill, isn't dinner ready yet? It's been ten minutes! What's wrong with that stove?'

'It's almost ready.' The stove showed a red signal light. The robant waiter had come out of the wall and was waiting expectantly to take the food.

Jill sat down and blew her small nose violently. In the living-room, Lester worked on unperturbed. His work. His research. Day after day. Lester was getting ahead; there was no doubt of that. His lean body was bent like a coiled spring over the tape scanner, cold gray eyes taking in the information feverishly, analyzing, appraising, his conceptual faculties operating like well-greased machinery.

Jill's lips trembled in misery and resentment. Gus – little Gus. How could she tell him? Fresh tears welled up in her eyes. Never to see the chubby little fellow again. He could never come back – because his childish laughter and play bothered Lester. Interfered with his research.

The stove clicked to green. The food slid out, into the arms of the robant. Soft chimes sounded to announce dinner.

'I hear it,' Lester grated. He snapped off the scanner and got to his feet. 'I suppose he'll come while we're eating.'

'I can vid Frank and ask – '

'No. Might as well get it over with.' Lester nodded impatiently to the robant. 'All right. Put it down.' His thin lips set in an angry line. 'Damn it, don't dawdle! I want to get back to my work!'

Jill bit back the tears.

Little Gus came trailing into the house as they were finishing dinner.

Jill gave a cry of joy. 'Gussie!' She ran to sweep him up in her arms. 'I'm so glad to see you!'

'Watch out for my tiger,' Gus muttered. He dropped his little gray kitten onto the rug and it rushed off, under the couch. 'He's hiding.'

Lester's eyes flickered as he studied the little boy and the tip of gray tail extending from under the couch.

'Why do you call it a tiger? It's nothing but an alley cat.'

Gus looked hurt. He scowled. 'He's a tiger. He's got stripes.'

'Tigers are yellow and a great deal bigger. You might as well learn to classify things by their correct names.'

'Lester, please – ' Jill pleaded.

'Be quiet,' her husband said crossly. 'Gus is old enough to shed childish illusions and develop a realistic orientation. What's wrong with the psych testers? Don't they straighten this sort of nonsense out?'

Gus ran and snatched up his tiger. 'You leave him alone!'

Lester contemplated the kitten. A strange, cold smile played about his lips. 'Come down to the lab some time, Gus. We'll show you lots of cats. We use them in our research. Cats, guinea pigs, rabbits – '

'Lester!' Jill gasped. 'How can you!'

Lester laughed thinly. Abruptly he broke off and returned to his desk. 'Now clear out of here. I have to finish these reports. And don't forget to tell Gus.'

Gus got excited. 'Tell me what?' His cheeks flushed. His eyes sparkled. 'What is it? Something for me? A *secret*?'

Jill's heart was like lead. She put her hand heavily on the child's shoulder. 'Come on, Gus. We'll go sit out in the garden and I'll tell you. Bring – bring your tiger.'

A click. The emergency vidsender lit up. Instantly Lester was on his feet. 'Be quiet!' He ran to the sender, breathing rapidly. 'Nobody speak!'

Jill and Gus paused at the door. A confidential message was sliding from the slot into the dish. Lester grabbed it up and broke the seal. He studied it intently.

'What is it?' Jill asked. 'Anything bad?'

'Bad?' Lester's face shone with a deep inner glow. 'No, not bad at all.' He glanced at his watch. 'Just time. Let's see, I'll need – '

'What is it?'

'I'm going on a trip. I'll be gone two or three weeks. Rexor IV is into the charted area.'

'Rexor IV? You're going there?' Jill clasped her hands eagerly. 'Oh, I've always wanted to see an old system, old ruins and cities! Lester, can I come along? Can I go with you? We never took a vacation, and you always promised – '

Lester Herrick stared at his wife in amazement. 'You?' he said. '*You* go along?' He laughed unpleasantly. 'Now hurry and get my things together. I've been waiting for this a long time.' He rubbed his hands together in satisfaction. 'You can keep the boy here until I'm back. But no longer. Rexor IV! I can hardly wait!'

'You have to make allowances,' Frank said. 'After all, he's a scientist.'

'I don't care,' Jill said. 'I'm leaving him. As soon as he gets back from Rexor IV. I've made up my mind.'

Her brother was silent, deep in thought. He stretched his feet out, onto the lawn of the little garden. 'Well, if you leave him you'll be free to marry again. You're still classed as sexually adequate, aren't you?'

Jill nodded firmly. 'You bet I am. I wouldn't have any trouble. Maybe I can find somebody who likes children.'

'You think a lot of children,' Frank perceived. 'Gus loves to visit you. But he doesn't like Lester. Les needles him.'

'I know. This past week has been heaven, with him gone.' Jill patted her soft blonde hair, blushing prettily. 'I've had fun. Makes me feel alive again.'

'When'll he be back?'

'Any day.' Jill clenched her small fists. 'We've been married five years and every year it's worse. He's so – so inhuman. Utterly cold and ruthless. Him and his work. Day and night.'

'Les is ambitious. He wants to get to the top in his field.' Frank lit a cigarette lazily. 'A pusher. Well, maybe he'll do it. What's he in?'

'Toxicology. He works out new poisons for Military. He invented the copper sulphate skin-lime they used against Callisto.'

'It's a small field. Now take me.' Frank leaned contentedly against the wall of the house. 'There are thousands of Clearance lawyers. I could work for years and never create a ripple. I'm content just to be. I do my job. I enjoy it.'

'I wish Lester felt that way.'

'Maybe he'll change.'

'He'll *never* change,' Jill said bitterly. 'I know that, now. That's why I've made up my mind to leave him. He'll always be the same.'

* * *

Lester Herrick came back from Rexor IV a different man. Beaming happily, he deposited his anti-grav suitcase in the arms of the waiting robant. 'Thank you.'

Jill gasped speechlessly. 'Les! What – '

Lester removed his hat, bowing a little. 'Good day, my dear. You're looking lovely. Your eyes are clear and blue. Sparkling like some virgin lake, fed by mountain streams.' He sniffed. 'Do I smell a delicious repast warming on the hearth?'

'Oh, Lester.' Jill blinked uncertainly, faint hope swelling in her bosom. 'Lester, what's happened to you? You're so – so different.'

'Am I, my dear?' Lester moved about the house, touching things and sighing. 'What a dear little house. So sweet and friendly. You don't know how wonderful it is to be here. Believe me.'

'I'm afraid to believe it,' Jill said.

'Believe what?'

'That you mean all this. That you're not the way you were. The way you've always been.'

'What way is that?'

'Mean. Mean and cruel.'

'I?' Lester frowned, rubbing his lip. 'Hmm. Interesting.' He brightened. 'Well, that's all in the past. What's for dinner? I'm faint with hunger.'

Jill eyed him uncertainly as she moved into the kitchen. 'Anything you want, Lester. You know our stove covers the maximum select-list.'

'Of course.' Lester coughed rapidly. 'Well, shall we try sirloin steak, medium, smothered in onions? With mushroom sauce. And white rolls. With hot coffee. Perhaps ice cream and apple pie for dessert.'

'You never seemed to care much about food,' Jill said thoughtfully.

'Oh?'

'You always said you hoped eventually they'd make intravenous intake universally applicable.' She studied her husband intently. 'Lester, what's happened?'

'Nothing. Nothing at all.' Lester carelessly took his pipe out and lit it rapidly, somewhat awkwardly. Bits of tobacco drifted to the rug. He bent nervously down and tried to pick them up again. 'Please go about your tasks and don't mind me. Perhaps I can help you prepare – that is, can I do anything to help?'

'No,' Jill said. 'I can do it. You go ahead with your work, if you want.'

'Work?'

'Your research. In toxins.'

'Toxins!' Lester showed confusion. 'Well, for heaven's sake! Toxins. Devil take it!'

'What dear?'

'I mean, I really feel too tired, just now. I'll work later.' Lester moved vaguely around the room. 'I think I'll sit and enjoy being home again. Off that awful Rexor IV.'

'Was it awful?'

'Horrible.' A spasm of disgust crossed Lester's face. 'Dry and dead. Ancient. Squeezed to a pulp by wind and sun. A dreadful place, my dear.'

'I'm sorry to hear that. I always wanted to visit it.'

'Heaven forbid!' Lester cried feelingly. 'You stay right here, my dear. With me. The – the two of us.' His eyes wandered around the room. 'Two, yes. Terra is a wonderful planet. Moist and full of life.' He beamed happily. 'Just right.'

'I don't understand it,' Jill said.

'Repeat all the things you remember,' Frank said. His robot pencil poised itself alertly. 'The changes you've noticed in him. I'm curious.'

'Why?'

'No reason. Go on. You say you sensed it right away? That he was different?'

'I noticed it at once. The expression on his face. Not that hard, practical look. A sort of mellow look. Relaxed. Tolerant. A sort of calmness.'

'I see,' Frank said. 'What else?'

Jill peered nervously through the back door into the house. 'He can't hear us, can he?'

'No. He's inside playing with Gus. In the living-room. They're Venusian otter-men today. Your husband built an otter slide down at his lab. I saw him unwrapping it.'

'His talk.'

'His what?'

'The way he talks. His choice of words. Words he never used before. Whole new phrases. Metaphors. I never heard him use a metaphor in all our five years together. He said metaphors were inexact. Misleading. And – '

'And what?' The pencil scratched busily.

'And they're *strange* words. Old words. Words you don't hear any more.'

'Archaic phraseology?' Frank asked tensely.

'Yes.' Jill paced back and forth across the small lawn, her hands in the pockets of her plastic shorts. 'Formal words. Like something – '

'Something out of a book?'

'Exactly! You've noticed it?'

'I noticed it.' Frank's face was grim. 'Go on.'

Jill stopped pacing. 'What's on your mind? Do you have a theory?'

'I want to know more facts.'

She reflected. 'He plays. With Gus. He plays and jokes. And he – he eats.'

'Didn't he eat before?'

'Not like he does now. Now he *loves* food. He goes into the kitchen and tries endless combinations. He and the stove get together and cook up all sorts of weird things.'

'I thought he'd put on weight.'

'He's gained ten pounds. He eats, smiles and laughs. He's constantly polite.' Jill glanced away coyly. 'He's even – romantic! He always said *that* was irrational. And he's not interested in his work. His research in toxins.'

'I see.' Frank chewed his lip. 'Anything more?'

'One thing puzzles me very much. I've noticed it again and again.'

'What is it?'

'He seems to have strange lapses of – '

A burst of laughter. Lester Herrick, eyes bright with merriment, came rushing out of the house, little Gus close behind.

'We have an announcement!' Lester cried.

'An announzelmen,' Gus echoed.

Frank folded his notes up and slid them into his coat pocket. The pencil hurried after them. He got slowly to his feet. 'What is it?'

'You make it,' Lester said, taking little Gus's hand and leading him forward.

Gus's plump face screwed up in concentration. 'I'm going to come live with you,' he stated. Anxiously he watched Jill's expression. 'Lester says I can. Can I? Can I, Aunt Jill?'

Her heart flooded with incredible joy. She glanced from Gus to Lester. 'Do you – do you really mean it?' Her voice was almost inaudible.

Lester put his arm around her, holding her close to him. 'Of course, we mean it,' he said gently. His eyes were warm and understanding. 'We wouldn't tease you, my dear.'

'No teasing!' Gus shouted excitedly. 'No more teasing!' He and Lester and Jill drew close together. 'Never again!'

Frank stood a little way off, his face grim. Jill noticed him and broke away abruptly. 'What is it?' she faltered. 'Is anything – '

'When you're quite finished,' Frank said to Lester Herrick, 'I'd like you to come with me.'

A chill clutched Jill's heart. 'What is it? Can I come, too?'

Frank shook his head. He moved toward Lester ominously. 'Come on, Herrick. Let's go. You and I are going to take a little trip.'

The three Federal Clearance Agents took up positions a few feet from Lester Herrick, vibro-tubes gripped alertly.

Clearance Director Douglas studied Herrick for a long time. 'You're sure?' he said finally.

'Absolutely,' Frank stated.

'When did he get back from Rexor IV?'

'A week ago.'

'And the change was noticeable at once?'

'His wife noticed it as soon as she saw him. There's no doubt it occurred on Rexor.' Frank paused significantly. 'And you know what that means.'

'I know.' Douglas walked slowly around the seated man, examining him from every angle.

Lester Herrick sat quietly, his coat neatly folded across his knee. He rested his hands on his ivory-topped cane, his face calm and expressionless. He wore a soft gray suit, a subdued necktie, French cuffs, and shiny black shoes. He said nothing.

'Their methods are simple and exact,' Douglas said. 'The original psychic contents are removed and stored – in some sort of suspension. The interjection of the substitute contents is instantaneous. Lester Herrick was probably poking around the Rexor city ruins, ignoring the safety precautions – shield or manual screen – and they got him.'

The seated man stirred. 'I'd like very much to communicate with Jill,' he murmured. 'She surely is becoming anxious.'

Frank turned away, face choked with revulsion. 'God. It's still pretending.'

Director Douglas restrained himself with the greatest effort. 'It's certainly an amazing thing. No physical changes. You could look at it and never know.' He moved toward the seated man, his face hard. 'Listen to me, whatever you call yourself. Can you understand what I say?'

'Of course,' Lester Herrick answered.

'Did you really think you'd get away with it? We caught the others – the ones before you. All ten of them. Even before they got here.' Douglas grinned coldly. 'Vibro-rayed them one after another.'

The color left Lester Herrick's face. Sweat came out on his forehead. He wiped it away with a silk handkerchief from his breast pocket. 'Oh?' he murmured.

'You're not fooling us. All Terra is alerted for you Rexorians. I'm surprised you got off Rexor at all. Herrick must have been extremely careless. We stopped the others aboard ship. Fried them out in deep space.'

'Herrick had a private ship,' the seated man murmured. 'He bypassed the check station going in. No record of his arrival existed. He was never checked.'

'*Fry it!*' Douglas grated. The three Clearance agents lifted their tubes, moving forward.

'No.' Frank shook his head. 'We can't. It's a bad situation.'

'What do you mean? Why can't we? We fried the others –'

'They were caught in deep space. This is Terra. Terran law,

not military law, applies.' Frank waved toward the seated man. 'And it's in a human body. It comes under regular civil laws. We've got to *prove* it's not Lester Herrick – that it's a Rexorian infiltrator. It's going to be tough. But it can be done.'

'How?'

'His wife. Herrick's wife. Her testimony. Jill Herrick can assert the difference between Lester Herrick and this thing. She knows – and I think we can make it stand up in court.'

It was late afternoon. Frank drove his surface cruiser slowly along. Neither he nor Jill spoke.

'So that's it,' Jill said at last. Her face was gray. Her eyes dry and bright, without emotion. 'I knew it was too good to be true.' She tried to smile. 'It seemed so wonderful.'

'I know,' Frank said. 'It's a terrible damn thing. If only – '

'*Why?*' Jill said. 'Why did he – did it do this? Why did it take Lester's body?'

'Rexor IV is old. Dead. A dying planet. Life is dying out.'

'I remember, now. He – it said something like that. Something about Rexor. That it was glad to get away.'

'The Rexorians are an old race. The few that remain are feeble. They've been trying to migrate for centuries. But their bodies are too weak. Some tried to migrate to Venus – and died instantly. They worked out this system about a century ago.'

'But it knows so much. About us. It speaks our language.'

'Not quite. The changes you mentioned. The odd diction. You see, the Rexorians have only a vague knowledge of human beings. A sort of ideal abstraction, taken from Terran objects that have found their way to Rexor. Books mostly. Secondary data like that. The Rexorian idea of Terra is based on centuries-old Terran literature. Romantic novels from our past. Language, customs, manners from old Terran books.

'That accounts for the strange archaic quality to *it*. It had studied Terra, all right. But in an indirect and misleading way.' Frank grinned wryly. 'The Rexorians are two hundred years behind the times – which is a break for us. That's how we're able to detect them.'

'Is this sort of thing – common? Does it happen often? It

seems unbelievable.' Jill rubbed her forehead wearily. 'Dream-like. It's hard to realize that it's actually happened. I'm just beginning to understand what it means.'

'The galaxy is full of alien life forms. Parasitic and destructive entities. Terran ethics don't extend to them. We have to guard constantly against this sort of thing. Lester went in unsuspect-ingly – and this thing ousted him and took over his body.'

Frank glanced at his sister. Jill's face was expressionless. A stern little face, wide-eyed, but composed. She sat up straight, staring fixedly ahead, her small hands folded quietly in her lap.

'We can arrange it so you won't actually have to appear in court,' Frank went on. 'You can vid a statement and it'll be presented as evidence. I'm certain your statement will do. The Federal courts will help us all they can, but they have to have *some* evidence to go on.'

Jill was silent.

'What do you say?' Frank asked.

'What happens after the court makes its decision?'

'Then we vibro-ray it. Destroy the Rexorian mind. A Terran patrol ship on Rexor IV sends out a party to locate the – er – original contents.'

Jill gasped. She turned toward her brother in amazement. 'You mean – '

'Oh, yes. Lester is alive. In suspension, somewhere on Rexor. In one of the old city ruins. We'll have to force them to give him up. They won't want to, but they'll do it. They've done it before. Then he'll be back with you. Safe and sound. Just like before. And this horrible nightmare you've been living will be a thing of the past.'

'I see.'

'Here we are.' The cruiser pulled to a halt before the imposing Federal Clearance Building. Frank got quickly out, holding the door for his sister. Jill stepped down slowly. 'Okay?' Frank said.

'Okay.'

When they entered the building, Clearance agents led them through the check screens, down the long corridors. Jill's high heels echoed in the ominous silence.

'Quite a place,' Frank observed.

'It's unfriendly.'

'Consider it a glorified police station.' Frank halted. Before them was a guarded door. 'Here we are.'

'Wait.' Jill pulled back, her face twisting in panic. 'I – '

'We'll wait until you're ready.' Frank signaled to the Clearance agent to leave. 'I understand. It's a bad business.'

Jill stood for a moment, her head down. She took a deep breath, her small fists clenched. Her chin came up, level and steady. 'All right.'

'You ready?'

'Yes.'

Frank opened the door. 'Here we are.'

Director Douglas and the three Clearance agents turned expectantly as Jill and Frank entered. 'Good,' Douglas murmured, with relief. 'I was beginning to get worried.'

The sitting man got slowly to his feet, picking up his coat. He gripped his ivory-headed cane tightly, his hands tense. He said nothing. He watched silently as the woman entered the room, Frank behind her. 'This is Mrs Herrick,' Frank said. 'Jill, this is Clearance Director Douglas.'

'I've heard of you,' Jill said faintly.

'Then you know our work.'

'Yes. I know your work.'

'This is an unfortunate business. It's happened before. I don't know what Frank has told you – '

'He explained the situation.'

'Good.' Douglas was relieved. 'I'm glad of that. It's not easy to explain. You understand, then, what we want. The previous cases were caught in deep space. We vibro-tubed them and got the original contents back. But this time we must work through legal channels.' Douglas picked up a vidtape recorder. 'We will need your statement, Mrs Herrick. Since no physical change has occurred we'll have no direct evidence to make our case. We'll have only your testimony of character alteration to present to the court.'

He held the vidtape recorder out. Jill took it slowly.

'Your statement will undoubtedly be accepted by the court. The court will give us the release we want and then we can go ahead. If everything goes correctly we hope to be able to set things exactly as they were before.'

Jill was gazing silently at the man standing in the corner with his coat and ivory-headed cane. 'Before?' she said. 'What do you mean?'

'Before the change.'

Jill turned toward Director Douglas. Calmly, she laid the vidtape recorder down on the table. 'What change are you talking about?'

Douglas paled. He licked his lips. All eyes in the room were on Jill. 'The change in *him*.' He pointed at the man.

'Jill!' Frank barked. 'What's the matter with you?' He came quickly toward her. 'What the hell are you doing? You know damn well what change we mean!'

'That's odd,' Jill said thoughtfully. 'I haven't noticed any change.'

Frank and Director Douglas looked at each other. 'I don't get it,' Frank muttered, dazed.

'Mrs Herrick – ' Douglas began.

Jill walked over to the man standing quietly in the corner. 'Can we go now, dear?' she asked. She took his arm. 'Or is there some reason why my husband has to stay here?'

The man and woman walked silently along the dark street.

'Come on,' Jill said. 'Let's go home.'

The man glanced at her. 'It's a nice afternoon,' he said. He took a deep breath, filling his lungs. 'Spring is coming – I think. Isn't it?'

Jill nodded.

'I wasn't sure. It's a nice smell. Plants and soil and growing things.'

'Yes.'

'Are we going to walk? Is it far?'

'Not too far.'

The man gazed at her intently, a serious expression on his face. 'I am very indebted to you, my dear,' he said.

Jill nodded.

'I wish to thank you. I must admit I did not expect such a – '

Jill turned abruptly. 'What is your name? Your *real* name.'

The man's gray eyes flickered. He smiled a little, a kind, gentle smile. 'I'm afraid you would not be able to pronounce it. The sounds cannot be formed . . .'

Jill was silent as they walked along, deep in thought. The city lights were coming on all around them. Bright yellow spots in the gloom. 'What are you thinking?' the man asked.

'I was thinking perhaps I will still call you Lester,' Jill said. 'If you don't mind.'

'I don't mind,' the man said. He put his arm around her, drawing her close to him. He gazed down tenderly as they walked through the thickening darkness, between the yellow candles of light that marked the way. 'Anything you wish. Whatever will make you happy.'

Adjustment Team

It was bright morning. The sun shone down on the damp lawns and sidewalks, reflecting off the sparkling parked cars. The Clerk came walking hurriedly, leafing through his instructions, flipping pages and frowning. He stopped in front of the small green stucco house for a moment, and then turned up the walk, entering the back yard.

The dog was asleep inside his shed, his back turned to the world. Only his thick tail showed.

'For heaven's sake,' the Clerk exclaimed, hands on his hips. He tapped his mechanical pencil noisily against his clipboard. 'Wake up, you in there.'

The dog stirred. He came slowly out of his shed, head first, blinking and yawning in the morning sunlight. 'Oh, it's you. Already?' He yawned again.

'Big doings.' The Clerk ran his expert finger down the traffic-control sheet. 'They're adjusting Sector T137 this morning. Starting at exactly nine o'clock.' He glanced at his pocket watch. 'Three hour alteration. Will finish by noon.'

'T137? That's not far from here.'

The Clerk's thin lips twisted with contempt. 'Indeed. You're showing astonishing perspicacity, my black-haired friend. Maybe you can divine why I'm here.'

'We overlap with T137.'

'Exactly. Elements from this Sector are involved. We must make sure they're properly placed when the adjustment begins.' The Clerk glanced toward the small green stucco house. 'Your particular task concerns the man in there. He is employed by a business establishment lying within Sector T137. It's essential that he be there before nine o'clock.'

The dog studied the house. The shades had been let up. The

kitchen light was on. Beyond the lace curtains dim shapes could be seen, stirring around the table. A man and woman. They were drinking coffee.

'There they are,' the dog murmured. 'The man, you say? He's not going to be harmed, is he?'

'Of course not. But he must be at his office early. Usually he doesn't leave until after nine. Today he must leave at eight-thirty. He must be within Sector T137 before the process begins, or he won't be altered to coincide with the new adjustment.'

The dog sighed. 'That means I have to summon.'

'Correct.' The Clerk checked his instruction sheet. 'You're to summon at precisely eight-fifteen. You've got that? Eight-fifteen. No later.'

'What will the eight-fifteen summons bring?'

The Clerk flipped open his instruction book, examining the code columns. 'It will bring A Friend with a Car. To drive him to work early.' He closed the book and folded his arms, preparing to wait. 'That way he'll get to his office almost an hour ahead of time. Which is vital.'

'Vital,' the dog murmured. He lay down, half inside his shed. His eyes closed. 'Vital.'

'Wake up! This must be done exactly on time. If you summon too soon or too late – '

The dog nodded sleepily. 'I know. I'll do it right. I *always* do it right.'

Ed Fletcher poured more cream in his coffee. He sighed, leaning back in his chair. Behind him the oven hissed softly, filling the kitchen with warm fumes. The yellow overhead light beamed down.

'Another roll?' Ruth asked.

'I'm full.' Ed sipped his coffee. 'You can have it.'

'Have to go.' Ruth got to her feet, unfastening her robe. 'Time to go to work.'

'Already?'

'Sure. You lucky bum! Wish I could sit around.' Ruth moved toward the bathroom, running her fingers through her long black hair. 'When you work for the Government you start early.'

'But you get off early,' Ed pointed out. He unfolded the *Chronicle*, examining the sporting green. 'Well, have a good time today. Don't type any wrong words, any double-entendres.'

The bathroom door closed, as Ruth shed her robe and began dressing.

Ed yawned and glanced up at the clock over the sink. Plenty of time. Not even eight. He sipped more coffee and then rubbed his stubbled chin. He would have to shave. He shrugged lazily. Ten minutes, maybe.

Ruth came bustling out in her nylon slip, hurrying into the bedroom. 'I'm late.' She rushed rapidly around, getting into her blouse and skirt, her stockings, her little white shoes. Finally she bent over and kissed him. 'Good-bye, honey. I'll do the shopping tonight.'

'Good-bye.' Ed lowered his newspaper and put his arm around his wife's trim waist, hugging her affectionately. 'You smell nice. Don't flirt with the boss.'

Ruth ran out the front door, clattering down the steps. He heard the click of her heels diminish down the sidewalk.

She was gone. The house was silent. He was alone.

Ed got to his feet, pushing his chair back. He wandered lazily into the bathroom, and got his razor down. Eight-ten. He washed his face, rubbing it down with shaving cream, and began to shave. He shaved leisurely. He had plenty of time.

The Clerk bent over his round pocket watch, licking his lips nervously. Sweat stood out on his forehead. The second hand ticked on. Eight-fourteen. Almost time.

'Get ready!' the Clerk snapped. He tensed, his small body rigid. 'Ten seconds to go!'

'*Time!*' the Clerk cried out.

Nothing happened.

The Clerk turned, eyes wide with horror. From the little shed a thick black tail showed. The dog had gone back to sleep.

'TIME!' the Clerk shrieked. He kicked wildly at the furry rump. 'In the name of God – '

The dog stirred. He thumped around hastily, backing out of the shed. 'My goodness.' Embarrassed, he made his way quickly to the fence. Standing up on his hind paws, he opened his mouth wide. 'Woof!' he summoned. He glanced apologetically at the Clerk. 'I beg your pardon. I can't understand how – '

The Clerk gazed fixedly down at his watch. Cold terror knotted his stomach. The hands showed eight-sixteen. 'You failed,' he grated. 'You failed! You miserable flea-bitten ragbag of a wornout old mutt! You failed!'

The dog dropped and came anxiously back. 'I failed, you say? You mean the summons time was – ?'

'You summoned too late.' The Clerk put his watch away slowly, a glazed expression on his face. 'You summoned too late. We won't get A Friend with a Car. There's no telling what will come instead. I'm afraid to see what eight-sixteen brings.'

'I hope he'll be in Sector T137 in time.'

'He won't,' the Clerk wailed. 'He won't be there. We've made a mistake. We've made things go wrong!'

Ed was rinsing the shaving cream from his face when the muffled sound of the dog's bark echoed through the silent house.

'Damn,' Ed muttered. 'Wake up the whole block.' He dried his face, listening. Was somebody coming?

A vibration. Then –

The doorbell rang.

Ed came out of the bathroom. Who could it be? Had Ruth forgotten something? He tossed on a white shirt and opened the front door.

A bright young man, face bland and eager, beamed happily at him. 'Good morning, sir.' He tipped his hat. 'I'm sorry to bother you so early – '

'What do you want?'

'I'm from the Federal Life Insurance Company. I'm here to see you about – '

Ed pushed the door closed. 'Don't want any. I'm in a rush. Have to get to work.'

'Your wife said this was the only time I could catch you.' The young man picked up his briefcase, easing the door open again. 'She especially asked me to come this early. We don't usually begin our work at this time, but since she asked me, I made a special note about it.'

'Okay.' Sighing wearily, Ed admitted the young man. 'You can explain your policy while I get dressed.'

The young man opened his briefcase on the couch, laying out heaps of pamphlets and illustrated folders. 'I'd like to show you some of these figures, if I may. It's of great importance to you and your family to – '

Ed found himself sitting down, going over the pamphlets. He purchased a ten-thousand-dollar policy on his own life and then eased the young man out. He looked at the clock. Practically nine-thirty!

'Damn.' He'd be late to work. He finished fastening his tie, grabbed his coat, turned off the oven and the lights, dumped the dishes in the sink, and ran out on the porch.

As he hurried toward the bus stop he was cursing inwardly. Life insurance salesmen. Why did the jerk have to come just as he was getting ready to leave?

Ed groaned. No telling what the consequences would be, getting to the office late. He wouldn't get there until almost ten. He set himself in anticipation. A sixth sense told him he was in for it. Something bad. It was the wrong day to be late.

If only the salesman hadn't come.

Ed hopped off the bus a block from his office. He began walking rapidly. The huge clock in front of Stein's Jewelry Store told him it was almost ten.

His heart sank. Old Douglas would give him hell for sure. He could see it now. Douglas puffing and blowing, red-faced, waving his thick finger at him; Miss Evans, smiling behind her typewriter; Jackie, the office boy, grinning and snickering; Earl Hendricks; Joe and Tom; Mary, dark-eyed, full bosom and long lashes. All of them, kidding him the whole rest of the day.

He came to the corner and stopped for the light. On the other side of the street rose a big white concrete building, the towering column of steel and cement, girders and glass windows – the office building. Ed flinched. Maybe he could say the elevator got stuck. Somewhere between the second and third floor.

The street light changed. Nobody else was crossing. Ed crossed alone. He hopped up on the curb on the far side –

And stopped, rigid.

The sun had winked off. One moment it was beaming down. Then it was gone. Ed looked up sharply. Gray clouds swirled above him. Huge, formless clouds. Nothing more. An ominous, thick haze that made everything waver and dim. Uneasy chills plucked at him. *What was it?*

He advanced cautiously, feeling his way through the mist. Everything was silent. No sounds – not even the traffic sounds. Ed peered frantically around, trying to see through the rolling haze. No people. No cars. No sun. Nothing.

The office building loomed up ahead, ghostly. It was an indistinct gray. He put out his hand uncertainly –

A section of the building fell away. It rained down, a torrent of particles. Like sand. Ed gaped foolishly. A cascade of gray debris, spilling around his feet. And where he had touched the building, a jagged cavity yawned – an ugly pit marring the concrete.

Dazed, he made his way to the front steps. He mounted them. The steps gave way underfoot. His feet sank down. He was wading through shifting sand, weak, rotted stuff that broke under his weight.

He got into the lobby. The lobby was dim and obscure. The overhead lights flickered feebly in the gloom. An unearthly pall hung over everything.

He spied the cigar stand. The seller leaned silently, resting on the counter, toothpick between his teeth, his face vacant. *And gray*. He was gray all over.

'Hey,' Ed croaked. 'What's going on?'

The seller did not answer. Ed reached out toward him. His hand touched the seller's gray arm – and passed right through.

'Good God,' Ed said.

The seller's arm came loose. It fell to the lobby floor, disintegrating into fragments. Bits of gray fiber. Like dust. Ed's senses reeled.

'Help!' he shouted, finding his voice.

No answer. He peered around. A few shapes stood here and there: a man reading a newspaper, two women waiting at the elevator.

Ed made his way over to the man. He reached out and touched him.

The man slowly collapsed. He settled into a heap, a loose pile of gray ash. Dust. Particles. The two women dissolved when he touched them. Silently. They made no sound as they broke apart.

Ed found the stairs. He grabbed hold of the banister and climbed. The stairs collapsed under him. He hurried faster. Behind him lay a broken path – his footprints clearly visible in the concrete. Clouds of ash blew around him as he reached the second floor.

He gazed down the silent corridor. He saw more clouds of ash. He heard no sound. There was just darkness – rolling darkness.

He climbed unsteadily to the third floor. Once, his shoe broke completely through the stair. For a sickening second he hung, poised over a yawning hole that looked down into a bottomless nothing.

Then he climbed on, and emerged in front of his own office: DOUGLAS AND BLAKE, REAL ESTATE.

The hall was dim, gloomy with clouds of ash. The overhead lights flickered fitfully. He reached for the door handle. The handle came off in his hand. He dropped it and dug his fingernails into the door. The plate glass crashed past him, breaking into bits. He tore the door open and stepped over it, into the office.

Miss Evans sat at her typewriter, fingers resting quietly on the keys. She did not move. She was gray, her hair, her skin, her clothing. She was without color. Ed touched her. His fingers went through her shoulder, into dry flakiness.

He drew back, sickened. Miss Evans did not stir.

He moved on. He pushed against a desk. The desk collapsed into rotting dust. Earl Hendricks stood by the water cooler, a cup in his hand. He was a gray statue, unmoving. Nothing stirred. No sound. No life. The whole office was gray dust – without life or motion.

Ed found himself out in the corridor again. He shook his head, dazed. What did it mean? Was he going out of his mind? Was he – ?

A sound.

Ed turned, peering into the gray mist. A creature was coming, hurrying rapidly. A man – a man in a white robe. Behind him others came. Men in white, with equipment. They were lugging complex machinery.

'Hey – ' Ed gasped weakly.

The men stopped. Their mouths opened. Their eyes popped.

'Look!'

'Something's gone wrong!'

'One still charged.'

'Get the de-energizer.'

'We can't proceed until – '

The men came toward Ed, moving around him. One lugged a long hose with some sort of nozzle. A portable cart came wheeling up. Instructions were rapidly shouted.

Ed broke out of his paralysis. Fear swept over him. Panic. Something hideous was happening. He had to get out. Warn people. Get away.

He turned and ran, back down the stairs. The stairs collapsed under him. He fell half a flight, rolling in heaps of dry ash. He got to his feet and hurried on, down to the ground floor.

The lobby was lost in the clouds of gray ash. He pushed blindly through, toward the door. Behind him, the white-clad men were coming, dragging their equipment and shouting to each other, hurrying quickly after him.

He reached the sidewalk. Behind him the office building wavered and sagged, sinking to one side, torrents of ash raining down in heaps. He raced toward the corner, the men just behind him. Gray cloud swirled around him. He groped his way across the street, hands outstretched. He gained the opposite curb –

The sun winked on. Warm yellow sunlight streamed down on him. Cars honked. Traffic lights changed. On all sides men and women in bright spring clothes hurried and pushed: shoppers, a blue-clad cop, salesmen with briefcases. Stores, windows, signs . . . noisy cars moving up and down the street . . .

And overhead was the bright sun and familiar blue sky.

Ed halted, gasping for breath. He turned and looked back the way he had come. Across the street was the office building – as it had always been. Firm and distinct. Concrete and glass and steel.

He stepped back a pace and collided with a hurrying citizen. 'Hey,' the man grunted. 'Watch it.'

'Sorry.' Ed shook his head, trying to clear it. From where he stood, the office building looked like always, big and solemn and substantial, rising up imposingly on the other side of the street.

But a minute ago –

Maybe he was out of his mind. He had seen the building crumbling into dust. Building – and people. They had fallen into gray clouds of dust. And the men in white – they had chased him. Men in white robes, shouting orders, wheeling complex equipment.

He was out of his mind. There was no other explanation. Weakly, Ed turned and stumbled along the sidewalk, his mind reeling. He moved blindly, without purpose, lost in a haze of confusion and terror.

The Clerk was brought into the top-level Administrative chambers and told to wait.

He paced back and forth nervously, clasping and wringing his hands in an agony of apprehension. He took off his glasses and wiped them shakily.

Lord. All the trouble and grief. And it wasn't his fault. But he would have to take the rap. It was his responsibility to get the Summoners routed out and their instructions followed. The miserable flea-infested Summoner had gone back to sleep – and *he* would have to answer for it.

The doors opened. 'All right,' a voice murmured, preoccupied. It was a tired, care-worn voice. The Clerk trembled and entered slowly, sweat dripping down his neck and into his celluloid collar.

The Old Man glanced up, laying aside his book. He studied the Clerk calmly, his faded blue eyes mild – a deep, ancient mildness that made the Clerk tremble even more. He took out his handkerchief and mopped his brow.

'I understand there was a mistake,' the Old Man murmured. 'In connection with Sector T137. Something to do with an element from an adjoining area.'

'That's right.' The Clerk's voice was faint and husky. 'Very unfortunate.'

'What exactly occurred?'

'I started out this morning with my instruction sheets. The material relating to T137 had top priority, of course. I served notice on the Summoner in my area that an eight-fifteen summons was required.'

'Did the Summoner understand the urgency?'

'Yes, sir.' The Clerk hesitated. 'But – '

'But what?'

The Clerk twisted miserably. 'While my back was turned the Summoner crawled back in his shed and went to sleep. I was occupied, checking the exact time with my watch. I called the moment – but there was no response.'

'You called at eight-fifteen exactly?'

'Yes, sir! Exactly eight-fifteen. But the Summoner was asleep. By the time I managed to arouse him it was eight-*sixteen*. He summoned, but instead of A Friend with a Car we got – A Life Insurance Salesman.' The Clerk's face screwed up with disgust. 'The Salesman kept the element there until almost nine-thirty. Therefore he was late to work instead of early.'

For a moment the Old Man was silent. 'Then the element was not within T137 when the adjustment began.'

'No. He arrived about ten o'clock.'

'During the middle of the adjustment.' The Old Man got to his feet and paced slowly back and forth, face grim, hands behind his back. His long robe flowed out behind him. 'A serious matter. During a Sector Adjustment all related elements from other Sectors must be included. Otherwise, their orientations remain out of phase. When this element entered T137 the adjustment had been in progress fifty minutes. The element encountered the Sector at its most de-energized stage. He wandered about until one of the adjustment teams met him.'

'Did they catch him?'

'Unfortunately, no. He fled, out of the Sector. Into a nearby fully energized area.'

'What – what then?'

The Old Man stopped pacing, his lined face grim. He ran a heavy hand through his long white hair. 'We do not know. We lost contact with him. We will reestablish contact soon, of course. But for the moment he is out of control.'

'What are you going to do?'

'He must be contacted and contained. He must be brought up here. There's no other solution.'

'Up *here*!'

'It is too late to de-energize him. By the time he is regained he will have told others. To wipe his mind clean would only complicate matters. Usual methods will not suffice. I must deal with this problem myself.'

'I hope he's located quickly,' the Clerk said.

'He will be. Every Watcher is alerted. Every Watcher and every Summoner.' The Old Man's eyes twinkled. 'Even the Clerks, although we hesitate to count on them.'

The Clerk flushed. 'I'll be glad when this thing is over,' he muttered.

Ruth came tripping down the stairs and out of the building, into the hot noonday sun. She lit a cigarette and hurried along the walk, her small bosom rising and falling as she breathed in the spring air.

'Ruth.' Ed stepped up behind her.

'Ed!' She spun, gasping in astonishment. 'What are you doing away from – ?'

'Come on.' Ed grabbed her arm, pulling her along. 'Let's keep moving.'

'But what – ?'

'I'll tell you later.' Ed's face was pale and grim. 'Let's go where we can talk. In private.'

'I was going down to have lunch at Louie's. We can talk there.' Ruth hurried along breathlessly. 'What is it? What's happened? You look so strange. And why aren't you at work? Did you – did you get fired?'

They crossed the street and entered a small restaurant. Men and women milled around, getting their lunch. Ed found a table in the back, secluded in a corner. 'Here.' He sat down abruptly. 'This will do.' She slid into the other chair.

Ed ordered a cup of coffee. Ruth had salad and creamed tuna on toast, coffee and peach pie. Silently, Ed watched her as she ate, his face dark and moody.

'Please tell me,' Ruth begged him.

'You really want to know?'

'Of course I want to know!' Ruth put her small hand anxiously on his. 'I'm your wife.'

'Something happened today. This morning. I was late to work. A damn insurance man came by and held me up. I was half an hour late.'

Ruth caught her breath. 'Douglas fired you.'

'No.' Ed ripped a paper napkin slowly into bits. He stuffed the bits in the half-empty water glass. 'I was worried as hell. I got off the bus and hurried down the street. I noticed it when I stepped up on the curb in front of the office.'

'Noticed what?'

Ed told her. The whole works. Everything.

When he had finished, Ruth sat back, her face white, hands trembling. 'I see,' she murmured. 'No wonder you're upset.' She drank a little cold coffee, the cup rattling against the saucer. 'What a terrible thing.'

Ed leaned intently toward his wife. 'Ruth. Do you think I'm going crazy?'

Ruth's red lips twisted. 'I don't know what to say. It's so strange . . .'

'Yeah. Strange is hardly the word for it. I poked my hands right through them. Like they were clay. Old dry clay. Dust. Dust figures.' Ed lit a cigarette from Ruth's pack. 'When I got out I looked back and there it was. The office building. Like always.'

'You were afraid Mr Douglas would bawl you out, weren't you?'

'Sure. I was afraid – and guilty.' Ed's eyes flickered. 'I know what you're thinking. I was late and I couldn't face him. So I had some sort of protective psychotic fit. Retreat from reality.'

He stubbed the cigarette out savagely. 'Ruth, I've been wandering around town since. Two and a half hours. Sure, I'm afraid. I'm afraid like hell to go back.'

'Of Douglas?'

'No! The men in white.' Ed shuddered. 'God. Chasing me. With their damn hoses and – and equipment.'

Ruth was silent. Finally she looked up at her husband, her dark eyes bright. 'You have to go back, Ed.'

'Back? Why?'

'To prove something.'

'Prove what?'

'Prove it's all right.' Ruth's hand pressed against his. 'You have to, Ed. You have to go back and face it. To show yourself there's nothing to be afraid of.'

'The hell with it! After what I saw? Listen, Ruth. I saw the fabric of reality split open. I saw – *behind*. Underneath. I saw what was really there. And I don't want to go back. I don't want to see dust people again. Ever.'

Ruth's eyes were fixed intently on him. 'I'll go back with you,' she said.

'For God's sake.'

'For *your* sake. For your sanity. So you'll know.' Ruth got abruptly to her feet, pulling her coat around her. 'Come on, Ed. I'll go with you. We'll go up there together. To the office of Douglas and Blake, Real Estate. I'll even go in with you to see Mr Douglas.'

Ed got up slowly, staring hard at his wife. 'You think I blacked out. Cold feet. Couldn't face the boss.' His voice was low and strained. 'Don't you?'

Ruth was already threading her way toward the cashier. 'Come on. You'll see. It'll all be there. Just like it was.'

'Okay,' Ed said. He followed her slowly. 'We'll go back there – and see which of us is right.'

They crossed the street together, Ruth holding on tight to Ed's arm. Ahead of them was the building, the towering structure of concrete and metal and glass.

'There it is,' Ruth said. 'See?'

There it was, all right. The big building rose up, firm and

solid, glittering in the early afternoon sun, its windows sparkling brightly.

Ed and Ruth stepped up onto the curb. Ed tensed himself, his body rigid. He winced as his foot touched the pavement –

But nothing happened: the street noises continued; cars, people hurrying past; a kid selling papers. There were sounds, smells, the noise of a city in the middle of the day. And overhead was the sun and the bright blue sky.

'See?' Ruth said. 'I was right.'

They walked up the front steps, into the lobby. Behind the cigar stand the seller stood, arms folded, listening to the ball game. 'Hi, Mr Fletcher,' he called to Ed. His face lit up good-naturedly. 'Who's the dame? Your wife know about this?'

Ed laughed unsteadily. They passed on toward the elevator. Four or five businessmen stood waiting. They were middle-aged men, well dressed, waiting impatiently in a bunch. 'Hey, Fletcher,' one said. 'Where you been all day? Douglas is yelling his head off.'

'Hello, Earl,' Ed muttered. He gripped Ruth's arm. 'Been a little sick.'

The elevator came. They got in. The elevator rose. 'Hi, Ed,' the elevator operator said. 'Who's the good-looking gal? Why don't you introduce her around?'

Ed grinned mechanically. 'My wife.'

The elevator let them off at the third floor. Ed and Ruth got out, heading toward the glass door of Douglas and Blake, Real Estate.

Ed halted, breathing shallowly. 'Wait.' He licked his lips. 'I – '

Ruth waited calmly as Ed wiped his forehead and neck with his handkerchief. 'All right now?'

'Yeah.' Ed moved forward. He pulled open the glass door.

Miss Evans glanced up, ceasing her typing. 'Ed Fletcher! Where on earth have you been?'

'I've been sick. Hello, Tom.'

Tom glanced up from his work. 'Hi, Ed. Say, Douglas is yelling for your scalp. Where have you been?'

'I know.' Ed turned wearily to Ruth. 'I guess I better go in and face the music.'

Ruth squeezed his arm. 'You'll be all right. I know.' She smiled, a relieved flash of white teeth and red lips. 'Okay? Call me if you need me.'

'Sure.' Ed kissed her briefly on the mouth. 'Thanks, honey. Thanks a lot. I don't know what the hell went wrong with me. I guess it's over.'

'Forget it. So long.' Ruth skipped back out of the office, the door closing after her. Ed listened to her race down the hall to the elevator.

'Nice little gal,' Jackie said appreciatively.

'Yeah.' Ed nodded, straightening his necktie. He moved unhappily toward the inner office, steeling himself. Well, he had to face it. Ruth was right. But he was going to have a hell of a time explaining it to the boss. He could see Douglas now, thick red wattles, big bull roar, face distorted with rage –

Ed stopped abruptly at the entrance to the inner office. He froze rigid. The inner office – it was *changed*.

The hackles of his neck rose. Cold fear gripped him, clutching at his windpipe. The inner office was different. He turned his head slowly, taking in the sight: the desks, chairs, fixtures, file cabinets, pictures.

Changes. Little changes. Subtle. Ed closed his eyes and opened them slowly. He was alert, breathing rapidly, his pulse racing. It was changed, all right. No doubt about it.

'What's the matter, Ed?' Tom asked. The staff watched him curiously, pausing in their work.

Ed said nothing. He advanced slowly into the inner office. The office had been *gone over*. He could tell. Things had been altered. Rearranged. Nothing obvious – nothing he could put his finger on. But he could tell.

Joe Kent greeted him uneasily. 'What's the matter, Ed? You look like a wild dog. Is something – ?'

Ed studied Joe. He was different. Not the same. What was it?

Joe's face. It was a little fuller. His shirt was blue-striped. Joe never wore blue stripes. Ed examined Joe's desk. He saw papers and accounts. The desk – it was too far to the right. And it was bigger. It wasn't the same desk.

The picture on the wall. It wasn't the same. It was a different picture entirely. And the things on top of the file cabinet – some were new, others were gone.

He looked back through the door. Now that he thought about it, Miss Evans' hair was different, done a different way. And it was lighter.

In here, Mary, filing her nails, over by the window – she was taller, fuller. Her purse, lying on the desk in front of her – a red purse, red knit.

'You always . . . have that purse?' Ed demanded.

Mary glanced up. 'What?'

'That purse. You always have that?'

Mary laughed. She smoothed her skirt coyly around her shapely thighs, her long lashes blinking modestly. 'Why, Mr Fletcher. What do you mean?'

Ed turned away. *He knew.* Even if she didn't. She had been redone – changed: her purse, her clothes, her figure, everything about her. None of them knew – but him. His mind spun dizzily. They were all changed. All of them were different. They had all been remolded, recast. Subtly – but it was there.

The wastebasket. It was smaller, not the same. The window shades – white, not ivory. The wallpaper was not the same pattern. The lighting fixtures . . .

Endless, subtle changes.

Ed made his way back to the inner office. He lifted his hand and knocked on Douglas's door.

'Come in.'

Ed pushed the door open. Nathan Douglas looked up impatiently. 'Mr Douglas – ' Ed began. He came into the room unsteadily – and stopped.

Douglas was not the same. Not at all. His whole office was changed: the rugs, the drapes. The desk was oak, not mahogany. And Douglas himself . . .

Douglas was younger, thinner. His hair, brown. His skin not so red. His face smoother. No wrinkles. Chin reshaped. Eyes green, not black. He was a different man. But still Douglas – a different Douglas. A different version!

'What is it?' Douglas demanded impatiently. 'Oh, it's you, Fletcher. Where were you this morning?'

Ed backed out. Fast.

He slammed the door and hurried through the inner office. Tom and Miss Evans glanced up, startled. Ed passed them by, grabbing the hall door open.

'Hey!' Tom called. 'What – ?'

Ed hurried down the hall. Terror leaped through him. He had to hurry. He had *seen*. There wasn't much time. He came to the elevator and stabbed the button.

No time.

He ran to the stairs and started down. He reached the second floor. His terror grew. It was a matter of seconds.

Seconds!

The public phone. Ed ran into the phone booth. He dragged the door shut after him. Wildly, he dropped a dime in the slot and dialed. He had to call the police. He held the receiver to his ear, his heart pounding.

Warn them. Changes. Somebody tampering with reality. Altering it. He had been right. The white-clad men . . . their equipment . . . going through the building.

'Hello!' Ed shouted hoarsely. There was no answer. No hum. Nothing.

Ed peered frantically out the door.

And he sagged, defeated. Slowly he hung up the telephone receiver.

He was no longer on the second floor. The phone booth was rising, leaving the second floor behind, carrying him up, faster and faster. It rose floor by floor, moving silently, swiftly.

The phone booth passed through the ceiling of the building and out into the bright sunlight. It gained speed. The ground fell away below. Buildings and streets were getting smaller each moment. Tiny specks hurried along, far below, cars and people, dwindling rapidly.

Clouds drifted between him and the earth. Ed shut his eyes, dizzy with fright. He held on desperately to the door handles of the phone booth.

Faster and faster the phone booth climbed. The earth was rapidly being left behind, far below.

Ed peered up wildly. *Where?* Where was he going? Where was it taking him?

He stood gripping the door handles, waiting.

* * *

The Clerk nodded curtly. 'That's him, all right. The element in question.'

Ed Fletcher looked around him. He was in a huge chamber. The edges fell away into indistinct shadows. In front of him stood a man with notes and ledgers under his arm, peering at him through steel-rimmed glasses. He was a nervous little man, sharp-eyed, with celluloid collar, blue serge suit, vest, watch chain. He wore black shiny shoes.

And beyond him –

An old man sat quietly, in an immense modern chair. He watched Fletcher calmly, his blue eyes mild and tired. A strange thrill shot through Fletcher. It was not fear. Rather it was a vibration, rattling his bones – a deep sense of awe, tinged with fascination.

'Where – what is this place?' he asked faintly. He was still dazed from his quick ascent.

'Don't ask questions!' The nervous little man snapped angrily, tapping his pencil against his ledgers. 'You're here to answer, not ask.'

The Old Man moved a little. He raised his hand. 'I will speak to the element alone,' he murmured. His voice was low. It vibrated and rumbled through the chamber. Again the wave of fascinated awe swept Ed.

'Alone?' The little fellow backed away, gathering his books and papers in his arms. 'Of course.' He glanced hostilely at Ed Fletcher. 'I'm glad he's finally in custody. All the work and trouble just for – '

He disappeared through a door. The door closed softly behind him. Ed and the Old Man were alone.

'Please sit down,' the Old Man said.

Ed found a seat. He sat down awkwardly, nervously. He got out his cigarettes and then put them away again.

'What's wrong?' the Old Man asked.

'I'm just beginning to understand.'

'Understand what?'

'That I'm dead.'

The Old Man smiled briefly. 'Dead? No, you're not dead. You're . . . visiting. An unusual event, but necessitated by circumstances.' He leaned toward Ed. 'Mr Fletcher, you have got yourself involved with something.'

'Yeah,' Ed agreed. 'I wish I knew what it was. Or how it happened.'

'It was not your fault. You were a victim of a clerical error. A mistake was made – not by you. But involving you.'

'What mistake?' Ed rubbed his forehead wearily. 'I – I got in on something. I saw *through*. I saw something I wasn't supposed to see.'

The Old Man nodded. 'That's right. You saw something you were not supposed to see – something few elements have been aware of, let alone witnessed.'

'Elements?'

'An official term. Let it pass. A mistake was made, but we hope to rectify it. It is my hope that – '

'Those people,' Ed interrupted. 'Heaps of dry ash. And gray. Like they were dead. Only it was everything: the stairs and walls and floor. No color or life.'

'That Sector had been temporarily de-energized. So the adjustment team could enter and effect changes.'

'Changes.' Ed nodded. 'That's right. When I went back later, everything was alive again. But not the same. It was all different.'

'The adjustment was complete by noon. The team finished its work and re-energized the Sector.'

'I see,' Ed muttered.

'You were supposed to have been in the Sector when the adjustment began. Because of an error you were not. You came into the Sector late – during the adjustment itself. You fled, and when you returned it was over. You saw, and you should not have seen. Instead of a witness you should have been part of the adjustment. Like the others, you should have undergone changes.'

Sweat came out on Ed Fletcher's head. He wiped it away. His stomach turned over. Weakly, he cleared his throat. 'I get the picture.' His voice was almost inaudible. A chilling premonition moved through him. 'I was supposed to be changed like the others. But I guess something went wrong.'

'Something went wrong. An error occurred. And now a

serious problem exists. You have seen these things. You know a great deal. And you are not coordinated with the new configuration.'

'Gosh,' Ed muttered. 'Well, I won't tell anybody.' Cold sweat poured off him. 'You can count on that. I'm as good as changed.'

'You have already told someone,' the Old Man said coldly.

'Me?' Ed blinked. 'Who?'

'Your wife.'

Ed trembled. The color drained from his face, leaving it a sickly white. 'That's right. I did.'

'Your wife knows.' The Old Man's face twisted angrily. 'A woman. Of all the things to tell – '

'I didn't know.' Ed retreated, panic leaping through him. 'But I know *now*. You can count on me. Consider me changed.'

The ancient blue eyes bored keenly into him, peering far into his depths. 'And you were going to call the police. You wanted to inform the authorities.'

'But I didn't know *who* was doing the changing.'

'Now you know. The natural process must be supplemented – adjusted here and there. Corrections must be made. We are fully licensed to make such corrections. Our adjustment teams perform vital work.'

Ed plucked up a measure of courage. 'This particular adjustment. Douglas. The office. What was it for? I'm sure it was some worthwhile purpose.'

The Old Man waved his hand. Behind him in the shadows an immense map glowed into existence. Ed caught his breath. The edges of the map faded off in obscurity. He saw an infinite web of detailed sections, a network of squares and ruled lines. Each square was marked. Some glowed with a blue light. The lights altered constantly.

'The Sector Board,' the Old Man said. He sighed wearily. 'A staggering job. Sometimes we wonder how we can go on another period. But it must be done. For the good of all. For *your* good.'

'The change. In our – our Sector.'

'Your office deals in real estate. The old Douglas was a shrewd man, but rapidly becoming infirm. His physical health was waning. In a few days Douglas will be offered a chance to purchase a large unimproved forest area in western Canada. It will require most of his assets. The older, less virile Douglas would have hesitated. It is imperative he not hesitate. He must purchase the area and clear the land at once. Only a younger man – a younger Douglas – would undertake this.

'When the land is cleared, certain anthropological remains will be discovered. They have already been placed there. Douglas will lease his land to the Canadian Government for scientific study. The remains found there will cause international excitement in learned circles.

'A chain of events will be set in motion. Men from numerous countries will come to Canada to examine the remains. Soviet, Polish, and Czech scientists will make the journey.

'The chain of events will draw these scientists together for the first time in years. National research will be temporarily forgotten in the excitement of these nonnational discoveries. One of the leading Soviet scientists will make friends with a Belgian scientist. Before they depart they will agree to correspond – without the knowledge of their governments, of course.

'The circle will widen. Other scientists on both sides will be drawn in. A society will be founded. More and more educated men will transfer an increasing amount of time to this international society. Purely national research will suffer a slight but extremely critical eclipse. The war tension will somewhat wane.

'This alteration is vital. And it is dependent on the purchase and clearing of the section of wilderness in Canada. The old Douglas would not have dared take the risk. But the altered Douglas, and his altered, more youthful staff, will pursue this work with wholehearted enthusiasm. And from this, the vital chain of widening events will come about. The beneficiaries will be *you*. Our methods may seem strange and indirect. Even incomprehensible. But I assure you we know what we're doing.'

'I know that now,' Ed said.

'So you do. You know a great deal. Much too much. No element should possess such knowledge. I should perhaps call an adjustment team in here . . .'

A picture formed in Ed's mind: swirling gray clouds, gray men and women. He shuddered. 'Look,' he croaked. 'I'll do anything. Anything at all. Only don't de-energize me.' Sweat ran down his face. 'Okay?'

The Old Man pondered. 'Perhaps some alternative could be found. There is another possibility . . .'

'What?' Ed asked eagerly. 'What is it?'

The Old Man spoke slowly, thoughtfully. 'If I allow you to return, you will swear never to speak of the matter? Will you swear not to reveal to anyone the things you saw? The things you know?'

'Sure!' Ed gasped eagerly, blinding relief flooding over him. 'I swear!'

'Your wife. She must know nothing more. She must think it was only a passing psychological fit – retreat from reality.'

'She thinks that already.'

'She must continue to.'

Ed set his jaw firmly. 'I'll see that she continues to think it was a mental aberration. She'll never know what really happened.'

'You are certain you can keep the truth from her?'

'Sure,' Ed said confidently. 'I know I can.'

'All right.' The Old Man nodded slowly. 'I will send you back. But you must tell no one.' He swelled visibly. 'Remember: you will eventually come back to me – everyone does, in the end – and your fate will not be enviable.'

'I won't tell her,' Ed said, sweating. 'I promise. You have my word on that. I can handle Ruth. Don't give it a second thought.'

Ed arrived home at sunset.

He blinked, dazed from the rapid descent. For a moment he stood on the pavement, regaining his balance and catching his breath. Then he walked quickly up the path.

He pushed the door open and entered the little green stucco house.

'Ed!' Ruth came flying, face distorted with tears. She threw her arms around him, hugging him tight. 'Where the hell have you been?'

'Been?' Ed murmured. 'At the office, of course.'

Ruth pulled back abruptly. 'No, you haven't.'

Vague tendrils of alarm plucked at Ed. 'Of course I have. Where else – ?'

'I called Douglas about three. He said you left. You walked out, practically as soon as I turned my back. Eddie – '

Ed patted her nervously. 'Take it easy, honey.' He began unbuttoning his coat. 'Everything's okay. Understand? Things are perfectly all right.'

Ruth sat down on the arm of the couch. She blew her nose, dabbing at her eyes. 'If you knew how much I've worried.' She put her handkerchief away and folded her arms. 'I want to know where you were.'

Uneasily, Ed hung his coat in the closet. He came over and kissed her. Her lips were ice cold. 'I'll tell you all about it. But what do you say we have something to eat? I'm starved.'

Ruth studied him intently. She got down from the arm of the couch. 'I'll change and fix dinner.'

She hurried into the bedroom and slipped off her shoes and nylons. Ed followed her. 'I didn't mean to worry you,' he said carefully. 'After you left me today I realized you were right.'

'Oh?' Ruth unfastened her blouse and skirt, arranging them over a hanger. 'Right about what?'

'About me.' He manufactured a grin and made it glow across his face. 'About . . . what happened.'

Ruth hung her slip over the hanger. She studied her husband intently as she struggled into her tight-fitting jeans. 'Go on.'

The moment had come. It was now or never. Ed Fletcher braced himself and chose his words carefully. 'I realized,' he stated, 'that the whole darn thing was in my mind. You were right, Ruth. Completely right. And I even realize what caused it.'

Ruth rolled her cotton T-shirt down and tucked it in her jeans. 'What was the cause?'

'Overwork.'

'Overwork?'

'I need a vacation. I haven't had a vacation in years. My mind isn't on the job. I've been daydreaming.' He said it firmly, but his heart was in his mouth. 'I need to get away. To the mountains. Bass fishing. Or – ' He searched his mind frantically. 'Or – '

Ruth came toward him ominously. 'Ed!' she said sharply. 'Look at me!'

'What's the matter?' Panic shot through him. 'Why are you looking at me like that?'

'*Where were you this afternoon*?'

Ed's grin faded. 'I told you. I went for a walk. Didn't I tell you? A walk. To think things over.'

'Don't lie to me, Eddie Fletcher! I can tell when you're lying!' Fresh tears welled up in Ruth's eyes. Her breasts rose and fell excitedly under her cotton shirt. 'Admit it! You didn't go for a walk!'

Ed stammered weakly. Sweat poured off him. He sagged helplessly against the door. 'What do you mean?'

Ruth's black eyes flashed with anger. 'Come on! I want to know where you were! Tell me! I have a right to know. What really happened?'

Ed retreated in terror, his resolve melting like wax. It was going all wrong. 'Honest. I went out for a – '

'Tell me!' Ruth's sharp fingernails dug into his arm. 'I want to know where you were – and who you were with!'

Ed opened his mouth. He tried to grin, but his face failed to respond. 'I don't know what you mean.'

'You know what I mean. Who were you with? Where did you go? Tell me! I'll find out sooner or later.'

There was no way out. He was licked – and he knew it. He couldn't keep it from her. Desperately he stalled, praying for time. If he could only distract her, get her mind on something else. If she would only let up, even for a second. He could invent something – a better story. Time – he needed more time. 'Ruth, you've got to – '

Suddenly there was a sound: the bark of a dog, echoing through the dark house.

Ruth let go, cocking her head alertly. 'That was Dobbie. I think somebody's coming.'

The doorbell rang.

'You stay here. I'll be right back.' Ruth ran out of the room, to the front door. 'Darn it.' She pulled the front door open.

'Good evening!' The young man stepped quickly inside,

loaded down with objects, grinning broadly at Ruth. 'I'm from the Sweep-Rite Vacuum Cleaner Company.'

Ruth scowled impatiently. 'Really, we're about to sit down at the table.'

'Oh, this will only take a moment.' The young man set down the vacuum cleaner and its attachments with a metallic crash. Rapidly, he unrolled a long illustrated banner, showing the vacuum cleaner in action. 'Now, if you'll just hold this while I plug in the cleaner – '

He bustled happily about, unplugging the TV set, plugging in the cleaner, pushing the chairs out of his way.

'I'll show you the drape scraper first.' He attached a hose and nozzle to the big gleaming tank. 'Now, if you'll just sit down I'll demonstrate each of these easy-to-use attachments.' His happy voice rose over the roar of the cleaner. 'You'll notice – '

Ed Fletcher sat down on the bed. He groped in his pocket until he found his cigarettes. Shakily he lit one and leaned back against the wall, weak with relief.

He gazed up, a look of gratitude on his face. 'Thanks,' he said softly. 'I think we'll make it – after all. Thanks a lot.'

The Impossible Planet

'She just stands there,' Norton said nervously. 'Captain, you'll have to talk to her.'

'What does she want?'

'She wants a ticket. She's stone deaf. She just stands there staring and she won't go away. It gives me the creeps.'

Captain Andrews got slowly to his feet. 'Okay. I'll talk to her. Send her in.'

'Thanks.' To the corridor Norton said, 'The Captain will talk to you. Come ahead.'

There was motion outside the control room. A flash of metal. Captain Andrews pushed his desk scanner back and stood waiting.

'In here.' Norton backed into the control room. 'This way. Right in here.'

Behind Norton came a withered little old woman. Beside her moved a gleaming robant, a towering robot servant, supporting her with its arm. The robant and the tiny old woman entered the control room slowly.

'Here's her papers.' Norton slid a folio onto the chart desk, his voice awed. 'She's three hundred and fifty years old. One of the oldest sustained. From Riga II.'

Andrews leafed slowly through the folio. In front of the desk the little woman stood silently, staring straight ahead. Her faded eyes were pale blue. Like ancient china.

'Irma Vincent Gordon,' Andrews murmured. He glanced up. 'Is that right?'

The old woman did not answer.

'She is totally deaf, sir,' the robant said.

Andrews grunted and returned to the folio. Irma Gordon was one of the original settlers of the Riga system. Origin unknown. Probably born out in space in one of the old sub-C ships. A strange feeling drifted through him. The little old creature. The centuries she had seen! The changes.

'She wants to travel?' he asked the robant.

'Yes, sir. She has come from her home to purchase a ticket.'

'Can she stand space travel?'

'She came from Riga, here to Fomalhaut IX.'

'Where does she want to go?'

'To Earth, sir,' the robant said.

'*Earth!*' Andrews' jaw dropped. He swore nervously. 'What do you mean?'

'She wishes to travel to Earth, sir.'

'You see?' Norton muttered. 'Completely crazy.'

Gripping his desk tightly, Andrews addressed the old woman. 'Madam, we can't sell you a ticket to Earth.'

'She can't hear you, sir,' the robant said.

Andrews found a piece of paper. He wrote in big letters:

CAN'T SELL YOU A TICKET TO EARTH

He held it up. The old woman's eyes moved as she studied the words. Her lips twitched. 'Why not?' she said at last. Her voice was faint and dry. Like rustling weeds.

Andrews scratched an answer.

NO SUCH PLACE

He added grimly:

MYTH – LEGEND – NEVER EXISTED

The old woman's faded eyes left the words. She gazed directly at Andrews, her face expressionless. Andrews became uneasy. Beside him, Norton sweated nervously.

'Jeez,' Norton muttered. 'Get her out of here. She'll put the hex on us.'

Andrews addressed the robant. 'Can't you make her understand? There is no such place as Earth. It's been proved a thousand times. No such primordial planet existed. All scientists agree human life arose simultaneously throughout the – '

'It is her wish to travel to Earth,' the robant said patiently. 'She is three hundred and fifty years old and they have ceased giving her sustenation treatments. She wishes to visit Earth before she dies.'

'But it's a myth!' Andrews exploded. He opened and closed his mouth, but no words came.

'How much?' the old woman said. 'How much?'

'I can't do it!' Andrews shouted. 'There isn't – '

'We have a kilo positives,' the robant said.

Andrews became suddenly quiet. 'A thousand positives.' He blanched in amazement. His jaws clamped shut, the color draining from his face.

'How much?' the old woman repeated. 'How much?'

'Will that be sufficient?' the robant asked.

For a moment Andrews swallowed silently. Abruptly he found his voice. 'Sure,' he said. 'Why not?'

'Captain!' Norton protested. 'Have you gone nuts? You know there's no such place as Earth! How the hell can we – '

'Sure, we'll take her.' Andrews buttoned his tunic slowly, hands shaking. 'We'll take her anywhere she wants to go. Tell her that. For a thousand positives we'll be glad to take her to Earth. Okay?'

'Of course,' the robant said. 'She has saved many decades for this. She will give you the kilo positives at once. She has them with her.'

'Look,' Norton said. 'You can get twenty years for this. They'll take your articles and your card and they'll – '

'Shut up.' Andrews spun the dial of the intersystem vidsender. Under them the jets throbbed and roared. The lumbering transport had reached deep space. 'I want the main information library at Centaurus II,' he said into the speaker.

'Even for a thousand positives you can't do it. Nobody can do it. They tried to find Earth for generations. Directorate ships tracked down every moth-eaten planet in the whole – '

The vidsender clicked. 'Centaurus II.'

'Information library.'

Norton caught Andrews' arm. 'Please, Captain. Even for *two* kilo positives – '

'I want the following information,' Andrews said into the vidspeaker. 'All facts that are known concerning the planet Earth. Legendary birthplace of the human race.'

'No facts are known,' the detached voice of the library monitor came. 'The subject is classified as metaparticular.'

'What unverified but widely circulated reports have survived?'

'Most legends concerning Earth were lost during the Centauran-Rigan conflict of 4-B33a. What survived is fragmentary. Earth is variously described as a large ringed planet with three moons, as a small, dense planet with a single moon, as the first planet of a ten-planet system located around a dwarf white – '

'What's the most prevalent legend?'

'The Morrison Report of 5-C2 1r analyzed the total ethnic and subliminal accounts of the legendary Earth. The final summation noted that Earth is generally considered to be a small third planet of a nine-planet system, with a single moon. Other than that, no agreement of legends could be constructed.'

'I see. A third planet of a nine-planet system. With a single moon.' Andrews broke the circuit and the screen faded.

'So?' Norton said.

Andrews got quickly to his feet. 'She probably knows every legend about it.' He pointed down – at the passenger quarters below. 'I want to get the accounts straight.'

'Why? What are you going to do?'

Andrews flipped open the master star chart. He ran his fingers down the index and released the scanner. In a moment it turned up a card.

He grabbed the chart and fed it into the robant pilot. 'The Emphor System,' he murmured thoughtfully.

'Emphor? We're going there?'

'According to the chart, there are ninety systems that show a third planet of nine with a single moon. Of the ninety, Emphor is the closest. We're heading there now.'

'I don't get it,' Norton protested. 'Emphor is a routine trading system. Emphor III isn't even a Class D check point.'

Captain Andrews grinned tightly. 'Emphor III has a single moon, and it's the third of nine planets. That's all we want.

Does anybody know any more about Earth?' He glanced downwards. 'Does *she* know any more about Earth?'

'I see,' Norton said slowly. 'I'm beginning to get the picture.'

Emphor III turned silently below them. A dull red globe, suspended among sickly clouds, its baked and corroded surface lapped by the congealed remains of ancient seas. Cracked, eroded cliffs jutted starkly up. The flat plains had been dug and stripped bare. Great gouged pits pocked the surface, endless gaping sores.

Norton's face twisted in revulsion. 'Look at it. Is anything alive down there?'

Captain Andrews frowned. 'I didn't realize it was so gutted.' He crossed abruptly to the robant pilot. 'There's supposed to be an auto-grapple some place down there. I'll try to pick it up.'

'A grapple? You mean that waste is inhabited?'

'A few Emphorites. Degenerate trading colony of some sort.' Andrews consulted the card. 'Commercial ships come here occasionally. Contact with this region has been vague since the Centauran-Rigan War.'

The passage rang with a sudden sound. The gleaming robant and Mrs Gordon emerged through the doorway into the control room. The old woman's face was alive with excitement. 'Captain! Is that – is that Earth down there?'

Andrews nodded. 'Yes.'

The robant led Mrs Gordon over to the big viewscreen. The old woman's face twitched, ripples of emotion stirring her withered features. 'I can hardly believe that's really Earth. It seems impossible.'

Norton glanced sharply at Captain Andrews.

'It's Earth,' Andrews stated, not meeting Norton's glance. 'The moon should be around soon.'

The old woman did not speak. She had turned her back.

Andrews contacted the auto-grapple and hooked the robant pilot on. The transport shuddered and then began to drop, as the beam from Emphor caught it and took over.

'We're landing,' Andrews said to the old woman, touching her on the shoulder.

'She can't hear you, sir,' the robant said.

Andrews grunted. 'Well, she can see.'

Below them the pitted, ruined surface of Emphor III was rising rapidly. The ship entered the cloud belt and emerged, coasting over a barren plain that stretched as far as the eye could see.

'What happened down there?' Norton said to Andrews. 'The war?'

'War. Mining. And it's old. The pits are probably bomb craters. Some of the long trenches may be scoop gouges. Looks like they really exhausted this place.'

A crooked row of broken mountain peaks shot past under them. They were nearing the remains of an ocean. Dark, unhealthy water lapped below, a vast sea, crusted with salt and waste, its edges disappearing into banks of piled debris.

'Why is it that way?' Mrs Gordon said suddenly. Doubt crossed her features. 'Why?'

'What do you mean?' Andrews said.

'I don't understand.' She stared uncertainly down at the surface below. 'It isn't supposed to be this way. Earth is green. Green and alive. Blue water and . . .' Her voice trailed off uneasily. '*Why?*'

Andrews grabbed some paper and wrote:

COMMERCIAL OPERATIONS EXHAUSTED SURFACE

Mrs Gordon studied his words, her lips twitching. A spasm moved through her, shaking the thin, dried-out body. 'Exhausted . . .' Her voice rose in shrill dismay. 'It's not supposed to be this way! I don't *want* it this way!'

The robant took her arm. 'She had better rest. I'll return her to her quarters. Please notify us when the landing has been made.'

'Sure.' Andrews nodded awkwardly as the robant led the old woman from the viewscreen. She clung to the guide rail, face distorted with fear and bewilderment.

'Something's wrong!' she wailed. 'Why is it this way? Why . . .'

The robant led her from the control room. The closing of the hydraulic safety doors cut off her thin cry abruptly.

Andrews relaxed, his body sagging. 'God.' He lit a cigarette shakily. 'What a racket she makes.'

'We're almost down,' Norton said frigidly.

Cold wind lashed at them as they stepped out cautiously. The air smelled bad – sour and acrid. Like rotten eggs. The wind brought salt and sand blowing up against their faces.

A few miles off the thick sea lay. They could hear it swishing faintly, gummily. A few birds passed silently overhead, great wings flapping soundlessly.

'Depressing damn place,' Andrews muttered.

'Yeah. I wonder what the old lady's thinking.'

Down the descent ramp came the glittering robant, helping the little old woman. She moved hesitantly, unsteady, gripping the robant's metal arm. The cold wind whipped around her frail body. For a moment she tottered – and then came on, leaving the ramp and gaining the uneven ground.

Norton shook his head. 'She looks bad. This air. And the wind.'

'I know.' Andrews moved back toward Mrs Gordon and the robant. 'How is she?' he asked.

'She is not well, sir,' the robant answered.

'Captain,' the old woman whispered.

'What is it?'

'You must tell me the truth. Is this – is this really Earth?'

She watched his lips closely. 'You swear it is? You *swear*?' Her voice rose in shrill terror.

'It's Earth!' Andrews snapped irritably. 'I told you before. Of course it's Earth.'

'It doesn't look like Earth.' Mrs Gordon clung to his answer, panic-stricken. 'It doesn't look like Earth, Captain. Is it really Earth?'

'Yes!'

Her gaze wandered toward the ocean. A strange look flickered across her tired face, igniting her faded eyes with sudden hunger. 'Is that water? I want to see.'

Andrews turned to Norton. 'Get the launch out. Drive her where she wants.'

Norton pulled back angrily. 'Me?'

'That's an order.'

'Okay.' Norton returned reluctantly to the ship. Andrews lit a cigarette moodily and waited. Presently the launch slid out of the ship, coasting across the ash toward them.

'You can show her anything she wants,' Andrews said to the robant. 'Norton will drive you.'

'Thank you, sir,' the robant said. 'She will be grateful. She has wanted all her life to stand on Earth. She remembers her grandfather telling her about it. She believes that he came from Earth, a long time ago. She is very old. She is the last living member of her family.'

'But Earth is just a – ' Andrews caught him. 'I mean – '

'Yes, sir. But she is very old. And she has waited many years.' The robant turned to the old woman and led her gently toward the launch. Andrews stared after them sullenly, rubbing his jaw and frowning.

'Okay,' Norton's voice came from the launch. He slid the hatch open and the robant led the old woman carefully inside. The hatch closed after them.

A moment later the launch shot away across the salt flat, toward the ugly, lapping ocean.

Norton and Captain Andrews paced restlessly along the shore. The sky was darkening. Sheets of salt blew against them. The mud flats stank in the gathering gloom of night. Dimly, off in the distance, a line of hills faded into the silence and vapors.

'Go on,' Andrews said. 'What then?'

'That's all. She got out of the launch. She and the robant. I stayed inside. They stood looking across the ocean. After a while the old woman sent the robant back to the launch.'

'Why?'

'I don't know. She wanted to be alone, I suppose. She stood for a time by herself. On the shore. Looking over the water. The wind rising. All at once she just sort of settled down. She sank down in a heap, into the salt ash.'

'Then what?'

'While I was pulling myself together, the robant leaped out and ran to her. It picked her up. It stood for a second and then it started for the water. I leaped out of the launch, yelling. It stepped into the water and disappeared. Sank down in the mud and filth. Vanished.' Norton shuddered. 'With her body.'

Andrews tossed his cigarette savagely away. The cigarette rolled off, glowing behind them. 'Anything more?'

'Nothing. It all happened in a second. She was standing there, looking over the water. Suddenly she quivered – like a dead branch. Then she just sort of dwindled away. And the robant was out of the launch and into the water with her before I could figure out what was happening.'

The sky was almost dark. Huge clouds drifted across the faint stars. Clouds of unhealthy night vapors and particles of waste. A flock of immense birds crossed the horizon, flying silently.

Against the broken hills the moon was rising. A diseased, barren globe, tinted faintly yellow. Like old parchment.

'Let's get back in the ship,' Andrews said. 'I don't like this place.'

'I can't figure out why it happened. The old woman.' Norton shook his head.

'The wind. Radio-active toxins. I checked with Centaurus II. The War devastated the whole system. Left the planet a lethal wreck.'

'Then we won't – '

'No. We won't have to answer for it.' They continued for a time in silence. 'We won't have to explain. It's evident enough. Anybody coming here, especially an old person – '

'Only nobody would come here,' Norton said bitterly. 'Especially an old person.'

Andrews didn't answer. He paced along, head down, hands in pockets. Norton followed silently behind. Above them, the single moon grew brighter as it escaped the mists and entered a patch of clear sky.

'By the way,' Norton said, his voice cold and distant behind Andrews. 'This is the last trip I'll be making with you. While I was in the ship I filed a formal request for new papers.'

'Oh.'

'Thought I'd let you know. And my share of the kilo positives. You can keep it.'

Andrews flushed and increased his pace, leaving Norton

behind. The old woman's death had shaken him. He lit another cigarette and then threw it away.

Damn it – the fault wasn't *his*. She had been old. Three hundred and fifty years. Senile and deaf. A faded leaf, carried off by the wind. By the poisonous wind that lashed and twisted endlessly across the ruined face of the planet.

The ruined face. Salt ash and debris. The broken line of crumbling hills. And the silence. The eternal silence. Nothing but the wind and the lapping of the thick stagnant water. And the dark birds overhead.

Something glinted. Something at his feet, in the salt ash. Reflecting the sickly pallor of the moon.

Andrews bent down and groped in the darkness. His fingers closed over something hard. He picked the small disc up and examined it.

'Strange,' he said.

It wasn't until they were out in deep space, roaring back towards Fomalhaut, that he remembered the disc.

He slid away from the control panel, searching his pockets for it.

The disc was worn and thin. And terribly old. Andrews rubbed it and spat on it until it was clean enough to make out. A faint impression – nothing more. He turned it over. A token? Washer? Coin?

On the back were a few meaningless letters. Some ancient, forgotten script. He held the disc to the light until he made the letters out.

E PLURIBUS UNUM

He shrugged, tossed the ancient bit of metal into a waste disposal unit beside him, and turned his attention to the star charts, and home . . .

Imposter

'One of these days I'm going to take time off,' Spence Olham said at first-meal. He looked around at his wife. 'I think I've earned a rest. Ten years is a long time.'

'And the Project?'

'The war will be won without me. This ball of clay of ours isn't really in much danger.' Olham sat down at the table and lit a cigarette. 'The newsmachines alter dispatches to make it appear the Outspacers are right on top of us. You know what I'd like to do on my vacation? I'd like to take a camping trip to those mountains outside of town, where we went that time. Remember? I got poison oak and you almost stepped on a gopher snake.'

'Sutton Wood?' Mary began to clear away the food dishes. 'The Wood was burned a few weeks ago. I thought you knew. Some kind of flash fire.'

Olham sagged. 'Didn't they even try to find the cause?' His lips twisted. 'No one cares anymore. All they can think of is the war.' He clamped his jaws together, the whole picture coming up in his mind, the Outspacers, the war, the needle-ships.

'How can we think about anything else?'

Olham nodded. She was right, of course. The dark little ships out of Alpha Centauri had bypassed the Earth cruisers easily, leaving them like helpless turtles. It had been one-way fights, all the way back to Terra.

All the way, until the protec-bubble was demonstrated by Westinghouse Labs. Thrown around the major Earth cities and finally the planet itself, the bubble was the first real defense, the first legitimate answer to the Outspacers – as the news-machines labeled them.

But to win the war, that was another thing. Every lab, every project was working night and day, endlessly, to find something more: a weapon for positive combat. His own project, for example. All day long, year after year.

Olham stood up, putting out his cigarette. 'Like the Sword of Damocles. Always hanging over us. I'm getting tired. All I want to do is take a long rest. But I guess everybody feels that way.'

He got his jacket from the closet and went out on the front porch. The shoot would be along any moment, the fast little bug that would carry him to the Project.

'I hope Nelson isn't late.' He looked at his watch. 'It's almost seven.'

'Here the bug comes,' Mary said, gazing between the rows of houses. The sun glittered behind the roofs, reflecting against the heavy lead plates. The settlement was quiet; only a few people were stirring. 'I'll see you later. Try not to work beyond your shift, Spence.'

Olham opened the car door and slid inside, leaning back against the seat with a sigh. There was an older man with Nelson.

'Well?' Olham said, as the bug shot ahead. 'Heard any interesting news?'

'The usual,' Nelson said. 'A few Outspace ships hit, another asteroid abandoned for strategic reasons.'

'It'll be good when we get the Project into final stage. Maybe it's just the propaganda from the newsmachines, but in the last month I've gotten weary of all this. Everything seems so grim and serious, no color to life.'

'Do you think the war is in vain?' the older man said suddenly. 'You are an integral part of it, yourself.'

'This is Major Peters,' Nelson said. Olham and Peters shook hands. Olham studied the older man.

'What brings you along so early?' he said. 'I don't remember seeing you at the Project before.'

'No, I'm not with the Project,' Peters said, 'but I know something about what you're doing. My own work is altogether different.'

A look passed between him and Nelson. Olham noticed it and he frowned. The bug was gaining speed, flashing across the barren, lifeless ground toward the distant rim of the Project building.

'What is your business?' Olham said. 'Or aren't you permitted to talk about it?'

'I'm with the government,' Peters said. 'With FSA, the security organ.'

'Oh?' Olham raised an eyebrow. 'Is there any enemy infiltration in this region?'

'As a matter of fact I'm here to see you, Mr Olham.'

Olham was puzzled. He considered Peters' words, but he could make nothing of them. 'To see me? Why?'

'I'm here to arrest you as an Outspace spy. That's why I'm up so early this morning. *Grab him Nelson –* '

The gun drove into Olham's ribs. Nelson's hands were shaking, trembling with released emotion, his face pale. He took a deep breath and let it out again.

'Shall we kill him now?' he whispered to Peters. 'I think we should kill him now. We can't wait.'

Olham stared into his friend's face. He opened his mouth to speak, but no words came. Both men were staring at him steadily, rigid and grim with fright. Olham felt dizzy. His head ached and spun.

'I don't understand,' he murmured.

At that moment the shoot car left the ground and rushed up, heading into space. Below them the Project fell away, smaller and smaller, disappearing. Olham shut his mouth.

'We can wait a little,' Peters said. 'I want to ask him some questions first.'

Olham gazed dully ahead as the bug rushed through space.

'The arrest was made all right,' Peters said into the vidscreen. On the screen the features of the security chief showed. 'It should be a load off everyone's mind.'

'Any complications?'

'None. He entered the bug without suspicion. He didn't seem to think my presence was too unusual.'

'Where are you now?'

'On our way out, just inside the protec-bubble. We're moving at a maximum speed. You can assume that the critical period is past. I'm glad the takeoff jets in this craft were in good working order. If there had been any failure at that point – '

'Let me see him,' the security chief said. He gazed directly at Olham where he sat, his hands in his lap, staring ahead.

'So that's the man.' He looked at Olham for a time. Olham said nothing. At last the chief nodded to Peters. 'All right. That's enough.' A faint trace of disgust wrinkled his features. 'I've seen all I want. You've done something that will be remembered for a long time. They're preparing some sort of citation for both of you.'

'That's not necessary,' Peters said.

'How much danger is there now? Is there still much chance that – '

'There is some chance, but not too much. According to my understanding it requires a verbal key phrase. In any case we'll have to take the risk.'

'I'll have the Moon base notified you're coming.'

'No.' Peters shook his head. 'I'll land the ship outside, beyond the base. I don't want it in jeopardy.'

'Just as you like.' The chief's eyes flickered as he glanced again at Olham. Then his image faded. The screen blanked.

Olham shifted his gaze to the window. The ship was already through the protec-bubble, rushing with greater and greater speed all the time. Peters was in a hurry; below him, rumbling under the floor, the jets were wide-open. They were afraid, hurrying frantically, because of him.

Next to him on the seat, Nelson shifted uneasily. 'I think we should do it now,' he said. 'I'd give anything if we could get it over with.'

'Take it easy,' Peters said. 'I want you to guide the ship for a while so I can talk to him.'

He slid over beside Olham, looking into his face. Presently he reached out and touched him gingerly, on the arm and then on the cheek.

Olham said nothing. *If I could let Mary know*, he thought again. *If I could find some way of letting her know.* He looked around the ship. How? The vidscreen? Nelson was sitting by the board, holding the gun. There was nothing he could do. He was caught, trapped.

But why?

'Listen,' Peters said, 'I want to ask you some questions. You know where we're going. We're moving Moonward. In an hour we'll land on the far side, on the desolate side. After we land you'll be turned over immediately to a team of men waiting there. Your body will be destroyed at once. Do you understand that?' He looked at his watch. 'Within two hours your parts will be strewn over the landscape. There won't be anything left of you.'

Olham struggled out of his lethargy. 'Can't you tell me – '

'Certainly, I'll tell you.' Peters nodded. 'Two days ago we received a report that an Outspace ship had penetrated the protec-bubble. The ship let off a spy in the form of a humanoid robot. The robot was to destroy a particular human being and take his place.'

Peters looked calmly at Olham.

'Inside the robot was a U-Bomb. Our agent did not know how the bomb was to be detonated, but he conjectured that it might be by a particular spoken phrase, a certain group of words. The robot would live the life of the person he killed, entering into his usual activities, his job, his social life. He had been constructed to resemble that person. No one would know the difference.'

Olham's face went sickly chalk.

'The person whom the robot was to impersonate was Spence Olham, a high-ranking official at one of the research Projects. Because this particular Project was approaching crucial stage, the presence of an animate bomb, moving toward the center of the Project – '

Olham stared down at his hands. '*But I'm Olham!*'

'Once the robot had located and killed Olham it was a simple matter to take over his life. The robot was released from the ship eight days ago. The substitution was probably accomplished over the last weekend, when Olham went for a short walk in the hills.'

'But I'm Olham.' He turned to Nelson, sitting at the controls. 'Don't you recognize me? You've known me for twenty years. Don't you remember how we went to college together?' He stood up. 'You and I were at the University. We had the same room.' He went toward Nelson.

'Stay away from me!' Nelson snarled.

'Listen. Remember our second year? Remember that girl? What was her name – ' He rubbed his forehead. 'The one with the dark hair. The one we met over at Ted's place.'

'Stop!' Nelson waved the gun frantically. 'I don't want to hear any more. You killed him! You . . . machine.'

Olham looked at Nelson. 'You're wrong. I don't know what happened, but the robot never reached me. Something must have gone wrong. Maybe the ship crashed.' He turned to Peters. 'I'm Olham. I know it. No transfer was made. I'm the same as I've always been.'

He touched himself, running his hands over his body. 'There must be some way to prove it. Take me back to Earth. An X-ray examination, a neurological study, anything like that will show you. Or maybe we can find the crashed ship.'

Neither Peters nor Nelson spoke.

'I am Olham,' he said again. 'I know I am. But I can't prove it.'

'The robot,' Peters said, 'would be unaware that he was not the real Spence Olham. He would become Olham in mind as well as body. He was given an artificial memory system, false recall. He would look like him, have his memories, his thoughts and interests, perform his job.

'But there would be one difference. Inside the robot is a U-Bomb, ready to explode at the trigger phrase.' Peters moved a little away. 'That's the one difference. That's why we're taking you to the Moon. They'll disassemble you and remove the bomb. Maybe it will explode, but it won't matter, not there.'

Olham sat down slowly.

'We'll be there soon,' Nelson said.

He lay back, thinking frantically, as the ship dropped slowly down. Under them was the pitted surface of the Moon, the endless expanse of ruin. What could he do? What would save him?

'Get ready,' Peters said.

In a few minutes he would be dead. Down below he could see a tiny dot, a building of some kind. There were men in the building, the demolition team, waiting to tear him to bits. They would rip him open, pull off his arms and legs, break him apart. When they found no bomb they would be surprised; they would know, but it would be too late.

Olham looked around the small cabin. Nelson was still holding the gun. There was no chance there. If he could get to a doctor, have an examination made – that was the only way. Mary could help him. He thought frantically, his mind racing. Only a few minutes, just a little time left. If he could contact her, get word to her some way.

'Easy,' Peters said. The ship came down slowly, bumping on the rough ground. There was silence.

'Listen,' Olham said thickly. 'I can prove I'm Spence Olham. Get a doctor. Bring him here – '

'There's the squad,' Nelson pointed. 'They're coming.' He glanced nervously at Olham. 'I hope nothing happens.'

'We'll be gone before they start work,' Peters said. 'We'll be out of here in a moment.' He put on his pressure suit. When he had finished he took the gun from Nelson. 'I'll watch him for a moment.'

Nelson put on his pressure suit, hurrying awkwardly. 'How about him?' He indicated Olham. 'Will he need one?'

'No.' Peters shook his head. 'Robots probably don't require oxygen.'

The group of men were almost to the ship. They halted, waiting. Peters signaled to them.

'Come on!' He waved his hand and the men approached warily; stiff, grotesque figures in their inflated suits.

'If you open the door,' Olham said, 'it means my death. It will be murder.'

'Open the door,' Nelson said. He reached for the handle.

Olham watched him. He saw the man's hand tighten around the metal rod. In a moment the door would swing back, the air in the ship would rush out. He would die, and presently they would realize their mistake. Perhaps at some other time, when there was no war, men might not act this way, hurrying an individual to his death because they were afraid. Everyone was frightened, everyone was willing to sacrifice the individual because of the group fear.

He was being killed because they could not wait to be sure of his guilt. There was not enough time.

He looked at Nelson. Nelson had been his friend for years. They had gone to school together. He had been best man at his wedding. Now Nelson was going to kill him. But Nelson was not wicked; it was not his fault. It was the times. Perhaps it had been the same way during the plagues. When men had shown a spot they probably had been killed, too, without a moment's hesitation, without proof, on suspicion alone. In times of danger there was no other way.

He did not blame them. But he had to live. His life was too precious to be sacrificed. Olham thought quickly. What could he do? Was there anything? He looked around.

'Here goes,' Nelson said.

'You're right,' Olham said. The sound of his own voice surprised him. It was the strength of desperation. 'I have no need of air. Open the door.'

They paused, looking at him in curious alarm.

'Go ahead. Open it. It makes no difference.' Olham's hand disappeared inside his jacket. 'I wonder how far you two can run?'

'Run?'

'You have fifteen seconds to live.' Inside his jacket his fingers twisted, his arm suddenly rigid. He relaxed, smiling a little. 'You were wrong about the trigger phrase. In that respect you were mistaken. Fourteen seconds, now.'

Two shocked faces stared at him from the pressure suits. Then they were struggling, running, tearing the door open. The air shrieked out, spilling into the void. Peters and Nelson bolted out of the ship. Olham came after them. He grasped the door and dragged it shut. The automatic pressure system chugged furiously, restoring the air. Olham let his breath out with a shudder.

One more second –

Beyond the window the two men had joined the group. The group scattered, running in all directions. One by one they threw themselves down, prone on the ground. Olham seated himself at the control board. He moved the dials into place. As the ship rose up into the air the men below scrambled to their feet and stared up, their mouths open.

'Sorry,' Olham murmured, 'but I've got to get back to Earth.'

He headed the ship back the way it had come.

It was night. All around the ship crickets chirped, disturbing the chill darkness. Olham bent over the vidscreen. Gradually the image formed; the call had gone through without trouble. He breathed a sigh of relief.

'Mary,' he said. The woman stared at him. She gasped.

'Spence! Where are you? What's happened?'

'I can't tell you. Listen, I have to talk fast. They may break this call off any minute. Go to the Project grounds and get Dr Chamberlain. If he isn't there, get any doctor. Bring him to the house and have him stay there. Have him bring equipment, X-ray, fluoroscope, everything.'

'But – '

'Do as I say. Hurry. Have him get it ready in an hour.' Olham leaned toward the screen. 'Is everything all right? Are you alone?'

'Alone?'

'Is anyone with you? Has . . . has Nelson or anyone contacted you?'

'No. Spence, I don't understand.'

'All right. I'll see you at the house in an hour. And don't tell anyone anything. Get Chamberlain there on any pretext. Say you're very ill.'

He broke the connection and looked at his watch. A moment later he left the ship, stepping down into the darkness. He had a half mile to go.

He began to walk.

One light showed in the window, the study light. He watched it, kneeling against the fence. There was no sound, no movement of any kind. He held his watch up and read it by starlight. Almost an hour had passed.

Along the street a shoot bug came. It went on.

Olham looked toward the house. The doctor should have already come. He should be inside, waiting with Mary. A thought struck him. Had she been able to leave the house? Perhaps they had intercepted her. Maybe he was moving into a trap.

But what else could he do?

With a doctor's records, photographs and reports, there was a chance, a chance of proof. If he could be examined, if he could remain alive long enough for them to study him –

He could prove it that way. It was probably the only way. His one hope lay inside the house. Dr Chamberlain was a respected man. He was the staff doctor for the Project. He would know, his word on the matter would have meaning. He could overcome their hysteria, their madness, with facts.

Madness – that was what it was. If only they would wait, act slowly, take their time. But they could not wait. He had to die, die at once, without proof, without any kind of trial or examination. The simplest test would tell, but they had no time for the simplest test. They could think only of the danger. Danger, and nothing more.

He stood up and moved toward the house. He came up on the porch. At the door he paused, listening. Still no sound. The house was absolutely still.

Too still.

Olham stood on the porch, unmoving. They were trying to be silent inside. Why? It was a small house; only a few feet away, beyond the door, Mary and Dr Chamberlain should be standing. Yet he could hear nothing, no sound of voices, nothing at all. He looked at the door. It was a door he had opened and closed a thousand times, every morning and every night.

He put his hand on the knob. Then, all at once, he reached out and touched the bell instead. The bell pealed, off some place in the back of the house. Olham smiled. He could hear movement.

Mary opened the door. As soon as he saw her face he knew.

He ran, throwing himself into the bushes. A security officer shoved Mary out of the way, firing past her. The bushes burst apart. Olham wriggled around the side of the house. He leaped up and ran, racing frantically into the darkness. A searchlight snapped on, a beam of light circling past him.

He crossed the road and squeezed over a fence. He jumped down and made his way across a backyard. Behind him men were coming, security officers, shouting to each other as they came. Olham gasped for breath, his chest rising and falling.

Her face – he had known at once. The set lips, the terrified, wretched eyes. Suppose he had gone ahead, pushed open the door and entered! They had tapped the call and come at once, as soon as he had broken off. Probably she believed their account. No doubt she thought he was the robot, too.

Olham ran on and on. He was losing the officers, dropping them behind. Apparently they were not much good at running. He climbed a hill and made his way down the other side. In a moment he would be back at the ship. But where to, this time? He slowed down, stopping. He could see the ship already, outlined against the sky, where he had parked it. The settlement was behind him; he was on the outskirts of the wilderness between the inhabited places, where the forests and desolation began. He crossed a barren field and entered the trees.

As he came toward it, the door of the ship opened.

Peters stepped out, framed against the light. In his arms was a heavy Boris gun. Olham stopped, rigid. Peters stared around him, into the darkness. 'I know you're there, some place,' he said. 'Come on up here, Olham. There are security men all around you.'

Olham did not move.

'Listen to me. We will catch you very shortly. Apparently you still do not believe you're the robot. Your call to the woman indicates that you are still under the illusion created by your artificial memories.

'But you *are* the robot. You are the robot, and inside you is the bomb. Any moment the trigger phrase may be spoken, by you, by someone else, by anyone. When that happens the bomb will destroy everything for miles around. The Project, the woman, all of us will be killed. Do you understand?'

Olham said nothing. He was listening. Men were moving toward him, slipping through the woods.

'If you don't come out, we'll catch you. It will only be a matter of time. We no longer plan to remove you to the Moon base. You will be destroyed on sight, and we will have to take the chance that the bomb will detonate. I have ordered every available security officer into the area. The whole county is being searched, inch by inch. There is no place you can go. Around this wood is a cordon of armed men. You have about six hours left before the last inch is covered.'

Olham moved away. Peters went on speaking; he had not seen him at all. It was too dark to see anyone. But Peters was right. There was no place he could go. He was beyond the settlement, on the outskirts where the woods began. He could hide for a time, but eventually they would catch him.

Only a matter of time.

Olham walked quietly through the wood. Mile by mile, each part of the county was being measured off, laid bare, searched, studied, examined. The cordon was coming all the time, squeezing him into a smaller and smaller space.

What was there left? He had lost the ship, the one hope of escape. They were at his home; his wife was with them, believing, no doubt, that the real Olham had been killed. He clenched his fists. Some place there was a wrecked Outspace needle-ship, and in it the remains of the robot. Somewhere nearby the ship had crashed and broken up.

And the robot lay inside, destroyed.

A faint hope stirred him. What if he could find the remains? If he could show them the wreckage, the remains of the ship, the robot –

But where? Where would he find it?

He walked on, lost in thought. Some place, not too far off, probably. The ship would have landed close to the Project; the robot would have expected to go the rest of the way on foot. He went up the side of the hill and looked around. Crashed and burned. Was there some clue, some hint? Had he read anything, heard anything? Some place close by, within walking distance. Some wild place, a remote spot where there would be no people.

Suddenly Olham smiled. Crashed and burned –

Sutton Wood.

He increased his pace.

*   *   *

It was morning. Sunlight filtered down through the broken trees, onto the man crouching at the edge of the clearing. Olham glanced up from time to time, listening. They were not far off, only a few minutes away. He smiled.

Down below him, strewn across the clearing and into the charred stumps that had been Sutton Wood, lay a tangled mass of wreckage. In the sunlight it glittered a little, gleaming darkly. He had not had too much trouble finding it. Sutton Wood was a place he knew well; he had climbed around it many times in his life, when he was younger. He had known where he would find the remains. There was one peak that jutted up suddenly, without a warning.

A descending ship, unfamiliar with the Wood, had little chance of missing it. And now he squatted, looking down at the ship, or what remained of it.

Olham stood up. He could hear them, only a little distance away, coming together, talking in low tones. He tensed himself. Everything depended on who first saw him. If it was Nelson, he had no chance. Nelson would fire at once. He would be dead before they saw the ship. But if he had time to call out, hold them off for a moment – that was all he needed. Once they saw the ship he would be safe.

But if they fired first –

A charred branch cracked. A figure appeared, coming forward uncertainly. Olham took a deep breath. Only a few seconds remained, perhaps the last seconds of his life. He raised his arms, peering intently.

It was Peters.

'Peters!' Olham waved his arms. Peters lifted his gun, aiming. 'Don't fire!' His voice shook. 'Wait a minute. Look past me, across the clearing.'

'I've found him,' Peters shouted. Security men came pouring out of the burned woods around him.

'Don't shoot. Look past me. The ship, the needle-ship. The Outspace ship. Look!'

Peters hesitated. The gun wavered.

'It's down there,' Olham said rapidly. 'I knew I'd find it here. The burned wood. Now you believe me. You'll find the remains of the robot in the ship. Look, will you?'

'There is something down there,' one of the men said nervously.

'Shoot him!' a voice said. It was Nelson.

'Wait.' Peters turned sharply. 'I'm in charge. Don't anyone fire. Maybe he's telling the truth.'

'Shoot him,' Nelson said. 'He killed Olham. Any minute he may kill us all. If the bomb goes off – '

'Shut up.' Peters advanced toward the slope. He stared down. 'Look at that.' He waved two men up to him. 'Go down there and see what that is.'

The men raced down the slope, across the clearing. They bent down, poking in the ruins of the ship.

'Well?' Peters called.

Olham held his breath. He smiled a little. It must be there; he had not had time to look, himself, but it had to be there. Suddenly doubt assailed him. Suppose the robot had lived long enough to wander away? Suppose his body had been completely destroyed, burned to ashes by the fire?

He licked his lips. Perspiration came out on his forehead. Nelson was staring at him, his face still livid. His chest rose and fell.

'Kill him,' Nelson said. 'Before he kills us.'

The two men stood up.

'What have you found?' Peters said. He held the gun steady. 'Is there anything there?'

'Looks like something. It's a needle-ship, all right. There's something beside it.'

'I'll look.' Peters strode past Olham. Olham watched him go down the hill and up to the men. The others were following after him, peering to see.

'It's a body of some sort,' Peters said. 'Look at it!'

Olham came along with them. They stood around in a circle, staring down.

On the ground, bent and twisted in a strange shape, was a grotesque form. It looked human, perhaps; except that it was bent so strangely, the arms and legs flung off in all directions. The mouth was open; the eyes stared glassily.

'Like a machine that's run down,' Peters murmured. Olham smiled feebly. 'Well?' he said.

Peters looked at him. 'I can't believe it. You were telling the truth all the time.'

'The robot never reached me,' Olham said. He took out a cigarette and lit it. 'It was destroyed when the ship crashed. You were all too busy with the war to wonder why an out-of-the-way wood would suddenly catch fire and burn. Now you know.'

He stood smoking, watching the men. They were dragging the grotesque remains from the ship. The body was stiff, the arms and legs rigid.

'You'll find the bomb now,' Olham said. The men laid the body on the ground. Peters bent down.

'I think I see the corner of it.' He reached out, touching the body.

The chest of the corpse had been laid open. Within the gaping tear something glinted, something metal. The men stared at the metal without speaking.

'That would have destroyed us all, if it had lived,' Peters said. 'That metal box there.'

There was silence.

'I think we owe you something,' Peters said to Olham. 'This must have been a nightmare to you. If you hadn't escaped, we would have – ' He broke off.

Olham put out his cigarette. 'I knew, of course, that the robot had never reached me. But I had no way of proving it. Sometimes it isn't possible to prove a thing right away. That was the whole trouble. There wasn't any way I could demonstrate that I was myself.'

'How about a vacation?' Peters said. 'I think we might work out a month's vacation for you. You could take it easy, relax.'

'I think right now I want to go home,' Olham said.

'All right, then,' Peters said. 'Whatever you say.'

Nelson had squatted down on the ground, beside the corpse. He reached out toward the glint of metal visible within the chest.

'Don't touch it,' Olham said. 'It might still go off. We better let the demolition squad take care of it later on.'

Nelson said nothing. Suddenly he grabbed hold of the metal, reaching his hand inside the chest. He pulled.

'What are you doing?' Olham cried.

Nelson stood up. He was holding on to the metal object. His face was blank with terror. It was a metal knife, an Outspace needle-knife, covered with blood.

'This killed him,' Nelson whispered. 'My friend was killed with this.' He looked at Olham. 'You killed him with this and left him beside the ship.'

Olham was trembling. His teeth chattered. He looked from the knife to the body. 'This can't be Olham,' he said. His mind spun, everything was whirling. 'Was I wrong?'

He gaped.

'But if that's Olham, then I must be – '

He did not complete the sentence, only the first phrase. The blast was visible all the way to Alpha Centauri.

James P. Crow

'You're a nasty little – *human being*,' the newly-formed Z Type robot shrilled peevishly.

Donnie flushed and slunk away. It was true. He was a human being, a human child. And there was nothing science could do. He was stuck with it. A human being in a robot's world.

He wished he were dead. He wished he lay under the grass and the worms were eating him up and crawling through him and devouring his brain, his poor miserable human's brain. The Z-236r, his robot companion, wouldn't have anybody to play with and it would be sorry.

'Where are you going?' Z-236r demanded.

'Home.'

'Sissy.'

Donnie didn't reply. He gathered up his set of fourth dimensional chess, stuffed it in his pocket, and walked off between the rows of ecarda trees, toward the human quarter. Behind him, Z236r stood gleaming in the late afternoon sun, a pale tower of metal and plastic.

'See if I care,' Z-236r shouted sullenly. 'Who wants to play with a human being, anyhow? Go on home. You – you smell.'

Donnie said nothing. But he hunched over a little more. And his chin sank lower against his chest.

'Well, it happened,' Edgar Parks said gloomily to his wife, across the kitchen table.

Grace looked quickly up. 'It?'

'Donnie learned his place today. He told me while I was changing my clothes. One of the new robots he was playing with. Called him a human being. Poor kid. Why the hell do they have to rub it in? Why can't they let us alone?'

'So that's why he didn't want any dinner. He's in his room. I knew something had happened.' Grace touched her husband's hand. 'He'll get over it. We all have to learn the hard way. He's strong. He'll snap back.'

Ed Parks got up from the table and moved into the living-room of his modest five-room dwelling unit, located in the section of the city set aside for humans. He didn't feel like eating. 'Robots.' He clenched his fists futilely. 'I'd like to get hold of one of them. Just once. Get my hands into their guts. Rip out handfuls of wires and parts. Just once before I die.'

'Maybe you'll get your chance.'

'No. No, it'll never come to that. Anyhow, humans wouldn't be able to run things without robots. It's true, honey. Humans haven't got the integration to maintain a society. The Lists prove that twice a year. Let's face it. Humans are inferior to robots. But it's their damn holding it up to us! Like today with Donnie. Holding it up to our faces. I don't mind being a robot's body servant. It's a good job. Pays well and the work is light. But when my kid gets told he's – '

Ed broke off. Donnie had come out of his room slowly, into the living-room. 'Hi, Dad.'

'Hi, son.' Ed thumped the boy gently on the back. 'How you doing? Want to take in a show tonight?'

Humans entertained nightly on the vid-screens. Humans made good entertainers. That was one area the robots couldn't compete in. Human beings painted and wrote and danced and sang and acted for the amusement of robots. They cooked better, too, but robots didn't eat. Human beings had their place. They were understood and wanted: as body servants, entertainers, clerks, gardeners, construction workers, repair-men, odd-jobbers and factory workers.

But when it came to something like civic control coordinator or traffic supervisor for the usone tapes that fed energy into the planet's twelve hydrosystems –

'Dad,' Donnie said, 'can I ask you something?'

'Sure.' Ed sat down on the couch with a sigh. He leaned back and crossed his legs. 'What is it?'

Donnie sat quietly beside him, his little round face serious. 'Dad, I want to ask you about the Lists.'

'Oh, yeah.' Ed rubbed his jaw. 'That's right. Lists in a few weeks. Time to start boning up for your entry. We'll get out some of the sample tests and go over them. Maybe between the two of us we can get you ready for Class Twenty.'

'Listen.' Donnie leaned close to his father, his voice low and intense. 'Dad, how many humans have ever passed their Lists?'

Ed got up abruptly and paced around the room, filling his pipe and frowning. 'Well, son, that's hard to say. I mean, humans don't have access to the C-Bank records. So I can't check to see. The law says any human who gets a score in the top forty per cent is eligible for classification with a gradual upward gradation according to subsequent showing. I don't know how many humans have been able to – '

'Has *any* human ever passed his List?'

Ed swallowed nervously. 'Gosh, kid. I don't know. I mean, I don't honestly know of any, when you put it like that. Maybe not. The Lists have been conducted only three hundred years. Before that the Government was reactionary and forbade humans to compete with robots. Nowadays, we have a liberal Government and we can compete on the Lists and if we get high enough scores . . .' His voice wavered and faded. 'No, kid,' he said miserably. 'No human ever passed a List. We're – just – not – smart enough.'

The room was silent. Donnie nodded faintly, expressionless. Ed didn't look at him. He concentrated on his pipe, hands shaking.

'It's not so bad,' Ed said huskily. 'I have a good job. I'm body servant to a hell of a fine N Type robot. I get big tips at Christmas and Easter. It gives me time off when I'm sick.' He cleared his throat noisily. 'It's not so bad.'

Grace was standing at the door. Now she came into the room, eyes bright. 'No, not bad. Not at all. You open doors for it, bring its instruments to it, make calls for it, run errands for it, oil it, repair it, sing to it, talk to it, scan tapes for it – '

'Shut up,' Ed muttered irritably. 'What the hell should I do? Quit? Maybe I should mow lawns like John Hollister and Pete

Klein. At least my robot calls me by name. Like a living thing. It calls me Ed.'

'Will a human ever pass a List?' Donnie asked.

'Yes,' Grace said sharply.

Ed nodded. 'Sure, kid. Of course. Someday maybe humans and robots will live together in equality. There's an Equality Party among the robots. Holds ten seats in the Congress. They think humans should be admitted without Lists. Since it's obvious – ' He broke off. 'I mean, since no humans have ever been able to pass their Lists so far – '

'Donnie,' Grace said fiercely, bending down over her son, 'Listen to me. I want you to pay attention. Nobody knows this. The robots don't talk about it. Humans don't know. But it's true.'

'What is it?'

'I know of a human being who – who's classified. He passed his Lists. Ten years ago. And he's gone up. He's up to Class Two. Someday he'll be Class One. Do you hear? A human being. And he's going up.'

Donnie's face showed doubt. 'Really?' The doubt turned to wistful hope. 'Class Two? No kidding?'

'It's just a story,' Ed grunted. 'I've heard that all my life.'

'It's true! I heard two robots talking about it when I was cleaning up one of the Engineering Units. They stopped when they noticed me.'

'What's his name?' Donnie asked, wide-eyed.

'James P. Crow,' Grace said proudly.

'Strange name,' Ed murmured.

'That's his name. I know. It's not a story. It's true! And sometime, someday, he'll be on the top level. On the Supreme Council.'

Bob McIntyre lowered his voice. 'Yeah, it's true, all right. James P. Crow is his name.'

'It's not a legend?' Ed demanded eagerly.

'There really is such a human. And he's Class Two. Gone all the way up. Passed his Lists like *that*.' McIntyre snapped his fingers. 'The robots hush it up, but it's a fact. And the news is spreading. More and more humans know.'

The two men had stopped by the service entrance of the enormous Structural Research Building. Robot officials moved busily in and out through the main doors, at the front of the building. Robot planners who guided Terran society with skill and efficiency.

Robots ran Earth. It had always been that way. The history tapes said so. Humans had been invented during the Total War of the Eleventh Millibar. All types of weapons had been tested and used; humans were one of many. The War had utterly wrecked society. For decades after, anarchy and ruin lay everywhere. Only gradually had society reformed under the patient guidance of robots. Humans had been useful in the reconstruction. But why they had originally been made, what they had been used for, how they had served in the War – all knowledge had perished in the hydrogen bomb blasts. The historians had to fill in with conjecture. They did so.

'Why such a strange name?' Ed asked.

McIntyre shrugged. 'All I know is he's sub-Advisor to the Northern Security Conference. And in line for the Council when he makes Class One.'

'What do the robs think?'

'They don't like it. But there's nothing they can do. The law says they have to let a human hold a job if he's qualified. They never thought a human would be qualified, of course. But this Crow passed his Lists.'

'It certainly is strange. A human, smarter than the robs. I wonder why.'

'He was an ordinary repairman. A mechanic, fixing machinery and designing circuits. Unclassified, of course. Then suddenly he passed his first List. Entered Class Twenty. He rose the next bi-annual to Class Nineteen. They had to put him to work.' McIntyre chuckled. 'Too damn bad, isn't it? They have to sit with a human being.'

'How do they react?'

'Some quit. Walk out, rather than sit with a human. But most stay. A lot of robs are decent. They try hard.'

'I'd sure like to meet this fellow Crow.'

McIntyre frowned. 'Well – '

'What is it?'

'I understand he doesn't like to be seen with humans too much.'

'Why not?' Ed bristled. 'What's wrong with humans? Is he too high and mighty, sitting up there with robots – '

'It's not that.' There was a strange look in McIntyre's eyes. A yearning, distant look. 'It's not just that, Ed. He's up to something. Something important. I shouldn't be saying. But it's big. Big as hell.'

'What is it?'

'I can't say. But wait until he gets on the Council. Wait.' McIntyre's eyes were feverish. 'It's so big it'll shake the world. The stars and the sun'll shake.'

'What is it?'

'I don't know. But Crow's got something up his sleeve. Something incredibly big. We're all waiting for it. Waiting for the day . . .'

James P. Crow sat at his polished mahogany desk, thinking. That wasn't his real name, of course. He had taken it after the first experiments, grinning to himself as he did so. Nobody would ever know what it meant; it would remain a private joke, personal and unannounced. But it was a good joke nonetheless. Biting and appropriate.

He was a small man. Irish-German. A little lean light-skinned man with blue eyes and sandy hair that fell down in his face and had to be brushed back. He wore unpressed baggy pants and rolled-up sleeves. He was nervous, high-strung. He smoked all day and drank black coffee and usually couldn't sleep at night. But there was a lot on his mind.

A hell of a lot. Crow got abruptly to his feet and paced over to the vidsender. 'Send in the Commissioner of Colonies,' he ordered.

The Commissioner's metal and plastic body pushed through the door, into the office. An R Type robot, patient and efficient. 'You wished to – ' It broke off, seeing a human. For a second its pale eye lens flickered doubtfully. A faint sheen of distaste spread across its features. 'You wished to see me?'

Crow had seen that expression before. Endless times. He was used to it – almost. The surprise, and then the lofty withdrawal, the cold, clipped formality. He was '*Mister* Crow.' Not Jim. The law made them address him as an equal. It hurt some of them more than others. Some showed it without restraint. This one held its feelings back a trifle; Crow was its official superior.

'Yes, I wished to see you,' Crow said calmly. 'I want your report. Why hasn't it come in?'

The robot stalled, still lofty and withdrawn. 'Such a report takes time. We're doing the best we can.'

'I want it within two weeks. No later.'

The robot struggled with itself, life-long prejudices versus the requirements of Governmental codes. 'All right, *sir*. The report will be ready in two weeks.' It moved out of the office. The door formed behind it.

Crow let his breath out with a rush. Doing the best they could? Hardly. Not to please a human being. Even if he was at Advisory Level, Class Two. They all dragged their feet, all the way down the line. Little things here and there.

His door melted and a robot wheeled quickly into the office. 'I say there, Crow. Got a minute?'

'Of course.' Crow grinned. 'Come in and sit down. I'm always glad to talk to you.'

The robot dumped some papers on Crow's desk. 'Tapes and such. Business trifles.' He eyed Crow intently. 'You look upset. Anything happen?'

'A report I want. Overdue. Somebody taking its time.'

L-87t grunted. 'Same old stuff. By the way : . . We're having a meeting tonight. Want to come over and make a speech? Should have a good turn out.'

'Meeting?'

'Party meeting. Equality.' L-87t made a quick sign with its right gripper, a sort of half-arc in the air. The Equality sign. 'We'd be glad to have you, Jim. Want to come?'

'No. I'd like to, but I have things to do.'

'Oh.' The robot moved toward the door. 'All right. Thanks anyhow.' It lingered at the door. 'You'd give us a shot in the arm, you know. Living proof of our contention that a human being is the equal of a robot and should be afforded such recognition.'

Crow smiled faintly. 'But a human isn't the equal of a robot.'

L-87t sputtered indignantly. 'What are you saying? Aren't you the living proof? Look at your List scores. Perfect. Not a mistake. And in a couple of weeks you'll be Class One. Highest there is.'

Crow shook his head. 'Sorry. A human isn't the equal of a robot anymore than he's the equal of a stove. Or a diesel motor. Or a snowplow. There are a lot of things a human can't do. Let's face facts.'

L-87t was baffled. 'But – '

'I mean it. You're ignoring reality. Humans and robots are completely different. We humans can sing, act, write plays, stories, operas, paint, design sets, flower gardens, buildings, cook delicious meals, make love, scratch sonnets on menus – and robots can't. But robots can build elaborate cities and machines that function perfectly, work for days without rest, think without emotional interruption, gestalt complex data without a time lag.

'Humans excel in some fields, robots in others. Humans have highly developed emotions and feelings. Esthetic awareness. We're sensitive to colors and sounds and textures and soft music mixed with wine. All very fine things. Worthwhile. But realms totally beyond robots. Robots are purely intellectual. Which is fine, too. Both realms are fine. Emotional humans, sensitive to art and music and drama. Robots who think and plan and design machinery. But that doesn't mean we're both the same.'

L-87t shook its head sadly. 'I don't understand you, Jim. Don't you want to help your race?'

'Of course. But realistically. Not by ignoring facts and making an illusionary assertion that men and robots are interchangeable. Identical elements.'

A curious look slid across L-87t's eye lens. 'What's your solution, then?'

Crow clamped his jaw tight. 'Stick around another few weeks and maybe you'll see.'

Crow headed out of the Terran Security Building and along the street. Around him robots streamed, bright hulls of metal and plastic and d/n fluid. Except for body servants, humans never came to this area. This was the managerial section of the city, the core, the nucleus, where the planning and organization went on. From this area the life of the city was controlled. Robots were everywhere. In the surface cars, on the moving ramps, the balconies, entering buildings, streaming out, standing in pale glowing knots here and there like Roman Senators, talking and discussing business.

A few greeted him, faintly, formally, with a nod of their metal heads. And then turned their backs. Most robots ignored him or pulled aside to avoid contact. Sometimes a clump of talking robots would become abruptly silent, as Crow pushed past. Robot eye lenses fixed on him, solemn and half astonished. They noticed his arm color, Class Two. Surprise and indignation. And after he had passed, a quick angry buzz of resentment. Backward glances at him as he threaded his way toward the human quarter.

A pair of humans stood in front of the Domestic Control Offices, armed with pruning shears and rakes. Gardeners, weeding and watering the lawns of the big public building. They watched Crow pass with excited stares. One waved nervously at him, feverish and hopeful. A menial human waving at the only human ever to reach classification.

Crow waved back briefly.

The two humans' eyes grew wide with awe and reverence. They were still looking after him when he turned the corner at the main intersection and mixed with the business crowds shopping at the trans-planet marts.

Goods from the wealthy colonies of Venus and Mars and Ganymede filled the open-air marts. Robots drifted in swarms, sampling and pricing and discussing and gossiping. A few humans were visible, mostly household servants in charge of maintenance, stocking up on supplies. Crow edged his way through and beyond the marts. He was approaching the human quarter of the city. He could smell it already. The faint pungent scent of humans.

The robots, of course, were odorless. In a world of odorless machines the human scent stood out in bold relief. The human quarter was a section of the city once prosperous. Humans had moved in and property values had dropped. Gradually the houses had been abandoned by robots and now humans exclusively lived there. Crow, in spite of his position, was obliged to live in the human quarter. His house, a uniform five-room dwelling, identical with the others, was located to the rear of the quarter. One house of many.

He held his hand up to the front door and the door melted. Crow entered quickly and the door reformed. He glanced at his watch. Plenty of time. An hour before he was due back at his desk.

He rubbed his hands. It was always a thrilling moment to come here, to his personal quarters, where he had grown up, lived as an ordinary unclassified human being – before he had come across *it* and begun his meteoric ascent into the upper-class regions.

Crow passed through the small silent house, to the work shed in back. He unlocked the bolted doors and slid them aside. The shed was hot and dry. He clicked off the alarm system. Complex tangles of bells and wires that were really unnecessary: robots never entered the human section, and humans seldom stole from each other.

Locking the doors behind him, Crow seated himself before a bank of machinery assembled in the center of the shed. He snapped on the power and the machinery hummed into life. Dials and meters swung into activity. Lights glowed.

Before him, a square window of gray faded to light pink and shimmered slightly. The Window. Crow's pulse throbbed painfully. He flicked a key. The Window clouded and showed a scene. He slid a tape scanner before the Window and activated it. The scanner clicked as the Window gained shape. Forms moved, dim forms that wavered and hesitated. He steadied the picture.

Two robots were standing behind a table. They moved quickly, jerkily. He slowed them down. The two robots were handling something. Crow increased the power of the image and the objects bloated up, to be caught by the scanning lens and preserved on tape.

The robots were sorting Lists. Class One Lists. Grading and

dividing them into groups. Several hundred packets of questions and answers. Before the table a restless crowd waited, eager robots waiting to hear their scores. Crow speeded the image up. The two robots leaped into activity, tossing and arranging Lists in a blur of energy. Then the master Class One List was held up –

The List. Crow caught it in the Window, dropping the velocity to zero. The List was held, fixed tight like a specimen on a slide. The tape scanner hummed away, recording the questions and answers.

He felt no guilt. No sting of conscience at using a Time Window to see the results of future Lists. He had been doing it ten years, all the way up from the bottom, from unclassified up to the top List, to Class One. He had never kidded himself. Without advance sight of the answers, he could never have passed. He would still be unclassified, at the bottom of the pile, along with the great undifferentiated mass of humans.

The Lists were geared to robot minds. Made up by robots, phased to a robot culture. A culture which was alien to humans, to which humans had to make difficult adjustment. No wonder only robots passed their Lists.

Crow wiped the scene from the Window and threw the scanner aside. He sent the Window back into time, spinning back through the centuries into the past. He never tired of seeing the early days, the days before the Total War wrecked human society and destroyed all human tradition. The days when man lived without robots.

He fiddled with the dials, capturing a moment. The Window showed robots building up their post-war society, swarming over their ruined planet, erecting vast cities and buildings, clearing away the debris. With humans as slaves. Second-class servant citizens.

He saw the Total War, the rain of death from the sky. The blossoming pale funnels of destruction. He saw man's society dissolve into radioactive particles. All human knowledge and culture lost in the chaos.

And once again, he caught his favorite of all scenes. A scene he had examined repeatedly, enjoying with acute satisfaction this unique sight. A scene of human beings in an undersurface lab, in the early days of the war. Designing and building the first robots, the original A Type robots, four centuries before.

Ed Parks walked home slowly, holding his son's hand. Donnie gazed down at the ground. He said nothing. His eyes were red and puffy. He was pale with misery.

'I'm sorry, Dad,' he muttered.

Ed's grip tightened. 'It's okay, kid. You did your best. Don't worry about it. Maybe next time. We'll get started practicing sooner.' He cursed under his breath. 'Those lousy metal tubs. Damn soul-less heaps of tin!'

It was evening. The sun was setting. The two of them climbed the porch steps slowly and entered the house. Grace met them at the door. 'No luck?' She studied their faces. 'I can see. Same old story.'

'Same old story,' Ed said bitterly. 'He didn't have a chance. Hopeless.'

From the dining-room came a murmur of sound. Voices, men and women.

'Who's in there?' Ed demanded irritably. 'Do we have to have company? For God's sake, today of all days – '

'Come on.' Grace pulled him toward the kitchen. 'Some news. Maybe it'll make you feel better. Come along, Donnie. This will interest you, too.'

Ed and Donnie entered the kitchen. It was full of people. Bob McIntyre and his wife Pat. John Hollister and his wife Joan and their two daughters. Pete Klein and Rose Klein. Neighbors, Nat Johnson and Tim Davis and Barbara Stanley. An eager murmur buzzed through the room. Everybody was grouped around the table, excited and nervous. Sandwiches and beer bottles were piled up in heaps. The men and women were laughing and grinning happily, eyes bright with agitation.

'What's up?' Ed grumbled. 'Why the party?'

Bob McIntyre clapped him on the shoulder. 'How you doing, Ed? We've got news.' He rattled a public news tape. 'Get ready. Brace yourself.'

'Read it to him,' Pete Klein said excitedly.

'Go on! Read it!' They all grouped around McIntyre. 'Let's hear it again!'

McIntyre's face was alive with emotion. 'Well, Ed. This is it. He made it. He's there.'

'Who? Who made what?'

'Crow. Jim Crow. He made Class One.' The tape spool trembled in McIntyre's hand. 'He's been named to the Supreme Council. Understand? He's in. A human being. A member of the supreme governing body of the planet.'

'Gosh,' Donnie said, awed.

'Now what?' Ed asked. 'What's he going to do?'

McIntyre grinned shakily. 'We'll know, soon. He's got something. We know. We can feel it. And we should start seeing it in action – any time, now.'

Crow strode briskly into the Council Chamber, his portfolio under his arm. He wore a slick new suit. His hair was combed. His shoes were shined. 'Good day,' he said politely.

The five robots regarded him with mixed feelings. They were old, over a century old. The powerful N Type that had dominated the social scene since its construction. And an incredibly ancient D Type, almost three centuries old. As Crow advanced toward his seat the five robots stepped away, leaving a wide path for him.

'You,' one of the N Types said. 'You are the new Council member?'

'That's right.' Crow took his seat. 'Care to examine my credentials?'

'Please.'

Crow passed over the card plate given him by the Lists Committee. The five robots studied it intently. Finally they passed it back.

'It appears to be in order,' the D admitted reluctantly.

'Of course.' Crow unzipped his portfolio. 'I wish to begin work at once. There's quite a lot of material to cover. I have some reports and tapes you'll find worth your while.'

The robots took their places slowly, eyes still on Jim Crow. 'This is incredible,' the D said. 'Are you serious? Can you really expect to sit with us?'

'Of course,' Crow snapped. 'Let's forgo this and get down to business.'

One of the N Types leaned toward him, massive and contemptuous, its patina-encrusted hull glinting dully. 'Mr Crow,' it said icily. 'You must understand this is utterly impossible. In spite of the legal ruling and your technical right to sit on this – '

Crow smiled calmly back. 'I suggest you check my Listing scoring. You'll discover I've made no errors in all twenty Lists. A perfect score. To my knowledge, none of you has achieved a perfect score. Therefore, according to the Governmental ruling contained in the official Lists Committee decree, I'm your superior.'

The word fell like a bomb shell. The five robots slumped down in their seats, stricken. Their eye lenses flickered uneasily. A worried hum rose in pitch, filling the chamber.

'Let's see,' an N murmured, extending his gripper. Crow tossed his List sheets over and the five robots each scanned them rapidly.

'It's true,' the D stated. 'Incredible. No robot has ever achieved a perfect score. This human outranks us, according to our own laws.'

'Now,' Crow said. 'Let's get down to business.' He spread out his tapes and reports. 'I won't waste any time. I have a proposal to make. An important proposal bearing on the most critical problem of this society.'

'What problem is that?' an X asked apprehensively.

Crow was tense. 'The problem of humans. Humans occupying an inferior position in a robot world. Menials in an alien culture. Servants of robots.'

Silence.

The five robots sat frozen. It had happened. The thing they had feared. Crow sat back in his chair, lighting a cigarette. The robots watched each motion, his hands, the cigarette, the smoke, the match as he ground it out underfoot. The moment had come.

'What do you propose?' the D asked at last, with metallic dignity. 'What is this proposal of yours?'

'I propose you robots evacuate Earth at once. Pack up and leave. Emigrate to the colonies. Ganymede, Mars, Venus. Leave Earth to us humans.'

The robots got instantly up. 'Incredible! We built this world. This is our world! Earth belongs to us. It has always belonged to us.'

'*Has it?*' Crow said grimly.

An uneasy chill moved through the robots. They hesitated, strangely alarmed. 'Of course,' the D murmured.

Crow reached toward his heap of tapes and reports. The robots watched his movement with fear. 'What is that?' an N demanded nervously. 'What do you have there?'

'Tapes,' Crow said.

'What kind of tapes?'

'History tapes.' Crow signaled and a gray-clad human servant hurried into the chamber with a tape scanner. 'Thanks,' Crow said. The human started out. 'Wait. You might like to stay and watch this, my friend.'

The servant's eyes bulged. He found a place in the back and stood trembling and watching.

'Highly irregular,' the D protested. 'What are you doing? What is this?'

'Watch.' Crow snapped on the scanner, feeding the first tape into it. In the air in the center of the Council table, a three-dimensional image formed. 'Keep your eyes on this. You'll remember this moment for a long time.'

The image hardened. They were looking into the Time Window. A scene from the Total War was in motion. Men, human technicians, working frantically in an undersurface lab. Assembling something. Assembling –

The human servant squawked wildly. 'An A! It's a Type A robot! They're making it!'

The five Council robots buzzed in consternation. 'Get that servant out of here!' the D ordered.

The scene changed. It showed the first robots, the original Type A, rising to the surface to fight the war. Other early robots appeared, snaking through the ruins and ash, approaching warily. The robots clashed. Bursts of white light. Gleaming clouds of particles.

'Robots were originally designed as soldiers,' Crow explained. 'Then more advanced types were produced to act as technicians and lab workers and machinists.'

The scene showed an undersurface factory. Rows of robots worked presses and stampers. The robots worked rapidly, efficiently – supervised by human foremen.

'These tapes are fake!' an N cried angrily. 'Do you expect us to believe this?'

A new scene formed. Robots, more advanced, types more complex and elaborate. Taking over more and more economic and industrial functions as humans were destroyed by the War.

'At first robots were simple,' Crow explained. 'They served simple needs. Then, as the War progressed, more advanced types were created. Finally, humans were making Types D and E. Equal to humans – and in conceptual faculties, superior to humans.'

'This is insane!' an N stated. 'Robots evolved. The early types were simple because they were original stages, primitive forms that gave rise to more complex forms. The law of evolution fully explains this process.'

A new scene formed. The last stages of the War. Robots fighting men. Robots eventually winning. The complete chaos of the latter years. Endless wastes of rolling ash and radioactive particles. Miles of ruin.

'All cultural records were destroyed,' Crow said. 'Robots emerged masters without knowing how or why, or in what manner they came into being. But now you see the facts. Robots were created as human tools. During the War they got out of hand.'

He snapped off the tape scanner. The image faded. The five robots sat in stunned silence.

Crow folded his arms. 'Well? What do you say?' He jerked his thumb at the human servant crouching in the rear of the chamber, dazed and astonished. 'Now you know and now he knows. What do you imagine he's thinking? I can tell you. He's thinking – '

'How did you get these tapes?' the D demanded. 'They can't be genuine. They must be fakes.'

'Why weren't they found by our archeologists?' an N shouted shrilly.

'I took them personally,' Crow said.

'*You* took them? What do you mean?'

'Through a Time Window.' Crow tossed a thick package onto the table. 'Here are the schematics. You can build a Time Window yourself if you want.'

'A time machine.' The D snatched up the package and leafed through the contents. 'You saw into the past.' Dawning realization showed on its ancient face. 'Then – '

'He saw ahead!' an N searched wildly. 'Into the future! That explains his perfect Lists. He scanned them in advance.'

Crow rattled his papers impatiently. 'You've heard my proposal. You've seen the tapes. If you vote down the proposal I'll release the tapes publicly. And the schematics. Every human in the world will know the true story of his origin, and yours.'

'So?' an N said nervously. 'We can handle humans. If there's an uprising we'll put it down.'

'Will you?' Crow got suddenly to his feet, his face hard. 'Consider. Civil war raging over the whole planet. Men on one side, centuries of pent-up hatred. On the other side robots suddenly deprived of their myth. Knowing they were originally mechanical tools. Are you sure you'll come out on top this time? Are you positive?'

The robots were silent.

'If you'll evacuate Earth I'll suppress the tapes. The two races can go on, each with its own culture and society. Humans here on Earth. Robots on the colonies. Neither one master. Neither one slave.'

The five robots hesitated, angry and resentful. 'But we worked centuries to build up this planet! It won't make sense. Our leaving. What'll we say? What'll we give as our reason?'

Crow smiled harshly. 'You can say Earth isn't adequate for the great original master race.'

There was silence. The four Type N robots looked at each other nervously, drawing together in a whispered huddle. The massive D sat silent, its archaic brass eye lens fixed intently on Crow, a baffled, defeated expression on its face.

Calmly, Jim Crow waited.

'Can I shake your hand?' L-87t asked timidly. 'I'll be going soon. I'm in one of the first loads.'

Crow stuck out his hand briefly and L-87t shook, a little embarrassed.

'I hope it works out,' L-87t ventured. 'Vid us from time to time. Keep us posted.'

Outside the Council Buildings the blaring voices of the street speakers were beginning to disturb the late afternoon gloom. All up and down the city the speakers roared out their message, the Council Directive.

Men, scurrying home from work, paused to listen. In the uniform houses in the human quarter men and women glanced up, pausing in their routine of living, curious and attentive. Everywhere, in all cities of Earth, robots and human beings ceased their activities and looked up as the Government speakers roared into life.

'This is to announce that the Supreme Council has decreed the rich colony planets Venus, Mars, and Ganymede, are to be set aside exclusively for the use of robots. No humans will be permitted outside of Earth. In order to take advantage of the superior resources and living conditions of these colonies, all robots now on Earth are to be transferred to the colony of their choice.

'The Supreme Council has decided that Earth is no fit place for robots. Its wasted and still partly-devastated condition renders it unworthy of the robot race. All robots are to be conveyed to their new homes in the colonies as quickly as adequate transportation can be arranged.

'In no case can humans enter the colony areas. The colonies are exclusively for the use of robots. The human population will be permitted to remain on Earth.

'This is to announce that the Supreme Council had decreed that the rich colony planets of Venus – '

Crow moved away from the window, satisfied.

He returned to his desk and continued assembling papers and reports in neat piles, glancing at them briefly as he classified them and laid them aside.

'I hope you humans will get along all right,' L-87t repeated. Crow continued checking the heaps of top-level reports, marking them with his writing stick. Working rapidly, with absorbed attention, deep in his work. He scarcely noticed the robot lingering at the door. 'Can you give me some idea of the government you'll set up?'

Crow glanced up impatiently. 'What?'

'Your form of government. How will your society be ruled, now that you've maneuvered us off Earth? What sort of government will take the place of our Supreme Council and Congress?'

Crow didn't answer. He had already returned to his work. There was a strange granite cast to his face, a peculiar hardness L-87t had never seen.

'Who'll run things?' L-87t asked. 'Who'll be the Government now that we're gone? You said yourself humans show no ability to manage a complex modern society. Can you find a human capable of keeping the wheels turning? Is there a human being capable of leading mankind?'

Crow smiled thinly. And continued working.

Planet for Transients

The late afternoon sun shone down blinding and hot, a great shimmering orb in the sky. Trent halted a moment to get his breath. Inside his lead-lined helmet his face dripped with sweat, drop after drop of sticky moisture that steamed his viewplate and clogged his throat.

He slid his emergency pack over to the other side and hitched up his gun-belt. From his oxygen tank he pulled a couple of exhausted tubes and tossed them away in the brush. The tubes rolled and disappeared, lost in the endless heaps of red-green leaves and vines.

Trent checked his counter, found the reading low enough, slid back his helmet for a precious moment.

Fresh air rushed into his nose and mouth. He took a deep breath, filling his lungs. The air smelled good – thick and moist and rich with the odor of growing plants. He exhaled and took another breath.

To his right a towering column of orange shrubbery rose, wrapped around a sagging concrete pillar. Spread out over the rolling countryside was a vast expanse of grass and trees. In the distance a mass of growth looked like a wall, a jungle of creepers and insects and flowers and underbrush that would have to be blasted as he advanced slowly.

Two immense butterflies danced past him. Great fragile shapes, multicolored, racing erratically around him and then away. Life everywhere – bugs and plants and rustling small animals in the shrubbery, a buzzing jungle of life in every direction. Trent sighed and snapped his helmet back in place. Two breathfuls was all he dared.

He increased the flow of his oxygen tank and then raised his transmitter to his lips. He clicked it briefly on. 'Trent. Checking with the Mine Monitor. Hear me?'

A moment of static and silence. Then, a faint, ghostly voice. 'Come in, Trent. Where the hell are you?'

'Still going North. Ruins ahead. I may have to bypass. Looks thick.'

'Ruins?'

'New York, probably. I'll check with the map.'

The voice was eager. 'Anything yet?'

'Nothing. Not so far, at least. I'll circle and report in about an hour.' Trent examined his wristwatch. 'It's half-past three. I'll raise you before evening.'

The voice hesitated. 'Good luck. I hope you find something. How's your oxygen holding out?'

'All right.'

'Food?'

'Plenty left. I may find some edible plants.'

'Don't take any chances!'

'I won't.' Trent clicked off the transmitter and returned it to his belt. 'I won't,' he repeated. He gathered up his blast gun and hoisted his pack and started forward, his heavy lead-lined boots sinking deep into the lush foliage and compost underfoot.

It was just past four o'clock when he saw them. They stepped out of the jungle around him. Two of them, young males – tall and thin and horny blue-gray like ashes. One raised his hand in greeting. Six or seven fingers – extra joints. 'Afternoon,' he piped.

Trent stopped instantly. His heart thudded. 'Good afternoon.'

The two youths came slowly around him. One had an ax – a foliage ax. The other carried only his pants and the remains of a canvas shirt. They were nearly eight feet tall. No flesh – bones and hard angles and large, curious eyes, heavily lidded. There were internal changes, radically different metabolism and cell structure, ability to utilize hot salts, altered digestive system. They were both looking at Trent with interest – growing interest.

'Say,' said one. 'You're a human being.'

'That's right,' Trent said.

'My name's Jackson.' The youth extended his thin blue horny

hand and Trent shook it awkwardly. The hand was fragile under his lead-lined glove. Its owner added, 'My friend here is Earl Potter.'

Trent shook hands with Potter. 'Greetings,' Potter said. His rough lips twitched. 'Can we have a look at your rig?'

'My rig?' Trent countered.

'Your gun and equipment. What's that on your belt? And that tank?'

'Transmitter – oxygen.' Trent showed them the transmitter. 'Battery operated. Hundred-mile range.'

'You're from a camp?' Jackson asked quickly.

'Yes. Down in Pennsylvania.'

'How many?'

Trent shrugged. 'Couple of dozen.'

The blue-skinned giants were fascinated. 'How have you survived? Penn was hard hit, wasn't it? The pools must be deep around there.'

'Mines,' Trent explained. 'Our ancestors moved down deep in the coal mines when the War began. So the records have it. We're fairly well set up. Grow our own food in tanks. A few machines, pumps and compressors and electrical generators. Some hand lathes. Looms.'

He didn't mention that generators now had to be cranked by hand, that only about half of the tanks were still operative. After three hundred years metal and plastic weren't much good – in spite of endless patching and repairing. Everything was wearing out, breaking down.

'Say,' Potter said. 'This sure makes a fool of Dave Hunter.'

'Dave Hunter?'

'Dave says there aren't any true humans left,' Jackson explained. He poked at Trent's helmet curiously. 'Why don't you come back with us? We've got a settlement near here – only an hour or so away on the tractor – our hunting tractor. Earl and I were out hunting flap-rabbits.'

'Flap-rabbits?'

'Flying rabbits. Good meat but hard to bring down – weigh about thirty pounds.'

'What do you use? Not the ax surely.'

Potter and Jackson laughed. 'Look at this here.' Potter slid a long brass rod from his trousers. It fitted down inside his pants along his pipe-stem leg.

Trent examined the rod. It was tooled by hand. Soft brass, carefully bored and straightened. One end was shaped into a nozzle. He peered down it. A tiny metal pin was lodged in a cake of transparent metal. 'How does it work?' he asked.

'Launched by hand – like a blow gun. But once the b-dart is in the air it follows its target forever. The initial thrust has to be provided.' Potter laughed. 'I supply that. A big puff of air.'

'Interesting.' Trent returned the rod. With elaborate casualness, studying the two blue-gray faces, he asked, 'I'm the first human you've seen?'

'That's right,' Jackson said. 'The Old Man will be pleased to welcome you.' There was eagerness in his reedy voice. 'What do you say? We'll take care of you. Feed you, bring you cold plants and animals. For a week, maybe?'

'Sorry,' Trent said. 'Other business. If I come through here on the way back . . .'

The horny faces fell with disappointment. 'Not for a little while? Overnight? We'll pump you plenty of cold food. We have a fine cooler the Old Man fixed up.'

Trent tapped his tank. 'Short on oxygen. You don't have a compressor?'

'No. We don't have any use. But maybe the Old Man could –'

'Sorry.' Trent moved off. 'Have to keep going. You're sure there are no humans in this region?'

'We thought there weren't any left anywhere. A rumor once in a while. But you're the first we've seen.' Potter pointed west. 'There's a tribe of rollers off that way.' He pointed vaguely south. 'A couple of tribes of bugs.'

'And some runners.'

'You've seen them?'

'I came that way.'

'And north there's some of the underground ones – the blind digging kind.' Potter made a face. 'I can't see them and their bores and scoops. But what the hell.' He grinned. 'Everybody has his own way.'

'And to the east,' Jackson added, 'where the ocean begins,

there's a lot of the porpoise kind – the undersea type. They swim around – use those big underwater air-domes and tanks – come up sometimes at night. A lot of types come out at night. We're still daylight-oriented.' He rubbed his horny blue-gray skin. 'This cuts radiation fine.'

'I know,' Trent said. 'So long.'

'Good luck.' They watched him go, heavy-lidded eyes still big with astonishment, as the human being pushed slowly off through the lush green jungle, his metal and plastic suit glinting faintly in the afternoon sun.

Earth was alive, thriving with activity. Plants and animals and insects in boundless confusion. Night forms, day forms, land and water types, incredible kinds and numbers that had never been catalogued, probably never would be.

By the end of the War every surface inch was radioactive. A whole planet sprayed and bombarded by hard radiation. All life subjected to beta and gamma rays. Most life died – but not all. Hard radiation brought mutation – at all levels, insects, plant and animal. The normal mutation and selection process was accelerated millions of years in seconds.

These altered progeny littered the Earth. A crawling teeming glowing horde of radiation-saturated beings. In this world, only those forms which could use hot soil and breathe particle-laden air survived. Insects and animals and men who could live in a world with a surface so alive that it glowed at night.

Trent considered this moodily, as he made his way through the steaming jungle, expertly burning creepers and vines with his blaster. Most of the oceans had been vaporized. Water descended still, drenching the land with torrents of hot moisture. This jungle was wet – wet and hot and full of life. Around him creatures scuttled and rustled. He held his blaster tight and pushed on.

The sun was setting. It was getting to be night. A range of ragged hills jutted ahead in the violet gloom. The sunset was going to be beautiful – compounded of particles in suspension, particles that still drifted from the initial blast, centuries ago.

He stopped for a moment to watch. He had come a long way. He was tired – and discouraged.

The horny blue-skinned giants were a typical mutant tribe.

Toads, they were called. Because of their skin – like desert horned-toads. With their radical internal organs, geared to hot plants and air, they lived easily in a world where he survived only in a lead-lined suit, polarized viewplate, oxygen tank, special cold food pellets grown underground in the Mine.

The Mine – time to call again. Trent lifted his transmitter. 'Trent checking again,' he muttered. He licked his dry lips. He was hungry and thirsty. Maybe he could find some relatively cool spot, free of radiation. Take off his suit for a quarter of an hour and wash himself. Get the sweat and grime off.

Two weeks he had been walking, cooped up in a hot sticky lead-lined suit, like a diver's suit. While all around him count-less life-forms scrambled and leaped, unbothered by the lethal pools of radiation.

'Mine,' the faint tinny voice answered.

'I'm about washed up for today. I'm stopping to rest and eat. No more until tomorrow.'

'No luck?' Heavy disappointment.

'None.'

Silence. Then, 'Well, maybe tomorrow.'

'Maybe. Met a tribe of toads. Nice young bucks, eight feet high.' Trent's voice was bitter. 'Wandering around with nothing on but shirts and pants. Bare feet.'

The Mine Monitor was uninterested. 'I know. The lucky stiffs. Well, get some sleep and raise me tomorrow AM. A report came in from Lawrence.'

'Where is he?'

'Due west. Near Ohio. Making good progress.'

'Any results?'

'Tribes of rollers, bugs and the digging kind that come up at night – the blind white things.'

'Worms.'

'Yes, worms. Nothing else. When will you report again?'

'Tomorrow,' Trent said. He cut the switch and dropped his transmitter to his belt.

Tomorrow. He peered into the gathering gloom at the distant range of hills. Five years. And always – tomorrow. He was the last of a great procession of men to be sent out. Lugging precious oxygen tanks and food pellets and a blast pistol. Exhausting their last stores in a useless sortie into the jungles.

Tomorrow? Some tomorrow, not far off, there wouldn't be any more oxygen tanks and food pellets. The compressors and pumps would have stopped completely. Broken down for good. The Mine would be dead and silent. Unless they made contact pretty damn soon.

He squatted down and began to pass his counter over the surface, looking for a cool spot to undress. He passed out.

'Look at him,' a faint faraway voice said.

Consciousness returned with a rush. Trent pulled himself violently awake, groping for his blaster. It was morning. Gray sunlight filtered down through the trees. Around him shapes moved.

The blaster . . . gone!

Trent sat up, fully awake. The shapes were vaguely human – but not very. Bugs.

'Where's my gun?' Trent demanded.

'Take it easy.' A bug advanced, the others behind. It was chilly. Trent shivered. He got awkwardly to his feet as the bugs formed a circle around him. 'We'll give it back.'

'Let's have it now.' He was stiff and cold. He snapped his helmet in place and tightened his belt. He was shivering, shaking all over. The leaves and vines dripped wet slimy drops. The ground was soft underfoot.

The bugs conferred. There were ten or twelve of them. Strange creatures, more like insects than men. They were shelled – thick shiny chitin. Multi-lensed eyes. Nervous, vibrating antennae by which they detected radiation.

Their protection wasn't perfect. A strong dose and they were finished. They survived by detection and avoidance and partial immunity. Their food was taken indirectly, first digested by smaller warm-blooded animals and then taken as fecal matter, minus radioactive particles.

'You're a human,' a bug said. Its voice was shrill and metallic. The bugs were asexual – these, at least. Two other types existed, male drones and a Mother. These were neuter warriors, armed with pistols and foliage axes.

'That's right,' Trent said.

'What are you doing here? Are there more of you?'

'Quite a few.'

The bugs conferred again, antennae waving wildly. Trent waited. The jungle was stirring into life. He watched a gelatin-like mass flow up the side of a tree and into the branches, a half-digested mammal visible within. Some drab day moths fluttered past. The leaves stirred as underground creatures burrowed silently away from the light.

'Come along with us,' a bug said. It motioned Trent forward. 'Let's get going.'

Trent fell in reluctantly. They marched along a narrow path, cut by axes some time recently. The thick feelers and probes of the jungle were already coming back. 'Where are we going?' Trent demanded.

'To the Hill.'

'Why?'

'Never mind.'

Watching the shiny bugs stride along, Trent had trouble believing they had once been human beings. Their ancestors, at least. In spite of their incredible altered physiology the bugs were mentally about the same as he. Their tribal arrangement approximated the human organic states, communism and fascism.

'May I ask you something?' Trent said.

'What?'

'I'm the first human you've seen? There aren't any more around here?'

'No more.'

'Are there reports of human settlements anywhere?'

'Why?'

'Just curious,' Trent said tightly.

'You're the only one.' The bug was pleased. 'We'll get a bonus for this – for capturing you. There's a standing reward. Nobody's ever claimed it before.'

A human was wanted here too. A human brought with him valuable *gnosis*, odds and ends of tradition the mutants needed to incorporate into their shaky social structures. Mutant cultures were still unsteady. They needed contact with the past. A human being was a shaman, a Wise Man to teach and instruct.

To teach the mutants how life had been, how their ancestors had lived and acted and looked.

A valuable possession for any tribe – especially if no other humans existed in the region.

Trent cursed savagely. *None?* No others? There *had* to be other humans – some place. If not north, then east. Europe, Asia, Australia. Some place, somewhere on the globe. Humans with tools and machines and equipment. The Mine couldn't be the only settlement, the last fragment of true man. Prized curiosities – doomed when their compressors burned out and their food tanks dried up.

If he didn't have any luck pretty soon . . .

The bugs halted, listening. Their antennae twitched suspiciously.

'What is it?' Trent asked.

'Nothing.' They started on. 'For a moment – '

A flash. The bugs ahead on the trail winked out of existence. A dull roar of light rolled over them.

Trent sprawled. He struggled, caught in the vines and sappy weeds. Around him bugs twisted and fought wildly. Tangling with small furry creatures that fired rapidly and efficiently with hand weapons and, when they got close, kicked and gouged with immense hind legs.

Runners.

The bugs were losing. They retreated back down the trail, scattering into the jungle. The runners hopped after them, springing on their powerful hind legs like kangaroos. The last bug departed. The noise died down.

'Okay,' a runner ordered. He gasped for breath, straightening up. 'Where's the human?'

Trent got slowly to his feet. 'Here.'

The runners helped him up. They were small, not over four feet high. Fat and round, covered with thick pelts. Little good-natured faces peered up at him with concern. Beady eyes, quivering noses and great kangaroo legs.

'You all right?' one asked. He offered Trent his water canteen.

'I'm all right.' Trent pushed the canteen away. 'They got my blaster.'

The runners searched around. The blaster was nowhere to be seen.

'Let it go.' Trent shook his head dully, trying to collect himself. 'What happened? The light.'

'A grenade.' The runners puffed with pride. 'We stretched a wire across the trail, attached to the pin.'

'The bugs control most of this area,' another said. 'We have to fight our way through.' Around his neck hung a pair of binoculars. The runners were armed with slug-pistols and knives.

'Are you really a human being?' a runner asked. 'The original stock?'

'That's right,' Trent muttered in unsteady tones.

The runners were awed. Their beady eyes grew wide. They touched his metal suit, his viewplate. His oxygen tank and pack. One squatted down and expertly traced the circuit of his transmitter apparatus.

'Where are you from?' the leader asked in his deep purr-like voice. 'You're the first human we've seen in months.'

Trent spun, choking. 'Months? Then . . .'

'None around here. We're from Canada. Up around Montreal. There's a human settlement up there.'

Trent's breath came fast. 'Walking distance?'

'Well, we made it in a couple of days. But we go fairly fast.' The runner eyed Trent's metal-clad legs doubtfully. 'I don't know. For you it would take longer.'

Humans. A human settlement. 'How many? A big settlement? Advanced?'

'It's hard to remember. I saw their settlement once. Down underground – levels, cells. We traded some cold plants for salt. That was a long time ago.'

'They're operating successfully? They have tools – machinery – compressors? Food tanks to keep going?'

The runner twisted uneasily. 'As a matter of fact they may not be there any more.'

Trent froze. Fear cut through him like a knife. 'Not there? What do you mean?'

'They may be gone.'

'Gone where?' Trent's voice was bleak. 'What happened to them?'

'I don't know,' the runner said. 'I don't know what happened to them. Nobody knows.'

He pushed on, hurrying frantically north. The jungle gave way to a bitterly cold fern-like forest. Great silent trees on all sides. The air was thin and brittle.

He was exhausted. And only one tube of oxygen remained in the tank. After that he would have to open his helmet. How long would he last? The first rain cloud would bring lethal particles sweeping into his lungs. Or the first strong wind, blowing from the ocean.

He halted, gasping for breath. He had reached the top of a long slope. At the bottom a plain stretched out – tree-covered – a dark green expanse, almost brown. Here and there a spot of white gleamed. Ruins of some kind. A human city had been here three centuries ago.

Nothing stirred – no sign of life. No sign anywhere.

Trent made his way down the slope. Around him the forest was silent. A dismal oppression hung over everything. Even the usual rustling of small animals was lacking. Animals, insects, men – all were gone. Most of the runners had moved south. The small things probably had died. And the men?

He came out among the ruins. This had been a great city once. Then men had probably gone down in air-raid shelters and mines and subways. Later on they had enlarged their underground chambers. For three centuries men – true men – had held on, living below the surface. Wearing lead-lined suits when they came up, growing food in tanks, filtering their water, compressing particle-free air. Shielding their eyes against the glare of the bright sun.

And now – nothing at all.

He lifted his transmitter. 'Mine,' he snapped. 'This is Trent.'

The transmitter sputtered feebly. It was a long time before it responded. The voice was faint, distant. Almost lost in the static. 'Well? Did you find them?'

'They're gone.'

'But . . .'

'Nothing. No one. Completely abandoned.' Trent sat down on a broken stump of concrete. His body was dead. Drained of life. 'They were here recently. The ruins aren't covered. They must have left in the last few weeks.'

'It doesn't make sense. Mason and Douglas are on their way. Douglas has the tractor car. He should be there in a couple of days. How long will your oxygen last?'

'Twenty-four hours.'

'We'll tell him to make time.'

'I'm sorry I don't have more to report. Something better.' Bitterness welled up in his voice. 'After all these years. They were here all this time. And now that we've finally got to them . . .'

'Any clues? Can you tell what became of them?'

'I'll look.' Trent got heavily to his feet. 'If I find anything I'll report.'

'Good luck.' The faint voice faded off into static. 'We'll be waiting.'

Trent returned the transmitter to his belt. He peered up at the gray sky. Evening – almost night. The forest was bleak and ominous. A faint blanket of snow was falling silently over the brown growth, hiding it under a layer of grimy white. Snow mixed with particles. Lethal dust – still falling, after three hundred years.

He switched on his helmet-beam. The beam cut a pale swath ahead of him through the trees, among the ruined columns of concrete, the occasional heaps of rusted slag. He entered the ruins.

In their center he found the towers and installations. Great pillars laced with mesh scaffolding – still bright. Open tunnels from underground lay like black pools. Silent deserted tunnels. He peered down one, flashing his helmet beam into it. The tunnel went straight down, deep into the heart of the Earth. But it was empty.

Where had they gone? What had happened to them? Trent wandered around dully. Human beings had lived here, worked here, survived. They had come up to the surface. He could see the bore-nosed cars parked among the towers, now gray with the night snow. They had come up and then – gone.

Where?

He sat down in the shelter of a ruined column and flicked on his heater. His suit warmed up, a slow red glow that made him feel better. He examined his counter. The area was hot. If he intended to eat and drink he'd have to move on.

He was tired. Too damn tired to move on. He sat resting, hunched over in a heap, his helmet-beam lighting up a circle of gray snow ahead of him. Over him the snow fell silently. Presently he was covered, a gray lump sitting among the ruined concrete. As silent and unmoving as the towers and scaffolding around him.

He dozed. His heater hummed gently. Around him a wind came up, swirling the snow, blowing it up against him. He slid forward a little until his metal and plastic helmet came to rest against the concrete.

Towards midnight he woke up. He straightened, suddenly alert. Something – a noise. He listened.

Far off, a dull roaring.

Douglas in the car? No, not yet – not for another two days. He stood up, snow pouring off him. The roar was growing, getting louder. His heart began to hammer wildly. He peered around, his beam flashing through the night.

The ground shook, vibrating through him, rattling his almost empty oxygen tank. He gazed up at the sky – and gasped.

A glowing trail slashed over the sky, igniting the early morning darkness. A deep red, swelling each second. He watched it, open-mouthed.

Something was coming down – landing.

A rocket.

The long metal hull glittered in the morning sun. Men were working busily, loading supplies and equipment. Tunnel cars raced up and down, hauling material from the undersurface levels to the waiting ship. The men worked carefully and efficiently, each in his metal-and-plastic suit, in his carefully sealed lead-lined protection shield.

'How many back at your Mine?' Norris asked quietly.

'About thirty.' Trent's eyes were on the ship. 'Thirty-three, including all those out.'

'Out?'

'Looking. Like me. A couple are on their way here. They should arrive soon. Late today or tomorrow.'

Norris made some notes on his chart. 'We can handle about fifteen with this load. We'll catch the rest next time. They can hold out another week?'

'Yes.'

Norris eyed him curiously. 'How did you find us? This is a long way from Pennsylvania. We're making our last stop. If you had come a couple days later . . .'

'Some runners sent me this way. They said you had gone they didn't know where.'

Norris laughed. 'We didn't know where either.'

'You must be taking all this stuff some place. This ship. It's old, isn't it? Fixed up.'

'Originally it was some kind of bomb. We located it and repaired it – worked on it from time to time. We weren't sure what we wanted to do. We're not sure yet. But we know we have to leave.'

'Leave? Leave Earth?'

'Of course.' Norris motioned him toward the ship. They made their way up the ramp to one of the hatches. Norris pointed back down. 'Look down there – at the men loading.'

The men were almost finished. The last cars were half empty, bringing up the final remains from underground. Books, records, pictures, artifacts – the remains of a culture. A multitude of representative objects, shot into the hold of the ship to be carried off, away from Earth.

'Where?' Trent asked.

'To Mars for the time being. But we're not staying there. We'll probably go on out, towards the moons of Jupiter and Saturn. Ganymede may turn out to be something. If not Ganymede, one of the others. If worse comes to worst we can stay on Mars. It's pretty dry and barren but it's not radioactive.'

'There's no chance here – no possibility of reclaiming the radioactive areas? If we could cool off Earth, neutralize the hot clouds and – '

'If we did that,' Norris said, 'they'd all die.'

'They?'

'Rollers, runners, worms, toads, bugs, all the rest. The endless varieties of life. Countless forms adapted to *this* Earth – this hot Earth. These plants and animals use the radioactive metals. Essentially the new basis of life here is an assimilation of hot metallic salts. Salts which are utterly lethal to us.'

'But even so – '

'Even so, it's not really our world.'

'We're the true humans,' Trent said.

'Not any more. Earth is alive, teeming with life. Growing wildly – in all directions. We're one form, an old form. To live here, we'd have to restore the old conditions, the old factors, the balance as it was three hundred and fifty years ago. A colossal job. And if we succeeded, if we managed to cool Earth, none of this would remain.'

Norris pointed at the great brown forest. And beyond it, towards the south, at the beginning of the steaming jungle that continued all the way to the Straits of Magellan.

'In a way it's what we deserve. *We* brought the War. *We* changed Earth. Not destroyed – *changed*. Made it so different we can't live here any longer.'

Norris indicated the lines of helmeted men. Men sheathed in lead, in heavy protection suits, covered with layers of metal and wiring, counters, oxygen tanks, shields, food pellets, filtered water. The men worked, sweated in their heavy suits. 'See them? What do they resemble?'

A worker came up, gasping and panting. For a brief second he lifted his viewplate and took a hasty breath of air. He slammed his plate and nervously locked it in place. 'Ready to go, sir. All loaded.'

'Change of plan,' Norris said. 'We're going to wait until this man's companions get here. Their camp is breaking up. Another day won't make any difference.'

'All right, sir.' The worker pushed off, climbing back down to the surface, a weird figure in his heavy lead-lined suit and bulging helmet and intricate gear.

'We're visitors,' Norris told him.

Trent flinched violently. '*What?*'

'Visitors on a strange planet. Look at us. Shielded suits and

helmets, spacesuits – for exploring. We're a rocket-ship stopping at an alien world on which we can't survive. Stopping for
a brief period to load up – and then take off again.'

'Closed helmets,' Trent said, in a strange voice.

'Closed helmets. Lead shields. Counters and special food and
water. Look over there.'

A small group of runners were standing together, gazing up
in awe at the great gleaming ship. Off to the right, visible
among the trees, was a runner village. Checker-board crops
and animal pens and board houses.

'The natives,' Norris said. 'The inhabitants of the planet.
They can breathe the air, drink the water, eat the plant-life.
We can't. This is their planet – not ours. They can live here,
build up a society.'

'I hope we can come back.'

'Back?'

'To visit – some time.'

Norris smiled ruefully. 'I hope so too. But we'll have to get
permission from the inhabitants – permission to land.' His eyes
were bright with amusement – and, abruptly, pain. A sudden
agony that gleamed out over everything else. 'We'll have to ask
them if it's all right. And they may say *no*. They may not want
us.'

Small Town

Verne Haskel crept miserably up the front steps of his house, his overcoat dragging behind him. He was tired. Tired and discouraged. And his feet ached.

'My God,' Madge exclaimed, as he closed the door and peeled off his coat and hat. 'You home already?'

Haskel dumped his briefcase and began untying his shoes. His body sagged. His face was drawn and gray.

'Say something!'

'Dinner ready?'

'No, dinner isn't ready. What's wrong this time? Another fight with Larson?'

Haskel stumped into the kitchen and filled a glass with warm water and soda. 'Let's move,' he said.

'Move?'

'Away from Woodland. To San Francisco. Anywhere.' Haskel drank his soda, his middle-aged flabby body supported by the gleaming sink. 'I feel lousy. Maybe I ought to see Doc Barnes again. I wish this was Friday and tomorrow was Saturday.'

'What do you want for dinner?'

'Nothing. I don't know.' Haskel shook his head wearily. 'Anything.' He sank down at the kitchen table. 'All I want is rest. Open a can of stew. Pork and beans. Anything.'

'I suggest we go out to Don's Steakhouse. On Monday they have good sirloins.'

'No. I've seen enough human faces today.'

'I suppose you're too tired to drive me over to Helen Grant's.'

'The car's in the garage. Busted again.'

'If you took better care of it – '

'What the hell do you want me to do? Carry it around in a cellophane bag?'

'Don't shout at me, Verne Haskel!' Madge flushed with anger. 'Maybe you want to fix your own dinner.'

Haskel got wearily to his feet. He shuffled toward the cellar door. 'I'll see you.'

'Where are you going?'

'Downstairs in the basement.'

'Oh, Lord!' Madge cried wildly. 'Those trains! Those toys! How can a grown man, a middle-aged man – '

Haskel said nothing. He was already half way down the stairs, feeling around for the basement light.

The basement was cool and moist. Haskel took his engineer's cap from the hook and fitted it on his head. Excitement and a faint surge of renewed energy filled his tired body. He approached the great plywood table with eager steps.

Trains ran everywhere. Along the floor, under the coal bin, among the steam pipes of the furnace. The tracks converged at the table, rising up on carefully graded ramps. The table itself was littered with transformers and signals and switches and heaps of equipment and wiring. And –

And the town.

The detailed, painfully accurate model of Woodland. Every tree and house, every store and building and street and fireplug. A minute town, each facet in perfect order. Constructed with elaborate care throughout the years. As long as he could remember. Since he was a kid, building and glueing and working after school.

Haskel turned on the main transformer. All along the track signal lights glowed. He fed power to the heavy Lionel engine parked with its load of freight cars. The engine sped smoothly into life, gliding along the track. A flashing dark projectile of metal that made his breath catch in his throat. He opened an electric switch and the engine headed down the ramp, through a tunnel and off the table. It raced under the workbench.

His trains. And his town. Haskel bent over the miniature houses and streets, his heart glowing with pride. He had built it – himself. Every inch. Every perfect inch. The whole town. He touched the corner of Fred's Grocery Store. Not a detail lacking. Even the windows. The displays of food. The signs. The counters.

The Uptown Hotel. He ran his hand over its flat roof. The sofas and chairs in the lobby. He could see them through the window.

Green's Drugstore. Bunion pad displays. Magazines. Frazier's Auto Parts. Mexico City Dining. Sharpstein's Apparel. Bob's Liquor Store. Ace Billiard Parlor.

The whole town. He ran his hands over it. He had built it; the town was his.

The train came rushing back, out from under the workbench. Its wheels passed over an automatic switch and a drawbridge lowered itself obediently. The train swept over and beyond, dragging its cars behind it.

Haskel turned up the power. The train gained speed. Its whistle sounded. It turned a sharp curve and grated across a cross-track. More speed. Haskel's hands jerked convulsively at the transformer. The train leaped and shot ahead. It swayed and bucked as it shot around a curve. The transformer was turned up to maximum. The train was a clattering blur of speed, rushing along the track, across bridges and switches, behind the big pipes of the floor furnace.

It disappeared into the coal bin. A moment later it swept out the other side, rocking wildly.

Haskel slowed the train down. He was breathing hard, his chest rising painfully. He sat down on the stool by the workbench and lit a cigarette with shaking fingers.

The train, the model town, gave him a strange feeling. It was hard to explain. He had always loved trains, model engines and signals and buildings. Since he was a little kid, maybe six or seven. His father had given him his first train. An engine and a few pieces of track. An old wind-up train. When he was nine he got his first real electric train. And two switches.

He added to it, year after year. Track, engines, switches, cars, signals. More powerful transformers. And the beginnings of the town.

He had built the town up carefully. Piece by piece. First, when he was in junior high, a model of the Southern Pacific

Depot. Then the taxi stand next door. The cafe where the drivers ate. Broad Street.

And so on. More and more. Houses, buildings, stores. A whole town, growing under his hands, as the years went by. Every afternoon he came home from school and worked. Glued and cut and painted and sawed.

Now it was virtually complete. Almost done. He was forty-three years old and the town was almost done.

Haskel moved around the big plywood table, his hands extended reverently. He touched a miniature store here and there. The flower shop. The theater. The Telephone Company. Larson's Pump and Valve Works.

That, too. Where he worked. His place of business. A perfect miniature of the plant, down to the last detail.

Haskel scowled. Jim Larson. For twenty years he had worked there, slaved day after day. For what? To see others advanced over him. Younger men. Favorites of the boss. Yes-men with bright ties and pressed pants and wide, stupid grins.

Misery and hatred welled up in Haskel. All his life Woodland had got the better of him. He had never been happy. The town had always been against him. Miss Murphy in high school. The frats in college. Clerks in the snooty department stores. His neighbors. Cops and mailmen and bus drivers and delivery boys. Even his wife. Even Madge.

He had never meshed with the town. The rich, expensive little suburb of San Francisco, down the peninsula beyond the fog belt. Woodland was too damn upper-middle class. Too many big houses and lawns and chrome cars and deck chairs. Too stuffy and sleek. As long as he could remember. In school. His job –

Larson. The Pump and Valve Works. Twenty years of hard work.

Haskel's fingers closed over the tiny building, the model of the Larson's Pump and Valve Works. Savagely, he ripped it loose and threw it to the floor. He crushed it underfoot, grinding the bits of glass and metal and cardboard into a shapeless mass.

God, he was shaking all over. He stared down at the remains, his heart pounding wildly. Strange emotions, crazy emotions, twisted through him. Thoughts he never had had before. For a long time he gazed down at the crumpled wad by his hose. What had once been the model of Larson's Pump and Valve Works.

Abruptly he pulled away. In a trance he returned to his workbench and sat stiffly down on the stool. He pulled his tools and materials together, clicking the power drill on.

It took only a few moments. Working rapidly, with quick, expert fingers, Haskel assembled a new model. He painted, glued, fitted pieces together. He lettered a microscopic sign and sprayed a green lawn into place.

Then he carried the new model carefully over to the table and glued it in the correct spot. The place where Larson's Pump and Valve Works had been. The new building gleamed in the overhead light, still moist and shiny.

WOODLAND MORTUARY

Haskel rubbed his hands in an ecstasy of satisfaction. The Valve Works was gone. He had destroyed it. Obliterated it. Removed it from the town. Below him was Woodland – without the Valve Works. A mortuary instead.

His eyes gleamed. His lips twitched. His surging emotions swelled. He had got rid of it. In a brief flurry of action. In a second. The whole thing was simple – amazingly easy.

Odd he hadn't thought of it before.

Sipping a tall glass of ice-cold beer thoughtfully, Madge Haskel said, 'There's something wrong with Verne. I noticed it especially last night. When he came home from work.'

Doctor Paul Tyler grunted absently. 'A highly neurotic type. Sense of inferiority. Withdrawal and introversion.'

'But he's getting worse. Him and his trains. Those damn model trains. My God, Paul! Do you know he has a whole town down there in the basement?'

Tyler was curious. 'Really? I never knew that.'

'All the time I've known him he's had them down there. Started when he was a kid. Imagine a grown man playing with trains! It's – it's disgusting. Every night the same thing.'

'Interesting.' Tyler rubbed his jaw. 'He keeps at them continually? An unvarying pattern?'

'Every night. Last night he didn't even eat dinner. He just came home and went directly down.'

Paul Tyler's polished features twisted into a frown. Across from him Madge sat languidly sipping her beer. It was two in the afternoon. The day was warm and bright. The living-room was attractive in a lazy, quiet way. Abruptly Tyler got to his feet. 'Let's take a look at them. The models. I didn't know it had gone so far.'

'Do you really want to?' Madge slid back the sleeve of her green silk lounge pajamas and consulted her wristwatch. 'He won't be home until five.' She jumped to her feet, setting down her glass. 'All right. We have time.'

'Fine. Let's go down.' Tyler caught hold of Madge's arm and they hurried down into the basement, a strange excitement flooding through them. Madge clicked on the basement light and they approached the big plywood table, giggling and nervous, like mischievous children.

'See?' Madge said, squeezing Tyler's arm. 'Look at it. Took years. All his life.'

Tyler nodded slowly. 'Must have.' There was awe in his voice. 'I've never seen anything like it. The detail . . . He has skill.'

'Yes, Verne is good with his hands.' Madge indicated the workbench. 'He buys tools all the time.'

Tyler walked slowly around the big table, bending over and peering. 'Amazing. Every building. The whole town is here. Look! There's my place.'

He indicated his luxurious apartment building, a few blocks from the Haskel residence.

'I guess it's all there,' Madge said. 'Imagine a grown man coming down here and playing with model trains!'

'Power.' Tyler pushed an engine along a track. 'That's why it appeals to boys. Trains are big things. Huge and noisy. Power-sex symbols. The boy sees the train rushing along the track. It's so huge and ruthless it scares him. Then he gets a toy train. A model, like these. He controls it. Makes it start, stop. Go slow. Fast. He runs it. It responds to him.'

Madge shivered. 'Let's go upstairs where it's warm. It's so cold down here.'

'But as the boy grows up, he gets bigger and stronger. He can shed the model-symbol. Master the real object, the real train. Get genuine control over things. Valid mastery.' Tyler shook his head. 'Not this substitute thing. Unusual, a grown person going to such lengths.' He frowned. 'I never noticed a mortuary on State Street.'

'A mortuary?'

'And this, Steuben Pet Shop. Next door to the radio repair shop. There's no pet shop there.' Tyler cudgeled his brain. 'What *is* there? Next to the radio repair place.'

'Paris Furs.' Madge clasped her arms. 'Brrrrr. Come on, Paul. Let's go upstairs before I freeze.'

Tyler laughed. 'Okay, sissy.' He headed toward the stairs, frowning again. 'I wonder why. Steuben Pets. Never heard of it. Everything is so detailed. He must know the town by heart. To put a shop there that isn't – ' He clicked off the basement light. 'And the mortuary. What's supposed to be there? Isn't the – '

'Forget it,' Madge called back, hurrying past him, into the warm living-room. 'You're practically as bad as he is. Men are such children.'

Tyler didn't respond. He was deep in thought. His suave confidence was gone; he looked nervous and shaken.

Madge pulled the venetian blinds down. The living-room sank into amber gloom. She flopped down on the couch and pulled Tyler down beside her. 'Stop looking like that,' she ordered. 'I've never seen you this way.' Her slim arms circled his neck and her lips brushed close to his ear. 'I wouldn't have let you in if I thought you were going to worry about *him*.'

Tyler grunted, preoccupied. 'Why *did* you let me in?'

The pressure of Madge's arms increased. Her silk pajamas rustled as she moved against him. 'Silly,' she said.

Big red-headed Jim Larson gaped in disbelief. 'What do you mean? What's the matter with you?'

'I'm quitting.' Haskel shoveled the contents of his desk into his briefcase. 'Mail the check to my house.'

'But – '

'Get out of the way.' Haskel pushed past Larson, out into the hall. Larson was stunned with amazement. There was a fixed expression on Haskel's face. A glazed look. A rigid look Larson had never seen before.

'Are you – all right?' Larson asked.

'Sure.' Haskel opened the front door of the plant and disappeared outside. The door slammed after him. 'Sure I'm all right,' he muttered to himself. He made his way through the crowds of late-afternoon shoppers, his lips twitching. 'You're damn right I'm all right.'

'Watch it, buddy,' a laborer muttered ominously, as Haskel shoved past him.

'Sorry.' Haskel hurried on, gripping his briefcase. At the top of the hill he paused a moment to get his breath. Behind him was Larson's Pump and Valve Works. Haskel laughed shrilly. Twenty years – cut short in a second. It was over. No more Larson. No more dull, grinding job, day after day. Without promotion or future. Routine and boredom, months on end. It was over and done for. A new life and beginning.

He hurried on. The sun was setting. Cars streaked by him, businessmen going home from work. Tomorrow they would be going back – but not him. Not ever again.

He reached his own street. Ed Tildon's house rose up, a great stately structure of concrete and glass. Tildon's dog came rushing out to bark. Haskel hastened past. Tildon's dog. He laughed wildly.

'Better keep away!' he shouted at the dog.

He reached his own house and leaped up the front steps two at a time. He tore the door open. The living-room was dark and silent. There was a sudden stir of motion. Shapes untangling themselves, getting quickly up from the couch.

'Verne!' Madge gasped. 'What are you doing home so early?'

Verne Haskel threw his briefcase down and dropped his hat and coat over a chair. His lined face was twisted with emotion, pulled out of shape by violent inner forces.

'What in the world!' Madge fluttered, hurrying toward him nervously, smoothing down her lounge pajamas. 'Has something happened? I didn't expect you so – ' She broke off, blushing. 'I mean, I – '

Paul Tyler strolled leisurely toward Haskel. 'Hi there, Verne,' he murmured, embarrassed. 'Dropped by to say hello and return a book to your wife.'

Haskel nodded curtly. 'Afternoon.' He turned and headed toward the basement door, ignoring the two of them. 'I'll be downstairs.'

'But Verne!' Madge protested. 'What's happened?'

Verne halted briefly at the door. 'I quit my job.'

'You *what*?'

'I quit my job. I finished Larson off. There won't be any more of him.' The basement door slammed.

'Good Lord!' Madge shrieked, clutching at Tyler hysterically. 'He's gone out of his mind!'

Down in the basement, Verne Haskel snapped on the light impatiently. He put on his engineer's cap and pulled his stool up beside the great plywood table.

What next?

Morris Home Furnishings. The big plush store. Where the clerks all looked down their noses at him.

He rubbed his hands gleefully. No more of them. No more snooty clerks, lifting their eyebrows when he came in. Only hair and bow ties and folded handkerchiefs.

He removed the model of Morris Home Furnishings and disassembled it. He worked feverishly, with frantic haste. Now that he had really begun he wasted no time. A moment later he was glueing two small buildings in its place. Ritz Shoeshine. Pete's Bowling Alley.

Haskel giggled excitedly. Fitting extinction for the luxurious, exclusive furniture store. A shoeshine parlor and a bowling alley. Just what it deserved.

The California State Bank. He had always hated the Bank. They had once refused him a loan. He pulled the Bank loose.

Ed Tildon's mansion. His damn dog. The dog had bit him on the ankle one afternoon. He ripped the model off. His head spun. He could do anything.

Harrison Appliance. They had sold him a bum radio. Off came Harrison Appliance.

Joe's Cigar and Smoke Shop. Joe had given him a lead quarter in May, 1949. Off came Joe's.

The Ink Works. He loathed the smell of ink. Maybe a bread factory, instead. He loved baking bread. Off came the Ink Works.

Elm Street was too dark at night. A couple of times he had stumbled. A few more streetlights were in order.

Not enough bars along High Street. Too many dress shops and expensive hat and fur shops and ladies' apparel. He ripped a whole handful loose and carried them to the workbench.

At the top of the stairs the door opened slowly. Madge peered down, pale and frightened. 'Verne?'

He scowled up impatiently. 'What do you want?'

Madge came downstairs hesitantly. Behind her Doctor Tyler followed, suave and handsome in his gray suit. 'Verne – is everything all right?'

'Of course.'

'Did – did you really quit your job?'

Haskel nodded. He began to disassemble the Ink Works, ignoring his wife and Doctor Tyler.

'But *why*?'

Haskel grunted impatiently. 'No time.'

Doctor Tyler had begun to look worried. 'Do I understand you're too busy for your job?'

'That's right.'

'Too busy doing *what*?' Tyler's voice rose; he was trembling nervously. 'Working down here on this town of yours? Changing things?'

'Go away,' Haskel muttered. His deft hands were assembling a lovely little Langendorf Bread Factory. He shaped it with loving care, sprayed it with white paint, brushed a gravel walk and shrubs in front of it. He put it aside and began on a park. A big green park. Woodland had always needed a park. It would go in place of State Street Hotel.

Tyler pulled Madge away from the table, off in a corner of the basement. 'Good God.' He lit a cigarette shakily. The cigarette flipped out of his hands and rolled away. He ignored it and fumbled for another. 'You see? You see what he's doing?'

Madge shook her head mutely. 'What is it? I don't – '

'How long has he been working on this? All his life?'

Madge nodded, white-faced. 'Yes, all his life.'

Tyler's features twisted. 'My God, Madge. It's enough to drive you out of your mind. I can hardly believe it. We've got to do something.'

'What's happening?' Madge moaned. 'What – '

'He's losing himself into it.' Tyler's face was a mask of incredulous disbelief. 'Faster and faster.'

'He's always come down here,' Madge faltered. 'It's nothing new. He's always wanted to get away.'

'Yes. Get away.' Tyler shuddered, clenched his fists and pulled himself together. He advanced across the basement and stopped by Verne Haskel.

'What do you want?' Haskel muttered, noticing him.

Tyler licked his lips. 'You're adding some things, aren't you? New buildings.'

Haskel nodded.

Tyler touched the little bread factory with shaking fingers. 'What's this? Bread? Where does it go?' He moved around the table. 'I don't remember any bread factory in Woodland.' He whirled. 'You aren't by any chance *improving* on the town? Fixing it up here and there?'

'Get the hell out of here,' Haskel said, with ominous calm. 'Both of you.'

'Verne!' Madge squeaked.

'I've got a lot to do. You can bring sandwiches down about eleven. I hope to finish sometime tonight.'

'Finish?' Tyler asked.

'Finish,' Haskel answered, returning to his work.

'Come on, Madge.' Tyler grabbed her and pulled her to the stairs. 'Let's get out of here.' He strode ahead of her, up to the stairs and into the hall. 'Come on!' As soon as she was up he closed the door tightly after them.

Madge dabbed at her eyes hysterically. 'He's gone crazy, Paul! What'll we do?'

Tyler was in deep thought. 'Be quiet. I have to think this out.' He paced back and forth, a hard scowl on his features. 'It'll come soon. It won't be long, not at this rate. Sometime tonight.'

'*What?* What do you mean?'

'His withdrawal. Into his substitute world. The improved model he controls. Where he can get away.'

'Isn't there something we can do?'

'Do?' Tyler smiled faintly. 'Do we want to do something?'

Madge gasped. 'But we can't just – '

'Maybe this will solve our problem. This may be what we've been looking for.' Tyler eyed Mrs Haskel thoughtfully. 'This may be just the thing.'

It was after midnight, almost two o'clock in the morning, when he began to get things into final shape. He was tired – but alert. Things were happening fast. The job was almost done.

Virtually perfect.

He halted work a moment, surveying what he had accomplished. The town had been radically changed. About ten o'clock he had begun basic structural alterations in the lay-out of the streets. He had removed most of the public buildings, the civic center and the sprawling business district around it.

He had erected a new city hall, police station, and an immense park with fountains and indirect lighting. He had cleared the slum area, the old run-down stores and houses and streets. The streets were wider and well-lit. The houses were now small and clean. The stores modern and attractive – without being ostentatious.

All advertising signs had been removed. Most of the filling stations were gone. The immense factory area was gone, too. Rolling countryside took its place. Trees and hills and green grass.

The wealthy district had been altered. There were now only a few of the mansions left – belonging to persons he looked favorably on. The rest had been cut down, turned into uniform two-bedroom dwellings, one story, with a single garage each.

The city hall was no longer an elaborate, rococo structure. Now it was low and simple, modeled after the Parthenon, a favorite of his.

There were ten or twelve persons who had done him special harm. He had altered their houses considerably. Given them war-time housing unit apartments, six to a building, at the far edge of town. Where the wind came off the bay, carrying the smell of decaying mud-flats.

Jim Larson's house was completely gone. He had erased Larson utterly. He no longer existed, not in this new Woodland – which was now almost complete.

Almost. Haskel studied his work intently. All the changes had to be made *now*. Not later. This was the time of creation. Later, when it had been finished, it could not be altered. He had to catch all the necessary changes now – or forget them.

The new Woodland looked pretty good. Clean and neat – and simple. The rich district had been toned down. The poor district had been improved. Glaring ads, signs, displays, had all been changed or removed. The business community was smaller. Parks and countryside took the place of factories. The civic center was lovely.

He added a couple of playgrounds for smaller kids. A small theater instead of the enormous Uptown with its flashing neon sign. After some consideration he removed most of the bars he had previously constructed. The new Woodland was going to be moral. Extremely moral. Few bars, no billiards, no red light district. And there was an especially fine jail for undesirables.

The most difficult part had been the microscopic lettering of the main office door of the city hall. He had left it until last, and then painted the words with agonizing care:

MAYOR
VERNON R. HASKEL

A few last changes. He gave the Edwardses a '39 Plymouth instead of a new Cadillac. He added more trees in the down-town district. One more fire department. One less dress shop. He had never liked taxis. On impulse, he removed the taxi stand and put in a flower shop.

Haskel rubbed his hands. Anything more? Or was it com-plete . . . Perfect . . . He studied each part intently. What had he overlooked?

The high school. He removed it and put in two smaller high schools, one at each end of town. Another hospital. That took almost half an hour. He was getting tired. His hands were less swift. He mopped his forehead shakily. Anything else? He sat down on his stool wearily, to rest and think.

All done. It was complete. Joy welled up in him. A bursting cry of happiness. His work was over.

'Finished!' Verne Haskel shouted.

He got unsteadily to his feet. He closed his eyes, held his arms out, and advanced toward the plywood table. Reaching, grasping, fingers extended, Haskel headed toward it, a look of radiant exaltation on his seamed, middle-aged face.

Upstairs, Tyler and Madge heard the shout. A distant booming that rolled through the house in waves. Madge winced in terror. 'What was that?'

Tyler listened intently. He heard Haskel moving below them, in the basement. Abruptly, he stubbed out his cigarette. 'I think it's happened. Sooner than I expected.'

'It? You mean he's – '

Tyler got quickly to his feet. 'He's gone, Madge. Into his other world. We're finally free.'

Madge caught his arm. 'Maybe we're making a mistake. It's so terrible. Shouldn't we – try to do something? Bring him out of it – try to pull him back.'

'Bring him back?' Tyler laughed nervously. 'I don't think we could, now. Even if we wanted to. It's too late.' He hurried toward the basement door. 'Come on.'

'It's horrible.' Madge shuddered and followed reluctantly. 'I wish we had never got started.'

Tyler halted briefly at the door. 'Horrible? He's happier, where he is, now. And you're happier. The way it was, nobody was happy. This is the best thing.'

He opened the basement door. Madge followed him. They moved cautiously down the stairs, into the dark, silent basement, damp with the faint night mists.

The basement was empty.

Tyler relaxed. He was overcome with dazed relief. 'He's gone. Everything's okay. It worked out exactly right.'

'But I don't understand,' Madge repeated hopelessly, as Tyler's Buick purred along the dark, deserted streets. 'Where did he go?'

'You know where he went,' Tyler answered. 'Into his substitute world, of course.' He screeched around a corner on two wheels. 'The rest should be fairly simple. A few routine forms. There really isn't much left, now.'

The night was frigid and bleak. No lights showed, except an occasional lonely streetlamp. Far off, a train whistle sounded mournfully, a dismal echo. Rows of silent houses flickered by on both sides of them.

'Where are we going?' Madge asked. She sat huddled against the door, face pale with shock and terror, shivering under her coat.

'To the police station.'

'Why?'

'To report him, naturally. So they'll know he's gone. We'll have to wait; it'll be several years before he'll be declared legally dead.' Tyler reached over and hugged her briefly. 'We'll make out in the meantime, I'm sure.'

'What if – they find him?'

Tyler shook his head angrily. He was still tense, on edge. 'Don't you understand? They'll never find him – he doesn't exist. At least, not in our world. He's in his own world. You saw it. The model. The improved substitute.'

'He's there?'

'All his life he's worked on it. Built it up. Made it real. He brought that world into being – and now he's in it. That's what he wanted. That's why he built it. He didn't merely dream about an escape world. He actually constructed it – every bit and piece. Now he's warped himself right out of our world, into it. Out of our lives.'

Madge finally began to understand. 'Then he really *did* lose himself in his substitute world. You meant that, what you said about him – getting away.'

'It took me awhile to realize it. The mind constructs reality. Frames it. Creates it. We all have a common reality, a common dream. But Haskel turned his back on our common reality and created his own. And he had a unique capacity – far beyond the ordinary. He devoted his whole life, his whole skill to building it. He's there now.'

Tyler hesitated and frowned. He gripped the wheel tightly

and increased speed. The Buick hissed along the dark street, through the silent, unmoving bleakness that was the town.

'There's only one thing,' he continued presently. 'One thing I don't understand.'

'What is it?'

'The model. It was also gone. I assumed he'd – shrink, I suppose. Merge with it. But the model's gone, too.' Tyler shrugged. 'It doesn't matter.' He peered into the darkness. 'We're almost there. This is Elm.'

It was then Madge screamed. '*Look!*'

To the right of the car was a small, neat building. And a sign. The sign was easily visible in the darkness.

WOODLAND MORTUARY

Madge was sobbing in horror. The car roared forward, automatically guided by Tyler's numb hands. Another sign flashed by briefly, as they coasted up before the city hall.

STEUBEN PET SHOP

The city hall was lit by recessed, hidden illumination. A low, simple building, a square of glowing white. Like a marble Greek temple.

Tyler pulled the car to a halt. Then suddenly shrieked and started up again. But not soon enough.

The two shiny-black police cars came silently up around the Buick, one on each side. The four stern cops already had their hands on the door. Stepping out and coming toward him, grim and efficient.

Souvenir

'Here we go, sir,' the robot pilot said. The words startled Rogers and made him look up sharply. He tensed his body and adjusted the trace web inside his coat as the bubble ship started dropping, swiftly and silently, toward the planet's surface.

This – his heart caught – was Williamson's World. The legendary lost planet – found, after three centuries. By accident, of course. This blue and green planet, the holy grail of the Galactic System, had been almost miraculously discovered by a routine charting mission.

Frank Williamson had been the first Terran to develop an outer-space drive – the first to hop from the Solar System toward the universe beyond. He had never come back. He – his world, his colony – had never been found. There had been endless rumors, false leads, fake legends – and nothing more.

'I'm receiving field clearance.' The robot pilot raised the gain on the control speaker, and clicked to attention.

'Field ready,' came a ghostly voice from below. 'Remember, your drive mechanism is unfamiliar to us. How much run is required? Emergency brake-walls are up.'

Rogers smiled. He could hear the pilot telling them that no run would be required. Not with this ship. The brake-walls could be lowered with perfect safety.

Three hundred years! It had taken a long time to find Williamson's World. Many authorities had given him up. Some believed he had never landed, had died out in space. Perhaps there was *no* Williamson's World. Certainly there had been no real clues, nothing tangible to go on. Frank Williamson and three families had utterly disappeared in the trackless void, never to be heard from again.

Until now . . .

The young man met him at the field. He was thin and red-haired and dressed in a colorful suit of bright material. 'You're from the Galactic Relay Center?' he asked.

'That's right,' Rogers said huskily. 'I'm Edward Rogers.'

The young man held out his hand. Rogers shook it awkwardly. 'My name is Williamson,' the young man said. 'Gene Williamson.'

The name thundered in Rogers' ears. 'Are you – '

The young man nodded, his gaze enigmatical. 'I'm his great-great-great-great-grandson. His tomb is here. You may see it, if you wish.'

'I almost expected to see him. He's – well, almost a god-figure to us. The first man to break out of the Solar System.'

'He means a lot to us, too,' the young man said. 'He brought us here. They searched a long time before they found a planet that was habitable.' Williamson waved at the city stretched out beyond the field. 'This one proved satisfactory. It's the System's tenth planet.'

Rogers' eyes began to shine. Williamson's World. Under his feet. He stamped hard as they walked down the ramp together, away from the field. How many men in the Galaxy had dreamed of striding down a landing ramp onto Williamson's World with a young descendant of Frank Williamson beside them?

'They'll all want to come here,' Williamson said, as if aware of his thoughts. 'Throw rubbish around and break off the flowers. Pick up handfuls of dirt to take back.' He laughed a little nervously. 'The Relay will control them, of course.'

'Of course,' Rogers assured him.

At the ramp-end Rogers stopped short. For the first time he saw the city.

'What's wrong?' Gene Williamson asked, with a faint trace of amusement.

They had been cut off, of course. Isolated – so perhaps it wasn't so surprising. It was a wonder they weren't living in caves, eating raw meat. But Williamson had always symbolized progress – development. He had been a man *ahead* of other men.

True, his space-drive by modern standards had been primitive, a curiosity. But the concept remained unaltered; Williamson the pioneer, and inventor. The man who built.

Yet the city was nothing more than a village, with a few dozen houses, and some public buildings and industrial units at its perimeter. Beyond the city stretched green fields, hills, and broad prairies. Surface vehicles crawled leisurely along the narrow streets and most of the citizens walked on foot. An incredible anachronism it seemed, dragged up from the past.

'I'm accustomed to the uniform Galactic culture,' Rogers said. 'Relay keeps the technocratic and ideological level constant throughout. It's hard to adjust to such a radically different social stage. But you've been cut off.'

'Cut off?' asked Williamson.

'From Relay. You've had to develop without help.'

In front of them a surface vehicle crept to a halt. The driver opened the doors manually.

'Now that I recall these factors, I can adjust,' Rogers assured him.

'On the contrary,' Williamson said, entering the vehicle. 'We've been receiving your Relay coordinates for over a century.' He motioned Rogers to get in beside him.

Rogers was puzzled. 'I don't understand. You mean you hooked onto the web and yet made no attempt to –'

'We receive your coordinates,' Gene Williamson said, 'but our citizens are not interested in using them.'

The surface vehicle hurried along the highway, past the rim of an immense red hill. Soon the city lay behind them – a faintly glowing place reflecting the rays of the sun. Bushes and plants appeared along the highway. The sheer side of the cliff rose, a towering wall of deep red sandstone; ragged, untouched.

'Nice evening,' Williamson said.

Rogers nodded in disturbed agreement.

Williamson rolled down the window. Cool air blew into the car. A few gnatlike insects followed. Far off, two tiny figures were plowing a field – a man and a huge lumbering beast.

'When will we be there?' Rogers asked.

'Soon. Most of us live away from the cities. We live in the

country – in isolated self-sufficient farm units. They're modeled on the manors of the Middle Ages.'

'Then you maintain only the most rudimentary subsistence level. How many people live on each farm?'

'Perhaps a hundred men and women.'

'A hundred people can't manage anything more complex than weaving and dyeing and paper pressing.'

'We have special industrial units – manufacturing systems. This vehicle is a good example of what we can turn out. We have communication and sewage and medical agencies. We have technological advantages equal to Terra's.'

'Terra of the twenty-first century,' Rogers protested. 'But that was three hundred years ago. You're purposely maintaining an archaic culture in the face of the Relay coordinates. It doesn't make any sense.'

'Maybe we prefer it.'

'But you're not free to prefer an inferior cultural stage. Every culture has to keep pace with the general trend. Relay makes actual a uniformity of development. It integrates the valid factors and rejects the rest.'

They were approaching the farm, Gene Williamson's 'manor.' It consisted of a few simple buildings clustered together in a valley, to the side of the highway, surrounded by fields and pastures. The surface vehicle turned down a narrow side road and spiraled cautiously toward the floor of the valley. The air became darker. Cold wind blew into the car, and the driver clicked his headlights on.

'No robots?' Rogers asked.

'No,' Williamson replied. 'We do all our own work.'

'You're making a purely arbitrary distinction,' Rogers pointed out. 'A robot is a machine. You don't dispense with machines as such. This car is a machine.'

'True,' Williamson acknowledged.

'The machine is a development of the tool,' Rogers went on. 'The ax is a simple machine. A stick becomes a tool, a simple machine, in the hands of a man reaching for something. A machine is merely a multi-element tool that increases the power ratio. Man is the tool-making animal. The history of man is the history of tools into machines, greater and more efficient functioning elements. If you reject machinery you reject man's essential key.'

'Here we are,' Williamson said. The vehicle came to a halt and the driver opened the doors for them.

Three or four wooden buildings loomed up in the darkness. A few dim shapes moved around – human shapes.

'Dinner's ready,' Williamson said, sniffing. 'I can smell it.'

They entered the main building. Several men and women were sitting at a long rough table. Plates and dishes had been set in front of them. They were waiting for Williamson.

'This is Edward Rogers,' Williamson announced. The people studied Rogers curiously, then turned back to their food.

'Sit down,' a dark-eyed girl urged. 'By me.'

They made a place for him near the end of the table. Rogers started forward, but Williamson restrained him. 'Not there. You're *my* guest. You're expected to sit with me.'

The girl and her companion laughed. Rogers sat down awkwardly by Williamson. The bench was rough and hard under him. He examined a handmade wooden drinking cup. The food was piled in huge wooden bowls. There was a stew and a salad and great loaves of bread.

'We could be back in the fourteenth century,' Rogers said.

'Yes,' Williamson agreed. 'Manor life goes back to Roman times and to the classical world. The Gauls. Britons.'

'These people here. Are they – '

Williamson nodded. 'My family. We're divided up into small units arranged according to the traditional patriarch basis. I'm the oldest male and titular head.'

The people were eating rapidly, intent on their food – boiled meat, vegetables, scooped up with hunks of bread and butter and washed down with milk. The room was lit by fluorescent lighting.

'Incredible,' Rogers murmured. 'You're still using electric power.'

'Oh, yes. There are plenty of waterfalls on this planet. The vehicle was electric. It was run by a storage battery.'

'Why are there no older men?' Rogers saw several dried-up old women, but Williamson was the oldest man. And he couldn't have been over thirty.

'The fighting,' Williamson replied, with an expressive gesture.

'Fighting?'

'Clan wars between families are a major part of our culture.' Williamson nodded toward the long table. 'We don't live long.'

Rogers was stunned. 'Clan wars? But – '

'We have pennants, and emblems – like the old Scottish tribes.'

He touched a bright ribbon on his sleeve, the representation of a bird. 'There are emblems and colors for each family and we fight over them. The Williamson family no longer controls this planet. There is no central agency, now. For a major issue we have the plebiscite – a vote by all the clans. Each family on the planet has a vote.'

'Like the American Indians.'

Williamson nodded. 'It's a tribal system. In time we'll be distinct tribes, I suppose. We still retain a common language, but we're breaking up – decentralizing. And each family to its own ways, its own customs and manners.'

'Just what do you fight for?'

Williamson shrugged. 'Some real things like land and women. Some imaginary. Prestige for instance. When honor is at stake we have an official semi-annual public battle. A man from each family takes part. The best warrior and his weapons.'

'Like the medieval joust.'

'We've drawn from all traditions. Human tradition as a whole.'

'Does each family have its separate deity?'

Williamson laughed. 'No. We worship in common a vague animism. A sense of the general positive vitality of the universal process.' He held up a loaf of bread. 'Thanks for all this.'

'Which you grew yourselves.'

'On a planet provided for us.' Williamson ate his bread thoughtfully. 'The old records say the ship was almost finished. Fuel just about gone – one dead, arid waste after another. If this planet hadn't turned up, the whole expedition would have perished.'

* * *

'Cigar?' Williamson said, when the empty bowls had been pushed back.

'Thanks.' Rogers accepted a cigar noncommittally. Williamson lit his own, and settled back against the wall.

'How long are you staying?' he asked presently.

'Not long,' Rogers answered.

'There's a bed fixed up for you,' Williamson said. 'We retire early, but there'll be some kind of dancing, also singing and dramatic acts. We devote a lot of time to staging, and producing drama.'

'You place an emphasis on psychological release?'

'We enjoy making and doing things, if that's what you mean.'

Rogers stared about him. The walls were covered with murals painted directly on the rough wood. 'So I see,' he said. 'You grind your own colors from clay and berries?'

'Not quite,' Williamson replied. 'We have a big pigment industry. Tomorrow I'll show you our kiln where we fire our own things. Some of our best work is with fabrics and screen processes.'

'Interesting. A decentralized society, moving gradually back into primitive tribalism. A society that voluntarily rejects the advanced technocratic and cultural products of the Galaxy, and thus deliberately withdraws from contact with the rest of mankind.'

'From the uniform Relay-controlled society only,' Williamson insisted.

'Do you know why Relay maintains a uniform level for all worlds?' Rogers asked. 'I'll tell you. There are two reasons. First, the body of knowledge which men have amassed doesn't permit duplication of experiment. There's no time.

'When a discovery has been made it's absurd to repeat it on countless planets throughout the universe. Information gained on any of the thousand worlds is flashed to Relay Center and then out again to the whole Galaxy. Relay studies and selects experiences and coordinates them into a rational, functional system with contradictions. Relay orders the total experience of mankind into a coherent structure.'

'And the second reason?'

'If uniform culture is maintained, controlled from a central source, there won't be war.'

'True,' Williamson admitted.

'We've abolished war. It's as simple as that. We have a homogeneous culture like that of ancient Rome – a common culture for all mankind which we maintain throughout the Galaxy. Each planet is as involved in it as any other. There are no backwaters of culture to breed envy and hatred.'

'Such as this.'

Rogers let out his breath slowly. 'Yes – you've confronted us with a strange situation. We've searched for Williamson's World for three centuries. We've wanted it, dreamed of finding it. It has seemed like Prester John's Empire – a fabulous world, cut off from the rest of humanity. Maybe not real at all. Frank Williamson might have crashed.'

'But he didn't.'

'He didn't, and Williamson's World is alive with a culture of its own. Deliberately set apart, with its own way of life, its own standards. Now contact has been made, and our dream has come true. The people of the Galaxy will soon be informed that Williamson's World has been found. We can now restore the first colony outside the Solar System to its rightful place in the Galactic culture.'

Rogers reached into his coat, and brought out a metal packet. He unfastened the packet and laid a clean, crisp document on the table.

'What's this?' Williamson asked.

'The Articles of Incorporation. For you to sign, so that Williamson's World can become a part of the Galactic culture.'

Williamson and the rest of the people in the room fell silent. They gazed down at the document, none of them speaking.

'Well?' Rogers said. He was tense. He pushed the document toward Williamson. 'Here it is.'

Williamson shook his head. 'Sorry.' He pushed the document firmly back toward Rogers. 'We've already taken a plebiscite. I hate to disappoint you, but we've already decided not to join. That's our *final* decision.'

* * *

The Class-One battleship assumed an orbit outside the gravity belt of Williamson's World.

Commander Ferris contacted the Relay Center. 'We're here. What next?'

'Send down a wiring team. Report back to me as soon as it has made surface contact.'

Ten minutes later Corporal Pete Matson was dropped overboard in a pressurized gravity suit. He drifted slowly toward the blue and green globe beneath, turning and twisting as he neared the surface of the planet.

Matson landed and bounced a couple of times. He got shakily to his feet. He seemed to be at the edge of a forest. In the shadow of the huge trees he removed his crash helmet. Holding his blast rifle tightly he made his way forward, cautiously advancing among the trees.

His earphones clicked. 'Any sign of activity?'

'None, Commander,' he signaled back.

'There's what appears to be a village to your right. You may run into someone. Keep moving, and watch out. The rest of the team is dropping, now. Instructions will follow from your Relay web.'

'I'll watch out,' Matson promised, cradling his blast rifle. He sighted it experimentally at a distant hill and squeezed the trigger. The hill disintegrated into dust, a rising column of waste particles.

Matson climbed a long ridge and shielded his eyes to peer around him.

He could see the village. It was small, like a country town on Terra. It looked interesting. For a moment he hesitated. Then he stepped quickly down from the ridge and headed toward the village, moving rapidly, his supple body alert.

Above him, from the Class-One battleship, three more of the team were already falling, clutching their guns and tumbling gently toward the surace of the planet . . .

Rogers folded up the Incorporation papers and returned them slowly to his coat. 'You understand what you're doing?' he asked.

The room was deathly silent. Williamson nodded. 'Of course. We're refusing to join your Relay system.'

Rogers' fingers touched the trace web. The web warmed into life. 'I'm sorry to hear that,' he said.

'Does it surprise you?'

'Not exactly. Relay submitted our scout's report to the computers. There was always the possibility you'd refuse. I was given instructions in case of such an event.'

'What are your instructions?'

Rogers examined his wristwatch. 'To inform you that you have six hours to join us – or be blasted out of the universe.' He got abruptly to his feet. 'I'm sorry this had to happen. Williamson's World is one of our most precious legends. But nothing must destroy the unity of the Galaxy.'

Williamson had risen. His face was ash white, the color of death. They faced each other defiantly.

'We'll fight,' Williamson said quietly. His fingers knotted together violently, clenching and unclenching.

'That's unimportant. You've received Relay coordinates on weapons development. You know what our war fleet has.'

The other people sat quietly at their places, staring rigidly down at their empty plates. No one moved.

'Is it necessary?' Williamson said harshly.

'Cultural variation must be avoided if the Galaxy is to have peace,' Rogers replied firmly.

'You'd destroy us to avoid war?'

'We'd destroy anything to avoid war. We can't permit our society to degenerate into bickering provinces, forever quarrelling and fighting – like your clans. We're stable because we lack the very concept of variation. Uniformity must be preserved and separation must be discouraged. The idea itself must remain unknown.'

Williamson was thoughtful. 'Do you think you can keep the idea unknown? There are so many semantic correlatives, hints, verbal leads. Even if you blast us, it may arise somewhere else.'

'We'll take that chance.' Rogers moved toward the door. 'I'll return to my ship and wait there. I suggest you take another vote. Maybe knowing how far we're prepared to go will change the results.'

'I doubt it.'

Rogers' web whispered suddenly. 'This is North at Relay.'

Rogers fingered the web in acknowledgment.

'A Class-One Battleship is in your area. A team has already been landed. Keep your ship grounded until it can fall back. I've ordered the team to lay out its fission-mine terminals.'

Rogers said nothing. His fingers tightened around the web convulsively.

'What's wrong?' Williamson asked.

'Nothing.' Rogers pushed the door open. 'I'm in a hurry to return to my ship. Let's go.'

Commander Ferris contacted Rogers as soon as his ship had left Williamson's World.

'North tells me you've already informed them,' Ferris said.

'That's right. He also contacted your team directly. Had it prepare to attack.'

'So I'm informed. How much time did you offer them?'

'Six hours.'

'Do you think they'll give in?'

'I don't know,' Rogers said. 'I hope so. But I doubt it.'

Williamson's World turned slowly in the viewscreen with its green and blue forest, rivers and oceans. Terra might have looked that way, once. He could see the Class-One battleship, a great silvery globe moving slowly in its orbit around the planet.

The legendary world had been found and contacted. Now it would be destroyed. He had tried to prevent it, but without success. He couldn't prevent the inevitable.

If Williamson's World refused to join the Galactic culture its destruction became a necessity – grim, axiomatic. It was either Williamson's World or the Galaxy. To preserve the greater, the lesser had to be sacrificed.

He made himself as comfortable as possible by the viewscreen, and waited.

At the end of six hours a line of black dots rose from the planet and headed slowly toward the Class-One battleship. He recognized them for what they were – old-fashioned jet-driven rocket ships. A formation of antiquated war vessels, rising up to give battle.

The planet had not changed its mind. It was going to fight. It was willing to be destroyed, rather than give up its way of life.

The black dots grew swiftly larger, became roaring blazing metal disks puffing awkwardly along. A pathetic sight. Rogers felt strangely moved, watching the jet-driven ships divide up for the contact. The Class-One battleship had secured its orbit, and was swinging in a lazy, efficient arc. Its banks of energy tubes were slowly rising, lining up to meet the attack.

Suddenly the formation of the ancient rocketships dived. They rumbled over the Class-One, firing jerkily. The Class-One's tubes followed their path. They began to reform clumsily, gaining distance for a second try, and another run.

A tongue of colorless energy flicked out. The attackers vanished.

Commander Ferris contacted Rogers. 'The poor tragic fools.' His heavy face was gray. 'Attacking us with those things.'

'Any damage?'

'None whatever.' Ferris wiped his forehead shakily. 'No damage to me at all.'

'What next?' Rogers asked stonily.

'I've declined the mine operation and passed it back to Relay. They'll have to do it. The impulse should already be – '

Below them, the green and blue globe shuddered convulsively. Soundlessly, effortlessly, it flew apart. Fragments rose, bits of debris and the planet dissolved in a cloud of white flame, a blazing mass of incandescent fire. For an instant it remained a miniature sun, lighting up the void. Then it faded into ash.

The screens of Rogers' ship hummed into life, as the debris struck. Particles rained against them, and were instantly disintegrated.

'Well,' Ferris said. 'It's over. North will report the original scout mistaken. Williamson's World wasn't found. The legend will remain a legend.'

Rogers continued to watch until the last bits of debris had ceased flying, and only a vague, discolored shadow remained. The screens clicked off automatically. To his right, the Class-One battleship picked up speed and headed toward the Riga System.

Williamson's World was gone. The Galactic Relay culture had been preserved. The idea, the concept of a separate culture with its own ways, its own customs, had been disposed of in the most effective possible way.

'Good job,' the Relay trace web whispered. North was pleased. 'The fission mines were perfectly placed. Nothing remains.'

'No,' Rogers agreed. 'Nothing remains.'

Corporal Pete Matson pushed the front door open, grinning from ear to ear. 'Hi, honey! Surprise!'

'Pete!' Gloria Matson came running, throwing her arms around her husband. 'What are you doing home? Pete – '

'Special leave. Forty-eight hours.' Pete tossed down his suitcase triumphantly. 'Hi there, kid.'

His son greeted him shyly. 'Hello.'

Pete squatted down and opened his suitcase. 'How have things been going? How's school?'

'He's had another cold,' Gloria said. 'He's almost over it. But what happened? Why did they – '

'Military secret.' Pete fumbled in his suitcase. 'Here.' He held something out to his son. 'I brought you something. A souvenir.'

He handed his son a handmade wooden drinking cup. The boy took it shyly and turned it around, curious and puzzled. 'What's a – a *souvenir*?'

Matson struggled to express the difficult concept. 'Well, it's something that reminds you of a different place. Something you don't have, where you are. You know.' Matson tapped the cup. 'That's to drink out of. It's sure not like our plastic cups, is it?'

'No,' the child said.

'Look at this, Gloria.' Pete shook out a great folded cloth from his suitcase, printed with multi-colored designs. 'Picked this up cheap. You can make a shirt out of it. What do you say? Ever seen anything like it?'

'No,' Gloria said, awed. 'I haven't.' She took the cloth and fingered it reverently.

Pete Matson beamed, as his wife and child stood clutching

the souvenirs he had brought them, reminders of his excursion to distant places. Foreign lands.

'Gee,' his son whispered, turning the cup around and around. A strange light glowed in his eyes. 'Thanks a lot, Dad. For the – *souvenir*.'

The strange light grew.

Survey Team

Halloway came up through six miles of ash to see how the rocket looked in landing. He emerged from the lead-shielded bore and joined Young, crouching down with a small knot of surface troops.

The surface of the planet was dark and silent. The air stung his nose. It smelled foul. Halloway shivered uneasily. 'Where the hell are we?'

A soldier pointed into the blackness. 'The mountains are over there. See them? The Rockies, and this is Colorado.'

Colorado . . . The old name awakened vague emotion in Halloway. He fingered his blast rifle. 'When will it get here?' he asked. Far off, against the horizon, he could see the Enemy's green and yellow signal flares. And an occasional flash of fission white.

'Any time now. It's mechanically controlled all the way, piloted by robot. When it comes it really comes.'

An Enemy mine burst a few dozen miles away. For a brief instant the landscape was outlined in jagged lightning. Halloway and the troops dropped to the ground automatically. He caught the dead burned smell of the surface of Earth as it was now, thirty years after the war began.

It was a lot different from the way he remembered it when he was a kid in California. He could remember the valley country, grape orchards and walnuts and lemons. Smudge pots under the orange trees. Green mountains and sky the color of a woman's eyes. And the fresh smell of the soil . . .

That was all gone now. Nothing remained but gray ash pulverized with the white stones of buildings. Once a city had been in this spot. He could see the yawning cavities of cellars, filled now with slag, dried rivers of rust that had once been buildings. Rubble strewn everywhere, aimlessly . . .

The mine flare faded out and the blackness settled back. They got cautiously to their feet. 'Quite a sight,' a soldier murmured.

'It was a lot different before,' Halloway said.

'Was it? I was born undersurface.'

'In those days we grew our food right in the ground, on the surface. In the soil. Not in underground tanks. We – '

Halloway broke off. A great rushing sound filled the air suddenly, cutting off his words. An immense shape roared past them in the blackness, struck someplace close, and shook the earth.

'The rocket!' a soldier shouted. They all began running, Halloway lumbering awkwardly along.

'Good news, I hope,' Young said, close by him.

'I hope, too,' Halloway gasped. 'Mars is our last chance. If this doesn't work we're finished. The report on Venus was negative; nothing there but lava and steam.'

Later they examined the rocket from Mars.

'It'll do,' Young murmured.

'You're sure?' Director Davidson asked tensely. 'Once we get there we can't come running back.'

'We're sure.' Halloway tossed the spools across the desk to Davidson. 'Examine them yourself. The air on Mars will be thin, and dry. The gravity is much weaker than ours. But we'll be able to live there, which is more than you can say for this God-forsaken Earth.'

Davidson picked up the spools. The unblinking recessed lights gleamed down on the metal desk, the metal walls and floor of the office. Hidden machinery wheezed in the walls, maintaining the air and temperature. 'I'll have to rely on you experts, of course. If some vital factor is not taken into account – '

'Naturally, it's a gamble,' Young said. 'We can't be sure of all factors at this distance.' He tapped the spools. 'Mechanical samples and photos. Robots creeping around, doing the best they can. We're lucky to have *anything* to go on.'

'There's no radiation at least,' Halloway said. 'We can count on that. But Mars will be dry and dusty and cold. It's a long way out. Weak sun. Deserts and wrinkled hills.'

'Mars is old,' Young agreed.

'It was cooled a long time ago. Look at it this way: We have eight planets, excluding Earth. Pluto to Jupiter is *out*. No chance of survival there. Mercury is nothing but liquid metal. Venus is still volcano and steam – pre-Cambrian. That's seven of the eight. Mars is the only possibility *a priori*.'

'In other words,' Davidson said slowly, 'Mars *has* to be okay because there's nothing else for us to try.'

'We could stay here. Live on here in the undersurface systems like gophers.'

'We could not last more than another year. You've seen the recent psych graphs.'

They had. The tension index was up. Men weren't made to live in metal tunnels, living on tank-grown food, working and sleeping and dying without seeing the sun.

It was the children they were really thinking about. Kids that had never been up to the surface. Wan-faced pseudo mutants with eyes like blind fish. A generation born in the subterranean world. The tension index was up because men were seeing their children alter and meld in with a world of tunnels and slimy darkness and dripping luminous rocks.

'Then it's agreed?' Young said.

Davidson searched the faces of the two technicians. 'Maybe we could reclaim the surface, revive Earth again, renew its soil. It hasn't really gone that far, has it?'

'No chance,' Young said flatly. 'Even if we could work an arrangement with the Enemy there'll be particles in suspension for another fifty years. Earth will be too hot for life the rest of this century. *And we can't wait.*'

'All right,' Davidson said. 'I'll authorize the survey team. We'll risk that, at least. You want to go? Be the first humans to land on Mars?'

'You bet,' Halloway said grimly. 'It's in our contract that I go.'

The red globe that was Mars grew steadily larger. In the control room Young and van Ecker, the navigator, watched it intently.

'We'll have to bail,' van Ecker said. 'No chance of landing at this velocity.'

Young was nervous. 'That's all right for us, but how about the first load of settlers? We can't expect women and children to jump.'

'By then we'll know more.' Van Ecker nodded and Captain Mason sounded the emergency alarm. Throughout the ship relay bells clanged ominously. The ship throbbed with scampering feet as crew members grabbed their jump-suits and hurried to the hatches.

'Mars,' Captain Mason murmured, still at the viewscreen. 'Not like Luna. This is the real thing.'

Young and Halloway moved toward the hatch. 'We better get going.'

Mars was swelling rapidly. An ugly bleak globe, dull red. Halloway fitted on his jump helmet. Van Ecker came behind him.

Mason remained in the control cabin. 'I'll follow,' he said, 'after the crew's out.'

The hatch slid back and they moved out onto the jump shelf. The crew were already beginning to leap.

'Too bad to waste a ship,' Young said.

'Can't be helped.' Van Ecker clamped his helmet on and jumped. His brake-units sent him spinning upward, rising like a balloon into the blackness above them. Young and Halloway followed. Below them the ship plunged on, downward toward the surface of Mars. In the sky tiny luminous dots drifted – the crew members.

'I've been thinking,' Halloway said into his helmet speaker.

'What about?' Young's voice came in his earphones.

'Davidson was talking about overlooking some vital factor. There is one we haven't considered.'

'What's that?'

'The Martians.'

'Good God!' van Ecker chimed in. Halloway could see him drifting off to his right, settling slowly toward the planet below. 'You think there *are* Martians?'

'It's possible. Mars will sustain life. If we can live there other complex forms could exist, too.'

'We'll know soon enough,' Young said.

Van Ecker laughed. 'Maybe they trapped one of our robot rockets. Maybe they're expecting us.'

Halloway was silent. It was too close to be funny. The red planet was growing rapidly. He could see white spots at the poles. A few hazy blue-green ribbons that had once been called *canals*. Was there a civilization down there, an organized culture waiting for them, as they drifted slowly down? He groped at his pack until his fingers closed over the butt of his pistol.

'Better get your guns out,' he said.

'If there's a Martian defense system waiting for us we won't have a chance,' Young said. 'Mars cooled millions of years ahead of Earth. It's a cinch they'll be so advanced we won't even be – '

'Too late now,' Mason's voice came faintly. 'You experts should have thought of that before.'

'Where are you?' Halloway demanded.

'Drifting below you. The ship is empty. Should strike any moment. I got all the equipment out, attached it to automatic jump units.'

A faint flash of light exploded briefly below, winked out. The ship, striking the surface . . .

'I'm almost down,' Mason said nervously. 'I'll be the first . . .'

Mars had ceased to be a globe. Now it was a great red dish, a vast plain of dull rust spread out beneath them. They fell slowly, silently, toward it. Mountains became visible. Narrow trickles of water that were rivers. A vague checker-board pattern that might have been fields and pastures . . .

Halloway gripped his pistol tightly. His brake-units shrieked as the air thickened. He was almost down. A muffled *crunch* sounded abruptly in his earphones.

'Mason!' Young shouted.

'I'm down,' Mason's voice came faintly.

'You all right?'

'Knocked the wind out of me. But I'm all right.'

'How does it look?' Halloway demanded.

For a moment there was silence. Then: 'Good God!' Mason gasped. 'A *city*!'

'A city?' Young yelled. 'What kind? What's it like?'

'Can you see them?' van Ecker shouted. 'What are they like? Are there a lot of them?'

They could hear Mason breathing. His breath rasped hoarsely in their phones. 'No,' he gasped at last. 'No sign of life. No activity. The city is – it looks deserted.'

'*Deserted?*'

'Ruins. Nothing but ruins. Miles of wrecked columns and walls and rusting scaffolding.'

'Thank God,' Young breathed. 'They must have died out. We're safe. They must have evolved and finished their cycle a long time ago.'

'Did they leave us anything?' Fear clutched at Halloway. 'Is there anything left for *us*?' He clawed wildly at his brake-units, struggling frantically to hurry his descent. 'Is it all gone?'

'You think they used up everything?' Young said. 'You think they exhausted all the – '

'I can't tell.' Mason's weak voice came, tinged with uneasiness. 'It looks bad. Big pits. Mining pits. I can't tell, but it looks bad . . .'

Halloway struggled desperately with his brake-units.

The planet was a shambles.

'Good God,' Young mumbled. He sat down on a broken column and wiped his face. 'Not a damn thing left. Nothing.'

Around them the crew were setting up emergency defense units. The communications team was assembling a battery-driven transmitter. A bore team was drilling for water. Other teams were scouting around, looking for food.

'There won't be any signs of life,' Halloway said. He waved at the endless expanse of debris and rust. 'They're gone, finished a long time ago.'

'I don't understand,' Mason muttered. 'How could they wreck a whole planet?'

'We wrecked Earth in thirty years.'

'Not this way. They've *used* Mars up. Used up everything. Nothing left. Nothing at all. It's one vast scrap-heap.'

Shakily Halloway tried to light a cigarette. The match burned feebly, then sputtered out. He felt light and dopey. His heart throbbed heavily. The distant sun beat down, pale and small. Mars was a cold, lonely dead world.

Halloway said, 'They must have had a hell of a time, watching their cities rot away. No water or minerals, finally no soil.' He picked up a handful of dry sand, let it trickle through his fingers.

'Transmitter working,' a crew member said.

Mason got to his feet and lumbered awkwardly over to the transmitter. 'I'll tell Davidson what we've found.' He bent over the microphone.

Young looked across at Halloway. 'Well, I guess we're stuck. How long will our supplies carry us?'

'Couple of months.'

'And then – ' Young snapped his fingers. 'Like the Martians.' He squinted at the long corroded wall of a ruined house. 'I wonder what they were like.'

'A semantics team is probing the ruins. Maybe they'll turn up something.'

Beyond the ruined city stretched out what had once been an industrial area. Fields of twisted installations, towers and pipes and machinery. Sand-covered and partly rusted. The surface of the land was pocked with great gaping sores. Yawning pits where scoops had once dredged. Entrances of underground mines. Mars was honeycombed. Termite-ridden. A whole race had burrowed and dug in trying to stay alive. The Martians had sucked Mars dry, then fled it.

'A graveyard,' Young said. 'Well, they got what they deserved.'

'You blame them? What should they have done? Perished a few thousand years sooner and left their planet in better shape?'

'They could have left us *something*,' Young said stubbornly. 'Maybe we can dig up their bones and boil them. I'd like to get my hands on one of them long enough to – '

A pair of crewmen came hurrying across the sand. 'Look at these!' They carried armloads of metal tubes, glittering cylinders heaped up in piles. 'Look what we found buried!'

Halloway roused himself. 'What is it?'

'Records. Written documents. Get these to the semantics team!' Carmichael spilled his armload at Halloway's feet. 'And this isn't all. We found something else – installations.'

'Installations? What kind?'

'Rocket launchers. Old towers, rusty as hell. There are fields of them on the other side of the town.' Carmichael wiped perspiration from his red face. 'They didn't die, Halloway. They took off. They used up this place, then left.'

Doctor Judde and Young pored over the gleaming tubes. 'It's coming,' Judde murmured, absorbed in the shifting pattern undulating across the scanner.

'Can you make anything out?' Halloway asked tensely.

'They left, all right. Took off. The whole lot of them.'

Young turned to Halloway. 'What do you think of that? So they didn't die out.'

'Can't you tell where they went?'

Judde shook his head. 'Some planet their scout ships located. Ideal climate and temperature.' He pushed the scanner aside. 'In their last period the whole Martian civilization was oriented around this escape planet. Big project, moving a society lock, stock and barrel. It took them three or four hundred years to get everything of value off Mars and on its way to the other planet.'

'How did the operation come out?'

'Not so good. The planet was beautiful. But they had to adapt. Apparently they didn't anticipate all the problems arising from colonization on a strange planet.' Judde indicated a cylinder. 'The colonies deteriorated rapidly. Couldn't keep the traditions and techniques going. The society broke apart. Then came war, barbarism.'

'Then their migration was a failure.' Halloway pondered. 'Maybe it can't be done. Maybe it's impossible.'

'Not a failure,' Judde corrected. 'They lived, at least. This place was no good any more. Better to live as savages on a strange world than stay here and die. So they say, on these cylinders.'

'Come along,' Young said to Halloway. The two men stepped outside the semantics hut. It was night. The sky was littered with glowing stars. The two moons had risen. They glimmered coldly, two dead eyes in the chilly sky.

'This place won't do,' Young stated. 'We can't migrate here. That's settled.'

Halloway eyed him. 'What's on your mind?'

'This was the last of the nine planets. We tested every one of them.' Young's face was alive with emotion. 'None of them will support life. All of them are lethal or useless, like this rubbish heap. The whole damn solar system is out.'

'So?'

'We'll have to leave the solar system.'

'And go where? *How?*'

Young pointed toward the Martian ruins, to the city and the rusted, bent rows of towers. 'Where *they* went. They found a place to go. An untouched world outside the solar system. And they developed some kind of outer-space drive to get them there.'

'You mean – '

'Follow them. This solar system is dead. But outside, some-place in some other system, they found an escape world. And they were able to get there.'

'We'd have to fight with them if we land on their planet. They won't want to share it.'

Young spat angrily on the sand. 'Their colonies deteriorated. Remember? Broke down into barbarism. We can handle them. We've got everything in the way of war weapons – weapons that can wipe a planet clean.'

'We don't want to do that.'

'What *do* we want to do? Tell Davidson we're stuck on Terra? Let the human race turn into underground moles? Blind crawling things . . .'

'If we follow the Martians we'll be competing for their world. They found it; the damn thing belongs to them, not us. And maybe we can't work out their drive. Maybe the schematics are lost.'

Judde emerged from the semantics hut. 'I've some more information. The whole story is here. Details on the escape planet. Fauna and flora. Studies of its gravity, air density, mineral possessions, soil layer, climate, temperature – everything.'

'How about their drive?'

'Breakdown on that, too. Everything.' Judde was shaking with excitement. 'I have an idea. Let's get the designs team on these drive schematics and see if they can duplicate it. If they can, we could follow the Martians. We could sort of *share* their planet with them.'

'See?' Young said to Halloway. 'Davidson will say the same thing. It's obvious.'

Halloway turned and walked off.

'What's wrong with him?' Judde asked.

'Nothing. He'll get over it.' Young scratched out a quick message on a piece of paper. 'Have this transmitted to David-son back on Terra.'

Judde peered at the message. He whistled. 'You're telling him about the Martian migration. And about the escape planet?'

'We want to get started. It'll take a long time to get things under way.'

'Will Halloway come around?'

'He'll come around,' Young said. 'Don't worry about him.'

Halloway gazed up at the towers. The leaning, sagging towers from which the Martian transports had been launched thousands of years before.

Nothing stirred. No sign of life. The whole dried-up planet was dead.

Halloway wandered among the towers. The beam from his helmet cut a white path in front of him. Ruins, heaps of rusting metal. Bales of wire and building material. Parts of uncompleted equipment. Half-buried construction sections sticking up from the sand.

He came to a raised platform and mounted the ladder cautiously. He found himself in an observation mount, surrounded by the remains of dials and meters. A telescopic sight stuck up, rusted in place, frozen tight.

'Hey,' a voice came from below. 'Who's up there?'

'Halloway.'

'God, you scared me.' Carmichael slid his blast rifle away and climbed the ladder. 'What are you doing?'

'Looking around.'

Carmichael appeared beside him, puffing and red-faced. 'Interesting, these towers. This was an automatic sighting station. Fixed the take-off for supply transports. The population was already gone.' Carmichael slapped at the ruined control board. 'These supply ships continued to take off, loaded by machines and dispatched by machines, after all the Martians were gone.'

'Lucky for them they had a place to go.'

'Sure was. The minerals team says there's not a damn thing left here. Nothing but dead sand and rock and debris. Even the water's no good. They took everything of value.'

'Judde says their escape world is pretty nice.'

'Virgin.' Carmichael smacked his fat lips. 'Never touched. Trees and meadows and blue oceans. He showed me a scanner translation of a cylinder.'

'Too bad we don't have a place like that to go. A virgin world for ourselves.'

Carmichael was bent over the telescope. 'This here sighted for them. When the escape planet swam into view a relay delivered a trigger charge to the control tower. The tower launched the ships. When the ships were gone a new flock came up into position.' Carmichael began to polish the encrusted lenses of the telescope, wiping the accumulated rust and debris away. 'Maybe we'll see their planet.'

In the ancient lenses a vague luminous globe was swimming. Halloway could make it out, obscured by the filth of centuries, hidden behind a curtain of metallic particles and dirt.

Carmichael was down on his hands and knees, working with the focus mechanism. 'See anything?' he demanded.

Halloway nodded. 'Yeah.'

Carmichael pushed him away. 'Let me look.' He squinted into the lens. 'Aw, for God's sake!'

'What's wrong? Can't you see it?'

'I see it,' Carmichael said, getting down on his hands and knees again. 'The thing must have slipped. Or the time shift is too great. But this is supposed to adjust automatically. Of course, the gear box has been frozen for – '

'What's wrong?' Halloway demanded.

'That's Earth. Don't you recognize it?'

'Earth!'

Carmichael sneered with disgust. 'This fool thing must be busted. I wanted to get a look at their dream planet. That's just old Terra, where we came from. All my work trying to fix this wreck up, and what do we see?'

'*Earth!*' Halloway murmured. He had just finished telling Young about the telescope.

'I can't believe it,' Young said. 'But the description fitted Earth thousands of years ago . . .

'How long ago did they take off?' Halloway asked.

'About six hundred thousand years ago,' Judde said.

'And their colonies descended into barbarism on the new planet.'

The four men were silent. They looked at each other, tight-lipped.

'We've destroyed two worlds,' Halloway said at last. 'Not one. Mars first. We finished up here, then we moved to Terra. And we destroyed Terra as systematically as we did Mars.'

'A closed circle,' Mason said. 'We're back where we started. Back to reap the crop our ancestors sowed. They left Mars this way. Useless. And now we're back here poking around the ruins like ghouls.'

'Shut up,' Young snapped. He paced angrily back and forth. 'I can't believe it.'

'We're Martians. Descendants of the original stock that left here. We're back from the colonies. Back home.' Mason's voice rose hysterically. 'We're home again, where we belong!'

Judde pushed aside the scanner and got to his feet. 'No doubt about it. I checked their analysis with our own archeological records. It fits. Their escape world was Terra, six hundred thousand years ago.'

'What'll we tell Davidson?' Mason demanded. He giggled wildly. 'We've found a perfect place. A word untouched by human hands. Still in the original cellophane wrapper.'

Halloway moved to the door of the hut, stood gazing silently out. Judde joined him. 'This is catastrophic. We're really stuck. What the hell are you looking at?'

Above them, the cold sky glittered. In the bleak light the barren plains of Mars stretched out, mile after mile of empty, wasted ruin.

'At that,' Halloway said. 'You know what it reminds me of?'

'A picnic site.'

'Broken bottles and tin cans and wadded up plates. After the picnickers have left. Only, the picnickers are back. They're back – and they have to live in the mess they made.'

'What'll we tell Davidson?' Mason demanded.

'I've already called him,' Young said wearily. 'I told him there was a planet, out of the solar system. Someplace we could go. The Martians had a drive.'

'A drive.' Judde pondered. 'Those towers.' His lips twisted. 'Maybe they did have an outer space drive. Maybe it's worth going on with the translation.'

They looked at each other.

'Tell Davidson we're going on,' Halloway ordered. 'We'll keep on until we find it. We're not staying on this God-forsaken junkyard.' His gray eyes glowed. 'We'll find it, yet. A virgin world. A world that's unspoiled.'

'*Unspoiled,*' Young echoed. 'Nobody there ahead of us.'

'We'll be the first,' Judde muttered avidly.

'It's wrong!' Mason shouted. 'Two are enough! Let's not destroy a third world!'

Nobody listened to him. Judde and Young and Halloway gazed up, faces eager, hands clenching and unclenching. As if they were already there. As if they were already holding onto the new world, clutching it with all their strength. Tearing it apart, atom by atom. . .

Prominent Author

'My husband,' said Mary Ellis, 'although he is a very prompt man, and hasn't been late to work in twenty-five years, is actually still some place around the house.' She sipped at her faintly scented hormone and carbohydrate drink. 'As a matter of fact, he won't be leaving for another ten minutes.'

'Incredible,' said Dorothy Lawrence, who had finished *her* drink, and now basked in the dermalmist spray that descended over her virtually unclad body from an automatic jet above the couch. 'What they won't think of next!'

Mrs Ellis beamed proudly, as if she personally were an employee of Terran Development. 'Yes, it is incredible. According to somebody down at the office, the whole history of civilization can be explained in terms of transportation techniques. Of course, I don't know anything about history. That's for Government research people. But from what this man told Henry – '

'Where's my briefcase?' came a fussy voice from the bedroom. 'Good Lord, Mary. I know I left it on the clothes-cleaner last night.'

'You left it upstairs,' Mary replied, raising her voice slightly. 'Look in the closet.'

'Why would it be in the closet?' Sounds of angry stirring around. 'You'd think a man's own briefcase would be safe.' Henry Ellis stuck his head into the living-room briefly. 'I found it. Hello, Mrs Lawrence.'

'Good morning,' Dorothy Lawrence replied. 'Mary was explaining that you're still here.'

'Yes, I'm still here.' Ellis straightened his tie, as the mirror revolved slowly around him. 'Anything you want me to pick up downtown, honey?'

'No,' Mary replied. 'Nothing I can think of. I'll vid you at the office if I remember something.'

'Is it true,' Mrs Lawrence asked, 'that *as soon as you step into it* you're all the way downtown?'

'Well, almost all the way.'

'A hundred and sixty miles! It's beyond belief. Why, it takes my husband two and a half hours to get his monojet through the commercial lanes and down at the parking lot then walk all the way up to his office.'

'I know,' Ellis muttered, grabbing his hat and coat. 'Used to take me about that long. But no more.' He kissed his wife good-bye. 'So long. See you tonight. Nice to have seen you again, Mrs Lawrence.'

'Can I – watch?' Mrs Lawrence asked hopefully.

'Watch? Of course, of course.' Ellis hurried through the house, out the back door and down the steps into the yard. 'Come along!' he shouted impatiently. 'I don't want to be late. It's nine-fifty-nine and I have to be at my desk by ten.'

Mrs Lawrence hurried eagerly after Ellis. In the backyard stood a big circular hoop that gleamed brightly in the mid-morning sun. Ellis turned some controls at the base. The hoop changed color, from silver to a shimmering red.

'Here I go!' Ellis shouted. He stepped briskly into the hoop. The hoop fluttered about him. There was a faint *pop*. The glow died.

'Good Heavens!' Mrs Lawrence gasped. 'He's gone!'

'He's in downtown N'York,' Mary Ellis corrected.

'I wish *my* husband had a Jiffi-scuttler. When they show up on the market commercially maybe I can afford to get him one.'

'Oh, they're very handy,' Mary Ellis agreed. 'He's probably saying hello to the boys right this minute.'

Henry Ellis was in a sort of tunnel. All round him a gray, formless tube stretched out in both directions, a sort of hazy sewer-pipe.

Framed in the opening behind him, he could see the faint outline of his own house. His back porch and yard, Mary standing on the steps in her red bra and slacks. Mrs Lawrence beside her in green-checkered shorts. The cedar tree and rows of petunias. A hill. The neat little houses of Cedar Groves, Pennsylvania. And in front of him –

New York City. A wavering glimpse of the busy street-corner in front of his office. The great building itself, a section of concrete and glass and steel. People moving. Skyscrapers. Monojets landing in swarms. Aerial signs. Endless white-collar workers hurrying everywhere, rushing to their offices.

Ellis moved leisurely toward the New York end. He had taken the Jiffi-scuttler often enough to know just exactly how many steps it was. Five steps. Five steps along the wavery gray tunnel and he had gone a hundred and sixty miles. He halted, glancing back. So far he had gone three steps. Ninety-six miles. More than half way.

The fourth dimension was a wonderful thing.

Ellis lit his pipe, leaning his briefcase against his trouser-leg and groping in his coat pocket for his tobacco. He still had thirty seconds to get to work. Plenty of time. The pipe-lighter flared and he sucked in expertly. He snapped the lighter shut and restored it to his pocket.

A wonderful thing, all right. The Jiffi-scuttler had already revolutionized society. It was now possible to go anywhere in the word *instantly*, with no time lapse. And without wading through endless lanes of other monojets, also going places. The transportation problem had been a major headache since the middle of the twentieth century. Every year more families moved from the cities out into the country, adding numbers to the already swollen swarms that choked the roads and jetlanes.

But it was all solved now. An *infinite* number of Jiffi-scuttlers could be set up; there was no interference between them. The Jiffi-scuttler bridged distances non-spacially, through another dimension of some kind (they hadn't explained that part too clearly to him). For a flat thousand credits any Terran family could have Jiffi-scuttler hoops set up, one in the back yard – the other in Berlin, or Bermuda, or San Francisco, or Port Said. Anywhere in the world. Of course, there was one drawback. The hoop had to be anchored in one specific spot. You picked your destination and that was that.

But for an office worker, it was perfect. Step in one end, step out the other. Five steps – a hundred and sixty miles. A hundred and sixty miles that had been a two-hour nightmare of grinding gears and sudden jolts, monojets cutting in and out, speeders, reckless flyers, alert cops waiting to pounce, ulcers and bad tempers. It was all over now. All over for him, at least, as an employee of Terran Development, the manufacturer of the Jiffi-scuttler. And soon for everybody, when they were commercially on the market.

Ellis sighed. Time for work. He could see Ed Hall racing up the steps of the TD building two at a time. Tony Franklin hurrying after him. Time to get moving. He bent down and reached for his briefcase –

It was then he saw them.

The wavery gray haze was thin there. A sort of thin spot where the shimmer wasn't so strong. Just a bit beyond his foot and past the corner of his briefcase.

Beyond the thin spot were three tiny figures. Just beyond the gray waver. Incredibly small men, no larger than insects. Watching him with incredulous astonishment.

Ellis gazed down intently, his briefcase forgotten. The three tiny men were equally dumbfounded. None of them stirred, the three tiny figures, rigid with awe. Henry Ellis bent over, his mouth open, eyes wide.

A fourth little figure joined the others. They all stood rooted to the spot, eyes bulging. They had on some kind of robes. Brown robes and sandals. Strange, unTerran costumes. Everything about them was unTerran. Their size, their oddly colored dark faces, their clothing – and their voices.

Suddenly the tiny figures were shouting shrilly at each other, squeaking a strange gibberish. They had broken out of their freeze and now ran about in queer, frantic circles. They raced with incredible speed, scampering like ants on a hot griddle. They raced jerkily, their arms and legs pumping wildly. And all the time they squeaked in their shrill high-pitched voices.

Ellis found his briefcase. He picked it up slowly. The figures watched in mixed wonder and terror as the huge bag rose, only a short distance from them. An idea drifted through Ellis's brain. Good Lord – could they come into the Jiffi-scuttler, through the gray haze?

But he had no time to find out. He was already late as it was. He pulled away and hurried towards the New York end of the tunnel. A second later he stepped out in the blinding sunlight, abruptly finding himself on the busy street-corner in front of his office.

'Hey, there, Hank!' Donald Potter shouted, as he raced through the doors into the TD building. 'Get with it!'

'Sure, sure.' Ellis followed after him automatically. Behind the entrance to the Jiffi-scuttler was a vague circle above the pavement, like the ghost of a soap-bubble.

He hurried up the steps and inside the offices of Terran Development, his mind already on the hard day ahead.

As they were locking up the office and getting ready to go home, Ellis stopped coordinator Patrick Miller in his office. 'Say, Mr Miller. You're also in charge of the research end, aren't you?'

'Yeah. So?'

'Let me ask you something. Just where does the Jiffi-scuttler go? It must go somewhere.'

'It goes out of this continuum completely.' Miller was impatient to get home. 'Into another dimension.'

'I know that. But – *where*?'

Miller unfolded his breast-pocket handkerchief rapidly and spread it out on his desk. 'Maybe I can explain it to you this way. Suppose you're a two dimensional creature and this handkerchief represents your –'

'I've seen that a million times,' Ellis said, disappointed. 'That's merely an analogy, and I'm not interested in an analogy. I want a factual answer. Where does my Jiffi-scuttler go, between here and Cedar Groves?'

Miller laughed. 'What the hell do you care?'

Ellis became abruptly guarded. He shrugged indifferently. 'Just curious. It certainly must go *some place*.'

Miller put his hand on Ellis's shoulder in a friendly big-brother fashion. 'Henry, old man, you just leave that up to us. Okay? We're the designers, you're the consumer. Your job is to use the 'scuttler, try it out for us, report any defects or failure so when we put it on the market next year we'll be sure there's nothing wrong with it.'

'As a matter of fact – ' Ellis began.

'What is it?'

Ellis clamped his sentence off. 'Nothing.' He picked up his briefcase. 'Nothing at all. I'll see you tomorrow. Thanks, Mr Miller. Goodnight.'

He hurried downstairs and out of the TD building. The faint outline of his Jiffi-scuttler was visible in the fading late-afternoon sunlight. The sky was already full of monojets taking off. Weary workers beginning their long trip back to their homes in the country. The endless commute. Ellis made his way to the hoop and stepped into it. Abruptly the bright sunlight dimmed and faded.

Again he was in the wavery gray tunnel. At the far end flashed a circle of green and white. Rolling green hills and his own house. His backyard. The cedar tree and flower beds. The town of Cedar Groves.

Two steps down the tunnel. Ellis halted, bending over. He studied the floor of the tunnel intently. He studied the misty gray wall, where it rose and flickered – and the thin place. The place he had noticed.

They were still there. *Still?* It was a different bunch. This time ten or eleven of them. Men and women and children. Standing together, gazing up at him with awe and wonder. No more than a half-inch high, each. Tiny distorted figures, shifting and changing shape oddly. Altering colors and hues.

Ellis hurried on. The tiny figures watched him go. A brief glimpse of their microscopic astonishment – and then he was stepping out into his backyard.

He clicked off the Jiffi-scuttler and mounted the back steps. He entered his house, deep in thought.

'Hi,' Mary cried, from the kitchen. She rustled towards him in her hip-length mesh shirt, her arms out. 'How was work today?'

'Fine.'

'Is anything wrong? You look – strange.'

'No. No, nothing's wrong.' Ellis kissed his wife absently on the forehead. 'What's for dinner?'

'Something choice. Siriusian mole steak. One of your favorites. Is that all right?'

'Sure.' Ellis tossed his hat and coat down on the chair. The chair folded them up and put them away. His thoughtful, preoccupied look still remained. 'Fine, honey.'

'Are you *sure* there's nothing wrong? You didn't get into another argument with Pete Taylor, did you?'

'No. Of course not.' Ellis shook his head in annoyance. 'Everything's all right, honey. Stop needling me.'

'Well, I *hope* so,' Mary said, with a sigh.

The next morning they were waiting for him.

He saw them the first step into the Jiffi-scuttler. A small group waiting within the wavering gray, like bugs caught in a block of jello. They moved jerkily, rapidly, arms and legs pumping in a blur of motion. Trying to attract his attention. Piping wildly in their pathetically faint voices.

Ellis stopped and squatted down. They were putting something through the wall of the tunnel, through the thin place in the gray. It was small, so incredibly small he could scarcely see it. A square of white at the end of a microscopic pole. They were watching him eagerly, faces alive with fear and hope. Desperate, pleading hope.

Ellis took the tiny square. It came loose like some fragile rose petal from its stalk. Clumsily, he let it drop and had to hunt all round for it. The little figures watched in an agony of dismay as his huge hands moved blindly around the floor of the tunnel. At last he found it and gingerly lifted it up.

It was too small to make out. *Writing?* Some tiny lines – but he couldn't read them. Much too small to read. He got out his wallet and carefully placed the square between the two cards. He restored his wallet to his pocket.

'I'll look at it later,' he said.

His voice boomed and echoed up and down the tunnel. At the sound the tiny creatures scattered. They all fled, shrieking in their shrill, piping voices, away from the gray shimmer, into the dimness beyond. In a flash they were gone. Like startled mice. He was alone.

Ellis knelt down and put his eye against the gray shimmer,

where it was thin. Where they had stood waiting. He could see something dim and distorted, lost in a vague haze. A landscape of some sort. Indistinct. Hard to make out.

Hills. Trees and crops. But so tiny. And dim . . .

He glanced at his watch. God, it was ten! Hastily he scrambled to his feet and hurried out of the tunnel, on to the blazing New York pavement.

Late. He raced up the stairs of the Terran Development building and down the long corridor to his office.

At lunchtime he stopped in at the Research Labs. 'Hey,' he called, as Jim Andrews brushed past, loaded down with reports and equipment. 'Got a second?'

'What do you want, Henry?'

'I'd like to borrow something. A magnifying glass.' He considered. 'Maybe a photon-microscope would be better. One- or two-hundred power.'

'Kids' stuff.' Jim found him a small microscope. 'Slides?'

'Yeah, a couple of blank slides.'

He carried the microscope back to his office. He set it up on his desk, clearing away his paper. As a precaution he sent Miss Nelson, his secretary, out of the room and off to lunch. Then carefully, cautiously, he got the tiny wisp from his wallet and slipped it between two slides.

It was writing, all right. But nothing he could read. Utterly unfamiliar. Complex, interlaced little characters.

For a time he sat thinking. Then he dialed his inter-department vidphone. 'Give me the Linguistics Department.'

After a moment Earl Peterson's good-natured face appeared. 'Hi, there, Ellis. What can I do for you?'

Ellis hesitated. He had to do this right. 'Say, Earl, old man. Got a little favor to ask you.'

'Like what? Anything to oblige an old pal.'

'You, uh – you have that Machine down there, don't you? That translating business you use for working over documents from non-Terran cultures?'

'Sure. So?'

'Think I could use it?' He talked fast. 'It's a screwy sort of a deal, Earl. I got this pal living on – uh – Centaurus VI, and he writes me in – uh – you know the Centauran native semantic system, and I – '

'You want the Machine to translate a letter? Sure, I think we could manage it. This once, at least. Bring it down.'

He brought it down. He got Earl to show him how the intake feed worked, and as soon as Earl had turned his back he fed in the tiny square of material. The Linguistics Machine clicked and whirred. Ellis prayed silently that the paper wasn't too small. Wouldn't fall out between the relay-probes of the Machine.

But sure enough, after a couple of seconds, a tape unreeled from the output slot. The tape cut itself off and dropped into a basket. The Linguistics Machine turned promptly to other stuff, more vital material from TD's various export branches.

With trembling fingers Ellis spread out the tape. The words danced before his eyes.

Questions. They were asking him questions. God, it was getting complicated. He read the questions intently, his lips moving. What was he getting himself into? They were expecting answers. He had taken their paper, gone off with it. Probably they would be waiting for him, on his way home.

He returned to his office and dialed his vidphone. 'Give me outside,' he ordered.

The regular vid monitor appeared. 'Yes, sir?'

'I want the Federal Library of Information,' Ellis said. 'Cultural Research Division.'

That night they were waiting, all right. But not the same ones. It was odd – each time a different group. Their clothing was slightly different, too. A new hue. And in the background the landscape had also altered slightly. The trees he had seen were gone. The hills were still there, but a different shade. A hazy gray-white. Snow?

He squatted down. He had worked it out with care. The answers from the Federal Library of Information had gone back to the Linguistics Machine for re-translation. The answers were now in the original tongue of the questions – but on a trifle larger piece of paper.

Ellis made like a marble game and flicked the wad of paper through the gray shimmer. It bowled over six or seven of the watching figures and rolled down the side of the hill on which they were standing. After a moment of terrified immobility the figures scampered frantically after it. They disappeared into the vague and invisible depths of their world and Ellis got stiffly to his feet again.

'Well,' he muttered to himself, 'that's that.'

But it wasn't. The next morning there was a new group – and a new list of questions. The tiny figures pushed their microscopic square of paper through the thin spot in the wall of the tunnel and stood waiting and trembling as Ellis bent over and felt around for it.

He found it – finally. He put it in his wallet and continued on his way, stepping out at New York, frowning. This was getting serious. Was this going to be a full-time job?

But then he grinned. It was the damn oddest thing he had ever heard of. The little rascals were cute, in their own way. Tiny intent faces, screwed up with serious concern. And terror. They were scared of him, really scared. And why not? Compared to them he was a giant.

He conjectured about their world. What kind of planet was theirs? Odd to be so small. But size was a relative matter. Small, though, compared to him. Small and reverent. He could read fear and yearning, gnawing hope, as they pushed up their papers. They were depending on him. Praying he'd give them answers.

Ellis grinned. 'Damn unusual job,' he said to himself.

'What's this?' Peterson said, when he showed up in the Linguistics Lab at noontime.

'Well, you see, I got another letter from my friend on Centaurus VI.'

'Yeah?' A certain suspicion flickered across Peterson's face. 'You're not ribbing me, are you, Henry? This Machine has a lot to do, you know. Stuff's coming in all the time. We can't afford to waste any time with – '

'This is really serious stuff, Earl.' Ellis patted his wallet. 'Very important business. Not just gossip.'

'Okay. If you say so.' Peterson gave the nod to the team operating the Machine. 'Let this guy use the Translator, Tommie.'

'Thanks,' Ellis murmured.

He went through the routine, getting a translation and then carrying the questions up to his vidphone and passing them over to the Library research staff. By nightfall the answers were back in the original tongue and with them carefully in his wallet, Ellis headed out of the Terran Development building and into his Jiffi-scuttler.

As usual, a new group was waiting.

'Here you go, boys,' Ellis boomed, flicking the wad through the thin place in the shimmer. The wad rolled down the microscopic countryside, bouncing from hill to hill, the little people tumbling jerkily after it in their funny stiff-legged fashion. Ellis watched them go, grinning with interest – and pride.

They really hurried; no doubt about that. He could make them out only vaguely, now. They had raced wildly off away from the shimmer. Only a small portion of their world was tangent to the Jiffi-scuttler, apparently. Only the one spot, where the shimmer was thin. He peered intently through.

They were getting the wad open, now. Three or four of them, unprying the paper and examining the answers.

Ellis swelled with pride as he continued along the tunnel and out into his own backyard. He couldn't read their questions – and when translated, he couldn't answer them. The Linguistics Department did the first part, the Library research staff the rest. Nevertheless, Ellis felt pride. A deep, glowing spot of warmth far down inside him. The expression on their faces. The look they gave him when they saw the answer-wad in his hand. When they realized he was going to answer their questions. And the way they scampered after it. It was sort of – satisfying. It made him feel damn good.

'Not bad,' he murmured, opening the back door and entering the house. 'Not bad at all.'

'What's not bad, dear?' Mary asked, looking quickly up from the table. She laid down her magazine and got to her feet. 'Why, you look so *happy*! What is it?'

'Nothing. Nothing at all!' He kissed her warmly on the mouth. 'You're looking pretty good tonight yourself, kid.'

'Oh, Henry!' Much of Mary blushed prettily. 'How sweet.'

He surveyed his wife in her two-piece wraparound of clear plastic with appreciation. 'Nice looking fragments you have on.'

'Why, Henry! What's come over you? You seem so – so *spirited*!'

Ellis grinned. 'Oh, I guess I enjoy my job. You know, there's nothing like taking pride in your work. A job well done, as they say. Work you can be proud of.'

'I thought you always said you were nothing but a cog in a great impersonal machine. Just a sort of cipher.'

'Things are different,' Ellis said firmly. 'I'm doing a – uh – a new project. A new assignment.'

'A new assignment?'

'Gathering information. A sort of – creative business. So to speak.'

By the end of the week he had turned over quite a body of information to them.

He began starting for work about nine-thirty. That gave him a whole thirty minutes to spend squatting down on his hands and knees, peering through the thin place in the shimmer. He got so he was pretty good at seeing them and what they were doing in their microscopic world.

Their civilization was somewhat primitive. No doubt of that. By Terran standards it was scarcely a civilization at all. As near as he could tell, they were virtually without scientific techniques; a kind of agrarian culture, rural communism, a monolithic tribal-based organization apparently without too many members.

At least, not at one time. That was the part he didn't understand. Every time he came past there was a different group of them. No familiar faces. And their world changed, too. The trees, the crops, fauna. The weather, apparently.

Was their time rate different? They moved rapidly, jerkily. Like a vidtape speeded up. And their shrill voices. Maybe that was it. A totally different universe in which the whole time structure was radically different.

As to their attitude towards him, there was no mistaking it. After the first couple of times they began assembling offerings, unbelievably small bits of smoking food, prepared in ovens and on open brick hearths. If he got down with his nose against the gray shimmer he could get a faint whiff of the food. It smelled good. Strong and pungent. Highly spiced. Meat, probably.

On Friday be brought a magnifying glass along and watched them through it. It was meat, all right. They were bringing ant-sized animals to be killed and cooked, leading them up to the ovens. With the magnifying glass he could see more of their faces. They had strange faces. Strong and dark, with a peculiar firm look.

Of course, there was only one look *he* got from them. A combination of fear, reverence, and hope. The look made him feel good. It was a look for him, only. Between themselves they shouted and argued – and sometimes stabbed and fought each other furiously, rolling in their brown robes in a wild tangle. They were a passionate and strong species. He got so he admired them.

Which was good – because it made him feel better. To have the reverent awe of such a proud, sturdy face was really something. There was nothing craven about them.

About the fifth time he came there was a rather attractive structure built. Some kind of temple. A place of religious worship.

To him! They were developing a real religion about him. No doubt of it. He began going to work at nine o'clock, to give himself a full hour with them. They had, by the middle of the second week, a full-sized ritual evolved. Processions, lighted tapers, what seemed to be songs or chants. Priests in long robes. And the spiced offerings.

No idols, though. Apparently he was so big they couldn't make out his appearance. He tried to imagine what it looked like to be on their side of the shimmer. An immense shape looming up above them, beyond a wall of gray haze. An indistinct being, something like themselves, yet not like them at all. A different kind of being, obviously. Larger – but different in other ways. And when he spoke – booming echoes up and down the Jiffi-scuttler. Which still sent them fleeing in panic.

An evolving religion. He was changing them. Through his actual presence and through his answers, the precise, correct responses he obtained from the Federal Library of Information and had the Linguistics Machine translate into their language. Of course, by *their* time-rate they had to wait generations for the answers. But they had become accustomed to it, by now. They waited. They expected. They passed up questions and after a couple of centuries he passed down answers, answers which they no doubt put to good use.

'What in the world?' Mary demanded, as he got home from work an hour late one night. 'Where have you been?'

'Working,' Ellis said carelessly, removing his hat and coat. He threw himself on the couch. 'I'm tired. Really tired.' He sighed with relief and motioned for the couch-arm to bring him a whiskey sour.

Mary came over by the couch. 'Henry, I'm a little worried.'

'Worried?'

'You shouldn't work so hard. You ought to take it easy, more. How long since you've had a real vacation? A trip off Terra. Out of the System. You know, I'd just like to call that fellow Miller and ask him why it's necessary for a man your age to put in so much – '

'A man my age!' Ellis bristled indignantly. 'I'm not so old.'

'Of course not.' Mary sat down beside him and put her arms around him affectionately. 'But you shouldn't have to do so much. You deserve a rest. Don't you think?'

'This is different. You don't understand. This isn't the same old stuff. Reports and statistics and the damn filing. This is – '

'What is it?'

'This is *different*. I'm not a cog. This gives me something. I can't explain it to you, I guess. But it's something I have to do.'

'If you could tell me more about it – '

'I can't tell you any more about it,' Ellis said. 'But there's nothing in the world like it. I've worked twenty-five years for Terran Development. Twenty-five years at the same reports, again and again. Twenty-five years – and I never felt this way.'

'Oh, yeah?' Miller roared. 'Don't give me that! Come clean, Ellis!'

Ellis opened and closed his mouth. 'What are you talking about?' Horror rolled through him. 'What's happened?'

'Don't try to give *me* the runaround.' On the vidscreen Miller's face was purple. 'Come into my office.'

The screen went dead.

Ellis sat stunned at his desk. Gradually, he collected himself and got shakily to his feet. 'Good Lord.' Weakly, he wiped cold sweat from his forehead. All at once. Everything in ruins. He was dazed with the shock.

'Anything wrong?' Miss Nelson asked sympathetically.

'No.' Ellis moved numbly towards the door. He was shattered. What had Miller found out? Good God! Was it possible he had –

'Mr Miller looked angry.'

'Yeah.' Ellis moved blindly down the hall, his mind reeling. Miller looked angry all right. Somehow he had found out. But why was he mad? Why did he care? A cold chill settled over Ellis. It looked bad. Miller was his superior – with hiring and firing powers. Maybe he'd done something wrong. Maybe he had somehow broken a law. Committed a crime. But what?

What did Miller care about *them*? What concern was it of Terran Development?

He opened the door to Miller's office. 'Here I am, Mr Miller,' he muttered. 'What's the trouble?'

Miller glowered at him with rage. 'All this goofy stuff about your cousin on Proxima.'

'It's – uh – you mean a business friend on Centaurus VI.'

'You – you swindler!' Miller leaped up. 'And after all the Company's done for you.'

'I don't understand,' Ellis muttered. 'What have – '

'Why do you think we gave you the Jiffi-scuttler in the first place?'

'Why?'

'To *test*! To try out, you wall-eyed Venusian stink-cricket! The Company magnanimously consented to allow you to operate a Jiffi-scuttler in advance of market presentation, and what do you do? Why, you – '

Ellis started to get indignant. After all, he had been with TD twenty-five years. 'You don't have to be so offensive. I plunked down my thousand gold credits for it.'

'Well, you can just mosey down to the accountant's office

and get your money back. I've already sent out a directive for a construction team to crate up your Jiffi-scuttler and bring it back to receiving.'

Ellis was dumbfounded. 'But *why*?'

'Why indeed! Because it's defective. Because it doesn't work. That's why.' Miller's eyes blazed with technological outrage. 'The inspection crew found a leak a mile wide in it.' His lip curled. 'As if you didn't know.'

Ellis's heart sank. 'Leak?' he croaked apprehensively.

'Leak. It's a damn good thing I authorized a periodic inspection. If we depended on people like you to – '

'Are you *sure*? It seemed all right to me. That is, it got me here without any trouble,' Ellis floundered. 'Certainly no complaints from my end.'

'No. No complaints from your end. That's exactly why you're not getting another one. That's why you're taking the monojet transport back home tonight. Because you didn't report the leak! And if you ever try to put something over on this office again – '

'How do you know I was aware of the – defect?'

Miller sank down in his chair, overcome with fury. 'Because,' he said carefully, 'of your daily pilgrimage to the Linguistic Machine. With your alleged letter from your grandmother on Betelgeuse II. Which wasn't any such thing. Which was an utter fraud. Which you got through the leak in the Jiffi-scuttler!'

'How do you know?' Ellis squeaked boldly, driven to the wall. 'So maybe there was a defect. But you can't prove there's any connection between your badly constructed Jiffi-scuttler and my – '

'Your missive,' Miller stated, 'which you foisted on our Linguistics Machine, was not a non-Terran script. It was not from Centaurus VI. It was not from any non-Terran system. It was ancient Hebrew. And there's only one place you could have got it, Ellis. So don't try to kid me.'

'Hebrew!' Ellis exclaimed, startled. He turned white as a sheet. 'Good Lord. The other continuum – the fourth dimension. Time, of course.' He trembled. 'And the expanding universe. That would explain their size. And it explains why a new group, a new generation – '

488   *Philip K. Dick*

'We're taking enough of a chance as it is, with these Jiffi-scuttlers. Warping a tunnel through other space-time continua.' Miller shook his head warily. 'You meddler. You *knew* you were supposed to report any defect.'

'I don't think I did any harm, did I?' Ellis was suddenly terribly nervous. 'They seemed pleased, even grateful. Gosh, I'm sure I didn't cause any trouble.'

Miller shrieked in insane rage. For a time he danced around the room. Finally he threw something down on his desk, directly in front of Ellis. 'No trouble. No, none. Look at this. I got this from the Ancient Artifacts Archives.'

'What is it?'

'Look at it! I compared one of your question sheets to this. The same. *Exactly* the same. All your sheets, questions and answers, every one of them's in here. You multi-legged Gany-medean mange beetle!'

Ellis picked up the book and opened it. As he read the pages a strange look came slowly over his face. 'Good Heavens. So they kept a record of what I gave them. They put it all together in a book. Every word of it. And some commentaries, too. It's all here – every single word. It *did* have an effect, then. They passed it on. Wrote all of it down.'

'Go back to your office. I'm through looking at you for today. I'm through looking at you forever. Your severance check will come through regular channels.'

In a trance, his face flushed with a strange excitement, Ellis gripped the book and moved dazedly towards the door. 'Say, Mr Miller. Can I have this? Can I take it along?'

'Sure,' Miller said wearily. 'Sure, you can take it. You can read it on your way home tonight. On the public monojet transport.'

'Henry has something to show you,' Mary Ellis whispered excitedly, gripping Mrs Lawrence's arm. 'Make sure you say the right thing.'

'The right thing?' Mrs Lawrence faltered nervously, a trifle uneasy. 'What is it? Nothing alive, I hope.'

'No, no.' Mary pushed her towards the study door. 'Just

smile.' She raised her voice. 'Henry, Dorothy Lawrence is here.'

Henry Ellis appeared at the door of his study. He bowed slightly, a dignified figure in silk dressing gown, pipe in his mouth, fountain pen in one hand. 'Good evening, Dorothy,' he said in a low, well-modulated voice. 'Care to step into my study a moment?'

'Study?' Mrs Lawrence came hesitantly in. 'What do you study? I mean, Mary says you've been doing something very interesting recently, now that you're not with – I mean, now that you're home more. She didn't give me any idea what it was, though.'

Mrs Lawrence's eyes roved curiously around the study. The study was full of reference volumes, charts, a huge mahogany desk, an atlas, globe, leather chairs, an unbelievably ancient electric typewriter.

'Good Heavens!' she exclaimed. 'How odd. All these old things.'

Ellis lifted something carefully from the bookcase and held it out to her casually. 'By the way – you might glance at this.'

'What is it? A book?' Mrs Lawrence took the book and examined it eagerly. 'My goodness. Heavy, isn't it?' She read the back, her lips moving. 'What does it mean? It looks old. What strange letters! I've never seen anything like it. *Holy Bible*.' She glanced up brightly. 'What is this?'

Ellis smiled faintly. 'Well – '

A light dawned. Mrs Lawrence gasped in revelation. 'Good Heavens! You didn't *write* this, did you?'

Ellis's smile broadened into a deprecating blush. A dignified hue of modesty. 'Just a little thing I threw together,' he murmured indifferently. 'My first, as a matter of fact.' Thoughtfully, he fingered his fountain pen. 'And now, if you'll excuse me, I really should be getting back to my work . . .'

Notes

All notes in italics are by Philip K. Dick. The year when the note was written appears in parentheses following the note. Most of these notes were written as story notes for the collections THE BEST OF PHILIP K. DICK (published 1977) and THE GOLDEN MAN (published 1980). A few were written at the request of editors publishing or reprinting a PKD story in a book or magazine.

When there is a date following the name of a story, it is the date the manuscript of that story was first received by Dick's agent, per the records of the Scott Meredith Literary Agency. Absence of a date means no record is available. The name of a magazine followed by a month and year indicates the first published appearance of a story. An alternate name following a story indicates Dick's original name for the story, as shown in the agency records.

These five volumes include all of Philip K. Dick's short fiction, with the exception of short novels later published as or included in novels, childhood writings, and unpublished writings for which manuscripts have not been found. The stories are arranged as closely as possible in chronological order of composition; research for this chronology was done by Gregg Rickman and Paul Williams.

THE COOKIE LADY 8/27/52. *Fantasy Fiction*, June 1953.

BEYOND THE DOOR 8/29/52. *Fantastic Universe*, Jan 1954.

SECOND VARIETY 10/3/52. *Space Science Fiction*, May 1953.
My grand theme – who is human and who only appears (masquerades) as human? – emerges most fully. Unless we can

individually and collectively be certain of the answer to this question, we face what is, in my view, the most serious problem possible. Without answering it adequately, we cannot even be certain of our own selves. I cannot even know myself, let alone you. So I keep working on this theme; to me nothing is as important a question. And the answer comes very hard. (1976)

JON'S WORLD ('Jon') 10/21/52. *Time to Come*, edited by August Derleth, New York, 1954.

THE COSMIC POACHERS ('Burglar') 10/22/52. *Imagination*, July 1953.

PROGENY 11/3/52. *If*, Nov 1954.

SOME KINDS OF LIFE ('The Beleaguered') 11/3/52. *Fantastic Universe*, Oct-Nov 1953 [under the pseudonym Richard Phillips].

MARTIANS COME IN CLOUDS ('The Buggies') 11/5/52. *Fantastic Universe*, June-July 1954.

THE COMMUTER 11/19/52. *Amazing*, Aug-Sept 1953.

THE WORLD SHE WANTED 11/24/52. *Science Fiction Quarterly*, May 1953.

A SURFACE RAID 12/2/52. *Fantastic Universe*, July 1955.

PROJECT: EARTH ('One Who Stole') 1/6/53. *Imagination*, Dec 1953.

THE TROUBLE WITH BUBBLES ('Plaything') 1/13/53. *If*, Sept 1953.

BREAKFAST AT TWILIGHT 1/17/53. *Amazing*, July 1954.
    There you are in your home, and the soldiers smash down the door and tell you you're in the middle of World War III. Something's gone wrong with time. I like to fiddle with the idea

of basic categories of reality, such as space and time, breaking down. It's my love of chaos, I suppose. (1976)

A PRESENT FOR PAT 1/17/53. *Startling Stories*, Jan 1954.

THE HOOD MAKER ('Immunity') 1/26/53. *Imagination*, June 1955.

OF WITHERED APPLES 1/26/53. *Cosmos Science Fiction and Fantasy*, July 1954.

HUMAN IS 2/2/53. *Startling Stories*, Winter 1955.
   To me, this story states my early conclusions as to what is human. I have not really changed my view since I wrote this story, back in the Fifties. It's not what you look like, or what planet you were born on. It's how kind you are. The quality of kindness, to me, distinguishes us from rocks and sticks and metal, and will forever, whatever shape we take, wherever we go, whatever we become. For me, Human Is *is my credo. May it be yours.* (1976)

ADJUSTMENT TEAM 2/11/53. *Orbit Science Fiction*, Sept-Oct 1954.

THE IMPOSSIBLE PLANET ('Legend') 2/11/53. *Imagination*, Oct 1953.

IMPOSTER 2/24/53. *Astounding*, June 1953.
   Here was my first story on the topic of: Am I a human? Or am I just programmed to believe I am human? When you consider that I wrote this back in 1953, it was, if I may say so, a pretty damn good new idea in sf. Of course, by now I've done it to death. But the theme still preoccupies me. It's an important theme because it forces us to ask: What is *a human? And – what isn't?* (1976)

JAMES P. CROW 3/17/53. *Planet Stories*, May 1954.

PLANET FOR TRANSIENTS ('The Itinerants') 3/23/53. *Fantastic Universe*, Oct-Nov 1953. [Parts of this story were adapted for the novel DEUS IRAE.]

SMALL TOWN ('Engineer') 3/23/53. *Amazing*, May 1954.
Here the frustrations of a defeated small person – small in terms of power, in particular power over others – gradually become transformed into something sinister: the force of death. In rereading this story (which is of course a fantasy, not science fiction) I am impressed by the subtle change which takes place in the protagonist from Trod-Upon to Treader. Verne Haskel initially appears as the prototype of the impotent human being, but this conceals a drive at his core self which is anything but weak. It is as if I am saying, The put-upon person may be very dangerous. Be careful as to how you misuse him; he may be a mask for thanatos: the antagonist of life; he may not secretly wish to rule, he may wish to destroy. (1979)

SOUVENIR 3/26/53. *Fantastic Universe*, Oct 1954.

SURVEY TEAM 4/3/53. *Fantastic Universe*, May 1954.

PROMINENT AUTHOR 4/20/53. *If*, May 1954.